PRAISE FOR MARIA V. SNYDER

"Snyder delivers another excellent adventure."

— PUBLISHER'S WEEKLY ON *FIRE STUDY*

"It's always such a joy to be back in this world, and Maria V. Snyder has done it again with a fantastic companion to the original series. These novels really do add a whole new dimension to the story, and I love getting to read about the adventures that were going on behind the scenes."

— ABI OF SCRIBBLES.AND.STORIES ON *THE STUDY OF MAGIC*

"Maria V. Snyder has managed to take a story most of us can tell by heart, and make it something brand new."

— MAKENNA M. LOYAL READER ON *THE STUDY OF MAGIC*

"This one is my favourite of the three. Valek literally was breaking my heart. There were moments that were hilarious and I loved all the one liners and the snide, sarcastic comments that were thrown in all over…I'm going to be feeling this one for a while, and I know everyone is going to absolutely LOVE it. You absolutely smashed this one."

— REEMA CROOKS ON *THE STUDY OF FIRE*

ALSO BY MARIA V. SNYDER

CHRONICLES OF IXIA & SITIA SERIES
In Reading Order

Diamond Study (short story)

Poison Study

The Study of Poisons

Assassin Study (short story)

Magic Study

The Study of Magic

Fire Study

The Study of Fire

Power Study (short story)

Storm Glass

Sea Glass

Ice Study (novella)

Spy Glass

Shadow Study

Night Study

Shattered Glass (novella)

Dawn Study

Diaper Study (short story)

Wedding Study (novella)

After Study (short story)

The Study Chronicles: Tales of Ixia & Sitia

THE ARCHIVES OF THE INVISIBLE SWORD SERIES

The Eyes of Tamburah

The City of Zirdai

The King of Koraha

THE SENTINELS OF THE GALAXY SERIES

Navigating the Stars

Chasing the Shadows

Defending the Galaxy

HEALER SERIES

Touch of Power

Scent of Magic

Taste of Darkness

INSIDER SERIES

Inside Out

Outside In

OTHER BOOKS

Up to the Challenge

(A Collection of SF & Fantasy Short Stories)

Storm Watcher

(A Middle Grade Novel)

Discover more titles by Maria V. Snyder at www.MariaVSnyder.com

The Study of Fire

Maria V. Snyder

Copyright © 2024 by Maria V. Snyder. All rights reserved.

No part of this book may be used or reproduced in any manner for the purpose of training artificial intelligence technologies or systems.

No part of this publication may be reproduced, distributed or transmitted in any form or by any means, including photocopying, recording, or other electronic or mechanical methods, without the prior written permission of the publisher, except in the case of brief quotations embodied in critical reviews and certain other noncommercial uses permitted by copyright law. For permission requests, contact the publisher.

This is a work of fiction. Names, characters, places, and incidents are a product of the author's imagination. Locales and public names are sometimes used for atmospheric purposes. Any resemblance to actual people, living or dead, or to businesses, companies, events, institutions, or locales is completely coincidental.

The Study of Fire / Maria V. Snyder

Cover design by Joy Kenney

Interior Art by Dema Harb & Hillary Bardin

Maps by Martyna Kuklis

Published by Maria V. Snyder

Paperback ISBN 9781946381262

Hardcover ISBN 9781946381286

Digital ISBN 9781946381279

To Rodney, Luke, and Jenna. You were all there at the start of Yelena and Valek's journey and have loved and supported me throughout the twenty plus year journey. You all endured my late night writing sessions, long absences due to conferences and book tours, and mood fluctuations as I worried over...well everything writing related! Thanks so much for accompanying me on this crazy writing adventure!

THE TERRITORY OF IXIA & THE CLANS OF SITIA
Designed by Martyna Kuklis

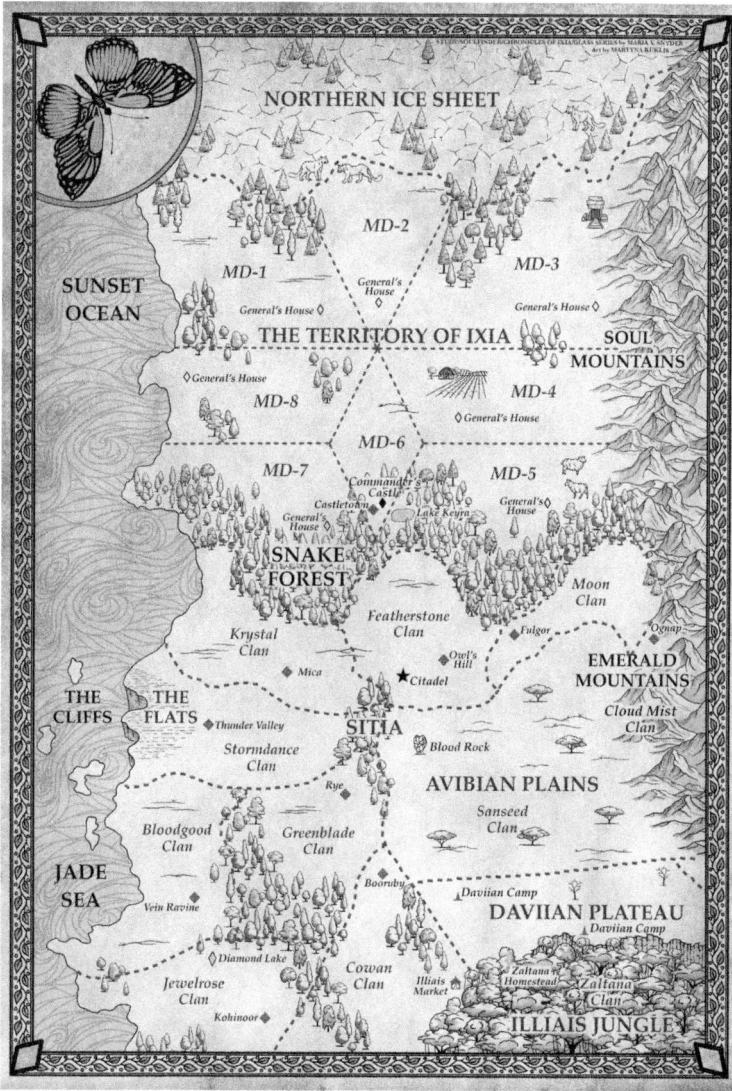

THE COMMANDER'S CASTLE COMPLEX
Designed by Martyna Kuklis

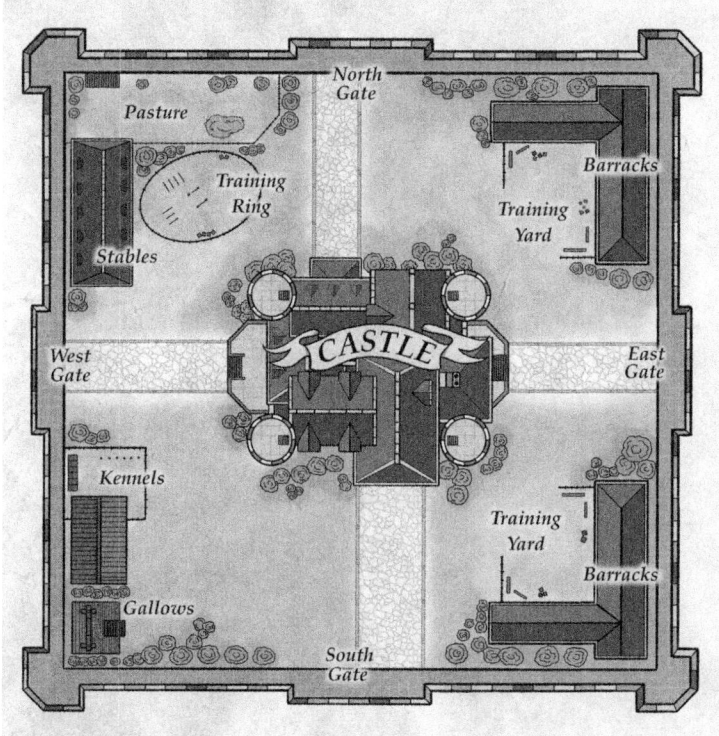

THE MAGICIAN'S KEEP
Designed by Martyna Kuklis

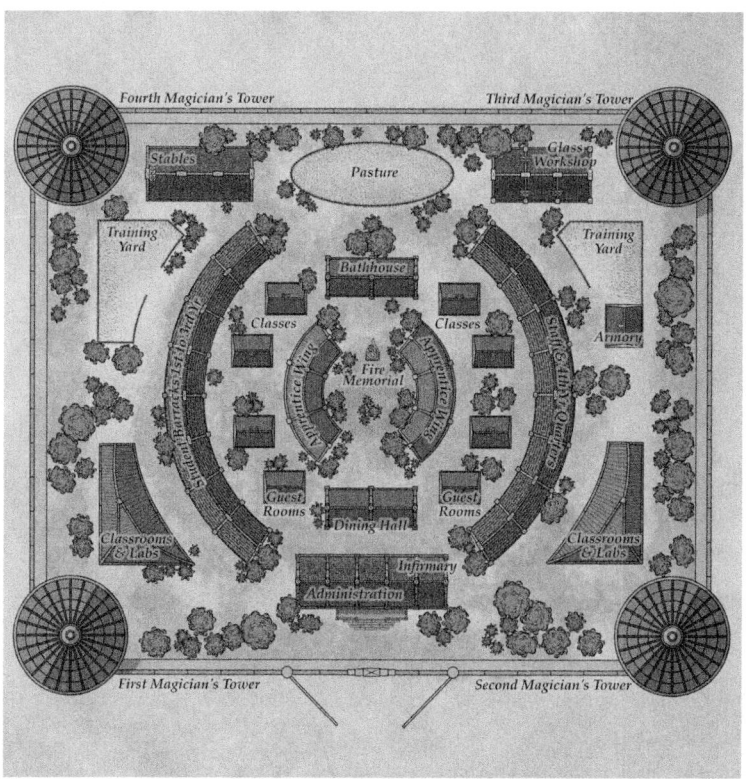

THE CITADEL
Designed by Martyna Kuklis

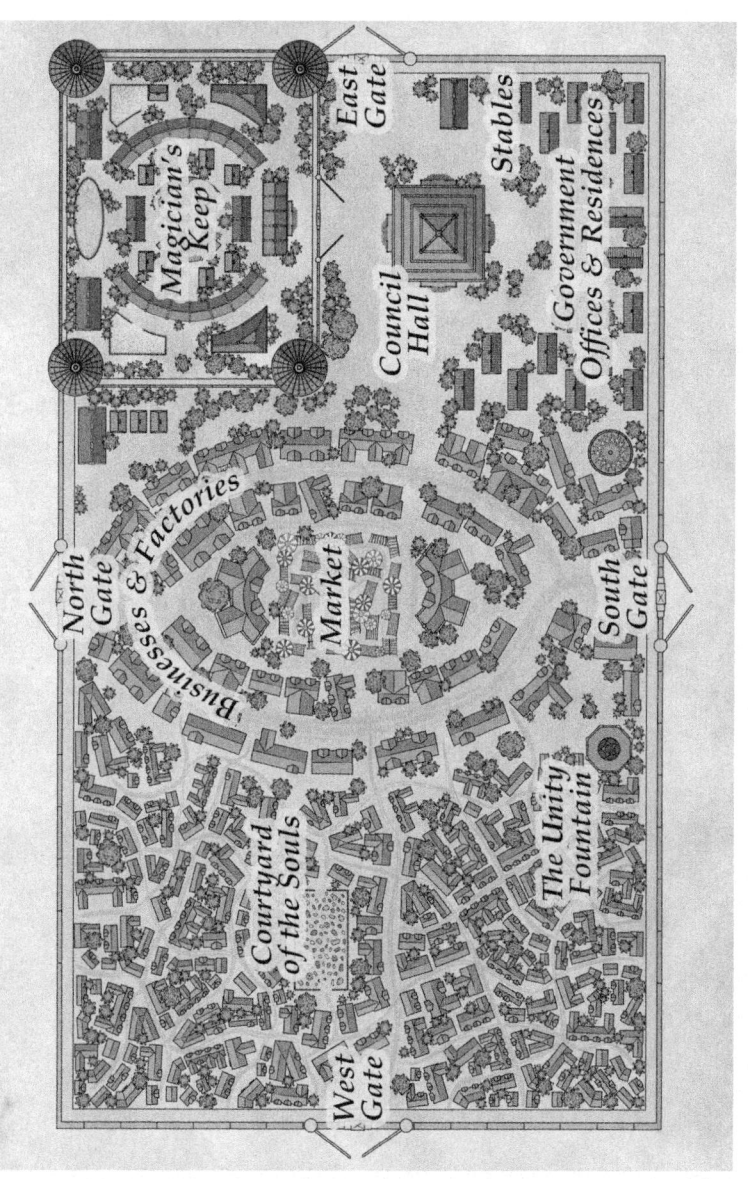

CHAPTER 1

Valek leaned on the fence, watching the soldiers train in the yard outside the castle complex's barracks. It was day thirty-six of the cooling season, and his breath fogged in the crisp morning air. However, his thoughts warmed him. They were on Yelena and their last night together.

Yelena had revealed she would be allowed to travel to Ixia now that the Commander's order for her execution had been nullified. Filled with joy over the news, he had said, "I'm looking forward to your first official visit as the liaison between Ixia and Sitia. But don't wait too long. Please." Valek had been only partially successful at keeping his pleading tone to a minimum.

A familiar ache throbbed in his chest at being parted from Yelena, but they both knew she needed to continue her magical studies. At least she had promised to visit soon.

"Fancy a challenge, sir?" Janco asked.

Valek's thoughts jerked to the present. He turned to Janco, who stood with his partner Ari, and Maren inside the training yard.

"It depends," Valek said.

Janco smiled at the familiar response. "On what?"

"Whether or not *you* can offer me a challenge."

"Normally, I'd be insulted, but you have a point. Which is why I'm not challenging you alone."

This was new. Valek straightened. "You're not?"

"No. *We* are. All *three* of us."

Interesting. "Is that allowed?" Valek asked.

"Nothing in the rules says it isn't," Ari said.

"There are rules?" Valek asked.

"Not officially." Ari gestured to the soldiers in the yard. "But we all know that if someone beats you in a fight, they'll win the right to be your second-in-command. You can turn down the challenge if you're so inclined, and, if you don't, the challenger chooses the weapon. That's it."

"There's nothing that says we can't team up," Janco said.

"Nothing official," Valek confirmed.

"So, make it official," Maren said with a huff of impatience. "Decide if we can attack en masse or not."

Valek had expected Ari and Janco to eventually team up and challenge him, adding Maren was a new wrinkle. It'd only been four days since they'd returned from their adventures with Ambassador Signe in Sitia, but Valek was well rested. The extra time spent in the Avibian Plains with Yelena had rejuvenated his body and soul.

He sized the three of them up. Long and lanky, Janco matched Valek's height of six feet. Ari stood another four inches taller than them. He had broad shoulders and thick muscles that belied his flexibility. With her athletic build, Maren could hold her own. As usual, her long blond hair had been pulled back into a ponytail.

"How long does it take to decide?" Janco asked. "Can we fight you three against one or not?"

"You can, but there will be rules," Valek said. "You can't gang up on me. No tackling me from behind."

"Gang up? Isn't that what we're doing?" Janco asked.

"It's different. Your goal will be to disarm me, but two of you can't grab and hold me while the other attacks."

"That's more like street fighting," Janco said. "And that would be cheating."

"Then you agree to my terms?" Valek asked.

"Yes, sir," all three said in unison.

"Weapon?"

"Bo staff."

Valek raised an eyebrow at Maren.

She shrugged. "It was a group decision."

Interesting. Four people wielding five-foot wooden staffs would need plenty of room to maneuver. They would attract a crowd. And he'd have to set some new rules if the threesome beat him. Valek didn't want large teams of soldiers attacking him.

The other soldiers had already sensed something unusual. They'd stopped training and were watching the exchange.

Valek removed his short cape and broadsword but left his uniform shirt on. He hopped the training yard's fence and Janco handed him a bo staff before he, Ari, and Maren walked out to the middle. The area immediately cleared of people, but they didn't go far. The onlookers formed a wide ring around the fighters. A heavy blanket of silence settled over everyone as the trio fanned out into a semicircle facing Valek.

All right then. Holding the bo in a ready position—horizontal in front of him with his hands about two feet apart—he moved closer to his opponents. There wasn't a referee, so they waited for his signal.

"Begin," he said.

Janco attacked first, moving fast as he swung his bo, aiming for Valek's ribs. "Three against one, this is gonna be fun."

Cries of encouragement sounded from the growing group of onlookers.

Valek jerked his bo upright and blocked the strikes while

keeping track of Ari and Maren in his peripheral vision. It made sense for the three of them to spread out and try to surround him.

Ari disappeared from sight, Valek spun in time to counter an overhead strike from Ari. His hands and the wooden staff vibrated with the force of the blow. The crowd *ooohhhed*.

Ari's next strike aimed for Valek's temple. He ducked under it and spun again. He needed to keep all three in front or to the sides of him.

Maren tried to sweep his feet, but he jumped onto her weapon, forcing it to the ground. The maneuver pulled the weapon from her grasp, and he shuffled close, jabbing the end of his bo into her solar plexus. Loud boos filled the air even though he hadn't hit her too hard; just enough to knock the wind from her lungs and push her to the ground, keeping her out of the fight for a few minutes.

How hard to hit his opponents was his biggest problem. He didn't want to break bones or cause any concussions, but he needed to slow them down. Ari and Janco immediately stepped between Maren and Valek, protecting their teammate.

They attacked in sync, aiming for Valek's ribs. The noises of the onlookers dimmed to a mere buzz as he backpedaled out of their range. No longer swinging their weapons, Ari and Janco pursued him. Perfect. Valek planted his back foot and charged toward them. Surprised by the sudden change in direction, they hesitated for a fraction of a second. Long enough that when Valek swung his bo, they couldn't properly block it.

He hit both of them on their wrists. Then he snapped a front kick to Janco's bo. It flew from his hand. However, a kick to Ari's bo was unsuccessful. Considering the corded muscle on Ari's forearms, it wasn't a surprise. While Janco scrambled after his weapon, Ari charged—an alarming sight—like a bull focused on a big red bullseye that happened to be on Valek's chest.

Rhythmic clacking sounded as Ari attacked with a series of

hard strikes that threatened to crack Valek's staff. Rib, rib, temple, temple, rib, temple. Uppercut. Valek jumped back and Ari's bo grazed his chin instead of catching him under his jaw. Too close for comfort.

Movement to his left alerted him. Valek ducked but he wasn't fast enough. Maren's bo slammed into his shoulder. Before the pain could register, Janco tried to sweep his legs. Valek lifted his right foot, letting the weapon hit his left ankle. Pain raced up his leg. He set his foot down and trapped the bo between his ankles. Spinning, he yanked it from Janco's grip again. Ari and Maren backed up as it swung around.

Valek caught sight of the Commander standing in the crowd. *Oh lovely. I better up my game and put on a show.* He went on the offensive.

Increasing the speed of his attacks and blocks, Valek kept moving. At one point, he planted his bo and used it to support his weight as he did a series of spinning kicks, hoping to crack their weapons and knock them off balance. Ducking and weaving, he shuffled in close, limiting his opponents' ability to swing, but allowing Valek to rap their knuckles. He also aimed for their thumbs and wrists. Too bad they figured out his strategy.

"Back off," Ari ordered, and they spread out. "Initiate phase two. Janco, you're up."

Phase two sounded ominous. Instead of attacking together, Ari and Maren stepped back, letting Janco engage with Valek. Janco poured on the speed, managing to get a few good solid hits to Valek's torso. Valek wasn't sure what was more alarming, the speed or the silence. For once, Janco didn't sing out his rhymes. It added a deadly intensity to his attack.

Just when Valek tuned into the cadence of the fight, Janco stepped back, allowing Ari to take a turn. The big man's hard blows didn't get through Valek's defenses, but each strike sent a wave of fatigue through his arms. When Maren replaced Ari, Valek realized their scheme. They planned to tire him out, while they rested. Waiting to implement this tactic until mid-fight was a genius move. If they'd started with one-on-one, he'd have had plenty of energy to defeat them.

Knowing their strategy didn't help Valek at all. He cursed under what was left of his ragged breath. They did another round of one-on-one.

"Phase three," Ari said. They attacked together.

Valek scrambled to block and dodge as his collection of bruises increased. His energy leaked at an alarming rate. No longer on the offensive, Valek was fighting to survive. His world shrank to the movements of the weapons and the sound of wood clacking wood.

In the middle of the melee, Ari dipped down and swung his bo toward Valek's ankles. Valek mistimed his jump, and the staff swept his feet out from underneath him. He landed hard on his back. The impact rattled his bones and knocked his bo from his hands. Valek looked up in time to see three bo staffs aimed at his neck, the ends less than an inch away from his skin. The threat was clear. One move, and they could crush his windpipe.

"Concede?" Ari asked.

CHAPTER 2

Valek had no more defensive moves left. No energy to spare.

"Yes." He conceded the match.

The crowd cheered as the trio's weapons were withdrawn, and Janco helped Valek to his feet. There were also some *boos* and jeers from the onlookers as coins were exchanged. No surprise the soldiers had bet on the outcome of the fight.

Janco *whooped* and danced around the training yard. Big grins spread on Maren's and Ari's faces as they high-fived in celebration.

Even though he'd lost the match, Valek couldn't help being proud of the trio. They'd worked as a true team, helping to maximize their individual strengths at the right time, keeping in sync with the others, and not trying to dominate. It was a rare dynamic, and he doubted another set of three people could achieve the same results.

Once Valek caught his breath, he projected his voice and addressed the crowd. "Congratulations to my opponents!" Another round of cheers sounded. "They have earned the right to become my seconds-in-command. However, if they don't want the job, they can choose any position in Ixia, with the exception of being Commander or a general."

A few laughs rippled through the onlookers. Maren's expression turned thoughtful.

"And there are new rules for my challenge. If you want to become my second-in-command, you must beat the current ones before you can face me. You have two choices. You can attack en masse, but with a maximum ratio of two against one. If your group wins against the seconds, you can fight me. The maximum ratio for our fight is three against one."

"If we beat your seconds and you, what happens? What's the prize?" a soldier called out.

"You will replace my seconds," Valek said.

"If six of us earn the right to fight you, what then?" another asked.

"I will fight each team of three separately. If you all defeat me, then I'll have six new seconds."

A murmur rose, and Valek raised his voice. "The second option is a one-on-one challenge. In that case, you must beat one of my seconds for the chance to fight me." This would weed out those who weren't ready to face Valek, saving him some time and aggravation. "Win against me and you'll replace the second who you beat."

"Two against one or one-on-one, it doesn't matter with this group of soldiers," Janco muttered as excited conversations broke out among the onlookers. "No one is getting through us. Valek's gonna be bored."

"Nothing's impossible," Ari said.

The noise from the various discussions died down as the Commander strode over to them.

"An impressive fight," the Commander said to the trio. "Congratulations." He shook each of their hands. Then he turned to Valek and lowered his voice. "That's an interesting set of new rules you created. Have them posted in the barracks to avoid confusion. And add the unspoken rules as well."

"Yes, sir."

"Unspoken?" Janco asked.

"Like the ones I set for our fight. Basically, no brawling," Valek explained. "Also, we can refuse a challenge. Or rather, reschedule. There are times when it's inconvenient or you're recovering from an injury. Eventually, you'll fight the challenger, but you'll have flexibility as to when."

By this time, the crowd had disbursed, everyone returning to work or to their training sessions.

"What's next?" Ari asked.

"The three of you will move out of my corps housing. There are suites down the hall from mine. You can each have one or share. Some have multiple bedrooms."

"I'll take my own," Maren said. "I spend way too much time with these guys. I don't need to hear them bickering all night long."

"Ari and I will share," Janco said without consulting his partner.

"What will our jobs entail?" Ari asked.

"Pretty much what you've been doing this past year," Valek said. "But you'll report directly to me instead of Kenda. And you'll get to be in charge if I'm out of town on a mission."

"What about our spy training?"

"I'd like you to finish it. While you already have a great deal of experience and knowledge, you can still learn some new skills in the art of subterfuge."

As the trio went off to celebrate, Valek grabbed his cape and sword and walked back to the castle with the Commander. Well, Valek might have limped a bit. His left ankle was still sore from Janco's blow.

The castle's asymmetrical shape really stood out among the rest of the buildings in the complex. Valek automatically scanned the canted roofs and cornices, seeking any hidden intruders.

"The winners can have any position. When did I agree to that?" the Commander asked, breaking the comfortable silence.

"You didn't have to agree. This is my challenge."

The Commander's expression hardened.

Valek rushed to continue. "Consider the person or persons who can beat me in a fight. You saw the match with Ari, Janco, and Maren. Those types aren't ordinary soldiers. We want them to be promoted. To be working with our leaders."

"I'm all for rewarding exceptional people, but I prefer to know a person before I have to work with them every day."

"You know Ari, Janco, and Maren. And I doubt there'll be another trio like them for a long while."

The Commander paused and looked at Valek. "You've favored them from the beginning. Did you throw the match?"

He huffed in indignation. "You saw the fight. They earned it."

"Don't get huffy. You weren't at your best."

"I've never fought three opponents with a bo staff before. Plus, they were relentless."

"True." The Commander continued walking as his expression grew thoughtful. "I only saw two thirds of the fight. They did a remarkable job of utilizing their strengths. Their teamwork was impressive as well. Usually, egos get in the way when you have more than two partners. Also, having Ari acting as the leader kept them on track. It was a successful strategy." He side-eyed Valek. "Are you injured? Ari's hits on your bo staff rattled my teeth."

"Bruised and sore, but nothing serious." Valek appreciated that they had pulled back on the hits to his body. It prolonged the fight, but far better to win with strategy and cunning than with brute strength. The other soldiers would respect them more for that.

"Good," the Commander said. "What are your thoughts on their new positions?"

Ah, good question. "I'm officially an adviser, so they should be advisers as well. Instead of reporting directly to you, they'll work with me."

"That's reasonable. And when you're away on a mission?"

"Then they'll be acting Chiefs of Security, unless they're with me," Valek said. Then he rushed to add, "They won't outrank the generals, though."

"Good." But then the Commander grinned at him. "Although, it could be fun if they did. Imagine setting Janco loose on the generals."

Valek laughed. "That would be very entertaining."

"It would. However, they will outrank the generals when they are acting as Chiefs of Security in your absence."

Wow, that spoke volumes of the Commander's trust in Valek's new seconds. "I'll let them know."

The hot water lapped at his chest as Valek reclined in the bath. Red and purple bruises mottled his skin with the biggest concentration of them on his torso, arms, and shoulders. He'd no idea there were so many, but now that he'd noticed them, they clamored for attention. He sank until the water reached his jaw. The abrasion on his chin burned. He closed his eyes and tried to relax his muscles.

As always during these quiet moments, his thoughts traveled to Yelena. It'd been four days since they'd parted, having teamed up and fought against two powerful enemies. Alea Daviian had first tried to kill the Commander and Valek in Ixia, and then set her sights on murdering Yelena. All to enact revenge for her brother Mogkan, whose death had been caused by a combination of Yelena's magic and Valek's blade.

Then there was Ferde. A magician on a quest for power, killing young women to harvest their souls. He'd hoped to complete an Efe ritual and become more powerful than all four master magicians together. If Ferde had been successful, he would have taken over Sitia and then set his sights on Ixia. And Yelena would have been killed. Valek shuddered despite the heat sinking into his skin.

He pulled his thoughts from the horrors with a reminder that Ferde had been captured and incarcerated, and Alea was dead. Valek wondered what reaction the Sitian Council and the master magicians had when Yelena returned to the Citadel as their new Liaison and Soulfinder.

It wouldn't be an easy road for her. Soulfinders had a bad reputation, as those in the past had abused their powers to manipulate a person's soul. Yelena had said she could gather one in her heart and then release it back into their body. She could also influence a person through their soul, but Valek wasn't sure what that entailed.

He did know that she'd managed to reach him in Ixia from the Citadel when she needed his help. Perhaps it was due to her Soulfinder magic. And while it would be a difficult time for her as she determined the extent of her powers, she'd been through worse. He'd no doubt that she'd persevere. Of course, that didn't stop him from wishing he could be by her side, helping when needed.

With a sigh, Valek stood, dried off, and donned a clean uniform. While the fight had felt like it lasted all morning, it was still early in the day and Valek had plenty of work to do.

His increasingly dusty office greeted him. Assigning a housekeeper to clean his office and suite was one of the items on his long to-do list. It was just—he pulled in a deep breath, detecting a faint hint of lavender—that he was reluctant to chase away Yelena's scent with the sharp aroma of cleaning solution. However, the Commander had ordered him to clean up his office. Perhaps the housekeepers had a lavender-scented furniture polish. He huffed in amusement. Most of the surfaces of his office were covered with stacks of books, half-burned candles, weapons, and his carving rocks.

Sitting behind his desk, Valek reviewed several reports before following up on a few promised tasks. He wrote the orders for Captain Silas's promotion. The captain had aided Valek when he had encountered trouble at Military District 3's garrison. The Commander had to sign the orders, but Valek didn't think he'd object.

Soon he was absorbed in his work, making notes. Reports came in weekly from his corps. They'd been assigned to all the garrisons, manor houses, and large cities in Ixia, as well as the Sitian Citadel and all the big cities in Sitia. It was a vast network that sent him information and updates. Most of it was routine and ordinary, but occasionally there was a tidbit that intrigued him, that hinted at potential trouble brewing. In that case, he'd send a message back, asking for details. Then he'd either give the agents instructions on how to follow up, or he'd dispatch more of his agents to help. In a few cases, he'd investigate himself.

Valek grinned. With the promotion of Ari, Janco, and Maren, he could go on more missions. Especially if those missions just happened to be in Sitia. Kenda, his corps manager, would fuss at him over the danger, but Valek didn't care if it meant seeing more of Yelena.

A knock interrupted his pleasant thoughts. "Come in."

Ari, Janco, and Maren strode in, surprising him. Between celebrating and moving to new quarters, Valek didn't expect to see them today. They wore their new adviser uniforms; the same one Valek wore every day. The all-black pants, belt, and tunic were plain. The only adornment was on their collars, where a red diamond shape had been stitched onto each side.

Janco held his arms out and did a little spin. "Nice, eh? This outfit commands respect." He'd bathed and his short brown hair was still wet.

"What else does it command?" Ari asked. His wide shoulders strained the seams of his tunic.

"Anything that has to do with security. The Commander's security, the castle's security, and Ixia's security. Overseeing security protocols, ensuring the guards are following those protocols, preventing treason and espionage," Valek said.

"Do we outrank the guards and officers of the Army?" Janco asked. Glee glowed in his dark eyes.

"Yes, but not the advisers, as they are your colleagues, or me, the Commander, or the generals."

"What if it's about security?" Ari asked.

"If I'm not here and you are acting as Chief of Security, then you outrank everyone and have the right to take the lead."

"What about the Commander?"

"Oh, he'll want to take charge, but his safety is the most important. More important than your own lives. So, you just have to tackle him to the ground when you hear the twang of a bow launching an arrow." Or, to avoid a sneeze. Ambrose was never going to let him forget that one.

"What about your corps?" Janco asked. "Are we in charge of them?"

"Not yet. You'll be working with Kenda for now, learning how the organization runs. Eventually, you'll have more oversight and will assume my role when I'm out of town." He scanned their concerned expressions. "You're my seconds. You aid me in my job and fill in for me when needed. Don't worry, there's bound to be some growing pains, mistakes, and miscommunications. What I want you all to remember is to not jump to conclusions. Thoroughly investigate everything, even if it's an offhand comment. Ensure the intent before getting insulted or offended or angry."

THE STUDY OF FIRE

They considered his comments in silence for a few moments.

"What do you need us to do right now?" Ari asked.

"Continue with your spy training. It's currently quiet." He held up a hand, stopping Janco's outburst. "I promise to bring you in when the next crisis happens. In my experience, these quiet spells don't last long."

While not happy, they agreed.

"Can we have a rematch with the puppy dogs?" Janco asked. He had not been happy when the corps' four youngest spy students had accused him, Ari, Maren, and Kimette of cheating at the last training session.

"Yes. We'll do another set."

"Same exercise?" Ari asked.

"No. I'll come up with something different. Perhaps more challenging for you since you're now my seconds."

"Ahhh, good," Janco said. "'Cause that last one—"

"Janco," Ari warned.

Somewhat mollified, Ari and Janco left his office, but Maren lingered. She hadn't said anything during the discussion. Her hair was wrapped in a tight bun, giving her a more mature and regal bearing. A tall woman with an athletic build, her posture was always military straight.

She ran a finger along his conference table, leaving a clean streak behind. "This is filthy."

"I'm aware. Do you need something?"

"I..." Maren inspected a pile of books.

Valek waited.

Turning toward him, she said, "I agreed to join Ari and Janco mostly for the satisfaction of beating you."

Understandable. "You don't want to be my second?"

"I..." She tugged the hem of her tunic. "I'm not sure I want to deal with all the subterfuge and undercover missions all the time. I mean...I enjoyed the smash and grab. And killing sand spiders was fun. But…I don't know…" She smoothed her collar and fiddled with the embroidered diamonds. "The spy training is interesting. It's just…" Maren met his gaze. "Can I be a part-time second? Or a when-you-really-need-me second? Is that possible?"

"I did say you can have any job. What else would you like to do?"

"I'd like to be a real adviser."

"You are a real adviser."

"To the Commander. I enjoy political machinations far more than security. And the generals, and Sitia…"

"Plenty of intrigue and drama?"

"Exactly."

"I'm okay with you being an as-needed second, but I need to check with the Commander about you reporting to him. Have you told Ari and Janco?"

"Yes. Janco pouted, of course. Cried I didn't love them anymore." Maren huffed in annoyance. "But Ari understood, and eventually Janco came around. I'm still going to finish the spy training, if that's okay."

"It's perfect. And if the Commander agrees, you'll have to go through his adviser training."

"Adviser training?"

"In diplomacy, politics, resource management, leadership, things like that. And there's an extensive course on self-defense, but I think you can skip that one."

"Oh, I don't know. Might be nice to have a class that I can ace." Maren fiddled with her sleeves. For the first time since Valek had known her, she appeared doubtful.

"I'm sure you'll ace them all."

"Really?"

"You wouldn't be standing here in an adviser's uniform if I thought differently. I'll let you know what the Commander decides."

THE STUDY OF FIRE

"Thank you." Maren grinned and strode from the room.

Conferring with the Commander was just a formality; he'd be a fool to not accept Maren. And the Commander was never a fool.

Kenda visited his office later that afternoon. "Exciting morning," she said as she settled on the chair in front of his desk. She held a stack of files.

"Did you see the fight?" he asked.

"Most of it. You made a number of mistakes."

"Thanks," he said dryly. "Guess I need to practice fighting multiple opponents again."

"Yes, you do. You upped the stakes for future challenges. Did you do that on purpose?"

"I couldn't make an exception for Ari, Janco, and Maren. Once I agreed to that fight, I couldn't say no to other groups."

"You're not getting any younger, you know."

"Gee, Kenda, no need to sugar-coat anything. Is there a reason, other than pointing out my flaws, for your visit?"

She held the files out. "This batch of reports came in this morning. I flipped through them, it's pretty standard stuff. You know, with your three new seconds, you can delegate and have them read all these."

"I'd need to teach them how to read between the lines first."

"I can—"

He took the reports from her. "You don't have the time." It was an old argument. She was in charge of assigning corps members, keeping track of them, and training the new recruits. Besides, Valek had so much practice at reading reports, he could scan them in half the time.

"How's Star?" he asked, changing the subject.

"Still grieving, which means she's not scheming. We have

bets on when she'll start planning her next treachery. I've a silver on mid-warming season."

The Commander had sent his elite unit to raid Star's operation. She had set up quite a network of illegal activities in two small towns in MD-7. When Major Granten had returned with prisoners, confiscated goods, and stacks of paperwork, gossip spread through the castle like a wildfire. It had been inevitable that Star would learn the fate of her organization. It had been a visible blow.

Kenda had reported that Star's confidence and bluster had died. The shattered woman moved through her days in a fog. Kenda had allowed Star some liberty while she mourned her organization's demise. She no longer stayed in the holding cells between tasting the Commander's food. Instead, she had a room in the servants' wing.

"I'll bet a silver that she starts before the cold season," Valek said.

"That early? Her people in Castletown were also arrested."

"Probably not all of them. I'm betting she'll soon be exploring her options and making trips into Castletown."

"It's your money." She shook her head as if to imply he was wasting it.

"Anything else of note?" he asked.

"I've upped the intensity of Trevar's training."

Ah. The young man—or young puppy dog according to Janco—had claimed to be bored with his current classes. "How so?"

"Random ambushes, late night assassination attempts, more complex knife drills. Poor guy hasn't gotten a good night's sleep in a while. Bright side, he's no longer bored."

"Good. Maybe he'll do better during the next round of exercises."

"Don't wait too long for that next round. Since your return from Sitia, Janco keeps suggesting creative ways for me to test

Trevar. I haven't been implementing them, but I'm afraid Janco will take the initiative—especially now that he's one of your seconds-in-command."

"He has no authority over you right now."

"Oh, I know, but his team's honor has been called into question. In this case, I don't think he cares about the chain of command."

"Noted."

Kenda left and Valek read through the new reports. It was best not to let them pile up. Gabor, his agent in the Sitian Citadel, mentioned Yelena had returned to the Magician's Keep and was currently living in Fourth Magician's, Irys Jewelrose's, tower.

That was new. Before, she had lived in the apprentice wing. Valek considered the change. Yelena was still learning the extent of her magic, still technically a student. But she had defeated Ferde and Alea, exhibiting master-level powers. Irys probably decided a full time apprenticeship would work better than Yelena attending various classes. Valek hoped it wasn't an attempt to keep Yelena under house arrest again.

He'd worry more, but Gabor had written, "all appears well."

By the time Valek reached the last report, his muscles had stiffened, and his bruises pulsed with pain. He either needed another hot soak, or to mix some pain powder in his now-cold tea. He'd missed dinner, and he was expected at his nightly meeting with the Commander soon. Unable to leave without finishing, Valek quickly scanned the information from his agents in MD-1.

They noted that General Kitvivan had sent out a large hunting party fully equipped with traps and large cages. Not unusual for this time of year. Game would be scarce during the cold season. So why would Kelia, Valek's agent, mention it? His gaze was drawn to the word 'large.' It was darker than the rest, as if Kelia wanted to emphasize it.

Valek mulled it over. General Kitvivan, like all the generals, had a bad scare. They had been targeted by a group of magicians and lost control of their thoughts and actions. Alea Daviian had led the group and been the only one to escape to Sitia. The Commander and Valek executed the others.

Had Kitvivan increased his security forces? Was that why he needed a bigger hunting party? But what about the large cages? Nothing unusual about capturing live squirrels, rabbits, and groundhogs to breed them for meat, but the hunters would use smaller cages.

An uneasy feeling bubbled in his chest. Valek remembered Kitvivan complaining about the snow cats coming down from the Northern Ice Pack during the cold season and killing their livestock. The Commander had forbidden the general from hunting the cats. However, it was clear that the general decided to ignore the Commander's order.

CHAPTER 3

The drink in Ambrose's hand paused midway to his mouth. "Are you *certain* Kitvivan plans to hunt snow cats?"

"What else could the cages be for?" Valek asked. They were sitting in the Commander's living room, having their nightly meeting. Like all the rooms Ambrose occupied, it was clean, neat, and sparsely furnished with minimal decorations. They sat on matching plain gray couches that faced each other, with a low table between them.

"Elk, deer, bears." He took a swallow of his brandy. "Wouldn't your agents know if he planned to hunt snow cats?"

"Not if Kitvivan kept his plans quiet. All the generals have been more cautious about who they trust since their encounter with the magicians."

"Still, it's a big leap in logic. Plus, snow cats are almost impossible to kill."

True. Except…Valek couldn't shake off his trepidation.

"Send a message to your agents. Ask them to investigate further," Ambrose said.

"All right."

"Anything else to report?"

"Yes. Maren wants to be a 'when-you-really-need-me' second-in-command."

"What does that mean?"

"That means she'd rather be one of your advisers, only helping me when needed."

"That's interesting. How do you feel about it?"

"I'll admit, I was disappointed. Maybe a little hurt. But I understand. Her interests are focused more on politics than intrigue. Plus, it's better to have her some of the time instead of none of the time."

Ambrose tapped his finger on his glass. "True. She has a unique set of skills that my other advisers don't have. And I have just the mission that needs those abilities."

"Oh?"

"The civilian watch in Rasmussen's Military District has a number of corrupt officers. The chain of command is a joke, and their judges are no longer adhering to the Code of Behavior's sentencing requirements."

Valek thought of Janco and how his judge gave him the option of going to prison or joining the army. Enlisting in the army had set Janco on the right path. Except, the Code of Behavior ruled that helping a prisoner escape jail resulted in ten years in prison. No exceptions. No deviations. No leniency for a first offense. No good-old-boy network. The exact same punishment was given to everyone. All Ixian citizens had to memorize the Code of Behavior. While Valek generally agreed with the Code's mandates, there were times when he felt they were too harsh. Good thing he was in a position to circumvent them.

"I thought the problems with the watch was only in the two towns Star had set up her operation," Valek said. Crooked Nook and Sectown were near the Sitian border, close enough to smuggle in black market goods with ease. They'd both been raided by the Commander's special unit of fifty soldiers, and Star's operation had been permanently shut down.

"Major Granten has interrogated the corrupt watch members and discovered it's a district-wide problem."

Ah. The civilian watch was under each Military District's general. The Commander could step in when needed, but he had enough to do with overseeing the country and the army.

"You think Maren would be a good person to send to General Rasmussen?"

"She has the military background and security knowledge. Maren can help the general to plan and implement a sweep of all the civilian watch stations and remove all those who are taking bribes or not following the Code of Behavior."

"A big job. Plus, General Rasmussen doesn't like to spend his money," Valek said.

"Then it's a good thing it isn't *his* money."

His cold tone warned Valek. "Can I tell Maren she's officially part of your staff?"

"As long as she doesn't become overprotective like Adviser Dema, Maren is welcome."

Valek laughed. "Dema was at MD-5, give her some time to recover and she'll stop acting like Mother Bear."

"She requested permission to learn how to fight," Ambrose said dryly.

Choking on his whiskey, Valek spluttered. "Give a guy warning, will you." He wiped his chin, chuckling.

"I'm glad you find it humorous." He huffed, but it was half-hearted.

"Did you give her permission?"

"Of course. I encourage my staff to continue learning new skills. I just hope she doesn't tackle me whenever anyone sneezes." Ambrose gave him a pointed look.

Valek failed to rise to the bait. He set his empty glass on the table between them, wincing as his muscles protested the movement. He would be sore for a few days.

"It's getting late." Ambrose finished his drink. "When do you think Maren will be ready to work with Rasmussen?"

He considered. "I'd wait until after she's gone through the course on diplomacy."

"Why?"

"She can be brutally frank, which I appreciate, but not many others do."

"I don't care if she upsets Rasmussen."

"Well, we can't *all* be the Commander." Valek held up his hand as Ambrose's expression hardened. "Rasmussen is passive aggressive when angry. Even though Maren's there on your orders, he won't implement any actions that she plans. Why would he? He's the one in charge. Eventually she'll get frustrated and message you, who, in turn will order Rasmussen to proceed with her campaigns. Rasmussen will invariably sabotage the efforts, they'll fail, and he'll blame it all on your brand-new adviser."

Ambrose gazed at him for a moment. "Is this something you've learned from experience?"

"I've seen it happen. My agents encounter this scenario on occasion. For Maren to succeed, she'll need to convince the general that this was more his idea than an order from the Commander. He needs to agree with her assessment and support her efforts. It's pure manipulation, which is why she needs to learn diplomacy."

"I'm glad I *am* the Commander and don't have to deal with all that bullshit."

"But you have done it. I've seen you pour on the charm when needed."

"Yes, because I *wish* to, not because I *have* to. Big difference." Ambrose smiled.

"Must be nice to be you." Valek teased.

"It is, until someone sets your uniform on fire."

Sobering, Valek remembered the attack six months ago. Eight rogue magicians had tried to assassinate the Commander and almost succeeded. Ambrose would always have a target on his back.

～

Maren hovered next to Valek's office door. It was only a few minutes past dawn, and, except for the kitchen staff and the Commander, the rest of the castle denizens were just stirring in their beds. He wondered how long she'd been waiting for him. By the anxious creases in her brow, he figured she wanted to know the Commander's decision.

"Couldn't sleep?" he asked as he unlocked his door.

"No. I love mornings. The earlier the better. It's quiet. And there is no one around to bother me." She followed him into his office.

"And no Janco to bug you."

"That, too." She hesitated, then asked, "Who am I reporting to today?"

Valek sat behind his desk. "The Commander has approved your new appointment."

Maren's brow smoothed and she grinned. Valek soaked it in. Good news should always be savored.

"Report to Adviser Carmia. She will schedule your classes. Tell her you need to start with the one on diplomacy."

"Yes, sir."

Maren left before he could warn her that Carmia was not a morning person. Oh well, it'd be her first lesson.

～

The quiet lasted four days. Long enough for some of Valek's bruises to fade. He was working in his office when Kenda entered with Ryda, the captain of Castletown's watch. The two of them together never boded well for anyone.

"What's wrong?" he asked as they approached his desk.

"I'll let you explain," Kenda said to Ryda.

Captain Ryda smoothed the tunic of her uniform. Her black hair had been braided and arranged in an artful knot on the top of her head. With wide hazel eyes and a long thin nose, she was rumored to be able to elicit a confession with one piercing glance.

While technically civilians, the watch's personnel were arranged in a military hierarchy with the captain overseeing the watch station. Depending on the size of the city, up to five lieutenants reported to the captain, and each lieutenant oversaw a dozen street patrollers.

Normally, Captain Ryda would report to Major Edan, who oversaw six cities in MD-6. If someone ascended high enough through the ranks, they would eventually reach the general of the district. But because Castletown was so close to the castle complex, Ryda sent reports to Valek as well. Unless it was serious. Then she came in person.

"I'm not quite sure what is wrong," Ryda said. "Which is why I'm here."

"Then sit down. Would you like a drink?" Valek stood and gestured to a row of bottles on his sideboard. "I've some iced gin from MD-2."

Ryda's expression brightened. "Yes, please." She settled in the seat. "Do you stock that gin just for me?"

He poured her a glass and handed it to her. "I do. It's your favorite."

"I'm debating if it's nice that you know that, or scary." She took a long swallow, and then relaxed back. "This could be nothing."

Valek waited.

"Like any town, we have our share of drunk and disorderly conduct, fights, petty thefts, pranks. Minor stuff. Except, these incidents have increased to numbers we usually deal with during the Fire Festival. We're heading toward the cold season and stuff like that tends to die down until the weather warms up.

"Also, what's puzzling is the people who are acting out are those who tend to be law-abiding citizens. We arrested a grandfather the other night for running through the streets naked." She shuddered. "And he wasn't drunk. Just convinced he was on fire."

"Sounds like a drug," Kenda said.

"We thought so, too. But there's no consistency to the symptoms. And those who have recovered, have no memory of taking anything. They're quite confused and alarmed that they're in a jail cell." Ryda met Valek's gaze. "It could be a new drug smuggled in from Sitia, but we've found nothing. No evidence."

Or it could be magic. There was a possibility that a young person living in Castletown had reached puberty and had developed magical power. A new magician had no control over their powers, which would explain the random strange actions of ordinary people. Valek's heart sank. Magicians were not tolerated in Ixia. When found, they were executed by him.

"I'll assign some of my corps to investigate," Valek said.

"Everyone's on edge. Strangers will be noticed," Ryda warned.

"Noted."

After Ryda left, Kenda asked, "Do you think the cause could be magic?"

"It's possible. I'd like to rule out the mundane reasons first."

"Who are you thinking for the job?"

Valek considered his agents. All could blend in, but it'd take longer to get the locals to trust them. "Trevar and Adrik."

"They're still in training."

"Yes, but Trevar grew up in Castletown. He's not a stranger."

"But he's been gone for almost a year."

"He disappeared when we arrested all the black market dealers. It makes sense that he moved to another town to avoid being captured. The fervor has died down, and no doubt there is another set of dealers setting up shop. The best baiter in town has returned and brought with him a new friend."

"He'll be thrilled with the assignment."

"Have them report to me."

"Yes, sir. Anything else?"

"Yes. Who on the housekeeping staff is totally trustworthy?"

Kenda glanced around his dust-covered office. "They're all vetted when hired."

"We both know not everyone is loyal."

"I can ask Inrick to test them out, see who's willing to sell information and who gets upset."

"That would be great. And the sooner the better."

"You mean you're not intentionally letting this place resemble a dungeon to intimidate your visitors? That cobweb in the window grows bigger by the day. It's seriously impressive, and I can't wait to get a glimpse of the spider. He must be massive."

"Your sarcasm has improved. Clearly, you've been hanging around Janco too long. Maybe I should send him and Ari to MD-1 to check if General Kitvivan is hunting snow cats this season."

Kenda's snarky smile died. "I hope he isn't. I'll let you know right away when I receive a message from our agents in MD-1."

"Thanks."

When she left, Valek turned around to study the square window behind his desk. Sunlight streamed in and glinted along the silky strands of the web. Some spy master. He'd failed to notice the growing net. He searched for the occupant. A black spider the size of a gold coin crouched in a shadow, waiting for his next meal. With the temperatures cooling daily, food would become scarce.

Careful not to disturb the web, Valek cracked the window open a notch. Hopefully a juicy moth or two would be attracted by the lantern light in his office and fly into the trap. As a fellow hunter, Valek respected spiders. They were intelligent, skilled, and patient. Too bad he couldn't recruit them. But he could ask his new housekeeper to leave the web alone until Mr. Spider left.

Valek returned to reading the reports that had been piled on his desk. It wasn't long before the silence was interrupted by a knock on his door. He called for the person to enter.

The door flew open, and Trevar rushed into his office with his weapon drawn. Valek hopped to his feet, but Trevar stopped and spun in a circle with his left hand out. His right hand clutched a dagger, which he kept tucked close to his chest. A textbook entry when a person suspected there might be an intruder or ambusher waiting inside a room. Once Trevar was satisfied no one would jump out at him, he relaxed and sheathed his knife.

He straightened. "Sorry, sir. I thought this might be a test."

Ah. Valek studied the young man. About twenty-three years old, he had sandy-blond hair and blue eyes. Normally, a handsome and affable fellow who tended to be cocky, the poor boy standing in front of him appeared haggard. Dark circles rimmed his eyes. Trevar's tousled hair was dull and looked as if he had scraped his hands through it in agitation. Two shades paler than normal, Trevar practically swayed on his feet.

"Come, sit down," Valek ordered.

Before sitting, Trevar picked up the chair and inspected it. Then he pressed his hands on the seat, testing that the legs wouldn't buckle. Or so Valek guessed. He settled his weight, only relaxing once nothing happened.

Valek grabbed his pitcher of water and filled a glass. "Drink this."

Trevar took the tumbler cautiously, sniffed at the water, sipped, and finally downed it.

Kenda had said she'd increased the intensity level of Trevar's training. However, she wasn't cruel. Mild sleep deprivation was one thing, but the poor boy was well beyond that and into the realm of paranoia. Something was going on.

"Where's Adrik?" Valek asked.

"He's...ah." Trevar blinked. "Shopping, I think. This is our day off." Another blink. "I think."

Valek muttered a curse. "How's your training going?"

Trevar flinched. "Ah...okay. I'm no longer bored." His laugh held a hysterical edge.

"Tell me what's been going on." Valek's flat tone belied the anger growing inside him.

"Ah... I'm being tested." He gestured vaguely. "All the time."

"By whom?"

"Ah...Everyone?"

That was the paranoia talking. "Kenda said—"

"Oh, no. She's... Well, yeah... She's done some... But she's grand."

"Then who?"

"The...Captain...er...Adviser Janco has taken a keen interest in my training."

Valek rubbed his face. It was easy to guess that once Kenda ignored Janco's suggestions, he had decided to go ahead and implement them. At least he hadn't tied the boy to a tree overnight with spearmint leaves shoved into his mouth. No, he would have used a dirty sock like Janco's cousins had once used on him.

He stood. "Come on, Trevar."

Panic flushed through his face. "Where are we going?"

Valek glanced at the window. The sunlight had faded into a gray twilight. "To have dinner." He lit a lantern and set it near the window before tucking a pile of reports under his arm. *Good hunting, Mr. Spider.*

If Trevar thought this was odd behavior, he didn't say anything as he followed Valek through the castle and into the kitchen. Trevar jumped at each clatter and loud noise caused by the staff preparing the evening meal.

Filling a tray with an obnoxious amount of food, Valek then led Trevar to his suite. He directed him to sit on the couch and set the tray on his lap.

Valek crouched in front of him. "You're safe here. Eat."

While Trevar devoured the food, Valek dropped the files onto his desk and then entered Yelena's old room. Dust coated the blanket on the bed and the night table. Unlike the other two rooms that lined the right wall of his living room, this one remained uncluttered. Actually, it remained exactly how Yelena had left it. A pang of loneliness echoed in his heart. But his mood improved when he realized that next time she visited Ixia, she'd share his bed.

He shook out the blanket. The scent of lavender mixed with the dust, and he coughed. The sheets underneath didn't look dirty, but he changed them anyway. He had started keeping a stack of clean linen in his suite after he'd fired Margg. Dust and cobwebs were one thing, but soiled sheets were another. He did have standards. After lighting the lantern by the bed, he rejoined Trevar.

"I left you some," Trevar said sheepishly. Some color had returned to his cheeks.

"Feel better?"

"A little."

"Good. You'll feel more like yourself after a good night's sleep." Valek gestured to Yelena's room.

"You want me to sleep here?" he asked with pure astonishment.

Valek suppressed a smile. "Yes. No one will test you tonight. I promise."

Uncertain, Trevar fingered the hilt of his knife as he glanced at the weapons displayed on the opposite wall. It was an impressive collection.

"They are all secured. Do you really believe anyone can get to you while you're under *my* protection?"

"No... Of course not. I'm just... Not thinking clearly."

"Understandable. Go. Sleep."

"Yes, sir." Trevar closed and locked the door behind him.

Did locking the door give Trevar a false sense of security, or did he hope the noise of someone picking the lock would rouse him?

Valek lit the lanterns hanging around his living room. The layout was the exact same as the Commander's, except piles of books, rocks, and miscellaneous items littered the floor. He also had a desk near the long windows since he frequently worked late into the night. The Commander never worked in his suite, claiming it was a place for rest.

Sitting at his messy desk, he ate the remaining food while reading reports. An hour later, Trevar came from the room.

"I can't sleep," he said. He had stripped down to his undershirt, boxers, and a pair of socks.

Not too surprising. The inability to fall asleep sometimes happened with extreme sleep deprivation. Valek palmed one of the darts hidden underneath his desk. "I know this great trick for settling your thoughts. Come on, I'll show you." He followed Trevar into the room. "Lie down and close your eyes."

Trevar did as instructed and Valek pricked him with the dart.

He sat up and demanded, "What was that?"

"Sleeping potion."

"Oh." He blinked at him for a few moments as if trying to decide on the proper response.

When he slumped over, Valek straightened him and covered him with the blanket. He returned to work for another few hours, then met briefly with the Commander, filling him in on Captain Ryda's visit.

He returned to his suite and grabbed his pillow and blanket. Clearing off the rest of his couch, he arranged his bedding before extinguishing the lanterns.

Valek squirmed into a comfortable position. The couch would do for a night or two. He had crashed on it a number of times when he was too exhausted to climb the stairs to his bedroom, and when he'd been feeling overprotective when Yelena slept in her room.

He dozed until the slight click of the window's latch woke him. A rush of cold air blew through the room before the window slid closed. Impressed that the intruder climbed the castle's walls in the dark to attain his suite, Valek waited until the black-clad figure reached Trevar's door.

"Leave the boy alone, Janco," he said.

The figure spun. "Shouldn't you be in bed?" Janco asked.

"I could ask the same of you."

"I'm just helping Kenda with the puppy dog's training."

"Did she ask you for help?"

"Well, no, but he needs to learn how to function in any physical condition."

"It's not your place to decide what Trevar needs to learn."

"He certainly needs a lesson in manners." Janco huffed.

"What you're doing is not a lesson. It's hazing, and borderline bullying." Valek continued before Janco could interrupt. "You are an adviser now. Second-in-command. This behavior is beneath you."

"But he—"

"Accused your team of cheating. I know. We'll do another set of exercises."

"I want an apology. A heartfelt apology and not ordered by anyone."

"Do you really think harassing him to the point of exhaustion is going to elicit an apology?"

"It's not like he has anything else to do."

"Again, it's not your place to determine that. I need him for a mission, but he's currently incapable of forming a complete sentence."

Janco perked up. "A mission? Ari and I have been bored to tears, we can—"

"No. Trevar and Adrik are best for this job."

"But they're still in training."

"Are you questioning my authority?"

Janco rushed to assure him. "No. It's just..." Another huff. "No one calls us cheaters and gets away with it."

"Did you cheat?"

"No! Of course not!" His outrage held an edge of betrayal, as if Valek just mortally wounded him.

"Then why are you so upset?"

"It's just..." Janco balled his hands into fists as he tensed. "My cousins accused me of cheating every time I won a game, or a race, or did anything better than them. They never acknowledged that I was good at something other than getting into trouble."

Ah, the real reason for the harassment.

"I understand your frustration and anger, but Trevar is not your cousin. He's your colleague. A young and inexperienced one that lost his temper over losing the exercise and said some things that I'm sure he's regretting. You can't get upset every time someone calls you a cheater. You are my second-in-command and need to learn to ignore all the comments and criticism and name calling that goes with being in a position of authority. Petty revenge and childish behavior is a thing of the past."

"It was just a bit of fun—" Janco protested.

"Fun? He might *not* recover. Do you understand? Even after he's caught up on his sleep, Trevar might jump at every shadow and noise for the rest of his life, rendering him useless as a spy."

"Oh. I hadn't thought of that."

"Obviously. Which is why we're having this chat. Now, do you understand?"

"Yes, sir."

"And you'll leave Trevar alone?"

"Yes, sir."

"Good. You're dismissed."

Janco headed toward the door.

"Where are you going?"

"Back to my suite."

"You came in through the window. You can exit the same way."

Janco paused a moment, then changed course. The window opened and closed with barely a whisper.

∽

Trevar slept for a day and a half. Dressed in his training uniform, he emerged from Yelena's room, blinking in the bright sunlight. The young man paled when he spotted Valek working at his desk.

"Uh. Sorry, sir?" Trevar ran a hand through his hair.

"For what?" Valek asked.

"I'm not sure. But…" He gestured to the living area. "I must have done something bad to end up here. Uh… No offense."

"If you'd done something bad, you would have woken up in a cell. How do you feel?"

"Better."

"Good. Go get cleaned up, grab something to eat, and find Adrik. Both of you are to report to me in my office in two hours."

"Yes, sir." Trevar strode to the door, but he stopped with his hand hovering over the knob.

"You passed the extra testing. No one is going to ambush you. Well, no one on *our* side. There's always a chance of an attack from our enemies."

"But it's a slim chance."

Valek thought about the Ambassador's recent visit to Sitia. It had not gone well and Ixia's relationship with the Council was currently strained. "It's always best to be prepared."

⁓

Adrik and Trevar arrived at the appointed hour. Some color had returned to Trevar's face, but he appeared to still be on edge. They sat in front of Valek's desk while he explained their mission in Castletown.

At the end, Trevar leaned forward. "Do you think it's a new drug?"

"I don't have enough information at this point to form an opinion. And you shouldn't either. If you think you're searching for a new drug, then you'll miss any clues that point in another direction. Keep an open mind. If anything strikes you as odd, don't dismiss it out of hand. Investigate it." Valek removed a pouch full of coins from his drawer and handed it to them. "This is for lodging, food, and bribes if needed. Also, if things get hot, leave town right away. I don't care if it blows your covers."

They exchanged a glance. Valek wondered if they thought of Sven, Adrik's father and one of Valek's corps. Sven had thought he could handle the heat and ended up being murdered.

"Take the rest of the day to gather supplies. Kenda will have the appropriate transfer paperwork for you. I'd suggest you arrive in Castletown tomorrow afternoon as if you've been traveling. I want weekly reports, unless you learn something important, then send word right away," Valek said. Although it was a rather straightforward mission, he asked if they had any questions.

"No, sir," they said in unison.

"Good. You're dismissed."

They left and Valek considered the other possibility. That magic was causing the citizens of Castletown to act strangely. He debated if he should go undercover as well, but decided to wait until Trevar and Adrik reported in.

Later that day, Kenda arrived in his office with a lanky young man at her heels. He had short dark brown hair, light brown eyes, and appeared to be in his early twenties.

"This is Brede, he works in housekeeping," Kenda said.

Careful not to squeeze Brede's long thin fingers too hard, Valek shook his hand. "Nice to meet you."

Half-distracted, Brede nodded as he took in the state of Valek's office and his eyes widened with glee.

Glee? Valek expected disapproval or distain or disgust.

"Oh, man," Brede said. "You said this place needed a good cleaning, but you didn't mention the sheer chaos. This is gonna be a challenge! I better get my cart and start right away." He dashed from the office.

Valek lifted an eyebrow, inviting Kenda to explain.

"You wanted someone trustworthy. He's the son of Adviser Abelard and he just about throttled our agent when he tried to bribe him to sell secrets. Brede was so outraged, he dragged the agent, who is twice his size, to my office and demanded I arrest him."

"Could have been an act. It seems odd that an adviser's son is working in housekeeping."

Kenda's expression turned cold. "What are you implying? That he's too good to scrub floors?"

"Not at all. Those positions are usually filled with people from other military districts who want an entry-level job in the castle. He grew up here. Most of those children either find apprenticeships or leave to work elsewhere."

"All I know is he enjoys his job and is trustworthy. Plus, the Commander approved. In fact, he's assigned Brede as your *personal* housekeeper."

Valek groaned. "Why do you hate me so much?"

She laughed. "For the record, I didn't go over your head. The Commander happened to be talking with the housekeeping manager when I went searching for a reliable staff member."

"Anything else you wish to torture me with?"

Kenda's humor faded. "I received a message from Kelia. She confirmed General Kitvivan is hunting snow cats."

CHAPTER 4

*C*ursing, Valek took the report from her and scanned the page. "And she doesn't have the clout to order him to stop."

"Her and her partner could sabotage the efforts."

"That would certainly work, but the general needs to know he's on thin ice."

"Ha. Ha." Kenda deadpanned. "Should I assign a couple more agents to aid them?"

"No. I think this is the perfect mission for our new seconds-in-command."

Now her laugh was genuine. "Good luck with that."

"Anything else?"

"Star is still sulking. It's nineteen days before the cold season starts. It's not looking good for you."

"There is still plenty of time."

Valek left his office with Kenda. They parted ways as she headed to the hexagon that housed his corps. He went in search of Ari and Janco, hoping to catch them before they left for dinner.

Ari opened the door when Valek knocked, inviting him into

their two-bedroom suite. The large common room held a couch, a couple comfy chairs, a table and chairs, and two desks. Doors on opposite sides of the room led to the bedrooms. Through the open doorways, Valek immediately recognized who occupied which bedroom. Ari's bed had been made with military precision. Janco's wasn't. The same could be said of their desks.

"I hope you have some good news," Janco said. He sat on the couch, juggling three knives.

"What would you consider good news?" Valek asked.

"A mission. An exercise with the puppy dogs. Anything other than lectures and studying."

"You're in luck. I've a mission for the two of you."

Ari straightened with interest. Janco whooped and threw his knives higher into the air.

"Where to?" Janco asked.

"MD-1."

"Ha. Ha. Right. Where are we *really* going?"

"MD-1, to stop General Kitvivan from hunting snow cats."

The weapons clattered to the floor. "Ow!" Janco sucked on a fingertip. "I'll pass. I'm not that bored."

"Details?" Ari asked.

Valek explained about the cages and Kelia's follow up report.

"How do we stop the general?" Ari asked.

"I suggest after the hunt is an utter failure, you introduce yourselves to General Kitvivan and let him know the Commander is extremely unhappy."

Janco perked up. "Ooohhh, thinly veiled threats. I like." Then he shuddered and wrapped his arms around his torso. "But I don't like the cold, and we might get stuck until the warming season when the snow melts."

"Which is why you're leaving tomorrow. Take the horses and lots of warm layers. Our seamstress, Dilana, can help kit you out with the proper clothing," Valek said.

"I'm assuming you expect us to leave at dawn." Another shudder.

"Stop moping, Janco," Ari cajoled. "We get to threaten a general and sabotage his hunt."

"Sabotage is always fun," Janco agreed. "Is Maren coming with us?" His voice held a hopeful tone.

"No. The Commander has another mission for her."

Janco slumped. "Boo."

"I'll bring your paperwork to the stables at dawn," Valek said.

"Paperwork?" Ari asked.

"You can't expect the general to trust that you're my new seconds-in-command without a missive from the Commander. The generals have been reluctant to trust anyone since the incident with the magicians."

"Magicians, *pah*," Janco spat.

"Just curious. Are there missions we can pass on?" Ari asked.

"It will depend on the reason. It has to be a damn good one and not something like Janco hating sand or the cold or mornings or magic."

"In my opinion, they are *all* excellent reasons." Janco huffed.

"Good to know," Ari said.

Valek left them to pack and get ready for the mission. When he reached his office, his door was slightly ajar. He had locked it, but hadn't engaged the other two, more complex locks because he'd known he wouldn't be gone long. Pulling out his cloud-kissed dagger, he eased the door wider. The lemon scent of cleaning solution hit him before he spotted Brede wiping dust from a pile of books on his conference table. A large rolling cart filled with brooms, feather dusters, and buckets sat nearby.

"How did you get in here?" Valek demanded.

The young man jumped a foot and let out a screech. He pressed the rag to his chest. "Uh…with…a key."

"Who gave you the key?"

"Uh…Kenda." He pulled out a leather tie from underneath

his shirt. Two keys hung like a pendant. "She said to guard these with my life. I swear they will never leave my person. Uh... except when I need to unlock this door or the one to your apartment." Brede tucked them back under his shirt.

Valek drew in a deep breath to steady his emotions. He imagined Kenda and the Commander sharing a conspiratorial smirk. "What are you doing here?"

"I'm cleaning. It's going to take me months to organize this mess."

"Oh no. You're not to move a thing. You can dust, sweep, scrub, whatever, but every book, file, and rock is to remain in its place. Understand?"

"But—"

"Understand?"

He sighed. "Yes."

"Good. And that cobweb stays." Valek pointed to the window. Two new silk-wrapped bugs hung in its strands. Mr. Spider had a successful night.

Brede moved closer to inspect the web. "Wow. That's a huge bat spider. Not to worry, though, his bite isn't venomous. Well, not to humans."

Curious. "How do you know?"

"As a member of the housekeeping staff, I've encountered all manner of critters that need to be evicted. I've found it advantageous to learn which ones are dangerous to us."

Valek's agents learned what creatures to avoid when on missions, but he never considered that information would help the housekeepers. "Did someone teach you?"

Brede's short burst of laughter implied the negative. "I found a couple books in the library. My colleagues thought I was weird." He shrugged.

Was. Past tense. "And now?"

"They're more accepting since Saril broke out in a fever last season. The medic couldn't figure out what was wrong with her.

But I recognized the tiny discolored welt on the back of her hand as a bite from a pink teacup spider."

"Impressive."

Another shrug. "Now I'm the designated critter ejector. Or DCE for short."

Valek couldn't resist asking, "Ejector?"

"I'm not gonna kill them." He sounded horrified at the notion. "They have the right to live. I capture them and rehome them."

So basically, Brede wouldn't harm a fly, and he was now working for Valek, who had harmed much more than flies. Lovely. In his imagination, the Commander and Kenda clinked their glasses and lifted them in a salute to Valek.

Suppressing a sigh, Valek decided to trust Kenda in her choice of housekeeper. "All right. You can clean my office in the evenings, and my apartment either in the afternoons or the mornings, but not both. You need time off."

"I'll take the mornings off," he said.

"Then follow me. I need to introduce you to the soldiers that guard the door to the Commander's and my suites."

Brede trotted at Valek's heels.

Lieutenant Millicent and Sergeant Dagon were on duty. They straightened to attention when they spotted Valek. At least they had stopped saluting him. He introduced Brede.

"Spread the word to your colleagues that he's allowed entry."

"And my cart," Brede added.

"And his cart of cleaning supplies."

"Yes, sir," they said in unison.

Valek led the young man into his suite of rooms and gave him the tour. "No need to bother with the two other rooms off the living area, I use them for storage. But I'd like to keep this one"—he gestured to Yelena's old room—"clean and ready in case I have guests."

Brede poked his head in and sniffed. "Will do." Then he

glanced around the living room. "You have so many books, perhaps I could arrange—"

"They stay on the floor. Everything remains in place."

He nodded despite the unhappy purse of his lips.

They climbed the stairs to the second floor. Valek pointed to the right. "I use the sitting area for storage."

To the left of the sitting room was a long hallway. The doorway to his carving room was closest to them. His boots crunched on the rock dust that had drifted onto the floor like snow when he strode inside. Piles of the gray rocks he used for his carvings littered the area. Toward the back was his table full of tools, his grinding wheel, and a half dozen finished statues.

"I don't normally let anyone in here, but the dust gets everywhere and should be cleaned up."

"No problem." Brede picked up a black frog statue and inspected it. The stone had streaks of silver though it and Valek had used bits of amber for the frog's eyes. "This is fantastic. Did you carve it?"

"Yes. Carving helps focus my mind when I'm working on a difficult problem."

"I know, right? When I'm scrubbing a floor, my mind is free to think about other things."

Interesting. Valek longed to ask what things but refrained.

Brede scanned the area. "Where are the pretty black rocks?"

"All around you." He picked up a small grey rock and sat down before the grinding wheel. He pumped the pedal with his foot a few times to set it spinning. Once it was fast enough, he pressed the rock to the whirling wheel for a few minutes. Then Valek blew the dust off and handed it to Brede. "See?"

"Wow. Look at that transformation! Like a caterpillar into a butterfly."

Valek's thoughts immediately went to Yelena and her transformation from a victim to a powerful Soulfinder. "Exactly."

After a brief stop in Valek's bedroom, they returned to the

lower level. Brede moved closer to inspect the weapons displayed on the wall.

"Be careful. They're still sharp, but they are secure."

"This dagger is dirty." He recoiled. "Is that blood on the blade?"

"Yes. Don't bother trying to clean it off. Actually, don't worry about the weapons at all. I oil them and keep them in good working condition."

"Why? They're useless."

"These weapons have served me well. I'm not going to allow them to rust or dull with age." And they were far from useless. Only Valek knew how to release them from the wall.

With the tour over, Valek handed Brede two more keys for his necklace. "There's three locks on my office door."

He raised his eyebrows.

"There's sensitive information in my office. And I have a number of enemies that would love to ambush me."

Brede paled. "Is it safe for me to be there at night?"

Good question. "I'll wait for you before I leave. And you can lock the door while you're inside cleaning. Do you know how to defend yourself?"

More color leaked from Brede's round face. "Uh…I took that self-defense class all the kids living in the castle had to take."

"You should attend a refresher course. Ask Kenda, she'll find you an instructor."

"Uh…yes, sir." His throat bobbed as he swallowed.

Ah hell. Valek had spooked him. "Come on, I'll escort you back."

When they returned, Brede immediately picked up his rag and attacked a layer of dust on a book cover.

"I know this place needs a great deal of work," Valek said. "Don't spend hours and hours here. A few hours each night is fine."

"But it's filthy! You can't live like this."

Valek laughed. "I can and have. I've spent weeks living in a bog for a mission. I think I can handle dust and dirt for a few more days."

"All right. What about the candles?"

"Candles?"

"You said not to move anything, but most of these are used."

"You can replace the candles, add oil to the lanterns, and fill the inkwells. Just make sure you leave the window open a crack for Mr. Spider before you leave."

He nodded. "That makes sense."

"What does?"

"That one predator would help another."

∼

Valek paused when he entered the Commander's suite. A chess set sat on the table between the couches. Ten years ago, Valek had carved it for Ambrose. The board, with its black and red squares, had been the hardest part to construct, while the pieces had been easier. Valek had transformed his gray rocks into the black side's pieces. Even after all this time, the silver still glittered in the lantern light. The red side's pieces were created from Lozen granite, a rare rock found only in the Soul Mountains. The granite had red diamond-shaped flecks mixed with the black and, once polished, the red metamorphosed into an eye-catching sparkle.

Valek hadn't seen the set in a long time. They used to play chess every night, but had stopped a few years ago because they knew each other's strategy so well, the game often ended in a stalemate.

Ambrose handed Valek a glass of whiskey as he settled on the opposite couch. "I thought I'd teach my advisers how to play chess."

"That's a great idea." He swallowed a large gulp of the smoky flavored alcohol. It warmed him from the inside out.

"It's been so long since I've played I need some practice."

Valek grinned. "Don't want to get trounced by a beginner?"

Ambrose gave him a flat look and moved a pawn. "Your move."

Ah right. Valek moved a pawn, and after a few more exchanges, they fell back into their old rhythm as if they had never stopped.

At one point, Ambrose asked, "Have you heard from MD-1?"

"Yes. My agents have confirmed the general is hunting snow cats." He braced for Ambrose's anger.

Instead, the man appeared thoughtful. "Those cats are wily. They're almost impossible to capture or kill. Almost." He tapped a fingernail on his rook. "I'm more concerned about why General Kitvivan thinks he can go against my orders."

"I'm sending Ari and Janco to handle the situation. I thought it would be a good first mission for my seconds-in-command."

Ambrose gazed at him with amusement. "While you remain here safe and warm."

"Exactly. I'm discovering quite a number of benefits to having seconds."

"Which I've been telling you about for *years*."

"You have? Funny, I don't recall—" Valek ducked as a small pillow flew over his head. He held up his hands in mock surrender. "Okay, okay. You were right."

"Nice of you to acknowledge it." Ambrose put down a second pillow and smoothed the fabric before moving his knight. "Check. When are Ari and Janco leaving?"

"Dawn." Valek pushed his king to safety.

"Stop by my office and I'll have their papers ready." Ambrose slid his bishop forward a few squares. "Check. Anything else of note?"

"Apparently, I have my very own housekeeper." Nudging his

king to the next spot, Valek glanced up. Amusement sparked in Ambrose's eyes. "I think it's excessive."

"I don't. Check."

Valek suppressed a sigh. He was running out of places to move his king. "Trevar and Adrik are also leaving on a mission in the morning." He explained about sending them to figure out Captain Ryda's puzzle.

"Aren't they still in training?" Ambrose asked.

"Yes, but Trevar's time as a baiter for the black market dealers gives him a unique insight into the citizens of Castletown. He's good at spotting those who could be coaxed into breaking the law."

"Have them report about the new group of black market dealers. Once they're feeling secure, I want you to do another raid."

"Yes, sir."

"Good." Ambrose moved his queen. "Check-mate."

~

Valek wasn't a fan of early mornings either, but there was something promising about the gradual arrival of sunlight. Night and shadows were an integral part of his trade. Within them, danger lurked and hunted. Seeing the sunrise after a nighttime op signaled survival.

The castle's stables, pasture, and training ring occupied the northwest corner of the complex. Ari and Janco had arrived before him. They had saddled their horses and were packing their supplies into leather knapsacks.

Steam puffed from the horses' nostrils as they stamped in anticipation of an adventure. The crisp air smelled of hay, grain, and that distinctive earthy scent of horse.

Valek handed them their official papers signed by the Commander.

Janco fiddled with the small scroll. "Kinda disappointing. I thought we'd get something...more."

"More?"

"Yeah. Badges or a special jacket. Something that says, I'm a second-in-command." Janco puffed out his chest.

Valek snapped his fingers. "I've the perfect thing for you."

"Ooohhh?" He rubbed his hands together. "Do tell!"

"It's a black cloak with a giant red bullseye on the back."

Janco's brows creased in confusion.

Ari laughed. "Nice. Don't worry, I'll explain it to him while we're on the road." He mounted. "Any last minute instructions?"

"Don't linger. It's a nine-day journey each way. I'd like you back home before the blizzards start."

"Yes, sir."

Janco hopped up into his saddle with ease. They clicked their tongues, urging their horses toward the east gate. Valek followed, watching until they both disappeared.

After a quick stop for breakfast, Valek returned to his office and paused as the pleasant scent of lemon greeted him. The thick dust that had coated everything except the top of his desk was gone. He hoped Brede hadn't worked too late into the night to get it all done. At least, everything remained in its place. It might appear that the clutter was haphazard and disorganized, but Valek knew exactly what each pile contained.

Over the next couple of days, Valek barely saw his new housekeeper, but there was plenty of evidence of his presence. New candle sticks waited to be lit each day. His inkpots practically overflowed. And fresh wood was stacked in the bin next to his brazier.

With the days, and especially the nights, becoming colder and colder, Brede had closed the window against the chill. Valek would have admonished him, but Mr. Spider had plenty of bugs in his web. He wondered if Brede had rehomed a few insects, letting them into Valek's office, hoping Mr. Spider's web would catch them. Perhaps Brede thought that, if the bugs were outside the castle walls, being eaten by a spider would be a natural death. Unfortunately, Valek had encountered plenty of spider webs in the wild—usually with his face. A shudder rippled up his spine at the memories.

Valek huffed at the direction his thoughts had gone. As if he didn't have anything else to do or worry about other than Brede's moral compass on insects. He settled behind his desk and read through reports.

Nothing worrisome caught his eye, and Valek enjoyed another three-day quiet spell. Normally, Valek would appreciate the downtime, but with Ari, Janco, Trevar, and Adrik on missions, the castle was too quiet.

A report from Trevar and Adrik arrived a week after they'd left. It had taken them several days just to get the baiters to talk to them, and the dealers still didn't trust them. Everyone was skittish, their nerves frayed. Trevar and Adrik hadn't found the source of the citizen's strange behavior. Yet.

He smiled at the dark lines under the word 'yet.' Trevar probably worried they'd be taken off the case for lack of results.

They reported that the incidents occurred at random intervals. Some nights two or three people ran amuck, while other nights no one.

Valek considered the information. They'd only been on the case for seven days, not enough time to really know if it was random or not. Then he remembered he had a book on statistical probabilities. Striding to his conference table, he reached his stack of math books. Except, the statistics manual wasn't on the top where he'd left it.

A quick scan of the spines revealed it to be the fourth one down. The books in this pile had been rearranged in alphabetical order by the author's last name. Valek checked the other piles. They'd all been alphabetized. He didn't know whether to be upset or impressed.

While technically the books had been moved, they also remained in their proper stacks. Valek could still easily find them. He decided it was a minor infraction and not worth mentioning to Brede.

Reading through the manual, Valek discovered he needed more data in order to establish if there was a pattern. He glanced out the window. If he hurried, he'd be able to catch Captain Ryda before she left for the day.

His suite was empty. Brede must have finished. Valek took the steps to his bedroom two at a time. After a quick check of his security measures, he entered. Stripping off his adviser's uniform shirt, he opened his closet. In order to not attract attention, he needed a disguise. Perhaps a kitchen uniform, or castle messenger uniform. Either one would work as long as they were in the Commander's colors of red and black. Even though Castletown was officially in MD-6, it was under the Commander's jurisdiction.

Valek paused. He had various uniforms tailored to fit him with the colors of all eight military districts. They all hung in his overflowing closet. Except, now they were grouped by color.

Brede.

Granted, finding what he needed was much quicker, but… He sighed, grabbed the messenger uniform and changed. He'd talk to Brede later. Maybe.

∽

The civilian watch house in Castletown resembled all the watch houses in Ixia. It was a sprawling two-story brick building with jail cells below ground level. The main entrance had a double-wide wooden door that led into a lobby. Uncomfortable chairs ringed the space. A handful of people occupied them. No one smiled, or made eye contact, or moved. They sat in silence, staring into the distance. Creepy.

A long desk blocked the only other doorway, but to get through that one, a person had to get permission from the patrol officer who sat behind the desk.

"I've a message for Captain Ryda," Valek said to the patrol officer.

Without looking up, the man held out a thick hand. "Give it here, I'll send it back."

"I've orders to give it to her directly."

"She's busy." He twitched his fingers, indicating Valek should hand over the message.

Valek lowered his voice and leaned in. "I have a message from Adviser Valek."

"Good for you. If you want to wait…" He stabbed a stubby finger at the chairs. "Be my guest." The patrol officer returned to his work.

Angling his body so the others in the room wouldn't see, Valek drew his cloud-kissed dagger in one smooth motion and pressed the tip to the officer's throat. The man froze and finally met Valek's gaze. He paled.

"I hope you enjoyed your little power trip, Officer, because it's over. My *boss* won't let me take no for an answer. Do you understand?"

"Yeah. But it's on you if she kicks you out."

"I'm willing to take that chance."

The man tipped his head. "Go on."

Valek returned his weapon to its sheath. All of his disguises had a long, slender, deep pocket, lined with thin leather, on his right hip to hide his dagger. Rounding the desk, Valek kept an eye on the patrol officer. The man ignored him.

The door opened into a buzz of activity. The main room of the building was filled with desks, and file cabinets. The proverbial bullpen. Weapons rested along the back wall. A few patrollers glanced at him and promptly dismissed him as harmless.

Valek wove through the chaos toward the left side, where a hallway led to the offices of the higher ranking officers. Captain Ryda occupied the room at the very end of the hall. The door was ajar, but he knocked.

"If it's not urgent, go away," she called.

He poked his head in. "Not urgent, but important."

"Oh, Adviser Valek. Come on in." She tucked the long strand of hair that had escaped her bun back behind her ear then gestured to the chair in front of her desk. "Do you have an update for me?"

Her office was a mix of organization and clutter. The desk and conference table were neat with plenty of workspace, but stacks of reports occupied every other flat surface except the floor.

"Sorry. No update, but I need more information."

"What do you need?"

"Did you map the places where each person was found?"

"No. We didn't think it was significant. It's not like a burglary ring or serial murders. At first, it appeared to be just disorderly conduct." She tapped her fingernails on her desk. "We have all the reports. I could assign a patroller to create a map from them." Ryda flipped through a chart. "Let me see who I can spare. We're shorthanded tonight, but I can ask Tivon to stay late."

"No need. I'll do it. Are the reports together?"

She glanced up. "Yes, they're in the FIIK room. I'll show you."

Ryda led him back down the hallway, across the bullpen and up a stairway.

"FIIK?" he asked.

They reached a large oval room with various sized tables, chalkboards, and maps on the walls.

"FIIK is an unofficial patrol designation. It means *Fuck If I Know*. This is where the unsolved cases end up. Every so often a young, ambitious patroller will try to make sense of one of them. And occasionally solve it. A few of the old timers will also revisit certain cold cases and have an epiphany."

Unfortunately, Valek also had a number of incidents over the years he hadn't been able to solve. He hadn't considered bringing in fresh eyes to take a look. Most of them were top secret, but he could have Ari and Janco read through them as part of their training.

Heading to a six-foot long desk, Ryda placed her hands on two stacks of files. "These are the reports you're looking for. If you clear off the other piles, I'll grab you a map to mark, a stylus, and some ink. Anything else you need?"

"Do you have colored ink?"

"Yes, what color do you want?"

"All of them."

She laughed. "All right." Striding to an oversized cabinet, she gathered the needed supplies.

After he created a workspace, Valek checked the lanterns on the other tables. Two had sufficient oil. The sunlight was fading rapidly so he brought them over and lit the elements. Then he pulled a chair over as Ryda set the requested items down.

"It's going to be a long night. Did you eat dinner?"

"No."

"I'll send something up."

"Thank you."

He sorted the files according to the date of the incidents. The first arrest had happened around the beginning of the cooling season. The most recent ones occurred two nights ago. A span of about seven weeks long. Valek had five different color inks, but he could mix a few so he'd have seven. One color for each week. Then he returned to the first week's cases, marking the locations in yellow ink.

The undertaking was time consuming and monotonous. Sometime during the effort, a steaming meat pie and a mug of ale had been delivered and consumed. Nearing the end of his task, one of the lanterns sputtered and died. He cursed at the delay. Running back to the bullpen, he exchanged the empty one for two lit ones.

"Hey, I need those," said the only person in the pen.

"So do I. And of the two of us, only you know where the extra oil is stored." Valek returned to the FIIK room.

He finished the last week of cases using purple ink. Then he set the lanterns on the edges of the map and stood up. Walking around the other tables, Valek waited for the colored dots to fade from his vision. With the extra illumination, he hoped to view the finished map as a single entity.

When enough time passed, he returned to the desk and glanced down. A rainbow of colors filled the map. The incidents had moved through the city during the seven weeks like a wave. And Valek now knew the next area of Castletown in its path.

CHAPTER 5

It was after midnight by the time Valek reached his corps' safe house in Castletown. Since he'd left the castle in such a hurry earlier, he had forgotten to send a message to the Commander explaining his absence. Now he'd missed their nightly meeting. It happened from time to time, and the Commander usually understood.

The safe house resembled all the others in the row. No lights shone through the windows, which meant the blackout curtains had been pulled closed. He used a special series of knocks to alert Hildred, the agent on duty. When the door opened, darkness loomed behind her figure.

He stepped into the vestibule. The door clicked shut and Hildred swept aside the curtains, revealing a living room that had been turned into an office. One lantern cast a puddle of yellow onto the desk.

"Something wrong?" Hildred asked.

"No. I need to talk to Trevar and Adrik. Do you know where they're staying?"

"They're at The Sole. It's the cheapest inn in town. Is this about the incidents they're investigating?"

"Yes. How did you know?"

"Trevar stopped here a few days after they arrived, wanted to see if we had any insights. We couldn't help him. None of our agents thought they were anything but drunk and disorderly conduct."

Still, it had been a good idea.

"He asked us to keep an eye out in case we see something odd," she added.

"Have you?"

"Not yet."

Too bad. "I also need a patroller uniform. When you do your rounds later, you can skip the Garden District. I'll be in that area until dawn."

"Yes, sir."

Each of his safe houses was equipped with disguises, supplies, weapons, and the necessary paperwork should the local watch discover their existence. Two agents lived there and took turns gathering information about the town and citizens. One worked the day shift while the other slept and vice versa. They discussed their findings at breakfast and dinner. If anything seemed off or piqued their interests, they would report it to Valek. The agents rotated to different cities every three seasons to avoid being spotted and to keep them engaged.

The second bedroom of this house had been converted into a changing room. Racks of clothing lined the walls. Valek sorted through the various sized patroller uniforms and found one that was close to his size. He didn't have time to return to his suite for one that fit better. Borrowing a knit hat, he pulled it down over his ears.

He said good-bye to Hildred and slipped out into the semi-darkness. Street lanterns in this part of town were few and far between. Keeping to the shadows, Valek headed for the Garden District. The majority of Castletown was a basic grid. Rows of homes were concentrated in some areas with businesses and factories clumped in others. They overlapped at the edges. The city was also divided into districts named after what that area was known for.

The Garden District had a mix of homes with large yards and small farms. The people who lived there were known for growing and selling fruits and vegetables. Valek walked the district, avoiding the patrol officers and seeking... Well, he wasn't quite sure.

According to his research, the next set of incidents would happen in this area. He didn't know if he'd encounter a victim or feel magic or something else. So, he kept his senses wide open.

By the time the night sky lightened with the first hint of dawn, Valek had covered the entire district and found nothing.

He returned to the safe house and changed back into his messenger uniform. Hildred also reported a quiet night in the other districts. The map he'd made had predicted the next area to be targeted, but there hadn't been a pattern to the timing. Guess he'd need to remain vigilant over the next few nights.

Valek entered The Sole right as the sun rose. A cheery bell rang when he opened the door. It was a stark contrast to the inn's dreary and cold common room. A thin man wearing an innkeeper's uniform bent over the hearth, stirring a fire to life while adding logs. Then he hung a metal tea pot over the flames.

When he straightened, he turned to Valek and eyed his uniform. "Can I help you?"

"Do you serve breakfast?"

"Yeah, but I just opened and haven't started cooking. I can get you a cup of tea while you wait."

"That would be lovely, thank you." A chill had settled into his bones despite being on the move all night. He avoided wearing his cloak for ops requiring stealth, it was too cumbersome. He'd layered extra clothing under his uniform and had a hat, but it hadn't been enough. Guess it was time to pull out his wool leggings and shirts.

The man disappeared into the kitchen, and Valek sat at the table that was the farthest from the door. He kept his back to the wall as he studied the room. The scarred and stained tables had been built with thin wood. Broken stools outnumbered the intact ones. No pictures hung on the walls, and the floor was just hard-packed dirt. Rusted lanterns lined the bar—or what had been the bar—but now appeared to be a storage area. There were three entrances to the room—the main door, the kitchen door, and a stairway in the corner that probably led up to the guest rooms.

The innkeeper returned with a mug of steaming tea and set it down.

"The Sole is an interesting name for an inn. It's why I stopped in," Valek said. He sipped the tea and was surprised by its robust flavor. "Is there a story behind it?"

After another measuring look, the man ran a hand through his short gray hair. "Depends on your perspective," he said. "To those who have limited funds, this place is the only affordable room in Castletown. To those who have extra funds, this place is on the bottom of their options, just like the sole of a foot." He shrugged. "You need a room?"

"No, I'm just passing through."

He grunted as if he didn't believe Valek. "The food'll be ready soon." Then he returned to the kitchen.

As Valek waited, he considered the man's explanation. Ixian citizens who had legitimate jobs earned a living wage and didn't need to stay at a place like The Sole. Unless they were thrifty and wanted to save a few coins. Those who chose to work illegal jobs, like the baiters for the black market dealers, earned a range of income. Some did very well, while others struggled to get by. Valek wondered if it was the uncertainty that attracted them. The possibility of hitting it big, versus a steady income.

Or was it the thrill and excitement that came with breaking the law? Probably a bit of both.

More customers arrived as Valek drank his tea. A few of the guests came downstairs. They all looked younger than twenty-five. The innkeeper served them tea.

Eventually, Valek spotted Trevar and Adrik at the bottom of the stairs. Like the other baiters, they wore merchant uniforms that had seen better days. Trevar's gaze swept the room. Would he spot Valek? Granted his disguise wasn't elaborate, but most people tended to look at the uniform and not the face. Unless they had been trained.

Trevar met his gaze without showing any signs of recognition, but he led Adrik over to Valek's table.

"Can we join you?" Trevar asked loud enough for the others to hear. "All the other tables are filled."

Well done. "Yes."

They sat. Once their backs were to the room, Trevar lowered his voice and asked, "Do you have news?"

He explained about the map. "I want you to concentrate your efforts in the Garden District."

"Yes, sir."

"Any progress with the black market dealers?" Valek asked.

"Some. We've been working for free to gain some trust. From the bits of gossip we've managed to pick up, it seems the dealers are just as freaked as everyone else over the incidents."

"It could all be an act," Adrik said. "If they're selling something that is causing it, they wouldn't admit it. No, they'd just keep taking everyone's money." Bitterness and anger hardened his tone.

Valek couldn't blame Adrik. Black market dealers had murdered his father. Those men had all been arrested and the one directly responsible had been executed, but it didn't bring back Sven.

"That's a good point," Valek said. "Keep working on earning their trust."

"Yes, sir."

The innkeeper set three plates filled with scrambled eggs and bacon on the table. Trevar and Adrik didn't hesitate to dig in.

"Doesn't he have someone to help him serve breakfast?" Valek asked.

"Nah," Trevar said with his mouth full. "Dallin does everything."

"Have you asked him if he knows what's going on?"

"Yeah. He has no idea. And if he catches you coming in drunk or on drugs, you're out on the street."

"Smart. Okay, keep up the good work. And send word if you learn anything."

"Yes, sir," they said in unison.

When Dallin returned to take the empty plates, Valek asked him how much the meal cost.

"Pay what you can," he said and left.

Adrik and Trevar each placed five coppers onto the table.

"Obviously we can afford more, but it would look suspicious," Trevar said.

Valek set a silver coin next to theirs. As a curious messenger, he could afford more. Besides, the simple meal had been delicious.

∼

Valek returned to the castle and headed straight to the Commander's office to explain his absence.

"Come in," the Commander said when he knocked.

He entered.

"Oh look, you're not dead," the Commander said dryly. "The kitchen staff will be disappointed. Many of them bet you were."

THE STUDY OF FIRE

The sarcasm was unexpected. Valek decided the best course of action was to ignore it. "Sorry for missing our meeting." He reported what he'd learned. "I'm planning on patrolling the Garden District for the next couple of nights, as well."

"Make sure you let Brede know. He was quite upset by your absence."

Ah, the reason for the Commander's snark. He'd have to have a word with his housekeeper. "I will."

"Good." The Commander stood. "Come with me."

Surprised, Valek followed his boss. When they mounted the spiral stairs in the northeast tower, Valek knew they were going to the war room. And for the life of him, Valek had no idea why. His lack of sleep must be catching up with him.

But the Commander stopped the floor below and unlocked the door, entering the map room. It was the same size and shape as the war room, except there were no stained-glass windows or oversized conference table. Instead, there were racks filled with maps of Ixia. All types, from mining maps to detailed maps of each military district.

The Commander scanned the labels and pulled out a map. He spread it on the table. It depicted Castletown. Sort of. Valek peered at it, trying to decipher it. There were no buildings, but there were named streets and strange lines marked with numbers. Then he saw the district labels and was able to get his bearings.

"Where did the incidents start?" the Commander asked.

Valek pointed to the Steel District in the northeast section of the city.

"And where does the wave go?"

He swept his hand over the areas, ending right before the Garden District.

The Commander studied the map for a few minutes, then straightened. "This is a groundwater map. See this circle?" He tapped the map. "It's a well. And see these lines?

That's the elevation of the ground. And these numbers record the depth of the groundwater. As you can see, the water flows from the northeast to the southwest." He pointed out more circles. "These are the other wells in town."

The water also flowed along the colored wave on Valek's map. "Are you suggesting someone could have put a drug in the Steel District's well to cause those incidents, and it flowed to the other wells?" He considered the problem. "But wouldn't it be diluted?"

"Not if it's insoluble."

"How long does it take the water to flow through the city?"

"It depends on the amount of rain. The more rain, the faster the water." The Commander paused. "All I'm suggesting is that it is a possibility."

"I should collect water from the wells in the Garden District and test it." But who would volunteer to drink it? Valek huffed a laugh as the answer sparked. "And I know the perfect person to taste the water."

The Commander smiled. "Yet another reason for Star to hate you."

"It might break her out of her sulk." Valek studied the map. "Can I borrow this to compare it to the map at the patrol house?"

"As long as you return it in good condition."

"I will." As Valek rolled it up, he asked, "Do you have groundwater maps for the other cities in Ixia?"

"Yes."

"Why?"

"You know why. You're just too tired to figure it out."

True. Valek followed him from the room and stopped as the answer popped into his head. The Commander had taken over Ixia by using subterfuge, bribery, and assassination, avoiding battles to limit the casualties of his followers. And now Valek realized the Commander had been fully prepared to poison the wells that provided water to his enemies.

The Commander gave him a cold smile. "Exactly."

∼

A tapping sound woke Valek. He squinted in the late afternoon sunlight, getting his bearings. He'd gone to bed right after talking to the Commander.

Tap. Clack. Pause. Tap. Clack. Tap. Tap. Clack. Clack. Pause.

The almost steady noise came from his door. Rolling out of bed, Valek pulled his dagger from underneath his pillow and crept closer. He twisted the knob and jerked it open. No one stood in the hallway. The tapping continued. Valek followed it to his carving room.

He peeked inside. Brede sat on the floor surrounded by gray rocks. He picked one up and tossed it onto a pile, the next one landed on a different mound. It took a moment for Valek to realize Brede was sorting the stones by size.

"Brede," he sighed.

The young man startled, jumping to his feet. "Buckets!" Then he recognized Valek. "You scared me."

"I didn't mean to frighten you."

He waved a dust-covered hand. "Not that. When you went missing."

Valek suppressed another sigh. "About that. I will disappear from time to time. And I'll try to let you know when I'll be gone, but there will be times, like last night, when I don't have enough time to send you a message."

"You could have left me a note on one of your desks."

Huh. "I didn't think of that. I'm not used to having a full time housekeeper." Or one that particularly cared about his whereabouts. "Next time, I will leave you a note. Although, when I'm on a mission, I won't always know how long I'll be gone. For example, I'm going out for the next few nights. It might be two or four or seven, I've no idea."

"Fair enough."

"I also might come back here to sleep during the day or not. So, I suggest you avoid cleaning up here when I'm out, just in case."

"Just in case?"

"I'm a light sleeper. If you come into my room unexpectedly, there's a good chance I'll throw my dagger first and ask questions second."

"Oh. Okay. Good to know." Brede swallowed a few times. "Uh, I guess, I should get back to work?"

"What were you doing?" He kept his tone neutral.

"Uh. Sorting."

"Is that part of your job description?"

"Well..." He wiped his dusty hands on his pants, leaving behind gray smudges. "I moved your rocks to clean underneath them, and then, I forgot which pile each rock was on, so..." He gestured to the half-built mounds. "Besides, it'll be so much easier for you to find the right sized stone!" The words gushed from his mouth. "How can that be a bad thing?"

"In this case, it's not a bad thing."

"When is organization ever bad? It makes life easy."

"Exactly. It makes it easy for someone who sneaks into my office to find the information they're seeking. That's the reason for the disorganization."

"Huh. I hadn't thought of it that way."

"There's a reason for everything I do. Next time, just ask me."

He gave Valek a panicked look. "Was there a reason all your disguises were all jumbled together?"

"Yes. That's because I'm lazy and just shove them into the closet when they come back from the laundry."

Brede laughed. "And now?"

Valek huffed. "I admit it is helpful, especially when I'm in a hurry."

"Ha!" Brede raised a hand in triumph. "And the rocks?"

"Okay, okay. You've made your point. Sometimes organization is a good thing."

Brede beamed.

"What else are you dying to organize?" Valek asked.

"Your books! Not the ones in your office, but in your suite. Do you really expect someone to creep in here to steal a book?"

"No, but those piles make sneaking around in the dark harder. And a knocked over stack makes enough noise to wake me."

He deflated a bit. "Hmmm. How about I organize the stacks by subject?"

"A fair compromise."

"Oh, and you could spread a few of your rocks underneath the windows in the living area. If someone climbs in, they'll lose their balance or roll their ankles."

"That's a good idea."

"See? We make a good team."

Valek hadn't considered their relationship as a team, but they'd both just learned something from the other. And they were working toward a common goal. "We do."

While Brede returned to sorting the rocks, Valek went back to his bedroom and changed into his patroller uniform. He filled his pack with a few essential items, including the groundwater map. It would be less time consuming for him to sleep in the safe house than return to the castle every morning.

He stopped in the kitchen for a quick bite and some supplies. Before he left the castle, he checked in with Kenda, updating her on the situation. "I'm going to send you a few bottles of water. Have Star taste the water first, then drink it all. One bottle per day. Let me know right away if she freaks out or has delusions or any effects from the water."

"You think someone spiked the wells?"

"The Commander thought it might be a possibility. Plus, it doesn't hurt to test the water."

"I doubt Star will agree with you."

"You can tell her the effects are temporary." He grinned. "Or not."

She laughed. "It'll depend on how much she annoys me that day. Did you tell Brede you'd be gone?"

"Did he—"

"Make a fuss? Yes, he did. When I didn't know where you were, he went to the Commander."

"At least someone cares about me."

She gave him a flat look. "We're used to your unexplained absences. Doesn't mean we don't care."

"I know. And, yes, I told Brede. Lesson learned."

"Well how about that! You can teach an old dog a new trick."

He growled. "Watch out I bite."

"I see Yelena hasn't finished housebreaking you yet."

"Cute. Are you done?"

"Never, but I'll let you know about Star."

"Thanks."

Valek exited the castle complex from the south gate and looped west to Castletown. The brisk air was refreshing. He'd been sweating inside with the wool layer underneath his patroller uniform.

He headed straight to the Garden District. Once there, he stopped at the first well and filled a bottle with water. Marking the cork with the location of the well, he examined the water in the fading sunlight. Nothing floated in the clear liquid. Valek moved to the next. There were five wells in the district. The water appeared clean. When he finished, Valek carried them to the safe house and gave them to Hildred.

"Please deliver these to Kenda," he said.

"Now?" she asked.

"You can wait until you've done your rounds. I'm going to be in the Garden District for the next couple nights and I'll sleep here on the couch during the day."

"All right. I'll let Inrick know your plans."

Valek stopped by the watch station to compare the Commander's groundwater map to the one he'd created the previous night. Getting inside was alarmingly easy, Valek walked to the back entrance the patrollers used and sauntered in with a couple officers. He'd have a conversation about that with Captain Ryda after they solved this puzzle.

She wasn't in her office, and he guessed she was gone for the day. So, he climbed the steps to the second level. When he entered the FIIK room, Ryda was sitting at the table, studying the map. He scuffed his boot on the floor, and she glanced up. It didn't take her long to recognize him.

"It's amazing how clear the pattern appears once you mapped it out," she said. "You must have been here for hours."

"Worth it." He joined her. "What do you see?"

"Whatever is causing the incidents is obviously moving to the southwest." She tapped the parchment. "It's not a drug, as that tends to spread out in roughly concentric circles around the people selling it. Perhaps it's from an animal's bite. Maybe the creature is sick and has been moving through the districts. No." She shook her head. "We didn't find any bite marks."

Valek considered. "How thoroughly did you examine the victims?"

"In those cases, we look for needle marks, discolored tongues, and smell their breath. Not a fun job especially when the person is still being affected. We found none of the signs, which is why I came to you."

Remembering Brede's comment about Saril's pink teacup spider bite, Valek wondered if the patrollers missed noticing a small welt. He made a mental note to ask Brede if there was a critter that could cause those symptoms.

Ryda glanced down. "I can assign extra patrollers in the Garden District."

"No need. I'm going to be covering the area for the next few nights."

Valek moved the stacks of files from the table then pulled out the groundwater map. Spreading it next to the incident map, he compared the markings to the flow of the water.

The captain moved closer. "Is that…a well?" She pointed to one of the circles.

"Yes." The pattern wasn't an exact match, but it was close enough that he couldn't discard the theory.

"Do you think someone dumped a drug in the well and it's spreading?"

"I can't rule it out." He told her about the water samples.

She laughed. "Serves Star right. That woman has been nothing but trouble since I was a patroller." Then she sobered. "She's dangerous and smart. Every time we figured out which patrollers she'd bribed for information, they ended up dead of suspicious circumstances."

"My people are keeping a close eye on her," he said.

"I thought so, too."

He met her serious gaze. "Consider me warned."

Ryda nodded. He rolled the groundwater map up, said goodbye to the captain, and headed to the safe house where he dropped off the map and his pack.

By the time Valek reached the Garden District, it was full dark. The lamplighters had filled and lit the lanterns that hung from posts. They were spaced about a hundred feet apart in this area. The distance between them lengthened on the streets that were further away from the central Market District.

Stars glittered in the night sky. The half-moon shone with just enough light to aid Valek, but not enough to expose him. A few citizens bustled along the sidewalks, finishing their day. There was only one tavern in the area, but it was closed. Most of the buildings in this part of town were residences and everyone was quick to get inside before it grew late.

Valek kept to the shadows, avoided the patrols, and let his instincts guide him. He covered the entire district twice over, but the night was quiet and still. At dawn, he returned to the safe house and stretched out on the couch.

Changing the direction of his route the next evening, he traversed the streets from the north to the south and back again, encountering nothing.

The third and fourth nights yielded the same results. If the cause had been a drug in the water, then perhaps it had lost its efficacy. Or somehow the person responsible knew Valek was hunting them.

Captain Ryda confirmed the quiet spell was the longest one since the incidents started. She hoped it signaled the end. But Valek suspected it wouldn't be that easy.

And he was right. Two hours past midnight on the sixth night, a woman's scream pierced the silence.

CHAPTER 6

"He's gonna find me!" the woman screamed. "He's gonna kill me!"

No longer keeping to the shadows, Valek ran toward the shrill voice. He raced down the empty streets, hoping to beat the Castletown patrollers to the woman.

"Gotta run! Gotta hide! He's close!"

Half a block away, a flash of white disappeared around a corner. Valek increased his pace. When he rounded the bend, he spotted the woman. Her feet were bare, her long hair flew behind her like a horse's tail, and she clutched the bottom of her nightgown to keep from tripping over it.

"Wake up, wake up!" she screeched. "Or you're gonna die!"

He caught up to her. "It's okay," he said. "You're safe."

She slowed and turned to him. Her wide eyes resembled a frightened animal, and tears streaked her face. When she met his gaze, she shrieked, "It's you! Don't kill me!" She kicked him before taking off.

Good thing he'd moved instinctively, otherwise she'd have hit his groin instead of his thigh. Valek sprinted after her. This time he didn't bother trying to soothe her. Tackling her, Valek twisted so he hit the ground hard on his back, skidding on the cobblestones while she landed on top of him.

She thrashed in his arms, but he held tight. Magic clung to the woman. He cursed. Flipping over and curling around her, he hoped to block the source of the power. After a few more attempts to elbow him, she went limp. Valek waited in case she was playing dead.

"What happened? Where am I?" she asked in a small, scared voice.

Valek sat up. He touched her shoulder. The magic was gone. He said, "Carrot Street, I think."

"Do you need assistance?" a masculine voice asked.

A patroller holding a baton stood a few feet away. Another officer ran toward them. She had also pulled her baton. Valek wondered if that was how they subdued the victims.

When she reached them, she asked, "Another one?"

Valek helped the woman to her feet. "No. She had a nightmare that seemed so real, she ran from her house screaming. As you can see, she's awake and not raving. I'll escort her back home."

The woman stared at him in shock, but thankfully didn't say anything. The patrollers weren't happy, but they didn't stop him. Valek suspected they would follow as he led her down the street.

"Where do you live?" he asked.

"Twenty-five Cucumber Court."

"What's your name?"

"Bea. Is that what really happened to me?"

"What do you remember?"

"I..." She shivered and wrapped her arms around her chest.

Valek took his uniform shirt off and draped it over her shoulders.

Taking a deep breath, Bea said, "It had to be a nightmare. Except, I couldn't wake from it. And you were there."

"I chased you."

"No. Before that."

Odd. "Me specifically? Or a patrol officer in general?"

"You, specifically. Not dressed like a patroller either. Dressed in all black." She stepped away from him. "You were coming to kill me."

He stilled as some of the pieces clicked into place. "Do you know who I am?"

Bea shook her head. "I've never seen you before tonight."

Not a surprise. Valek tried to keep a low profile among the general population. But a magician afraid of being caught in Ixia would be terrified of Valek.

"You had a name in the dream." Bea jerked with recognition and backed away from him. "Please don't kill me."

"I've no intention of harming you. The nightmare you experienced wasn't your own."

"But that's impos— I don't have magic! Don't kill me!" She held her hands up in a pleading gesture.

Normally, Valek didn't mind his reputation, but there were times when it was bloody inconvenient. "I'm not going to kill you. You are the victim, not the perpetrator."

"Oh." Bea's body quivered as if she was ready to bolt.

Conscious that they probably had an audience, Valek said in his most soothing tone, "You're freezing. Let's get you home. I'll explain on the way."

She hesitated for a few heartbeats, then keeping her distance from him, she resumed walking.

"My theory is that there is a magician in Castletown. They are naturally afraid of me catching and executing them. At night, they have nightmares of me hunting them and, because they're asleep, they don't have control of their magic. They must have projected their nightmare onto you."

Bea pulled his shirt tighter around her shoulders. "Do you think this magician is the one causing all the problems?"

"At this point, I'm not sure. That's why I'm investigating." He stopped and turned to her. "And I need you to promise not to say anything to anyone about me being here. Or about your nightmare."

"What if it happens again?"

"None of the other victims were targeted twice." Probably because the magician moved locations to avoid the extra patrols, which was why Valek wanted to keep this incident a secret so as to not spook the person into relocating again. Bea might have another nightmare, but he didn't want her to have trouble sleeping. Besides, Valek planned to be nearby. "Do you promise?"

"Will you let me know when they are caught?"

"I will."

"Then I promise."

When they reached her house, she handed him his shirt. "Thank you for waking me up."

"You're welcome." He waited until she closed the door. Then he disappeared into a shadow and watched the street. The two patrollers had hung back, but now they approached Bea's house and glanced around. Finding nothing, they left.

Valek scanned the nearby buildings. Bea's place was in a small cul-de-sac. Two houses bookended hers, and behind them was a tight row of residences. No light shone from any of the windows facing him.

His thoughts whirled as he considered his new theory. He hadn't been entirely truthful with Bea. Magicians who had control of their magic didn't lose that control while they were asleep. The ones that did were adolescents whose powers had just awakened. And now Valek needed to track down the teenager before they could do any more harm.

Once found, he'd have to decide what to do with them. A heavy weight sank in his chest. If the person was close to flaming out, he'd have no choice but to end their life. The disruption to the blanket of magic power that surrounded the world would be disastrous. While the Commander would probably give him another medal if he helped ruin the source of the magicians' magic, Valek couldn't do that to Yelena and those who used their powers to help others. Since being with Yelena, he'd dreaded the thought of killing another magician. However, if they were abusing their power to harm, like Alea Daviian and Mogkan, he had no problem dispatching them.

Valek looped around the neighborhood, seeking magic. Since he was immune, the magic didn't affect him, but he'd feel a sticky sensation on his skin when it was in use nearby. The main streets remained quiet and there were no signs anyone was awake at this late hour. All the windows were black. When he entered the alley behind Bea's house, he paused to allow his eyes to adjust to the darkness. The moon was waning toward new and not as bright as previous nights. Plus, the residences to each side blocked most of the moonlight.

He moved carefully down the narrow alley. Having used them often in his line of work, Valek appreciated their existence. Unfortunately, so did others. While this neighborhood appeared to be safe, he assumed danger lurked in every shadow.

Halfway through the alley, Valek spotted a thin yellow glow coming from a second story window. Someone was awake. The magician or a person unable to sleep? Only one way to find out. Valek climbed up the wall of the house. When he reached the window, he peeked in through the small gap.

A young girl, perhaps fifteen years old, paced the length of her bedroom. Her eyes were puffy and red, and she clutched a handkerchief in one hand and a stuffed dog in another. Stopping suddenly, she perched on the edge of the bed. She pressed the dog to her chest, closed her eyes, and took a few deep breaths.

Magic brushed his face and retreated. He waited for a cry of alarm or for her to jump up and extinguish the lantern, but nothing happened. Another pulse touched him, and then a third. Confused at first, Valek realized she must be practicing how to control her magic. While he could sense her power, he couldn't determine what she was trying to do. However, he suspected she had the ability to mentally communicate with another person, which was why poor Bea and the others experienced the new magician's nightmares.

Valek climbed down to the alley. The number forty-three was on the back door. Circling around to the front, he noted the street's name was Peach Lane, which meant the alley was called Peach Alley by default. He patrolled the streets in case the magician returned to bed and accidentally targeted another victim.

Before he could plan how to solve the problem, Valek needed more information. If the magician had been moving from house to house to avoid detection, he needed to know who organized the effort.

At dawn, he returned to the safe house. Inrick and Hildred sat at the table eating breakfast. Valek joined them.

"Another boring night?" Inrick asked as he set a cup of tea in front of Valek.

"No. I rescued a damsel-in-distress." He explained about the encounter with Bea, and how he found the person responsible for the incidents.

"Your persistence paid off. Well done," Hildred said.

"Did you...er...take care of her?" Inrick asked.

"Not yet. We need to discover who else is involved. Inrick, I want you to watch the house today and see who comes and goes. I'll keep an eye on it at night in case she loses control again."

"There are records of all the home and business owners at the watch station," Hildred said. "Do you want me to request permission to view them?"

"That's a great idea. But I'll do it this morning."

After breakfast, Hildred went to bed, Inrick left for his stake out, and Valek headed to the watch station. The records room was open to the public, but a person had to have a good reason for wanting to access them.

"Busy night?" Captain Ryda asked when he stopped in her office.

"Did your patrollers report me?"

"Not you specifically. They said they didn't recognize you as one of their team members and the situation seemed dodgy. That woman wasn't like the others, so they let you go. However, they followed you to twenty-five Cucumber Court and then lost you. Did you find the person responsible for the incidents?" Hope laced her voice.

"I think so. I'm going to need a few days to sort it out. Can you keep your patrollers away from the area during that time?"

"Yes. Why?"

"I don't want to spook them into moving to another location."

"All right. Do you need any help from my people?"

"Not at this time, but I do need access to the records room."

"I already checked. Twenty-five Cucumber Court is owned by Bea and Evert. She works for a baker, and he works for a local farmer, picking fruit and vegetables. No criminal history for either of them. No children."

"That's good to know, but I need to look up their neighbors."

"Of course." Ryda led him downstairs.

There were two wings of the underground level. One contained the jail cells and the other held the town's records.

A patroller guarded the door. He was slouched against it with his eyes half closed, but he straightened to attention when he spotted the captain. "Back so soon, Captain?"

She smiled. "Please let this man into the records room. He can stay as long as he needs."

"Yes, sir."

"Thank you." Then to Valek, "Let me know if you need anything else."

"I will."

She left. The patroller eyed Valek with curiosity, but he unlocked the door. It opened into a foyer. A bench filled with lanterns, oil, and matches lined the left wall.

"Light your lantern here. No open flames are allowed inside," the man said in a tone that implied he had given the speech a million times. "If you knock the lantern over, don't hesitate to extinguish the flames. There are plenty of buckets of sand within reach. Removal of any records is strictly prohibited. Your pack will be searched prior to your exit."

Valek wasn't carrying one, but he said, "Thanks." Lighting a lantern, Valek entered the main room.

File cabinets stacked to the ceiling lined the walls and created new walls within the space. Step stools littered the floor. Thank fate each drawer was labeled. The deeds to all the buildings in Castletown filled two entire floor-to-ceiling cabinets. Each district had its own drawer. He pulled the one labeled Garden District out, hoping they were organized by street address and not by owner's names.

Luck was with him. He sorted through them and found forty-three Peach Lane. A few desks had been scattered around. Each had a bucket of sand next to it. Valek sat down and opened the file. The owner of the house was not a person, but a corporation—Secure, Trustworthy, and Reliable, Incorporated.

Valek wasn't familiar with the company. If he had to guess, it might be one of the caravans that transported goods between military districts. The name was a bit over the top, though. Too earnest. And the only reason for them to purchase a house was probably for the owner of the company and their family. However, something about it just didn't sit right. He wondered if the company owned other buildings in Castletown.

He took the lantern and strode to the record room's entrance. The same bored patroller stood guard.

"I'll be right back." Valek set the lantern onto the bench in the foyer.

The man yawned.

Valek hurried to the FIIK room. He took the map and half the incident reports and carried them to the record room. He made a second trip for the rest of the stack. Then he spread the map out on the desk.

Bea lived two houses away from forty-three Peach Lane. Good thing he had organized the reports by date. He opened the first one. The address of the victim had been recorded along with their name. Valek located the residence on the map and then began the very tedious process of checking the owners of each of the houses nearby.

The owners' names didn't spark any inspiration, but the fourth house he checked was also owned by Secure, Trustworthy, and Reliable, Incorporated. And it was close enough to victim numbers two, three, and four.

Valek spent the rest of the day checking addresses. Sure enough, a building owned by Secure, Trustworthy, and Reliable, Incorporated was near all the victims' houses. Were they providing safe houses for new magicians? He needed to investigate the company. Good thing he was in the record room.

The files on the companies registered in Castletown filled three cabinets. Thank fate they were alphabetized. Secure, Trustworthy, and Reliable, Incorporated claimed to be a general contractor available for any and all jobs. The company was owned by Gestirn. Valek didn't recognize the name. Not a surprise.

Valek wrote down all the information. Perhaps Kenda would have some insight. By the time he finished his research, it was close to sunset.

Suddenly ravenous, he hurried back to the safe house. Hildred and Inrick had waited for him.

"Report," he said to Inrick as they sat down for dinner.

"No one left or entered the house all day."

Disappointing, but typical. "I'll keep watch tonight."

"Aren't you exhausted?" Hildred asked.

"It's been a while since I've had to stay up multiple nights, but I've plenty of experience."

Valek talked a good game, but after hours of nothing but silence, he struggled to stay awake. He walked in circles around forty-three Peach Lane to keep alert. No one raced through the streets screaming. Nothing happened.

He dragged his body back to the safe house, updated Hildred and Inrick, and collapsed onto the couch.

∽

Waking in time for dinner, Valek dressed and joined his agents. "Anything?" he asked.

"Yes," Inrick said. "A man arrived in the afternoon. He carried a couple bags filled with food."

"Did you recognize him?"

"Yes. But for the life of me, I can't remember his name." Inrick slapped his forehead. "Sorry."

"Describe him."

"He wore a merchant uniform. He's around fifty years old. About six feet tall. In good shape. I'm sure I've seen him, but I can't place him."

"It'll come to you eventually. How long did he stay?"

"An hour or so. Not long. I followed him when he left. He stopped in the Black Cat Tavern. I waited a few minutes before going in, and I discovered something very interesting." Inrick leaned back with a cat-that-caught-the-mouse expression.

"Go on," Valek urged.

"The man was sitting and talking with our infamous food taster, Star."

It hit Valek like a bolt of lightning. Star! Or rather STaR, Inc., Secure, Trustworthy, and Reliable, Incorporated. He smiled. It was four days before the cold season, and he'd won the bet. Then he sobered. It shouldn't have taken him that long to make the connection. He blamed it on lack of sleep.

Nothing happened of note the following two days. But on the day before the start of the cold season, Valek's midnight vigils paid off. Deep in the night, two men entered Peach Alley. They knocked lightly on number forty-three.

The door opened and two people joined the men. By their silhouettes, Valek guessed the slight and shorter figure was the young girl he had seen inside. Beside her was another man, but it was too dark to discern any facial features.

All four exited the alley and headed south. Valek followed. They kept to the shadows for the most part and avoided the patrols. However, they couldn't avoid all the streetlamps. When they crossed a puddle of light, he caught a glimpse of the men. Two he didn't recognize, but the man from the house was Porter. The Commander's kennel master, and the person Inrick couldn't name.

That was a surprise and yet not. Porter had some magical ability, and it was obvious he was helping this new magician escape Ixia. Valek knew Porter had helped others in the past, but he hadn't interfered. In fact, he had been glad. Had shutting down Star's operations effected Porter's efforts? Was that why they had to keep moving the young girl to different houses throughout Castletown?

Valek continued to trail them. They reached the edge of the Snake Forest and stopped. Inching closer, Valek stayed in the shadows. Porter handed the one man a pouch. It jingled with coins. Then he gave another pouch to the young girl.

Porter crouched down to her eye level. "Message me when

you get to Sitia. You can send letters with the trade caravans going to Ixia. That's not illegal. Okay?"

"I will," she said. "I know I caused you and all those poor people so much trouble." She lunged into his arms. "Thank you so very much."

He hugged her back. "You can thank me by learning how to control your magic and living a happy life in Sitia."

They said goodbye. The girl accompanied the men into the forest, and Porter headed north, presumably to the castle. Valek could find the kennel master at any time, so he followed the group into the dark woods. The moon was barely a sliver, but he noticed there was a narrow path. Probably an old smuggler's route.

After a hundred feet or so, they lit a small bullseye lantern and shone the thin beam of light onto the ground. It was risky. The light could be spotted by the border patrol, but they avoided tripping over roots or walking into trees. Besides, the patrols stayed near the border. And it would take a good eight hours to walk that far.

Valek decided he'd ensure the young girl reached Sitia. He would distract the border guards if they spotted the smugglers. In his opinion, the Commander's view on magicians was overly harsh, and Valek had helped quite a number of new ones escape Ixia.

The group trekked until dawn. Then they rested as they ate breakfast. Valek's stomach grumbled. He'd left his pack at the safe house, but he had a few sticks of beef jerky tucked into his pockets. They resumed their walk and reached the border with Sitia a few hours later.

The Snake Forest undulated like a snake from the Soul Mountains in the east to the Sunset Ocean in the west. It was the official border between Ixia and Sitia. The Commander had cleared the last hundred feet of the forest to make it harder for people to enter or exit Ixia illegally. Of course, people found ways to cross. Nighttime was the easiest. The sheer length of the border made it impossible to cover every mile. If a person was patient and waited for a patrol to move through an area, they could cross in the daylight without worry.

That was what the men did. Finding hiding spots, they hunkered down in the forest. Wearing dark gray cloaks, they blended in. A few hours later, a patrol came through. Valek watched the unit. The team did a decent job of searching for intruders, but they missed checking some obvious spots. Valek remembered the exercise he had done with Trevar, Adrik, Ari, Janco, and the others. Adrik had told his teammates to poke at large shadows with a stick. It had been a good idea and could be used even in the daylight to poke dense spots of greenery or, for the cold season, the dead spots. Perhaps Valek would assign Ari and Janco to give the patrols a refresher course.

The trio waited another hour before leaving their hiding spots and crossing the clearing into Sitia. Valek stopped at the edge of the forest, watching. Would the two men abandon the young girl as soon as they crossed into Sitia? However, it appeared they planned to stay with her until they reached a town. Probably Robin's Nest in the Featherstone Clan's lands, but he wasn't quite sure how far west they had drifted. Sitia had eleven official clans, and one illegal clan that called themselves the Daviians because they hid in the Daviian Plateau.

Alea had been from that clan. Ferde had been another Daviian, but he was defeated by Yelena before he could finish the Efe ritual and was currently in jail. Valek hoped the Sitian Council had executed him by now, but he doubted it. They ruled by committee, and it took them ages to make decisions.

Tired, hungry, and thirsty, Valek trudged back to Castletown, arriving at the safe house a few hours after dinner. Inrick waited inside.

"Phew," Inrick said. "We were worried." He held up a hand. "Yeah, I know we're not supposed to be, but I sat outside that house all day and I just knew it was empty."

"Where's Hildred?"

"She relieved me at dinner. We didn't want to take eyes off that place just in case."

Valek explained about the nighttime escape. However, he didn't tell Inrick about Porter. Either his agent would recognize him or not. Porter had one of those average faces that was forgettable. Plus, he kept to himself and most of Valek's agents didn't use dogs for their missions.

"So, Star's getting back into smuggling," Inrick said.

"It appears so, but I need to do some more investigating to find out the extent." And decide what to do about it.

"At least there's some good news," Inrick said. "No more night terrors for the locals. What are you going to tell Captain Ryda?"

"Let's wait a couple nights to ensure that the magician caused the incidents. I'd hate to tell her too soon."

"All right. What about Hildred?"

"You can tell her I'm back but have her remain in the Garden District tonight just in case."

Valek ate a large portion of the leftover stew and collapsed into bed. When he worked as an assassin fifteen years ago, he could go days without sleep. Now he felt every one of his thirty-five years. Getting old sucked.

∾

Over the next few nights, all remained quiet and calm. As promised, Valek visited Bea to tell her the news. Then he headed to Ryda's office to update her on the situation.

"We've solved the problem. You shouldn't have any more unexplained drunk and disorderly incidents."

"Was it something in the well water?" she asked.

"No. It was due to magic. A young person came into her powers and had limited control."

"Have you…" She swallowed the rest of her words. Even experienced watch captains balked at the thought of killing a young person.

"Yes. I've taken care of the problem." Sort of. He still needed to figure out a few things, but one crisis at a time.

Ryda paled as she assumed the worst, adding more fuel to Valek's reputation. To distract her, he told her about how easy it had been for him to get into the station.

"I'll need to resume training and hire more officers," she said. "When you arrested all of Star's employees, I lost a few patrollers who were corrupt." She cleared her throat. "Thanks for the help. Anytime you need assistance, just let me know."

"Will do."

Valek left the station. It was the fourth day of the cold season. A light snow fell, dusting the town with a layer of white. He wrapped his short cape over his shoulders, covering the top half of his uniform. After spending the last dozen nights outside wearing only a few layers of clothing, Valek thought he'd never be warm again.

He longed for his apartment, imagining an evening sitting on his couch with a book in hand next to the blazing hearth. However, he had one more stop to make. As daylight drained from the cloud-covered sky, Valek hurried to The Sole. When he entered, the patrons frowned at the cold air and snow sweeping in his wake. He hurried to shut the door before heading to the table in the corner.

Glancing around, Valek was relieved he had arrived before Trevar and Adrik. Again, he noted the younger crowd.

Dallin, the innkeeper, grunted at him as he set a mug down. "Yer back."

"I come through Castletown from time to time and I liked the eggs."

Another grunt. "Tonight's pork and beans." He disappeared into the kitchen.

Valek sipped the golden liquid in the mug. It was warm and tasted like apples and cinnamon. The drink hit his stomach like a hot coal, sending a wave of heat right through him. Damn good stuff. He considered removing his cape but didn't want to expose his patroller's uniform and scare the customers away. His black pants were standard issue for many different jobs. He already stood out as the oldest patron in the inn.

Trevar and Adrik entered. They said hello to a few people before winding their way to Valek's table, once again asking to join him.

"Any news?" Trevar asked.

Valek updated them. "There shouldn't be any more problems."

He frowned. "Does this mean our mission is over?"

"What's been going on with the black market dealers?"

"We're slowly earning their trust. And now that the strange incidents are over, they'll eventually relax."

Valek considered. Knowing the names and locations of all the new dealers in Castletown would be beneficial. And experience was just as important as schooling when it came to spying. "Keep gaining their trust. We can reevaluate your status in a few weeks."

They both grinned.

"Do our reports meet your expectations?" Trevar asked.

"Your first one was fine, but I haven't been back to the castle in almost two weeks. Do you have any new information?"

Trevar's blue eyes lit with delight. "Oh, you're going to love this. We spotted Star in town." He waited.

"She's allowed to come to town during her time off," Valek said.

"I know, but she was in the Black Cat Tavern. She's planning on getting back into business."

"How do you know?"

"She's recruiting people."

CHAPTER 7

Valek knew Star was looking into restarting her business, but to actively recruit people in the Black Cat Tavern was bold. Too bold? Was this a trick to make Valek focus his attention on her antics at the Black Cat, while she secretly built another empire? He'd be a fool to underestimate her.

"Was she successful?" Valek asked Trevar.

Before he could answer, Dallin came over to their table and set down three steaming bowls of pork and beans. Valek asked for a refill of the drink.

"Good, eh? I make it myself."

"What do you call it?"

"It depends on your perspective." Dallin scanned Valek. "For yours, I'd call it The Ball Thawer." Dallin bustled away.

Impressive and accurate. Trevar and Adrik tried to hide their grins.

Continuing their conversation, Trevar said, "Star hired a couple of muscles, but everyone knows what happened to her organization, so they're playing it safe."

He mulled over the information as they ate. Bacon, brown sugar, and mustard had been added, transforming the usually dull meal into a flavorful experience. And he wasn't the only one scraping the bottom of the bowl with his spoon.

"Did Star recognize either of you?" Valek asked.

"No. And I doubt she would. We haven't had any interaction with her," Trevar said.

"The only reason we recognized her was because Star interrupted a lesson," Adrik added. "She stormed into the training room, yelling at Kenda for some reason, but Kenda tossed her out on her ass."

Valek would have loved to see that. However, the fact that Star didn't know Trevar or Adrik might work in his favor. "I've a mission for you, but this is voluntary as it might get perilous."

Excited by the idea, they leaned forward. *Boys.*

"What do you think about getting recruited by Star and working for her?"

"Ooohhh, that would be perfect," Trevar said.

"Then we'll know what she's planning, instead of having to wait and guess," Adrik said.

"You have to do it right, though," Valek said. "You can't be too eager to join. There needs to be some reluctance. Let her reel you in."

"Do we need new cover stories?" Trevar asked.

"No. Play up how little money you're making for baiting people. And with your extensive knowledge of the dealers, she'll see you as potential protegees."

"We're in," Adrik said.

Valek met each of their gazes until their grins faded. "She's dangerous. Trust your instincts. Request help if you need it. If you get the sense things are getting hot, leave immediately. Do you understand?"

"Yes, sir," they said in unison.

"Good. I want twice weekly reports. You can deliver them to the agents at the safe house."

"Yes, sir."

Leaving seven coppers each for the meal, they took their mugs over to the hearth, joining the others who had gathered there. The group laughed and chatted. They seemed comfortable as if they did this every night.

Valek waited until Dallin returned to clear the bowls. He gave the innkeeper a small pouch filled with five gold coins. "I appreciate what you're doing here."

"That so? And what am I doing?" Dallin asked with a suspicious squint.

"It depends on your perspective." Valek smiled.

He left the warmth of the inn. When the first blast of cold, snowy air hit him in the face, he wished he had asked Trevar to steal the recipe for The Ball Thawer.

∼

Valek opened the door to his suite. The scent of lavender nearly brought him to his knees. Hope and fear tangled in his throat. "Yelena?" He could barely speak.

No answer. He left the door open, letting in the weak light from the hallway. Fumbling for a lantern, he lit it with trembling fingers.

He shone the light around the living room. "Yelena?"

No one. Disappointment crashed over him, and he sank onto his couch to keep from toppling. He'd been keeping busy, staying focused. Yet one whiff of lavender had felled him. Valek drew in a deep breath, inhaling her scent. It had been roughly half a season since he last held her in his arms. How in the world had he lasted almost a year without seeing her before?

After allowing loneliness and pity to run its course, Valek

stood. He lit a few more lanterns and stopped in amazement. His apartment hadn't been this clean since… Never. And it explained the lavender scent. But why would Brede switch? He'd been using lemon cleaner prior to Valek's departure.

Valek was too tired to second guess Brede's intentions. Instead, he built a big, beautiful fire and dragged his couch closer to the flames. Ahhh.

While the warmth from the flames soaked into his skin, Valek mulled over Porter's involvement with Star. He'd been helping new magicians escape to Sitia, and, apparently, had hired Star's people to safeguard them. When Valek had destroyed her organization, he'd inadvertently hindered Porter's network. The kennel master must have been unable to find anyone to escort the young magician. Instead, she had moved from place to place in Castletown until Star had time to recruit a couple people to take the girl to Sitia.

Despite it being illegal, Valek had no issue with Porter's network. And if that was all Star was up to, Valek would allow it to continue. Except, he doubted Star would be content with such small stakes. If he had to stop Star again, Valek would ensure Porter's network remained in business.

Valek dozed for a couple hours, waking in time for his nightly meeting with the Commander. Knocking on Ambrose's door, he stifled a yawn.

It swung open. "I heard a rumor you were back. Come in."

Valek followed him into the living area and settled in his spot.

Ambrose brought over a glass of fire whiskey and handed it to Valek. "You look like you could use it." He relaxed on the opposite couch.

"That bad?" Valek asked.

Cocking his head slightly, he scanned Valek. "You lost some weight, and there are dark smudges underneath your eyes."

Valek raised his glass, acknowledging the comment. He took a long sip.

"Tell me a bedtime story," Ambrose said. "Did you capture the villain and save the day?"

He laughed. "Singlehandedly."

"Of course. Isn't that what all dashing heroes do?"

"Dashing? Aww, you missed me."

"Like a toothache."

"Nice." Valek updated him.

"Magic and not a drug." Ambrose stared into the distance. "If you think about it, magic could be considered a drug. Magicians abuse it, crave it, and are willing to do anything to get more of it. But I digress. The magician?"

"Is no longer a problem."

"Good. Anything else?"

"Star's back to her old tricks." He explained.

"She's been a problem since the beginning. Kill her and train a new taster."

"I would, but I just discovered her company. Which makes me worry about what else I may have I missed."

"Does it matter?"

"Yes, because if she could set up such a complex network right under our noses, then so could someone else. I need to see how it all works so I can prevent others from doing the same thing. And this time, I have agents on the ground floor." Plus, he needed to decide what to do about Porter. If Valek killed Star, the kennel master might bolt.

"Do what you need, but if she gets too troublesome, I won't hesitate to put a permanent end to her schemes."

"Understood. What have I missed while I was gone?"

"I sent Adviser Maren to help General Rasmussen with his civilian watch problem. She finished her course in diplomacy." He took a sip of his brandy. "I talked with her at length. Patience and tact are not Maren's strongest skills, but she's intelligent. I think she plans on the old 'I'll help you and you'll help me and we'll both keep the Commander happy' tack."

"That's a good one. I've used it many times. And occasionally I manage to make the other person think it was their idea."

"As long as she gets results, and I don't have General Rasmussen complaining to me, I'm content."

"Did you give her a timeline?"

"No. I didn't want to rush her. If she doesn't get results or the general remains stubborn, then I'll have to send a more influential adviser." Ambrose gave Valek a pointed look.

Valek refrained from groaning aloud. Instead, he put his glass in the air and said, "Here's hoping Maren has a successful mission."

Ambrose clinked glasses and drank.

Valek entered Kenda's office early the next morning. He updated her about the incidents in Castletown, and Trevar and Adrik's new mission. "And I won the bet. Star was actively recruiting people for her network before the cold season started."

Frowning, she reached into her desk. She pulled out a small purse bulging with coins and slapped it into his palm. "Those boys are playing with fire. Star isn't easily fooled."

"I've warned them, and I'll have Hildred and Inrick keep an eye on them."

"Don't let her get too far with rebuilding her network. The more complex it becomes, the harder it is for us to unravel."

"I won't."

"Do you want me to dig deeper into her corporation?"

"Yes, please." With that taken care of, Valek switched subjects. "Have you heard from Ari and Janco?"

"Just a brief report that they'd arrived in MD-1. I don't expect we'll get another. After they finish their mission, they'll be on the way home. Unless they get stuck by the blizzards, and then the messengers are trapped as well."

Valek wasn't worried about the power twins, but he'd like them to return soon. "I think Janco is highly motivated to get the job done quickly."

Kenda laughed. "Janco apologized in the message for his shaking handwriting, claiming he was shivering uncontrollably."

There was a knock on Kenda's door. "Come in."

A castle guard entered. He carried a small wooden crate. Red ribbon had been wrapped around it. The bow held a scroll the size of a cigar. "This came for the Commander."

"From whom?"

"The man said it was given to him by a Sitian merchant at the exchange. He was told it's from the Sitian Council."

Valek straightened. Ever since relations had deteriorated with the Sitians, the merchant caravans have been exchanging goods at the border. Ixian merchandise heading to Sitia was given to Sitian caravans at the border and vice versa.

"Set it on the table please." Kenda thanked the guard, dismissing him.

Screening of all packages addressed to the Commander was the standard safety procedure prior to delivery. After the man left, Valek and Kenda approached the crate.

He held a hand over the crate, seeking the sticky strands of magic. Finding none, he touched it. "No magic." Pulling the scroll from the bow, Valek broke the seal and read the letter. "It's from the Sitian Council. They are apologizing for the way Ambassador Signe's visit ended. And they'd like to reestablish diplomatic communications. The crate is a peace offering."

"Is it legit?"

"The paper is expensive, and the words are written with authoritative strokes."

She put her hands on her hips. "How can you tell that?"

"There are no hitches. The letters flow together, and it's obviously written by a person who does this for a living."

"If you say so. Since it's from the Sitian Council, maybe we should let the Commander open it?"

"No exceptions, Kenda." Valek studied the crate. Except, for the thin gaps between boards, it was well constructed. "The top is nailed down. I'll go get a crowbar."

He strode down the hallway to their weapons cache, which was a fancy word for the medium sized storage room that had been converted into an armory for Valek's corps. A variety of swords, knives, crossbows, blow pipes, darts, bo staffs, and sais had been arranged so they were easy to find and grab when in a hurry. Other tools and manacles hung on the back wall. Valek found the stack of crowbars. They came in handy for a smash and grab operation or a raid. When there was no time for picking locks, just break the windows and force open the doors.

Kenda was studying the scroll in the patch of sunlight that streamed through her hexagonal window. "Do you find it odd that the signature is just 'The Sitian Council?' I thought all the eleven clan members and four master magicians had to sign a document to make it legal."

"They do for official documents like laws and treaties. But I don't think it's required for a friendly letter. Otherwise, they'd have to sign everything and that would be tedious and a logistical nightmare in tracking down all fifteen people."

Valek shoved the thin end of the crowbar underneath the crate's lid. "Hold the bottom, please."

Kenda grabbed it as he levered the crowbar up. The nails creaked as the lid parted. Then it popped off, landing on the floor with a bang. Green coils filled the inside of the crate.

It took a couple heartbeats for Valek to recognize the shape rising slowly from the box.

"Snake!" he yelled.

Kenda jumped back just as it lunged for her arm. The creature reared for another strike. Valek pulled his dagger and leapt onto the table. It swiveled and bit into his leather boots. Before it could disengage, Valek swooped down and cut its head off.

"For the love of mischief, did someone just try to assassinate the Commander?" Kenda had retreated to the other side of her desk.

"It depends." Careful to avoid its fangs, he pulled the creature's head from his boot and tossed it on top of the body. Then he eased off the table. "If the person who sent it knows about our safety protocols, they wouldn't expect the snake to reach the Commander. In that case, they're sending either a warning or trying to cause trouble between Ixia and Sitia." He cleaned the ichor from his blade.

"And if they didn't know that we open all packages for the Commander, then it was an assassination attempt." Kenda stood as far away from the dead snake as possible.

"Yes, with the Sitian Council implicated." Except, he didn't think the council would try to assassinate the Commander. "It could be from Cahil, the Wannabe King. He might be trying to provoke the Commander into retaliating against the council, which would aid in his we-should-attack-Ixia-before-they-attack-us campaign."

"And if it was from the council?"

"That would be a declaration of war." Valek covered the crate with the lid. "I need to find out what type of snake this is. It might not be venomous."

"Why would anyone send a nonvenomous snake?"

Valek shrugged. "Perhaps as a gift. Maybe sending a snake is a Sitian gesture of good faith or something. I'm not going to jump to conclusions until I know more."

"You're taking that thing with you, right?"

"Ah, Kenda, I didn't know you're scared of snakes."

"I didn't know either. Not until one popped up in my office and tried to bite me."

Valek carried the crate to his office. The clean scent of lemon filled the warm air. Either Brede had kept the brazier burning, or he'd heard Valek had returned from Castletown. He moved a few piles on his conference table, making room for his new acquisition. Once he had more information, he'd inform the Commander of the "gift."

He grabbed a number of books on wildlife then went to his desk. Mr. Spider and his web were missing. It was the cold season, and the arachnid had lasted longer than he should, but Valek was still sad to see him gone.

Ignoring the stacks of reports on his desk, he sat in his chair and read through the books. After a few hours, he realized the texts focused only on creatures found in Ixia. Then he remembered he had a few more books in his apartment. Valek grabbed the crate.

In his suite, he set the crate onto the floor near the hearth. Brede had finished arranging his books by subject. He found the books in no time and settled onto his couch to read.

The snick of the lock opening sent him to his feet with his dagger in hand. But it was only Brede, who was equally surprised.

"Sorry, I didn't know you'd returned," Brede said, pushing his cart into the living area. "Good to see you hale and whole."

"I got back late last night. What are you doing here?"

"Uh, cleaning like I always do."

"What's left to clean? This place is immaculate."

"Thank you, but the windows need to be washed. Unless you'd rather I come back later?"

"No, that's okay." Valek resumed reading until the scent of lavender distracted him. "Brede?"

"Yes?" He paused with his rag on the window and glanced over.

"Why lavender? Why switch from lemon?"

"Oh, it's a soothing scent. For relaxing and sleeping. I thought it was better than the sharp citrus scent, which is more energizing. Do you not like it? I can find—"

"It's fine. I was just curious."

Valek flipped through the books but found no reference to Sitian snakes. The library might have— An idea sparked. "Brede, can you come here a minute?"

"Sure." He dropped his rag into a bucket of water. "What do you need?"

"You mentioned that you encountered all manner of critters while cleaning, have you found any snakes?"

"A few. They come in during the cold season, seeking warmth."

"Any venomous?"

"The Black Rattler is, but it goes dormant during the cold weather."

Valek might have found an expert. He opened the crate. "Do you know what type of snake this is?"

Brede sucked in a harsh breath. "He's dead!"

"It was him or me," Valek said wryly.

"Oh. Sorry." He pointed. "May I?"

"Go ahead."

Brede picked up the snake's head and examined it. Then he set it down and pulled the rest of its body from the crate. "Wow, he's six feet, at least. And take a look at this pattern on his scales. It's very distinctive. I know I've seen this before." He tapped a fingernail on his chin. "It's not native to Ixia." Then he snapped his fingers. "There's a book in the library about snakes."

"Can you find out what type of snake this guy was? I need to know where they live and if they're venomous or not."

"Now?"

"Yes. The windows can wait."

"Can I take him with me?"

"Yes. But bring him back to my office before dinner. And if you find that book, bring it along as well."

"Will do!" Brede returned the snake to its box and left.

~

Valek was slowly going through fifteen days' worth of reports. Paying particular attention to Gabor's recent update, he read it twice. No mention or hint of trouble within the council, except the debate about Yelena's status as a Soulfinder. Many people worried she'd abuse her power, while others championed her abilities.

Valek was glad Yelena moved closer to Irys. Together, they were quite formidable. And if he included her brother Leif, and Moon Man, Yelena had a strong network of people to back her up. He'd hoped she would soon make an official visit as the Liaison between Sitia and Ixia, but she was focusing on her magic at the moment, which made sense and was what she had planned. Although, Valek's heart still thumped its impatience. It didn't care about logic or plans.

A knock sounded. The door swung open before Valek could respond. Brede hustled in.

"Found it!" He set the crate down on Valek's desk. A book rested on top. Brede flipped it open to a page, then showed it to Valek. "It's a fer-de-lance snake."

Dread filled Valek. Ferde, the man who had killed eleven young ladies in order to increase his magic, was given his moniker by one of his victims. Tula Cowan had compared him to a fer-de-lance snake and had shortened the name to Ferde.

Brede peered at him quizzically as he waited for a response.

"Good work. Are they venomous?"

"Very. No one survives their bite." He tapped the crate. "How long was this inside the castle?"

"Ten to fifteen minutes. Why?"

"That is what saved you. These snakes are fast, but he was probably still recovering from the cold air, that would have slowed him down."

"Don't tell Kenda that." Valek considered. "Where do they typically live?"

"In the southern clans of Sitia. Mostly in the Jewelrose and Cowan Clans. They like it hot and dry."

"What about the Avibian Plains or the Daviian Plateau?"

"The plateau for sure, but only the southern part of the plains."

Most likely, the gift had not come from the Sitian Council but from the unsanctioned Daviian Clan. Moon Man had called their magicians warpers and the rest vermin. It didn't matter what you called them; the Commander was not going to be happy.

"Thanks, Brede, this is all great information."

"Uh, what are you going to do with the snake?"

"I'm going to show it to the Commander and then throw it out."

"Can I have it?"

Valek stilled. "Why?"

"I can repurpose much of it. The meat is edible and quite tasty. The skin can be turned into leather. And you can have the venom to slay your enemies."

He stared at his housekeeper with an entirely new perspective. "That's rather devious. You'd better be careful, or I might try to recruit you for my corps."

"No, thank you. I'm content here."

"When I'm done with it, you can repurpose the snake."

"Goody." Brede bounced on the balls of his feet. "I'd better get back to your windows."

That reminded him. "What happened to Mr. Spider?"

"What do you mean?"

"He's not next to the window."

"Oh! I relocated him." Brede walked to the brazier. "See? He's much warmer here, but it's getting harder and harder to find insects for him."

Ah, Brede kept his office warm not for him, but for Mr. Spider. Good to know where his priorities lay. Valek thanked Brede.

Once his housekeeper was gone, Valek mulled over the implications of the gift for the Commander. The best official response was to ignore it. Unofficially…

Valek had assigned a couple agents to watch the Daviians when he had returned to Ixia. They might be able to deliver an unofficial message. Except…

He returned to his desk and sorted through his files. It had been almost a month; they should have reported in by now. But he found nothing. Perhaps Kenda hadn't processed their report yet. Valek headed for her office.

"If you have that snake with you, go away," Kenda said when he appeared at her door.

"It's dead."

"Yeah, well…" She shuddered. "Did you find out where it came from?"

"Yes." He explained his theories about the Daviian Clan. "Have we heard from the agents we sent to the plateau?"

Kenda glanced at the schedule. Written in code on an oversized chalkboard were all their agents' locations and when they last reported in. "Not yet. But they're pretty far south. It probably took them a good two weeks to get down there and to establish a cover. Another week to investigate. Then the closest safe house is in Booruby, a city in the Cowan Clan's land. And a message from Booruby takes about eight days via horse to reach Ixia. Add in the transfer at the border, and it's been thirty-one days total. So, I'd expect a report any day now."

Valek relaxed. The snake hadn't been a message that the Daviians discovered his agents. Besides, they'd probably send Valek their heads or another identifying body part. Unfortunately, that had happened before.

"When the report comes in, please make it a priority."

"Will do."

Valek had one more stop before informing the Commander about the snake. He wove through the crowded and noisy throne room, heading toward Adviser Ilom's desk. The adviser had done him a favor by allowing Valek to pretend to be him when they were in Sitia. Being rather easy going, Ilom thought it'd been an adventure. Plus, he appreciated the bottle of his favorite bourbon that Valek had given to thank him.

"Ah, Adviser Valek, what do I owe the pleasure?" Ilom asked. "Do you need a doppelganger again? I've been growing my hair just in case."

Valek was glad to see that the scratches Ilom received from the Wannabe King had healed without leaving a scar.

He laughed. "Is that what you tell the Commander when he comments on your unmilitary hairstyle?"

"It hasn't grown that long, but I'm sure to get a snide comment from our fearless leader soon. It's unfair that you get to keep yours longer."

"Perks of the job." Valek set the crate on the desk. "Speaking of the job, since you're the expert in Sitian diplomacy, do you know what the Sitian Council would send to Ixia as a peace offering?"

Ilom straightened in his chair. "Are they trying to reconcile? I haven't heard."

"I'm still working that out."

The adviser glanced at the box, but when Valek didn't offer an explanation, he said, "From what I know of the Sitians, they enjoy discovering what a person likes and gifting that item. For example, when they traveled to Ixia for the trade treaty, Fourth Magician brought a bottle of their most expensive cognac because it's well known the Commander enjoys the drink. Which is why I never believed they would poison the cognac. Anyway, I'd say they would send a collection of Sitian teas, an assortment of their finest liqueurs, and a box of Greenblade cigars as a peace offering."

"What would they send as a warning?"

"They might send a letter expressing their displeasure, or one of their master magicians to intimidate or threaten us." Ilom leaned back. "Why are you asking?"

Valek handed him the scroll. "Is this legit?"

Ilom unrolled it, scanned the words, then rubbed it between his fingers. "High quality parchment and ink. I don't recognize the handwriting, but we get so few letters from Sitia. What was the peace offering?"

Valek pulled the lid open.

Ilom jumped to his feet with a cry. When nothing happened, he pressed his hand to his chest. "You could have warned me."

"That's no fun."

"That's no gift, either. The council would never send a snake. That'd be a declaration of war."

"That's what I thought, but I wanted to double check this wasn't some Sitian custom."

"Next time, omit the dramatics and just ask." Ilom sank back into his seat. "Good thing I still have some of that bourbon left."

Valek laughed. Now that he had done his due diligence, he was ready to report to the Commander.

"Come in," the Commander called.

He entered and set the crate on the Commander's desk. "This package came for you today." Valek handed him the scroll.

The Commander scanned the note and raised an eyebrow. "A peace offering?"

"Not quite." Valek revealed the snake and explained his theory.

"This confirms that the Daviians are dangerous," the Commander said. "Let's wait for the report from your agents before we take any action."

"And if we don't get a report?"

"Then I expect you to personally deliver my response."

"Yes, sir."

∼

Valek was just about to finish his work for the day when a knock sounded on his apartment door. He froze. No one ever knocked. Brede had a key and no one else was allowed passed the guards. Except, Yelena and—

Ah, right. He hurried to open the door. Ari and Janco waited in the hallway.

"We're back!" Janco said. "Did you miss us?"

Glad they had returned before the storms, he refrained from using the Commander's toothache comeback. "It's late. Did you run into problems on the road?" He scanned them. They were rumpled and disheveled. Fatigue lined their faces.

"Nah, we just wanted to avoid another night sleeping in a cold travel shelter." Janco rubbed his back. "I think the ground is softer than those beds."

"We weren't sure if you wanted us to report in right away or wait until the morning," Ari said.

"Is there anything time sensitive?" Valek asked.

"No, sir."

"Then go get some sleep. Report to the Commander's office after breakfast, I'll meet you there."

"Yes, sir."

The next morning, Valek calculated how long Ari and Janco had been gone. They'd returned on the ninth day of the cold season, which meant they had spent ten days up in MD-1 and seventeen days traveling. It should have been eighteen, but it sounded like they'd pushed to get home.

Both men waited for Valek outside the Commander's office. Wearing clean uniforms, they looked refreshed.

Valek knocked and entered with Ari and Janco right behind him. The three of them stood in front of the Commander's desk. If he was glad to see Ari and Janco, he didn't give any indication.

"Report," the Commander said.

Janco glanced at Ari as if to say, 'you go first.'

"We arrived in MD-1 on the fifty-first day of the cooling season," Ari said. "We rendezvoused with Agent Kelia and her partner, Agent Cyrus, and they updated us on the situation. They had figured out that General Kitvivan's hunting party planned on capturing snow cats by correctly deducing that the large steel traps and live sheep were for the cats, and not for other game."

"How do you know they were correct?" the Commander asked.

"We observed teams of hunters setting the traps at various spots on the Northern Ice Pack. After they secured a sheep in each cage, they retreated."

The Commander's gaze turned icy. "Did they capture any snow cats?"

Janco scoffed. "Those cats are too smart to fall for a bunch of bleating sheeps."

"No, sir," Ari said, keeping his formal tone despite shooting his partner an exasperated look. No doubt because of Janco's insistence that sheeps is the correct plural form of sheep. "We sabotaged their efforts."

Intrigued, Valek asked, "How?"

"Well, first we released all those poor sheeps. Took them to a local farmer who promised to only shear them and not harm them."

"We replaced them with mock snow cats," Ari said.

"Mock?"

"You should have seen them!" Janco chortled. "Kelia sculpted them out of snow. We gathered bits of rocks and sticks and stuff for their face, teeth, and claws. I swear at ten paces out, they looked alive. She's super talented."

Valek hid his grin.

"When the hunters returned, they thought they had captured the cats," Ari said. "They were so focused on their prize; they didn't notice us."

"My mother always told me to be aware of my surroundings," Janco said. "Those guys obviously don't know my mother. Otherwise, they wouldn't have gotten caught in their own traps."

"We rounded up the wagons and horses and brought the full cages back to General Kitvivan."

"A thoughtful present, but the general disagreed." Janco *tsked*. "However, it was a convincing visual to back up our credentials."

"I'd say. What did Kitvivan do?" Valek asked.

"At first, he threatened to throw us in jail, and then he tried to bribe us. He's a very disagreeable fellow. But Mr. Unflappable here"—Janco hooked a thumb toward Ari—"just stared him down. Told him if he didn't stop hunting snow cats, we'd be back with the Commander's elite guard and a newly promoted general of MD-1."

"That was rather bold," the Commander said to Ari.

"I determined the general is the type of man who values his

position over all else. The threat worked and he promised not to hunt them anymore."

"How can you be certain he'll keep his word?"

"I can't, but Kelia and Cyrus will remain vigilant," Ari said.

"And if he tries again?"

Ari met the Commander's gaze. "You've told him not to hunt the cats, and we've warned him. What's the next step if he breaks his promise?"

The Commander laughed. "I'll send my elite guard and promote another colonel to general."

Proud of how his seconds handled the situation, Valek smiled. "I'd recommend Colonel Laban. In fact, why wait? Be proactive and promote them now."

"I'm well aware of your opinions about the generals, Valek," the Commander said. "Well done, Ari and Janco, you're dismissed."

"Yes, sir," they said, then left.

He moved to follow, but the Commander called him back. "I think they're going to work out. Well done, Valek."

"Thank you."

When he exited the office, both Ari and Janco fell into step with him.

"What did he say?" Janco asked anxiously. "I should have kept my mouth shut like we planned. Did I overstep?"

"If you did, he would have told you." Valek waited until they were away from the throne room and in a quieter part of the castle. Then he stopped and turned to them. "The Commander doesn't say 'well done' very often. When he does, it means he's very pleased. You did an excellent job, and you'll have to tell me exactly how you managed to capture all the hunters."

"Caught that omission, did you?" A gleam shone in Janco's eyes.

"That's because the hunters triggered the traps when they

entered to remove the fake snow cats," Ari said. "They were so angry about the ruse, they forgot."

"Aww, Ari. You can't just tell him everything. We could have bargained for that information."

"No, you technically can't," Valek said. "But how about I buy you both an ale at the pub tonight to celebrate your successful mission?"

Janco pressed both his hands to his heart. "Best boss ever!"

~

Worry gnawed on Valek's thoughts. Kenda had just delivered a combination of good and bad news. Trevar and Adrik had been successfully recruited by Star and their first mission for her was to find out who was supplying illegal goods to the black market dealers, which was also what Valek needed to know. The bad was the continuing silence from his agents sent to the Daviian Plateau.

Valek knew from experience that not all missions went as planned. In fact, most didn't. So, he'd waited an extra week for them to report in. But now it was the fourteenth day of the cold season and still no word. He debated whether he should send Ari and Janco to investigate or not.

A knock in the late afternoon interrupted his thoughts. "Come in."

Agent Gabor entered. The spy should be down in the Sitian Citadel, keeping an eye on the council and Yelena. And not here with snowflakes melting on the short strands of his black hair and the shoulders of his cloak.

Fear immediately coiled around Valek's heart. "Yelena?"

"As far as I know, Yelena's fine," Gabor said.

That brought Valek no comfort. "Why are you here?"

"Because I couldn't trust *this* news to a messenger."

"That bad?"

"Yes, and *that* sensitive, which is why I came straight to you."

Valek cursed. It had to be about the Sitian Council. "Let's go. You can report it to both me and the Commander."

As they hurried to the Commander's office, Valek asked about the missing agents. "Have you seen any of our corps in the Citadel?"

"No one has come through recently. Why?"

He explained. Now Gabor cursed, but he just shook his head at Valek's questioning glance.

The Commander was having a meeting with three of his advisers. But he took one look at Valek's expression and Gabor's presence and dismissed the trio.

"This better be important," the Commander said once the others left.

"I assure you, sir, it is of the upmost importance," Gabor said.

"Well then, report."

"The Sitian Council has been very quiet about the status of the criminal named Ferde Daviian. According to all my sources, the man was locked in the special holding cells for magicians in the bowels of the Council Hall. I've learned that Ferde has not only escaped, but Cahil Ixia aided him."

An icy dread flowed through Valek's veins. He really should have killed Cahil when he'd had the chance. "When did this happen?" he asked.

"That's the thing. It happened soon after Ambassador Signe left Sitia, in the middle of the cooling season."

"I'm amazed they managed to keep it a secret for so long," the Commander said. "How did you find out?"

Gabor glanced at Valek. "Liaison Yelena Zaltana left the Magician's Keep quite suddenly on day four of the cold season. She was with her brother Leif, and another man. I managed to discover that they'd received a tip about Ferde and Cahil's location from someone named Moon Man."

"That makes sense," Valek said. "Ferde is running home to

the Daviian Plateau. And I guess Cahil made a deal with him. Something along the lines of 'I'll free you if you help me conquer Ixia.' That snake must be their declaration of war."

"What snake?" Gabor asked.

Valek explained.

"Ah, that probably also explains about the missing agents. They've probably been discovered and killed," Gabor said.

"It's obvious that the Sitian Council, despite having four master magicians, cannot handle this Daviian situation," the Commander said. "They've bungled it from the start." His gaze sent a chill right through Valek's body.

"Valek, I want you to assassinate the entire Sitian Council."

CHAPTER 8

Valek rocked back on his heels. Assassinate the entire Sitian Council? He thought the Commander was overreacting, but now wasn't the time to point it out.

"And when they're dead? What happens next?" he asked instead.

"I'll send my army into the chaos and restore order. Then we'll annihilate those Daviians."

"May I make a suggestion?" Valek asked.

"I doubt I could stop you." The Commander's cold tone warned Valek to choose his words with care.

"I propose that I go to the Citadel and assess the situation. By now, Yelena could have returned with Ferde and Cahil in custody and all might be well. If the situation is dire, then I can evaluate if assassinating the council would be advantageous to us or not. Or if we could use them to solve the problem of the Daviians."

"And then assassinate them?"

"If it would be to our advantage." Valek held his breath.

The Commander's icy expression remained for several

heartbeats. "All right. Assess and evaluate. Take Ari and Janco with you for back up."

"Yes, sir."

"And don't hesitate to assassinate if it's a viable option."

"Yes, sir."

Valek and Gabor left before the Commander could change his mind.

"Wow," Gabor said. "I didn't expect that response."

"I think the snake rattled him more than I realized." Valek quickened his pace. "Tell me what's been going on with the council."

"They certainly don't think the Daviians are a threat. They're more worried about Yelena's Soulfinding magic."

"What about Cahil's people? Are they with him?"

"No. He left them behind. In fact, he brutally beat Captain Marrok. Left the poor man for dead."

Valek had warned the captain that might happen once Cahil found out the truth about his birth. Marrok and his team had been lying to him since he was a boy, telling Cahil that he was the King of Ixia's nephew, but Valek had assassinated the King and his entire royal family. Valek had also thought that Cahil might sulk and do nothing. The man was unstable and unpredictable and if anyone was going to be assassinated during Valek's trip to Sitia, it would be Cahil.

"Did Marrok recover?" Valek strangely liked the captain.

"Yes. The healers saved his life." Gabor snapped his fingers. "I'd bet he's the one that went with Yelena and Leif. I didn't see them leave, but the kid who reported it described the man and it just now clicked."

"Kid?"

Gabor smiled. "Yeah. A bunch of kids without homes have formed a Helper's Guild in the Citadel. They aid shoppers in finding and bargaining for goods, they carry packages and do odd jobs. They're smart and observant and invisible to most people. I've been buying information from them."

Valek remembered the young boy who had helped Yelena. "Is their leader named Fisk?"

"Yes. Do you know him?"

"He and a few of his friends helped me escape the Citadel." Valek thought about the enterprising young lad. He might know what was really going on with the council. Worth a try.

"What do you need me to do?" Gabor asked.

"Have dinner and rest tonight. We'll leave in the morning for Sitia."

"Yes, sir."

~

"...that's not the signal for sword. It's more like this," Janco said.

"That means knife," Ari countered.

"It's a pointy stabby weapon. Close enough."

Ari and Janco's argument echoed off the castle walls before they appeared around the corner. When they came into view, they spotted Valek waiting by their door and stopped.

"Uh oh," Janco said. "I've a bad feeling about this."

"We've a new mission," Valek said. "Prep for covert ops in Sitia. I'll meet you in the stables at dawn."

"Yes, sir."

Valek hurried away. He had much to do and would update them on the journey south.

Behind him, Janco said, "Dawn. See I knew it was bad."

"Brightside, we're going to Sitia. It's warmer there," Ari said.

And best of all, Yelena might be there as well. Valek fervently hoped she had returned from her mission.

Valek spent the remaining day updating Kenda about Gabor's intel and the Commander's response, ensuring Brede knew about his absence, and packing his bag with Sitian clothing, coins, and the various tools—disguises, lock picks, weapons, blow pipe, darts, poisons—for all his assassinating needs.

After a restless night of sleep, Valek joined Ari and Janco in the stables.

"And here I was thinking it'd be at least a season before I had to ride a horse again." Janco rubbed his backside.

"That's your problem right there," Ari said.

"Where?"

"Thinking. I believe that for our new jobs we shouldn't expect anything. Right, Valek?"

"Correct. Anything goes. Missions are rarely predictable. If you can't adapt quickly, then find a new job." Valek checked Onyx's legs for hot spots. The horse snuffled his hair.

Gabor arrived. "Should I saddle a horse?"

"No. You can ride with Janco, since only the three of us will be returning to Ixia." Valek grabbed Onyx's tack.

The Stable Master filled feed bags and helped them get the three horses ready. With five of them working, they were soon mounted and exiting the south gate of the castle complex.

The trip to the Citadel took two and a half days. During the journey, Valek and Gabor updated Ari and Janco on the situation with the council and the Daviians.

"You know what we really need," Janco said. He didn't wait for a response. "Permission to assassinate all the magicians in Sitia. Except Yelena, of course."

"That won't work," Ari said. "There's always a few that will escape. Plus, they're born with the ability. It's not predictable which families will birth magicians."

"But it works for Ixia. There're no magicians there."

"That we know of," Valek added. "Some could be in hiding, some flee to Sitia, and some have no idea they're using magic."

"We need more Valeks," Janco said. When they all glanced at him in confusion, he waved his hand in a circular motion. "You know, people who can detect magic. People who are immune to its effects." Then he brightened. "More Jancos, too. Since I'm sensitive to it."

They groaned in unison at the thought.

"That's how we'll defeat the Daviians," Ari said. "Send an army of Jancos. The enemy will commit suicide."

"Ha. Ha." Janco deadpanned. "It's just a shame that there isn't a way for normal folk to know when magic is in use."

"That would certainly even the playing field," Valek said.

~

They changed into Sitian clothing and approached the Citadel from the north. The high white, marble walls that encompassed the capital of Sitia reflected the sunshine. As they drew closer, the thin green veins that lined the stone became visible.

Since it was mid-afternoon and plenty of traffic flowed through the gate, they entered without trouble. They stopped at Horses on Mane Street Stables; the farm would take care of their horses while they were in the Citadel. Then they split up into two teams. Valek and Gabor headed southeast, while Ari and Janco went southwest. They would rendezvous at the safe house.

Even though it was the seventeenth day of the cold season, the sun warmed the air. Taking advantage of the good weather, the citizens bustled through the streets. The Citadel's rectangular shape contained six quadrants, with the market located dead center. Valek and Gabor walked through the oval rings of businesses and factories that filled the inner heart of the city. The Magician's Keep occupied the northeast corner, the Council Hall and all the government buildings were in the southeast section. A labyrinth of residences sprawled throughout both the northwest and southwest quadrants.

Their safe house was located in the southwest section.

Tucked in the middle of a row of houses, it was a few blocks from the outer ring. Looping around to the alley, they entered and left the door unlocked for Ari and Janco.

Valek's throat tightened as the memories of his last visit threatened to overwhelm him. Cahil had captured him and tried to strangle him by hanging. That had been the closest he'd come to dying in a long time. If he hadn't been rescued by Gabor, his partner Brigi, and Ambassador Signe, Valek wouldn't be alive.

Shaking off the dire thoughts, Valek set his pack on the couch and hung his cloak on a hook along the long hallway. "When will Brigi return?" he asked Gabor.

"Her shift at the council's stables ends at dusk. How about some tea while we wait?" Gabor piled logs in the hearth and lit a fire.

Ari and Janco arrived, joining them in the kitchen. The space suddenly seemed too small to house four men.

"I call dibs on the extra bed," Janco said.

"There isn't an extra," Gabor said. "This place has only two bedrooms, and the second room is where all our disguises are located."

"You share a bed with your partner?"

"Not at the same time. She has the day shift." Gabor filled a kettle with water and hung it over the growing fire.

They were sipping their tea when Brigi entered. She waved a hand in front of her face. "*Oof* boys, you need to visit the bathhouse."

"Hello to you, too," Janco said.

She smiled. "I call it as I smell it." Then she sobered. "There hasn't been any more news about the escape. And Yelena hasn't returned from her mission."

Disappointment burned in his chest, but Valek ignored it to focus on the job at hand. At this point, collecting information was vital.

"Starting tomorrow morning, I want eyes on the entrances

THE STUDY OF FIRE

to the Council Hall and the Magician's Keep at all times," he said. "Janco, there's a group of beggars who squat at the base of the Council Hall. I want you to disguise yourself as a beggar and join them. There's a man named Minel who was part of that group. If he's still there, make friends with him. He's sharp and might know something of value. Also, if Yelena returns to the Keep, let me know as soon as possible."

"Join them, as in during the day?" Janco asked, sounding hopeful.

Valek suppressed a smile. "As in all night and day. In fact, don't bathe, it'll help with your disguise. Sorry Brigi."

His hopeful expression fell. "You're serious?"

"Yes."

Janco stared at Valek in horror. "But that's... It's... I'm..." His mouth continued to move, but no sounds escaped.

"All part of the job, Janco. I once lived on the streets of Jeweltown for a week, during the cold season and dressed like a woman."

"Jeweltown?" Ari asked. "Is that when you were hunting the royal family?"

"It was the only way I could get close to the queen." Valek had befriended the queen's hairdresser, Parveen, by pretending to save her from a mugger. She had given him a job in her shop, and he'd learned how to cut and style hair. After a season, he filled in when poor Parveen had been too sick to tend to the queen. He had impressed the queen so much, she'd hired him, giving him access to the royal suite and the royal family.

"I'd ask for more details, but I don't think we have the time," Ari said. "What's my job for this mission?"

"You'll be stationed at the Keep. Go and apply for a job, they always need people. If you see Yelena, let me know. There's a chance she might return tonight."

"Yes, sir."

121

"I'd say I was jealous." Janco rubbed at the scar that replaced the bottom half of his right ear. "But the Keep creeps me out."

"Gabor and Brigi, continue with your regular duties, I'm going to find Fisk at the market and see what he knows."

∽

After Ari left for the Keep with a forged letter of recommendation, Valek helped Janco with his disguise. "Living on the streets is a hard life," he said. "Infrequent baths, little to no food, and limited possessions. These people have figured out how to survive and they're resourceful. You can learn a great deal from them."

Janco stroked the stubble on his cheeks. "No place to shave?"

"No. In fact, you might want to darken that scruff a bit, so you don't look like a newbie."

"I *am* a newbie. Maybe I shouldn't try to pretend to be street smart. Being new would explain any mistakes I make and be a good excuse for asking lots of questions."

"That's an excellent idea."

Janco beamed. "I have my moments."

"Then why do you let Ari tease you?"

"Because I also have my moments in the opposite direction, and Ari's very good at saving my ass. He has earned the right to tease me all he wants."

"I'm sure you've saved his ass as well."

"Well, yeah. We're partners, that's what we do."

Valek considered his relationship with Yelena. He longed for the day when they would become true partners. When they could reminisce over dozens of shared experiences, when they knew more about each other than any other person in the world, and when they spent more time together than apart.

Switching his knit cap for another one that wasn't so

THE STUDY OF FIRE

battered, Janco adjusted his clothing for his role as a newbie beggar.

"What's your backstory?" Valek asked.

Janco adjusted his belt, cinching it so his seen-better-days-but-still-useable pants didn't fall down. "Fired from my job for reasons that I'll swear weren't true. Can't find another position because my old boss holds a grudge and told all his buddies not to hire me. Ran out of money and was kicked out of my place. No family or friends to mooch off because nothing is my fault so I'm not about to apologize for anything to anyone."

"And the reasons that you were fired?"

His sly expression was full of mischief. "Vague enough to imply an impropriety without confirming anyone's guesses. And I'll swear the boss got bent out of shape over nothing. Stuff like that."

"Sounds like a good story."

Since he was planning to be a newbie, Janco was able to pack a few comfort items like a couple sticks of beef jerky, a bedroll, and a thicker blanket.

"Keep them close if you don't want them to get stolen," Valek warned. "Most folks will be kind and help you out, but there's always those who will take advantage of the newbie."

"Huh. Maybe I should let my stuff get stolen. It would track with my cover."

Impressed, Valek said, "Up to you."

Once Janco was ready, Valek clapped him on the shoulder and wished him good hunting. After he left, Valek checked his own disguise. He wore the typical Sitian clothing of gray pants, tunic, and a short gray cape. He used makeup on his face, wrists, and the back of his hands to blend in better with the Citadel's inhabitants. Even though they were a mix of skin tones, Valek would still stand out.

Growing up in MD-1 near the Northern Ice Pack, Valek had endured long cold winters and scant sunshine. His family had lived there for decades, and they were all as pale as snow on a cloudy day. Valek wondered if his father was still tanning hides. When he had left to enact revenge on the men who murdered his three older brothers, his parents told him to never return. Of course, he had assigned his agents to watch and protect them if needed, but he never asked for details of their lives. It would be too painful.

Satisfied with his clothing, Valek tucked his hair up into a wool cap. He headed for the market. It buzzed with activity. The weak morning sunlight cast long shadows. Young children trotted at shoppers' heels, their arms loaded with packages. Valek guessed they ranged in age from six to twelve years old.

He found an unobtrusive spot to watch the kids for a while, searching for Fisk. They had quite the operation. Darting up to hesitant shoppers or to those glancing around in confusion, they offered their services. And pointing those in need of help out to his guild members was Fisk.

The boy's brown hair was shaggy. He moved with confidence. The market was obviously his domain. Valek waited until Fisk was between customers.

Approaching him, Valek said, "I'm in need of assistance."

Fisk studied him. Maturity far beyond his ten years shone from his light brown eyes. "You're in need of a better disguise, Mister Valek."

He glanced around to check if anyone nearby had overheard. "How do you know my name?"

Fisk sighed. "It was easy to figure out after I helped you escape the Citadel. If I'd known before, I wouldn't have taken the job, even though you're a friend of Yelena's."

"Does that mean you won't help me now?"

"Depends on what you want."

The conversation was a bit surreal. Fisk looked ten but spoke as if he was thirty years old. "I'm willing to pay for information," Valek said.

Fisk brightened. "Nothing illegal in that, but I won't give away Sitian secrets."

"All right. I'd like to know what the council has been debating lately."

"That'll cost you a gold coin."

"Nice try. How about a silver? And if the info is good, I'll give you another one."

"Seven silvers up front."

"Three."

"Five."

"Deal." He dug out the coins. When he handed them over, they disappeared in the blink of an eye. "The council?"

Fisk told him the gossip. Most of the information matched what Gabor had reported. The council was more concerned about Yelena than the Daviians. However, Fisk mentioned the strange arrival of a group of Sandseed Warriors late the previous night.

"Why is that odd?" Valek asked.

"They almost never leave the Avibian Plains. Only their Councilor travels to the Citadel."

Yelena's friend, Moon Man was a Sandseed Story Weaver—a warrior with magical powers. And he had sent her a message about Ferde. Valek wondered if the Sandseeds' presence in the Citadel was connected.

"Do you know why they're here?"

"Not yet. But give me a couple days." Fisk grinned.

"And it'll cost me?"

"Of course. Nothing is free."

Such a sad statement. Valek met Fisk's hard gaze. "You're wrong. Lots of things are free."

"Yeah? Name one?"

"Friendship. Love. Kindness."

"Yeah, well, you can't buy food with those."

"Are you sure?"

"I've been living on the streets for my entire life. I'm sure."

"And you used to beg. Right? Getting coins from others to buy food?"

"That's not kindness. That's pity. That's shame."

"So, when Yelena gave you all her coins—"

"That's different. Yelena's different."

"While I agree that Yelena is unique in so many wonderful ways, there are other people who also give because of kindness and not due to pity or shame."

Uncertain, Fisk stared at him. "Come to the market in the mornings. If I have more information for you, I'll let you know." He disappeared into the crowd.

∼

Valek spent the rest of the day watching the guards at the Council Hall. The multi-story building was located across from the entrance to the Magician's Keep. Stone steps led up to the main doors. These steps extended the full length of the building. He would eventually need to get into the hall, which he could easily do dressed as a citizen, but he wanted access to the council meetings and not all of them were open to the public. He could change into a guard uniform once inside. However, the ideal time to get in would be when the guards changed shifts.

Huddled in his blanket on the steps, Janco looked miserable. As people left and entered the Council Hall, a group of beggars approached them, but Janco pouted, appearing to be too proud to beg. Impressed by his acting abilities, Valek suspected there was much more to Janco than the easy-going, overly dramatic, and irreverent persona he had donned.

Despite his lackluster posture, Janco spotted Valek. He signaled by raising his eyebrows, which meant, 'What's up?' Valek replied, motioning that all was well. Once Valek had

THE STUDY OF FIRE

marked the late afternoon shift change, he returned to the safe house.

Gabor had just woken up for his shift. Yawning, he cooked eggs and tried to smooth the wayward strands of his black hair. Soon after, Ari arrived.

"You weren't exaggerating when you said they needed people," Ari said. "The Keep's manager took one look at my shoulders and hired me to work in the infirmary."

That was unexpected. Valek had guessed he would be assigned as a gardener or be trained as a guard. "Doing what?"

"Working as an orderly. Apparently, unconscious people are heavy. And crazed patients are strong." He shrugged. "Doesn't sound like it happens too often, but my boss, Healer Hayes, said I could help with other duties. He wants me to stay in a small furnished apartment near the infirmary, just in case they need me at night. I told him I had to pack my stuff and tell my mother about my new job. He's expecting me back tomorrow morning."

"Good work. What's your cover name?"

"Denus Krystal. I'm too pale to be a Bloodgood. Too bad, that's a great clan name."

Ari's full name was Ardenus. "Perfect. Did you find anything out about Yelena?"

"Not yet."

Brigi joined them in the kitchen. "What a fun day!" She laughed. "Worth the stink to see Janco in action."

"You can see him from the stables?" Valek asked.

"Yeah. He mostly hung out on the east side of the hall. It has the best view of the Keep."

Which was why Brigi worked in the stables. That, and her knowledge and experience with horses was extensive. "Brigi, do you know the Council Hall guards' schedule?"

"By heart. Why?"

Valek stifled a groan. Of course she would know. Why

hadn't he thought of that before? "I need it, along with the Council's meeting schedule."

"Twice a season, they hold public meetings. Each day for two weeks, they have a two-hour public session to discuss various issues in the morning. The closed-door sessions for just the Council are in the afternoons. You're in luck, this is week two of the first set of public meetings for the cold season. Also, they don't meet at all during the hot season. Unless there's an emergency, then they meet as soon as possible. That applies for any time of the year."

"Has there been any emergency assemblies lately?"

"Not since the Scourge of Sitia escaped back to Ixia." She gave him a pointed look. "When he was here last season, though, there were lots of panicked gatherings."

"Nice," Ari said.

"I'll need that schedule," Valek said. "I plan to attend tomorrow's meeting."

~

In the morning, Valek stopped by the market. Fisk and his friends hustled among the stands. One young boy helped Ari purchase a few items to fill out a medium-sized bag. Ari hadn't wanted Healer Hayes to wonder why his new orderly only carried one small pack.

Fisk eventually made eye contact with Valek. He shook his head. A universal sign that the boy didn't have any additional information. Valek returned to the safe house to enhance his disguise. Being inside the Council Hall was dangerous, he would be surrounded by Sitian guards and there would be limited exits. If anyone recognized him, Valek would be in serious trouble.

With his sculpting putty, he softened his nose, turning it pudgy. He donned a pair of eyeglasses and added a few more wrinkles to his face. Satisfied, he headed to the Council Hall and joined the flow of people entering for the public meeting. The guards barely glanced at him, and he followed the others into the great hall.

The hall stretched three stories high and had been decorated with fifteen colorful banners, representing the eleven Sitian clans and the four master magicians. A U-shaped table filled the back third of the room. Currently, the seats were empty. Facing the table was a series of benches that had been arranged in rows. People settled on them. A tall podium had been set at the top of the U.

Valek picked a spot in the fourth row. He inspected the rafters in the ceiling, seeking hiding places. The banners offered great cover. And best of all, the high windows not only provided light, but would be perfect access points. If he could climb the outer walls. Unfortunately, marble was notoriously slick.

The murmur of voices ceased as soon as the councilors entered through a door behind the table. Everyone stood. The clan leaders split, six going to the chairs on the right arm of the U and five heading to the ones on the left. Three master magicians stopped at the bend of the U, while First Magician Roze Featherstone approached the podium.

Regal, powerful, and the leader of the council, Roze was a tall woman with midnight skin and short white hair. She banged a gavel on the wood, even though the entire room was silent. "I call this meeting to order," she said, scanning the crowd.

Magic brushed Valek's face as Roze used her powers. Since one of her many skills was mental communication, he guessed she searched for anyone who planned to disrupt the session or cause harm. Glad his immunity kept her from sensing him, Valek wondered if she also scanned the rafters with her magic.

"The topics for today's assembly are the tax increase proposal, the permit application for renovating the Hart Iron

Works building, and the bids to build a new east-west travel route through the Greenblade Clan's land. The council will discuss each issue, then we will allow comments from those in attendance before moving on to the next agenda item." Roze sat in the chair at the middle of the bend, signaling to everyone they could be seated as well.

The council launched into a debate about increasing taxes. Valek considered it all a colossal waste of time. Too many opinions, too many egos to smooth, too many stupid comments. While in Ixia, the Commander decided and it was done.

Bored, Valek studied the other master magicians. Second Magician Bain Bloodgood was the oldest. He wore navy blue robes, which contrasted with his wild, curly white hair. His eyes kept drifting closed, probably bored as well. At age twenty-one, Third Magician Zitora Cowan was the youngest and newest master. She took copious notes despite her long braids getting in the way. Zitora was a pretty woman, with a heart-shaped face and pale yellow eyes.

Valek was most familiar with Fourth Magician, Irys Jewelrose. Irys kept her long hair tied in a tight bun; a few white strands lurked among the glossy black. Not as many as the Commander's, even though they were close in age. Valek considered Irys a friend. She had traveled to Ixia to deal with Yelena's uncontrolled magic, intending to kill Yelena before she flamed out and caused a serious disruption in the blanket of power. Valek foiled her first attempt, and, by the second try, Yelena had gained control. In the end, Irys had helped stop General Brazell and Mogkan's attempt to overthrow the Commander.

As if she could sense Valek's scrutiny, Irys glanced at the audience. He stilled as her gaze swept his row, but she showed no signs of recognition. The last time she found out that Valek was in Sitia, she had told Yelena to warn him to leave right away. A smart plan, except he couldn't leave Yelena to deal with

Ferde and Cahil on her own. Even if the decision had almost killed him. He'd gladly give his life for Yelena's.

The other councilors had all been elected to represent their clans. Probably also to protect their interests. He paid particular attention to Councilor Harun Sandseed. Similar to all the Sandseed warriors, he was a tall muscular man with dark skin. Harun appeared distracted and kept tugging at the collar of his tunic. Yelena had told Valek the Sandseed Clan members were nomadic, and some preferred not to wear clothing. However, Valek wondered if Harun's discomfort was due to the unusual arrival of his clan members.

To keep from falling asleep, Valek tested his memory on the other councilors' names. He had met Bavol Zaltana, the leader of Yelena's clan when Valek had pretended to be Adviser Ilom. The others were Tama Moon, Shaba Greenblade, Leuel Stormdance, Ruy Cloudmist, Thema Cowan, Adya Krystal, Glynn Featherstone, Emlyn Jewelrose, and Kyler Bloodgood.

Finally, the meeting was over. The council left first by the back entrance. The attendees filed out the main doors. A few people hung together, talking animatedly. No one seemed in a hurry to leave, so Valek wandered around, examining the walls as the room slowly emptied.

"Can I help you, sir?" a masculine voice asked him.

Valek turned. A guard stood a few feet away.

"Do you know how they hang them all the way up there?" Valek gestured to the banners.

The guard chuckled. "First time in the great hall?"

He met his gaze and gave him a sheepish grin. "That obvious?"

"A bit. The banners look like they're secured to the rafters, but they are really hanging from metal rods. We can lower them to clean the banners or swap them with different decorations."

"Clever."

"Indeed." He gestured to the exit. "Now if you would, sir. The afternoon session is closed to the public."

"Oh, of course." He glanced around. "Is it starting now?"

"No, sir. Not until after lunch." The guard smiled. "But I need to clear this room so I can have my lunch, too."

"Ah, I see. Thank you for your time." Valek hurried out.

The guard had inadvertently given him a way to climb into the rafters. If they raised and lowered the rods, that meant there were pulleys and ropes that he could climb. Except, he hadn't seen any. Probably because they were hidden by a magical illusion. Finding them shouldn't be too difficult, Valek just needed to figure out how to get into the great hall without being seen.

When he left, the guard closed and locked the doors. Another guard moved to stand in front of them. Valek wondered if the door the council used was also protected. He guessed it led to the councilors' offices, which were also open to visiting clan members. Valek thought back to when he'd visited as Adviser Ilom, and he remembered the small side room they had waited in before being invited into the great hall. Perfect.

Valek found an empty room and changed into a guard's uniform. Then he strode through the hallways as if on a mission. No one looked at him twice. Most stepped out of his way. Fun.

The waiting room was unguarded. However, it was locked. Removing his lock pick and tension wrench, Valek quickly aligned the pins using his pick and turned the cylinder. He slipped inside. A few narrow windows let in the sunlight. The door to the great hall was on the opposite side. This one was locked as well. Not for long.

When Valek pulled it open, he encountered a sticky wall of magic. It resisted at first, but he pushed forward. It was like walking through a waterfall made of syrup. A syrupfall? That sounded like something Janco would say. Thankfully, it wasn't thick.

The great hall remained empty. When Valek turned around, the door had disappeared from sight. Ah. It had been concealed by a magical illusion. Probably so no one knew about the side room. Smart. He ran his hands along the walls, seeking magic. Sticky strands met his fingertips on the same side as the hidden door. He'd found the ropes.

Once he grabbed them, he could see them. Double checking that they were securely tied, Valek pulled his body off the floor and wrapped his legs around them. Shimmying up the rope, Valek's hands and shoulders burned with the effort. But it was far better than trying to find hand and foot holds on slick marble blocks.

A thick layer of dust coated the rafters. Valek stepped onto the wood, trying not to disturb the layer too much. The last thing he needed was for a dust cloud to give him away. Glancing down at the table, he settled into position behind a banner, which hid him from the majority of those seated below. The spot also allowed him to lean against the wall.

Eventually, voices sounded. Valek peeked. The council had returned. They resumed their appointed seats. Except for Councilor Harun Sandseed; his seat was empty. The others didn't seem to be concerned and the meeting started.

Valek settled back, concentrating on their discussion. Unfortunately, there was no mention of Yelena's status or of Ferde's escape. They argued about the strained relationship with the Commander. Some wished to send a gift with a request for another meeting. Perhaps at the border, which was neutral territory. Others countered that the Commander should apologize to *them*. After all, he had to have known his assassin was in Sitia.

Roze Featherstone was the most vocal, insisting they do neither. "The Commander is the enemy," she said. Her words held power but not the magical kind. "He might not attack tomorrow, or next season, or next year, but he will. That is a guarantee. And if we're not prepared, our clans will be transformed into military districts and assigned numbers. Our customs and our culture will be erased as our citizens are forced to wear uniforms and follow his Code of Behavior. We *must* be prepared for an attack."

"I disagree," Irys said. "He hired Yelena to be a liaison between our countries. Why do that if he planned to attack?"

"So we won't be prepared," Roze countered. "So he catches us off guard."

"Have you forgotten the history of the Ixian takeover?" Bain Bloodgood asked. "He won't attack us with an army, that's not his strategy. He'll send Valek to assassinate all of us. He'll bribe our soldiers and convince our younger generation that his way of life is better. He'll promise the beggars and those without homes that they'll all get jobs with equal wages for equal work."

True. And the people of Sitia would be better off. Except, the Commander had no interest in taking over Sitia before this mess with Ferde and the Daviians. If the council wasn't able to stop them from gaining power, the Daviians would become a direct threat to Ixia. The Commander sought to stop that chain of events to protect his people.

"Then we need to be prepared for those tactics as well." Roze wasn't backing down. "Our current security is not up to the challenge. Far from it. At least, let us start implementing the measures we need to keep the council safe."

For once, the council was in total agreement. Valek silently applauded their decision. The extra efforts wouldn't stop Valek, but they would make it harder for the Daviians to reach them.

The door banged open. Valek peered around a banner. Councilor Harun Sandseed entered. He swayed and pressed a hand against the wall. His dark face had an unhealthy hue. The rest of the council members jumped to their feet.

Irys was next to him in an instant. She cupped his elbow. "Harun, what happened? Are you all right?"

He looked at her with horror-filled eyes. "My clan…" Gulping, he tried again. "My clan was attacked. Killed. Decimated."

Irys helped him to her chair. He sank down and buried his face into his hands. Sobs sounded as shock zipped through the others. Anger followed. Then the questions started. Who? What? How?

Shaken, Valek's grip on the rafter tightened. An entire clan gone.

When Harun regained control of his emotions, he said, "Gede, a Story Weaver of my clan, arrived at my office today after our morning session. He said… He said the vermin…the Daviians…attacked our people without warning. They…killed almost everyone. Only about a dozen people survived."

Valek wondered if the Sandseeds Fisk spotted in the Citadel were those survivors. But why wait two days to inform their councilor of the massacre?

"But your warriors and Story Weavers are legendary fighters," Irys said.

"They weren't there. They'd gone to the plateau to clear out a nest of vermin. It was a decoy to lure them away. And when they returned…" Harun's voice hitched. "When they returned, they walked right into an ambush. The vermin pretended to be our clan. Our warriors…died as well." He reburied his face.

The councilors glanced at each other in horror. Fear fogged the air. If the Daviians could slaughter the Sandseed Clan, theirs could be next.

Valek worried about Yelena, Leif, and Moon Man. Had they been killed as well? Breathing became difficult, he rested his head on the wall as the voices buzzed in his ears. If they had killed Yelena, Valek silently promised he would decimate every last Daviian before he joined her in death.

Eventually, he reigned in his emotions and tucked them away. The council had also settled down.

"…send a battalion to the plains to aid with burials," Roze

said. "I doubt the vermin will still be there, but if they are, our soldiers will attack with the intent to kill."

"And the rest of the army?" Councilor Krystal asked.

"Will prepare for war. The Daviians must be stopped."

Valek and the rest of the council were in complete agreement. And now that the paralyzing fear had subsided, he could think clearly. The answer to why the Daviians attacked the Sandseeds was obvious. They were a threat. A bigger one than the Sitian army. With them out of the way, the Daviians had a better chance of gaining control of Sitia.

~

The next morning's council session was as boring as the day before. Other than the absence of Councilor Sandseed, there was no mention of the clan's slaughter, which wasn't a surprise. The council wouldn't want to panic the citizens of Sitia. Not until they had more information.

Valek had worn a different disguise and sat on the hard bench in another row. He stifled a yawn. He'd had a rough night. Unable to sleep, he'd prowled through the streets of the Citadel, fighting the desire to get Onyx and travel to the plains to search for Yelena.

To stay awake, he considered the Daviians attack. He couldn't assassinate the council now, that would just help the enemy. The council might be inept and unorganized, but they didn't hesitate to respond to the crisis.

At the end of the meeting, he left the great hall with the crowd, but didn't follow them outside. Instead, he climbed the grand staircase. Halfway up, a commotion exploded in the lobby. He stopped and turned.

A group of people had pushed their way into the lobby. It took Valek a moment to sort out the scene below, but in the middle of the confusion stood Ferde and Cahill. They had been captured.

CHAPTER 9

Valek would have whooped with happiness if he wasn't standing on the grand staircase in the Sitian Council Hall. Instead, he silently celebrated the capture of Ferde and Cahil. Their wrists had been manacled behind their backs, and they were escorted by a ring of guards. Leif and Marrok also accompanied them. Scanning the rest of the crowd in the lobby, Valek searched for Yelena. She had to be with them. Except, she wasn't in sight. Neither was Moon Man.

He kept his emotions in check. There were a dozen logical reasons for her absence. She could have headed to the Keep to find Irys and the other master magicians. Or she could be at the stables, taking care of Kiki before coming inside. Or she could have been killed in the Daviian's attack.

Sucking in a steadying breath, Valek focused on the afternoon council session. It would be very informative. No doubt they would interrogate the prisoners, and he might learn Yelena's fate. Valek needed to get into position before the session started.

Valek settled in the rafters just in time. The back door to the great hall flew open. Multiple voices shouted over each other, asking questions. Apparently, the councilors had not been informed of Ferde's escape or Cahil's involvement. Interesting.

Roze banged her gavel a dozen times before everyone quieted. "All your questions will be answered in time." Then, she projected her voice, "I call Cahil Ixia to appear before the council."

Valek leaned forward to get a better angle. The side door suddenly popped into view. It opened, and Cahil followed a guard inside. Two others walked behind him. Cahil's blond hair and beard were matted and dirty. Dark circles lined his light blue eyes, and his rumpled and torn clothing indicated he'd had a rough trip to the Citadel. Valek hoped it was Cahil's blood staining his shirt.

"Remove the manacles and leave," Roze ordered the guards.

They hurried to release Cahil and left through the still visible side door. Cahil rubbed his raw wrists and winced before standing behind the podium and facing the council.

"Cahil Ixia, report," Roze ordered.

"The mission was going well, until Yelena showed up with her goons," he said.

Valek stilled. What was Cahil up to?

"Start at the beginning. The mission is no longer classified," Roze said.

"I'd say not." Cahil's arrogant tone bordered on belligerence.

Harun Sandseed stood up. "Were you and Ferde part of the massacre of my clan?" he demanded.

"What?" Cahil gripped the podium. "What happened?"

"The vermin killed my clan!"

"I'm...so sorry, Councilor. I'd no idea. We weren't there. When did this happen?"

"Harun, please sit down," Roze said with compassion. "I

know it's difficult for you, and for all of us, but let Cahil report what he knows. Go on, Cahil."

Cahil took a breath and said, "I went down to the special cells in the Council Hall to check on Ferde Daviian. My people had been hired to increase the number of guards watching him, and I wished to see how they were faring. When I arrived, Ferde was missing, and the guards were unconscious. Captain Marrok had been on duty, yet he was nowhere to be seen. I tracked him down. He refused to answer my questions. I knew time was critical, so I..." He swallowed, then cleared his throat. "Sorry. It's been a rough couple of days. May I please have a drink?" His scratchy voice added a nice touch to his plea.

Cahil was quite the actor. Despite his hatred of the man, Valek was impressed.

"Yes, of course," Roze said.

Pitchers of water had been set on the conference table. Cahil poured a glass and returned to the podium. After gulping half the liquid, he resumed his story.

"I forced..." He performed another emotional pause. "Marrok to answer my questions. He admitted to me that he helped Ferde escape, and that he planned to meet up with the Ferde at Blood Rock in the Avibian Plains."

"Did he say why he committed this crime?" Councilor Sandseed asked. "Why he planned to collude with the Warper?"

"Marrok wanted to frame me for Ferde's escape. He wanted to take my place, leading my people. He also confirmed I'm the King's nephew and the true leader of Ixia."

Denial? Or was Cahil angling to be put in charge of Ixia when Sitia finally decided to attack Ixia?

"What did you do next?" Harun asked.

"Once I knew where Ferde was heading, I reported everything to First Magician Roze Featherstone."

A collective gasp sounded as all gazes turned to Roze.

"I asked him to travel to the rendezvous location and

convince Ferde that he wanted to join him," Roze explained. "The goal of the mission was to learn the Daviian's plans, to identify their leaders, and learn the location of their camps."

A murmurer of unhappiness rumbled. Valek approved of the scheme, it was something he'd assign to a pair of his corps. But he didn't believe Cahil's story for a second. Which meant, either Roze was somehow involved in the escape, or she had seen it as an opportunity to learn more about the Daviians.

Roze raised her hand. "I didn't inform the council because the mission was top secret. These Daviians have magical powers, and they could have learned of the plot from any one of you. I did inform the other master magicians of Ferde's escape. Except, I said Cahil helped him escape. I didn't tell them about Captain Marrok. If he recovered from his injuries and thought he had gotten away with freeing Ferde, I wanted to track his next movements. I found it very interesting that he joined Yelena and Leif when they left to visit Moon Man."

Smooth. Too smooth. Valek studied Bain's and Irys's expressions. Both of their faces were creased with concern and a bit of confusion. Unfortunately, Zitora was all in. She stared at Roze in amazement.

"Was your mission a success?" Bain asked Cahil.

"Partly. I managed to discover some of their plans. Again, Councilor Sandseed, I didn't know about their scheme to attack your clan. But I managed to recruit a few Daviians to our side."

"And their plans?"

"The Daviians are in league with the Commander of Ixia. Together, they plan to assassinate the councilors and master magicians. In the ensuing chaos, the Daviians will take over control of Sitia and, with the Commander's help, turn Sitia's government into a dictatorship."

Nice twist. Cries of dismay ringed the room. Except for the conspiracy with the Commander, it was exactly as Roze had predicted just a day ago. How very convenient. There was a conspiracy all right, and Valek would bet a dozen gold coins it was between Roze and Cahil.

It took a while for everyone to calm down. Valek waited for them to sort through the logic. Bain Bloodgood didn't disappoint him.

"Do you have any evidence of this treachery with the Commander?" Bain asked.

"They wouldn't have been so bold to attack the Sandseed Clan if they didn't have the Commander's support. Otherwise, it would be suicide. I would have gotten all the evidence you'd want, but I was interrupted. Yelena and Leif swallowed Marrok's lies. They joined with Moon Man. The Sandseeds had spotted the Daviians in the plateau. Oh"—Cahil glanced at Harun—"Is that when...the attack happened?"

"We are still working out the timeline," Roze said. "Please continue."

"At the time, I was in Booruby with Ferde, trying to get more information. Yelena and her goons attacked us there."

Valek sagged with relief. Yelena hadn't been killed in the massacre.

"What happened in Booruby?"

"They arrested us, and Yelena destroyed Ferde's mind. No way to find out who the leaders are or where the Daviians are hiding now."

"Destroyed his mind? Are you sure?" Irys asked.

"Oh yes."

"How?"

"I'm guessing with her Soulfinder powers. He now has the mental ability of a two year old."

Roze looked smug, but Irys frowned at Cahil. Yelena must have had a good reason to do it. In Valek's opinion, the man deserved to die, this worked just as well.

"Cahil, you may return to the waiting room," Roze said. "I call Ferde Daviian to appear before the council."

Ferde was surrounded by guards, but it was obvious he was no longer a threat. Unable to comprehend or answer any questions, he was sent back to the cells.

Roze then called Leif Zaltana to appear.

When Leif arrived, he looked exhausted. Yelena's brother had the same green eyes as his sister, but that was where their similarities ended. While her face was oval, his was square. He had brown hair and a muscularly stocky build, which was the opposite of her black hair and lithe grace.

"Leif, report," Roze ordered.

Leif gave a tired laugh. "How much time do you have?" He gazed at the council and sighed. "I hope you're comfortable."

"Leif," Roze warned.

"Fifteen days ago, Yelena received a message from Moon Man, implying the Sandseed Clan had found Ferde. We traveled to the Avibian Plains to meet up with him."

"Why did you take Marrok with you?" Roze asked.

"He said he could convince Cahil to surrender, could talk some sense into the idiot. Yelena read Marrok's intentions and confirmed he was telling the truth. Plus, he's a good tracker and we might have had need of his skills. Turned out we were right."

"What happened after you reached the plains?"

"The Sandseeds had found a vermin camp in the plateau and planned on attacking it. Moon Man thought Cahil and Ferde might be hiding with them. We joined the warriors for the ambush, except it was an illusion. Instead of a bustling, crowded settlement, it was empty. Well, except for the warper who created the illusion. He killed himself before we could interrogate him."

"Didn't they trick you the same way before?" Roze asked with an exasperated tone.

Valek remembered when he had joined Leif, Yelena, Moon Man, and his warriors. They didn't exterminate the Daviians as planned, but Valek had killed Alea, which he considered a win.

"Not quite. Last time the illusion showed only a few people in a camp when, in reality, there was a large force waiting for us. This time was the opposite. However, there were signs that the area had been occupied by dozens of people. With Marrok's help, we tracked them to a trench they had dug. Apparently, they knew they were being watched by the Sandseeds and used the trench to relocate to the northeast without being seen. We also discovered that a much smaller group went west. Worried about the clan members they had left behind, the Sandseed warriors headed home, while I went west with Yelena, Marrok, Moon Man, and Tauno."

The councilors exchanged glances at this news, but no one told Leif that the warriors had been ambushed and killed when they returned home. Valek wondered if they didn't wish to distract Leif.

"Who is Tauno?" Bain asked.

"A Sandseed tracker of some renown," Harun Sandseed said. "He's one of our best."

"He's also the one who found the vermin camp," Leif said. "The five of us located a cave west of the encampment. I used my magic to determine that some vermin and Cahil used that cave. We entered and eventually reached the Illiais Jungle."

Councilor Bavol Zaltana jumped to his feet in panic. "Our clan?"

"They're fine. Mostly."

"What does that mean?"

"I'm getting there." Leif rubbed a hand over his face. "When we exited the cave, we were ambushed by the vermin."

Valek held his breath and squashed the urge to yell at Leif to hurry up and tell them about Yelena. He reasoned that she had to be okay. Otherwise, Leif would be grieving. The siblings were growing close when he'd last seen them together.

"We didn't sense them. They hid behind a null shield and hit us with arrows dipped in Curare."

"Hold on," Councilor Shaba Greenblade said. "What is a null shield?"

"Another magic skill that the Sandseeds Story Weavers, and now the Daviian Warpers, have learned. It's an invisible shield that blocks magic. The warpers hid behind this shield so when Yelena used her magic to sense if anyone was lurking in the jungle, it couldn't pierce the null shield and detect them. Fun, eh?" Leif's tone was far from jovial. "Thank fate Yelena brought along Theobroma and was able to counter the paralyzing effects of the Curare for herself and Moon Man. Together, they rescued us. But while we were under their control, the warpers talked about performing an ancient ritual on us called the Kirakawa."

"Another ancient ritual?" Shaba turned to Harun. "These Daviian Warpers are originally from your clan. How many rituals have you been hiding?"

"We have not hidden anything. The knowledge about how to perform them was destroyed long ago."

"Yet everyone seems to know about them. The information must still be available," Shaba said in exasperation. "Tell us, Leif, what horrors does this one entail?"

Leif glanced at Roze, who nodded.

"I don't have any details on how it works or why. But the premise is the warper traps a person's soul in their blood. Then the warper cuts into the person's body and removes their still beating heart. The blood inside the heart is tattooed into the Warper's skin, increasing their magical power."

Irys paled, then looked at Bain. "Blood magic."

"Whatever you call it, it's powerful. The warpers we've encountered are strong and apparently can keep increasing their power with each victim," Leif said. "In fact, one man has achieved the power to stand in a fire without burning. We call him the Fire Warper. His command of the flames is unbelievable. We barely escaped."

"Fire warpers and this Kirakawa ritual are hard to believe," Councilor Ruy Cloudmist said. "Are you sure the vermin weren't telling you lies to scare you?"

Valek had the same thought. Disinformation and psychological warfare were an effective strategy.

Leif stared at the man as he spoke in an icy tone, "I witnessed this ritual firsthand. My cousin Stono and my father were captured by a second group of warpers that had been hiding in the jungle. They were staked to the ground, and the warpers were about to pull Stono's heart from his chest. My father was going to be next. Yelena ran into the clearing to stop them when a man appeared in the flames of the fire and stepped over the stone ring."

"Yelena has no fire magic," Roze said. "How did she escape?"

"With help. Moon Man, Tauno, and I provided a distraction. We freed my father and Stono. Yelena healed him while Moon Man and Tauno chased the warpers. The Fire Warper disappeared back into the flames."

"How's Stono doing?" Bavol asked.

"He's traumatized, but he's alive."

"Did the others capture the warpers?"

"No, but they did track them to Booruby. Cahil and Ferde found out we were there and captured Marrok. Then they tried to grab us, but we defeated them and brought them here."

"Where are Yelena and Moon Man?" Irys asked.

Finally! Valek almost fell off the rafter as he leaned forward.

"They headed to the Avibian Plains with Tauno to check on the Sandseed Clan. If all is well, she should be back in a couple days."

Valek leaned his head back against the wall. He was emotionally exhausted. Yelena had headed into an ambush. Yet, she had her Soulfinder powers. Would her magic warn her in time? Every fiber of his being hoped so.

Irys glanced at Harun. The Councilor clutched the arms of his chair in a death grip.

"Leif, you're dismissed. Go get some sleep," Roze said.

Valek wondered why she didn't inform him of the massacre. Was it kindness, or did she worry he'd mount up his horse, Rusalka, and head into the plains? Rusalka was a Sandseed horse, and they had a unique gait that allowed them to travel twice as fast when in the Avibian Plains. Leif would beat the Sitian soldiers to the massacre site.

"I call Marrok Ixia to appear before the council," Roze said.

Marrok entered. He, too, appeared tired. His rumpled clothes were similar to Leif's. His hair had turned white since Valek saw him last. Probably a result of being beaten to within an inch of his life.

"Marrok Ixia, report," Roze said.

"I joined Yelena and Leif on their mission because I wanted to help recapture Ferde and talk to Cahil."

"Start at the beginning."

"That is—"

"No, before you were beaten."

"That has nothing to do with Ferde's escape. That's between me and Cahil."

"Cahil claims he beat you to find out why you helped Ferde escape. Would you like to confess now and save us all some time?"

Marrok gaped at Roze. "That's not what happened. Cahil was angry because Valek told him he wasn't the King's nephew. He found out we'd been lying to him for years. He flew into a rage."

"Why did you lie to him?"

"We wanted revenge on the Commander. He killed the entire royal family, including the children. We were supposed to protect them. We decided we would do everything we could to kill the Commander and put a King back on the Ixian throne. Cahil might not have royal blood, but he was born in Ixia."

"And we're supposed to believe that after you recovered from almost dying, you joined Yelena and Leif to help? And not to get *revenge* on the man who beat you?"

"Uh, yes." Marrok looked flustered. "Cahil wasn't thinking clearly. He has a temper. I don't know why he freed Ferde, but I practically raised him, and I know him better than anyone. I was hoping he'd surrender without a fight."

"After you joined Yelena and her brother, what happened next?"

Marrok's report matched Leif's until they separated in the Illiais Jungle.

"Moon Man, Tauno, and I chased them through the jungle, but then Moon Man faltered. He said Yelena needed extra energy to heal that poor man whose stomach had been cut wide open." Marrok shuddered. "By the time Moon Man recovered, the warpers were gone. We waited until morning and then tracked them to Booruby, where we lost them. Tracking is near impossible in a city. We rented a room at one of the inns to wait while Moon Man returned to the jungle to let Yelena and Leif know what happened. Every day we went out to search for the warpers. A few days later the others joined us, and we continued to search."

"How long did it take to find them?" Roze asked.

"They found us. Well, me and Tauno. We were jumped and taken to an abandoned building. They beat poor Tauno, but Cahil pulled me aside. He told me he'd been working undercover, that we were hindering his efforts even though we'd just corroborated his cover story. But he acted like he was glad to learn that I survived and even joked." Marrok drew in a deep breath. "I know I said I knew Cahil the best, but I fell for his lies. He pumped me for information that night, and once he had what he wanted..." He rubbed his jaw. "They had released

Tauno, and I managed to escape to warn the others. Cahil and the warpers followed me, and there was a brief skirmish at the inn. We won, Cahil was arrested, and Ferde…was neutralized."

"Do you know why Yelena used such extreme measures?" Irys asked.

"We were outnumbered at the inn. The fight wasn't going in our favor, and the fire in the hearth started growing. I think the Fire Warper was coming. Yelena did what she had to in order to save us. Again."

"Marrok, you may return to the waiting room," Roze said.

That wasn't a good sign.

Roze stood and walked to the podium. "We've all heard the reports. As for who helped Ferde escape, it's a matter of Cahil's word against Marrok's."

"You talked to Cahil after he learned about the escape," Irys said. "Did you use your magic to determine if he told the truth? Yelena used hers on Marrok. She wouldn't have allowed him to join her if he'd been lying."

True. She would have turned him in to the authorities.

"You're way too fond of her," Roze said. "We can't trust you to be impartial."

"And you didn't answer my question."

"Using my magic would have been a breach of our Ethical Code. Besides, Cahil came to me. Why would he do that if he'd aided in Ferde's escape? He's well aware of my powers."

Powers that she claimed she wouldn't use. Didn't she listen to her own words?

"Leif corroborated Marrok's claim," Irys countered.

"He had gotten the information second hand. Yelena could have lied about Marrok's intentions." Roze held up a hand. "Plus, we all know Leif tends to exaggerate and see danger where there is none. I've no doubt he'd fall for the Daviian's lies. I propose we release Cahil until Yelena returns. He discovered valuable information about the Daviian's plans by risking his own life. I'd also like to detain Marrok until that time. I fear he's a flight risk."

"What happens if Yelena doesn't return?" Irys asked.

"We will have an official trial where I can use my magic to determine the truth," Roze said.

"And if she returns?"

"I will assess her involvement in these events."

"No," Irys said. "It's obvious you hate her. You won't be impartial. She can make her report in front of the council like the others."

"No. That is too dangerous. She *destroyed* Ferde's mind. You all saw him. If she survived the massacre, her mental state might be further unhinged. I won't risk the council. However, Bain and Zitora are welcome to witness my assessment. Will that appease you?"

"No. I need to be there as well."

"Your objectivity is compromised by your friendship with Yelena," Councilor Thema Cowan said. "I think First Magician is being reasonable."

In the end, the council agreed to Roze's proposal. They filed out of the room while Valek mulled over the reports, teasing out the inconsistencies. Cahil had to be lying. Had Roze backed him up because he provided evidence that the Commander had allied with the Daviians to attack Sitia? That would give Roze a legitimate reason to go after both Ixia and the Daviians. But why not include Ferde's release to Cahil's tale? Why implicate Marrok? Because purposely releasing Ferde from jail was too dangerous for the council to accept. However, if Marrok did it and Cahil swooped in to save the day, that was more palatable.

One question remained. Would Roze go after Ixia and the Daviians at the same time or focus on one before the other?

After the great hall had been empty for a while, Valek shimmied down the ropes and exited through the waiting room. He had to send a warning to the Commander.

When he left the Council Hall, he signaled Janco. Valek needed to update him. He'd send a message to Ari in the morning. Gabor and Brigi pounced on Valek the second he entered the safe house, asking him questions without taking a breath.

He held up his hands. "Slow down. One at a time."

Gabor gestured to Brigi.

"I saw they brought in Cahil and another man. Was that the infamous Ferde?"

"Yes, and I'll tell you all about what happened when Janco gets here."

As if on cue, Janco entered through the back door.

Brigi wrinkled her petite nose. "Perhaps we can have the meeting in the park."

"On behalf of all the people without homes, I'm insulted," Janco said. "Don't worry, I left my smelly blanket and cloak hidden in the alley."

Valek studied Janco. His clothes were still in good shape, and his scruff was thicker. And...he sniffed...he didn't stink. But, then again, he'd only been on the streets for three days.

Janco noticed the sniff. "Your friend, Minel, badgered me into bathing. There's a free bathhouse near the market. The rest *charge* you to use their baths." Janco's tone was outraged. "Clearly, we're not in Ixia anymore."

"That's because the Sitian government doesn't fund them like the Commander does," Gabor said. "They have to charge a fee so they can pay their staff and buy supplies."

"Why is the one by the market free?"

"The market stall owners fund that one. It's to lure shoppers to the market."

Janco creased his brow. "But they're the only game in town."

"Not really. There are shops in the residential districts."

"I haven't been there yet." He eyed the kitchen. "Any chance there's tea? And a chicken roasting? Or a steer? Or a pig? Perhaps all three?"

Gabor laughed. "Coming right up."

"I'm assuming this meeting is due to the excitement this morning," Janco said. He scootched his chair close to the fire and warmed his hands. "My new friends have a ton of wild theories. All were overjoyed to see Cahil arrested. He not only refuses to give them a single coin, but he's nasty to them. One lady claims she saw him kick a child who got in his way. They're hoping he is hung for treason."

The sound of the back door opening brought them all to their feet. Valek drew his dagger and investigated. Ari stood by the door. He removed his cloak and hung it on a hook, revealing a white uniform.

"White?" Valek returned his dagger to its sheath.

"I didn't have time to change. I saw Cahil in the Keep's infirmary."

Alarmed, Valek asked, "Did he see you?"

"No. I stayed out of sight. Healer Hayes healed his wrists; they were raw from manacles. But he wasn't under guard. He acted like a free man. I followed him to the bathhouse and then to his house in the Citadel. Then I came here. Do you know what's going on?"

"Come into the kitchen, I was just about to update everyone. Do you need to be back soon?" Valek asked Ari.

"No. I told Healer Hayes I was going to visit my mother. He told me to check in with him when I got back."

In the kitchen, Ari was greeted with a warm welcome. Janco teased him about working in the infirmary, but Ari just shrugged.

"I'm helping people heal, what's not to like?" he countered.

After the tea was poured, Valek updated the team on what happened. The tale took many cups of tea and ran through their entire meal. The jovial mood drained with each revelation.

"That lying sack of potatoes," Janco said. "If Yelena's hurt, I'm gonna peel that beard from Cahil's face and give him a brand-new red smile just under his chin."

"She can handle herself," Ari said. "No way she walks into an ambush. She's too smart."

Valek appreciated the words, but he wondered if Ari was trying to convince himself.

"What's the plan?" Janco asked. "You want me to pick up Cahil and bring him here for a private chat?"

"Not yet," Valek said. "Gabor, I need you to deliver a message to the Commander. You can take one of our horses. Janco and Ari, continue with your undercover surveillance. I'll keep spying on the council meetings."

"The public sessions have all been cancelled," Brigi said. "But they aren't calling for emergency meetings. From what you said, I think they're trying not to scare the public."

That made sense. "They'll still have discussions that I can listen to."

"Too bad you can't get into Roze Featherstone's office," Ari said.

"I could, but it'd be very difficult. Why?"

"It's obvious she's working with Cahil. To go after both the Daviians and the Commander will be a tremendous effort. She has to know her army isn't up to both tasks. I think there's more going on there, but I don't know what."

Valek had similar suspicions. "If I get the opportunity to eavesdrop on Cahil and Roze, I'll take it."

Ari walked with Janco to the back exit. "How's it going? You okay?"

"Yeah. It's not fun, and I'm not getting any sleep on the Council Hall's steps. The guards shoo everyone off them every couple hours, but we return like the tide. It's pointless, but they do it every night. And then there's the grind. You know? The uncertainty if there's gonna be another meal. I know I'm not going to starve, but they don't. The worry constantly gnaws at them. Even if they get food, the relief is only temporary. I want to bring them all to Ixia, tell them they'd be treated so much better there, but I can't."

Ari put his big hand on Janco's shoulder and squeezed.

Janco smiled. "It's not the worst assignment. Remember the mud? I'd take this over the mud any day." He gave them a jaunty wave and left.

"Mud?" Valek asked.

Ari shook his head. "You don't want to know. If you need to contact me, send a messenger. Say it's from my mother. Apparently, we're very close, so it won't seem strange." He donned his cloak and slipped out the door.

Valek spent the next hour writing a message to the Commander. It was proving harder than he'd expected. Too much information and the Commander would send his army to make a preemptive strike. A battle wasn't his style, but if time was a factor, it was the quickest way to conquer. Valek had to convince him to wait, to trust him, but to still be ready just in case. Easier said than done.

With the message in hand, Gabor left for Ixia early in the morning. Valek hoped it would be well received. In the meantime, he donned a new disguise and went to the Council Hall. Since the morning meetings had been cancelled, the Council Hall was closed to the public.

He looped around the building, but there wasn't an easy climbing route. Plus, it was daylight, and the beggars kept drifting his way. Valek would have to switch into a guard's uniform and return during the shift change later that afternoon. He doubted anything new would be discussed at the council session, but he still hated to miss it.

As he walked away, footsteps sounded behind him. He glanced back.

Janco approached with his hand out. "Spare a copper, sir?"

Valek fumbled in his pocket for a coin.

"None of the councilors or magicians are in the hall today," Janco whispered. "Only Roze and the general of the Sitian army."

He dropped a few coppers into Janco's palm. "Thanks."

Janco nodded and returned to the building. A couple beggars surrounded him. One clapped him on the back. Valek wondered if he was Janco's first mark. The timing worked out for the newbie to finally swallow his pride to survive.

Since he had unexpected free time, Valek went to the market. He purchased a few supplies, but he kept an eye out for Fisk.

After thirty minutes, the boy appeared by his side. "That's a much better disguise."

"Yet, you still recognized me."

"You have a certain…way." Fisk motioned with his hand as if to pull the right words from the air. "You know, gait. How you walk. It's…smooth. Like a dancer."

Interesting. Valek had altered his appearance, his speech, and clothing, but he never considered modifying his gait. "Not everyone is as observant as you."

"That's good for you. Or the guards would be swarming." Fisk glanced at the two people patrolling along the edges of the market. "Anyway, I've got some news."

"How much?"

"A gold."

"Four silvers and if it's something I don't know, I'll give you two more."

"Nope. I don't trust you to tell me the truth. Nine silvers."

"Seven."

Fisk sighed dramatically. "I've a family to feed."

THE STUDY OF FIRE

Valek smiled. "That line only works if you're an adult."

"Yeah? Tell my parents that. They have it backwards. Eight."

His grin faded as a pang squeezed his heart. "Eight, then. What do you know?"

"Those Sandseeds who arrived yesterday are not Sandseeds."

"Who are they?"

"I dunno. They split up and are staying at different inns and are haunting different locations. Sandseeds stick together. Like the group that arrived the day before yesterday, the ones who brought the bad news that their clan was attacked and most of them were killed. Who would do such a terrible thing?" Fisk's young face creased with sadness.

"There are terrible people in this world, Fisk. And it's one of my jobs to track them down and stop them."

He brightened a bit. "And I'm helping."

"You are." It was impressive that Fisk learned the news of the massacre. And figured out about the not Sandseeds. No doubt they were Daviians sent to observe the council's reaction to the Sandseed genocide. "Do you know who attacked the Sandseeds?"

"No. But the people around here are more worried over the council's silence. And there are more Sandseeds arriving. They could be survivors or more not Sandseeds." He shrugged.

"Do you know where these new Sandseeds are staying?"

"No, but I can find out."

"No. Never mind. It's too dangerous."

"No, it isn't. People like me are invisible. They'll never notice."

"I think these people will notice. Besides, it's not that important. Here." Valek handed him a gold coin.

Fisk flashed him a smile. "Happy doing business with you."

Valek watched him disappear into the crowd. Then he found a place to observe the people in the market. Soon enough, he spotted a few shoppers who resembled the tall and muscular

Sandseed warriors. They didn't make any effort to blend in. In fact, their gait—as Fisk would say—was confident. Their demeanors were bold. And they didn't appear to be grieving.

Fear swirled around Valek's heart. The Daviians used to be Sandseed warriors before they left to form their own unsanctioned clan.

One of the men reached for an apple on a seller's cart. His sleeve snagged on the edge of the wood, exposing his forearm. Red tattoos swirled on his skin.

Not Sandseeds. Daviian Warpers.

CHAPTER 10

Warpers were in the Citadel. Warpers who had enhanced their magical powers with that Kirakawa ritual.

Warpers who would be hard to fight with mundane tactics. Valek could kill a few, but how many of them were already here? Enough to overrun the council and take over? This was bad.

Valek hurried back to the safe house. Now that he'd seen them, he spotted them everywhere. He'd been so focused on the council; he hadn't given any thought to what the Daviians might do after they'd decimated the Sandseed Clan. It made complete sense that they would attack the council before they had time to respond to the massacre.

He had to warn the council. Scoffing, he imagined the Scourge of Sitia informing the Sitian Council they were about to be attacked by warpers. That would not go over well. Should he gather his people and leave? No. The only thing he could do was warn Irys. She was the only person who might trust him. Valek just needed to figure out the best time and place to approach the Master Magician.

"I've news," Brigi said, when she returned from her shift at the stables.

"Go on." Valek set the kettle on the hearth. A storm had swept in from the north and sleet rattled against the windows. Poor Janco.

"There's going to be a special meeting tomorrow morning," she said.

"An emergency session?" Maybe they already knew about the warpers. One could hope.

"No. This is different. More of a strategy conference. They invited their aides and specialists. I think they're planning their attack, deciding which clans are providing soldiers, and working on logistics. Stuff like that."

At least it was progress. But it might be too late. "I'll make sure I'm in position." He'd slip inside during the early morning shift change. "Have you noticed more Sandseeds in the Citadel?"

She cocked her head at the change in subject but creased her brow in thought. "Actually, yes. I assumed they were the survivors. Yes, I know, I know. Never assume. Sorry!"

"I missed it as well. My ego took a serious blow when a ten year old boy pointed it out to me."

She smiled. "What does it mean?"

"It means you need to be ready to leave if things go south."

"I don't think I will be a target. They would go after the councilors and magicians, but I'm part of the work force. It doesn't make sense for them to kill everyone. Yes, they did murder all the Sandseeds, but like you said, they were a real threat. I think having someone on the inside would be beneficial. I could send messages."

"You would risk your life for the Sitians?"

"Of course. They're not our enemy. Sure, they bark at the

Commander because they're afraid, but the real villains in this case are the Daviians."

True.

~

Trudging through the semi-darkness of dawn, Valek fought the wind and pulled his hood down to protect his face from the sleet. What a miserable start to the day. He arrived at the Council Hall at the tail end of the shift change. His boots crunched on the slush as he climbed the steps and entered the building.

All the guards who had arrived for duty were shaking off the sleet and grumbling about the weather. Valek followed them to the guard's room. He hung his cloak on a peg. As they dispersed for their posts, he headed toward the waiting room. Soon, he was in the rafters. This time, he'd brought a small pack of supplies. He suspected he might be up here all day.

Councilors, magicians, and aides started arriving an hour later. Maps were spread on the tables, pots of tea were brought in, and conversations buzzed. Obviously, this would be a more casual gathering. Yet, something had changed. An undercurrent of fear hummed. Valek wondered what had happened yesterday to alter everyone's... No, not everyone, only the councilors' demeanors.

The answer walked in with Cahil. He brought four Daviians with him. Vermin or warpers? Hard to tell who wielded magic and who didn't since their plain brown tunics and pants covered their skin. Councilor Harun scowled at all of them except the man standing next to him. Valek guessed he was a Sandseed warrior. One of the survivors? The man glared at everyone. No one dared approach him.

Cahil introduced his new Daviian friends as those he had converted to their side. The councilors stiffened and shook hands awkwardly. Irys and Bain kept exchanging confused glances. They must have also noticed the Councilor's fear. No, not fear. Terror. Had the council realized that the Daviians had already invaded the Citadel?

The session began with a discussion of moving soldiers from the southern garrisons north, toward the border. That answered the question of who the Sitians would attack first. The councilors agreed to everything Roze proposed, eliciting alarmed looks between Irys and Bain. The Daviians stayed out of the debate but had moved to the edges of the group, as if assuming a protective position. Or was it a defensive stance? Were they waiting for reinforcements?

Sweat trickled down Valek's back. Was he about to witness the fall of the Sitian government?

Valek listened to their plans, but nothing snagged his full attention. It was as if they were just going through the motions. The meeting ended and everyone drifted into groups. One of the Citadel's guards rushed into the great hall. He headed directly to Roze and interrupted her conversation. Bold. It must be important.

She frowned at whatever news he'd brought. Then she dismissed him and strode over to Irys. Fourth Magician's tight expression at Roze's approach relaxed as they spoke. Irys smiled and nodded. Still unhappy, Roze turned on her heel and joined Cahil.

Valek's heart thumped a question. What would make Irys happy and Roze scowl? Or rather *who*? He ignored it. Speculation would only lead to disappointment. By the time Irys sought out Bain, her smile had faded. And Valek was glad he hadn't allowed his heart to hope.

About ten minutes later, three people entered the great hall. His heart swelled in smug satisfaction while the rest of him melted with relief. Yelena scanned the great hall while her companions, Moon Man and another Sandseed warrior, headed straight for Councilor Sandseed. She hung back, uncertain, and Valek wanted to swoop down, throw her over his shoulder, and carry her away from all this danger. Then tuck her into bed. She looked exhausted.

Irys spotted her and hurried toward her. Yelena took one look at her friend's dire expression and scanned the room again. When she spotted Cahil, Yelena was no longer uncertain. Anger flashed in her green eyes, and she stepped toward the man.

Grabbing her arm, Irys pulled Yelena aside. "Now is not the time."

"What's going on?" Yelena demanded.

Irys glanced around at the councilors hovering nearby. Then she stared at Yelena. Valek guessed they were mentally communicating with their magic. Handy skill, especially when you were surrounded by enemies. He had his nonverbal signals, but they weren't as effective as having a conversation.

At one point during their silent discussion Yelena jolted as if shocked. *Yes, love, Cahil has managed to convince the Sitian Council he was on a mission for Roze and those Daviians you see are allies.*

Moon Man and the other Sandseed finished their conversation with their Councilman and joined Yelena and Irys.

"There are about a dozen Sandseed survivors," Moon Man said. "They came to the Citadel and are staying here for now. Only one Story Weaver besides me survived. It is Gede, and he is the one we need to talk to about the Fire Warper."

Irys said, "Who—"

Moon Man kept talking. "You said Master Bloodgood has a few books about the Efe, right?"

"Yes," Yelena said.

"We should examine them. Gede and I will come to the Keep tomorrow morning." Moon Man turned and walked away.

"That was rather abrupt," Irys said.

Valek agreed. Moon Man was one of Yelena's friends.

"He's been through a lot."

"And so have you." Irys linked her arm with Yelena's. They headed toward the exit. "Tell me about this Fire Warper. Leif had only sketchy details."

Valek suppressed a groan as she disappeared from sight. And now he was stuck in the rafters until everyone was gone. To pass the time, he considered Moon Man's comment about books on the Efe.

They had been an ancient tribe and the ancestors of the current Sandseed Clan. Known for their powerful magic, they also created a number of rites and rituals to increase their power. One of the rituals was named the Efe. Ferde had used it to harvest the souls of his victims before killing them. The twelfth victim had to go to him willingly, and once their soul was obtained, Ferde would have gained enough magical power to counter all four master magicians. Thankfully, Yelena stopped him before he finished the ritual. And now, he would never be a threat again. *Well done, love.*

⁓

It was dark before he could escape the Council Hall. Every muscle had stiffened, and his back hurt from sitting on the hard wood. He gazed at the Keep as a cold wind froze the slush piles, turning the puddles into ice.

As much as he longed to find Yelena, Valek knew she needed her rest. She would forgo sleep to get reacquainted. And to pump him for information. They'd be up all night talking. No, best she had a peaceful night. He'd find her tomorrow.

Brigi had returned to the safe house along with Janco, who sat on the edge of the hearth, warming his backside. They were both excited that Yelena was alive and safe inside the Citadel.

"It is just as dangerous here," Valek said. "We'll have to see what the council decides about her actions with Ferde. They're

THE STUDY OF FIRE

normally logical, but something has spooked them." He explained about their behavior during the meeting.

"Now that she's back, am I off duty?" Janco asked with a hopeful tone.

"Not yet. I need you to keep an eye on the movements of the Daviians."

Janco wilted.

"There's wool socks and wool long johns upstairs with the disguises," Brigi said. "No one will see them underneath your clothes."

He sighed. "Thanks. The others have built a campfire back behind the hall to keep warm. But that ruins my night vision."

"It's only for another couple nights," Valek said. "I get the sense things are about to blow up." He filled them in on what he'd learned.

∼

Dressed as one of the cooking staff in a gray tunic and pants, Valek headed toward the Magician's Keep. Fast footsteps sounded behind him. He whirled around, but it was only Fisk. And from the gleam in the boy's eyes, he had some hot gossip for Valek.

"How much this time?"

"This news is worth five silvers. It comes directly from one of the housekeeping staff."

Valek didn't bother haggling; he just handed over the coins.

"The Sitian Council is going to have a special trial tonight. Someone named Captain Marrok has agreed to testify under oath, which means the First Magician can use her magic to ensure he's telling the truth."

Interesting and worth the five silvers. "Thanks, Fisk."

"Anytime!" He took off, running back the way he'd come.

Considering the recent news, Valek believed it to be a good

move. Marrok's testimony would reveal Cahil's lies and reveal Roze's involvement in freeing Ferde.

He entered the Magician's Keep without trouble. From what he'd overheard yesterday, Moon Man and someone named Gede would visit Bain Bloodgood to examine his books. No doubt Yelena and Irys would also be in attendance.

Valek arrived just in time to see Yelena and Irys exit the dining hall. They headed toward the southeast corner of the Keep, entering Bain Bloodgood's tower. There were four towers that stood in each corner of the Keep. These towers housed the master magicians. Since there were currently four masters, they each had their own. But with ten levels, they could easily share. Yelena was living in Irys's tower in the northwest corner.

Valek found a hidden spot to watch. After a few minutes, Moon Man and Gede arrived. Gede was the man who had been with Councilor Harun. Did that mean the man who entered the great hall with Moon Man and Yelena had been Tauno? He'd find out when he was reunited with Yelena. That thought warmed him.

Unfortunately, after the meeting at Bain's, Yelena went into the infirmary. Immediate worry bloomed in his chest. Was she wounded? No. Her stride had been easy. Perhaps she was checking on the patients. Yelena had powerful healing magic.

As Valek waited for her, Bain and Irys crossed the campus toward Roze Featherstone's tower. But halfway there, Irys turned into the Administration building, while Bain continued on. His white hair blew in the wind. Valek wondered why Bain would leave his tower at all. With the ability to communicate with the other master magicians, he could be warm and cozy next to his hearth instead of facing the elements. In fact, they all could work separately. Instead, they had offices in the Administration building and in the Council Hall, and also had their studies in their towers.

Eventually, Yelena left the infirmary and headed toward

THE STUDY OF FIRE

Roze's tower. Keeping to the shadows, he followed her. She hesitated outside the doorway. This was the second time Valek had witnessed her hesitate. Something wasn't right. And then he remembered Roze planned to assess Yelena when she returned from her mission. To test if she was a danger to others.

The door opened and Bain peered out. "Come in, child. It is cold outside."

Yelena followed him. Valek wished he could go with her. She would be facing three master magicians. But she had her Soulfinding power and had withstood Roze's attack before. Well, with his help. And he'd been far away in Ixia at the time. Now, he was much closer. If she needed him, he wouldn't hesitate to give her all of his strength.

After an hour, Yelena left. Her worried expression, quick pace, and fisted hands didn't bode well. She went straight to Irys's tower and didn't bother to lock the door behind her. Another bad sign. The tap of her boots sounded above him, and he followed her up the steps.

On the third level, he spotted Yelena standing in the middle of a round room with her back to him. It was sparsely furnished with an armoire, a desk, a single bed, and a night table. He doubted she spent much time here.

Yelena laughed.

He leaned against the doorway and crossed his arms. "What's so funny?"

She jerked in surprise and whirled around. "I was thinking about curtains." She grinned and moved toward him.

"Curtains are funny?"

"In comparison to all my other thoughts, yes, curtains can be amusing. But you, sir, are the best thing that's happened to me all day, all week and, now that I think about it, all season."

Two steps and she was wrapped in his arms. Joy raced through his veins. He breathed in her lavender scent. "That's the best welcome I've had all day." All year, if he was being honest.

"Do I want to know why you're here?" she asked.

"No."

She sighed. "Should I know why you're here?"

"Yes. But not now." He leaned over and his lips met hers. The world and all his problems disappeared. Nothing else mattered but the woman in his arms.

∼

Spooned around Yelena on the narrow bed, Valek slept peacefully. Until she nudged him in the ribs with her elbow. It was late afternoon, and the air in the room was icy.

Valek moved to get up. "I'll make a fire—"

"No!" She grabbed his arm, stopping him.

He peered at her in concern. Yelena looked almost frightened.

"You'll need to reapply your makeup," she said, brushing a black strand of hair away from his face.

He took her hand in his. "Nice try, but you *are* going to tell me why you don't want a fire."

"Only if you tell me why you're here." She countered.

"Agreed."

She told Valek about Ferde's escape, Cahil's involvement, and the appearance of the Fire Warper. And by the way her voice hitched and trembled slightly, he knew exactly who she was afraid of. No fire in the room meant that the Fire Warper couldn't reach her. He also learned that she had saved Stono's life by collecting his soul and returning it to his healed body.

Then she recounted her conversation with Irys in the Council Hall. Valek knew most of the information, but it was still important to hear her side of the story and get her impressions.

"According to Cahil, the Daviians are in league with the Commander of Ixia," Yelena said.

"It's ridiculous to think the Commander is working with these Daviians." Valek considered her comments. "So, the Wannabe King has chosen to ignore the truth about his birth. You've got to admit his ability to dupe the entire council is impressive."

"Not the entire council. Irys doesn't believe Cahil and I'm sure there are others." She waved her hand in a shooing motion. "Doesn't matter. It's not my concern. I've been told to be a good little student and mind my own business."

Valek snorted. "Like *you* would listen to them."

"I agreed."

He laughed long and hard. "You. Not. Get involved." Valek paused to catch his breath. "You've been in the midst of trouble ever since you became the Commander's food taster, love. You would never walk away." It'd been ages since he had a good laugh. He wiped tears from his cheeks.

"This is different," she argued. "Then I didn't have a choice."

"Oh? And you have a choice now?"

"Yes. I'll let the council deal with these Daviians, and I'll stay out of trouble."

"But you know they can't counter them."

"They don't want my help."

Valek sobered. Yelena never backed down. The Fire Warper had rattled her confidence. Despite her fear, this wasn't the time to be a good little student. "What happens when the Daviians win?" he asked.

"I'll stay with you in Ixia."

While he'd love that, it wasn't so simple. "What about your parents? Leif? Moon Man? Irys? Do they come with you? And what happens when these Daviian Warpers with their incredible blood magic decide to follow you to Ixia? What choice will you have then?" He studied her face. "You can't let your fear of the Fire Warper stop you from—"

Annoyed, she snapped. "The council has stopped me. They're the ones who are against me."

Against her? Now she was being paranoid. "You just said there are a few councilors on your side. Once the council hears Marrok's evidence tonight, they'll believe you about the Wannabe King."

"How did you know about Marrok?" she demanded.

"Servants. Their information network is far superior to a corps of trained spies." And it appeared young Fisk's and his helper's guild were on track to rival them. "I'll tell you about the session later tonight."

"You rat! It's a closed meeting. Only you would try to pull it off."

"You know me, love." He didn't tell her he'd been snooping all along, just in case Irys or one of the other master magicians read her thoughts. He knew they had an Ethical Code, but from what he had learned about Roze, she would ignore it in a heartbeat if she thought it would benefit Sitia.

"I know. You crave a challenge and you're cocky."

He grinned. "I wouldn't call it cocky. A certain amount of self-confidence is needed, especially in my line of work." He sobered. "And for yours."

She ignored the implication. "Speaking of work, we made a deal. Why are you here?"

He stretched his arms over his head and yawned, considering how best to answer her question.

"Valek," she warned, poking him in the ribs. "Tell me."

"The Commander sent me."

"Why?"

"To assassinate the Sitian Council."

She gaped in surprise. "You're not—"

"No. It's the wrong thing to do right now. The Commander based his decision on the state of Sitian affairs before these Daviian Warpers showed up. He allowed me a degree of flexibility on this mission. We need to find out what's going on. The council meeting tonight might reveal crucial information."

"We?"

"Yes. *We.*" He needed her help. Plus, the old adage about being thrown off a horse applied to this situation. The only way for Yelena to regain her confidence was to get back on that cantankerous horse.

She sighed. They both hunted for the pieces of their hastily discarded clothing.

"What are you doing tonight?" he asked, pulling on his pants.

"I've a meeting with Gede Sandseed in one of the Citadel's guest quarters. He's also a Story Weaver, and he said he could help me learn about how to be a Soulfinder."

"I thought you knew how to be a Soulfinder?"

"Apparently, there's more to it." She rubbed her hands along her sleeves as she shuddered.

"What about Moon Man? Isn't he your Story Weaver?"

"He was. We had a bit of a falling out. Gede offered to help me without using cryptic and mysterious language. And in order to regain the trust of the council, I need to work with Gede." She scowled. "I've learned one thing already. There's this…shadow world. It's exactly like our world except it's all gray. According to Moon Man, it's the world's shadow. Moon Man said the souls of his people haunt that world."

Valek had heard about it. "He told me that you and Leif were in the shadow world when you had to…uh…untangle your relationship."

"That makes sense. I think the Story Weavers use it as a stage to show people the threads of their lives. Those Sandseed souls are part of my story."

"It's not your fault they died."

"I know, but I took the emotional turmoil of the massacre from Moon Man. It threatened to drown him. And I promised to help the souls somehow. But not now."

"Good. The dead can wait. We need to protect the living." He kissed her long and hard. It was a promise.

Valek left. Muscling through the cold wind, he hurried across the campus. There wasn't much time for him to switch into his guard's uniform and report for the evening shift change.

～

He'd just reached his rafter when the councilors and master magicians entered the great hall. Settling on the narrow wooden beam, he exhaled a long breath. That was close.

Roze pounded her gavel, and everyone quieted. Valek noted that Cahil and a few of his pet Daviians were also in attendance.

"I call Marrok Ixia to appear before the council," Roze said.

Marrok entered. He strode to the podium despite being flanked by two guards.

Once he faced the council, Roze said. "Marrok Ixia, please tell the council why you are here."

"I am here to set the record straight about the events surrounding the escape of Ferde Daviian."

"May I have your permission to use magic to confirm your statement?" Roze asked.

"You may," he said formally.

This should be interesting. Valek leaned forward to get a better look. Not that he could see Roze's magic, but Marrok's grip on the podium tightened as if he fought to stay upright against a strong gale.

"Marrok Ixia, report," Roze ordered.

His mouth moved, but no words came out. Marrok gazed at Roze in panic.

"You cannot lie. You can only speak the truth."

"I..." He swallowed, then the words gushed from his mouth. "I freed Ferde."

Gasps and murmurs sounded. Cahil smirked. Poor Marrok had been forced to spew a lie.

Roze leaned back, giving him a smug smile. "Continue."

"I planned to frame Cahil, so he'd be arrested, and I would be promoted to team leader. Once in charge of the soldiers, I would then join Ferde and the Daviians in their attempt to provoke a war with Ixia. But Cahil figured it out. He beat the information from me, and then went to join Ferde in my place."

"Freeing a prisoner from the Council Hall's special cells is a difficult task," Roze said. "Did you work alone, or did you have accomplices?"

"I had help." Sweat glistened on his forehead.

"Who helped you?" she asked.

Marrok's body shook. "Yelena and Leif Zaltana."

CHAPTER 11

A stunned silence filled the room. Its sharp edges dug into Valek's heart. Marrok was obviously being forced to accuse Yelena and her brother, but no one spoke in her defense. Not even Irys. But Bain and her appeared to be mentally communicating. Perhaps they considered it too dangerous to speak up at this time.

Roze dismissed Marrok, thanking him for his confession. Marrok stared at her blankly until the guards grabbed his elbows and led him away. Cahil trotted after them.

"We've always known Soulfinders are dangerous. Now, we have proof that Yelena is just like her predecessors. She has also recruited her brother to help with her schemes. I suspected this would happen, and I have already written up an arrest warrant for them. Once captured, Leif will be interrogated to determine if his involvement was by his own choice or if he was forced to comply. If it was by choice, he will join Yelena in the special cells until we can safely execute them."

Fear zipped through him. Yelena certainly wasn't being paranoid when she had said the council was against her. Or was it just Roze? They all quickly signed the warrant. Perhaps not.

Valek noticed that Bain and Irys left the great hall before it was their turn to sign the document. Perhaps Yelena had some allies after all.

But it wouldn't help if she was captured. Sudden heat scorched his heart. Yelena needed him, but not his strength. Odd. Regardless, he couldn't wait until the room emptied. Valek climbed higher, reaching the windows. He opened one, climbed out, and hung from his fingertips until he found a couple toeholds.

With the cold wind whipping and his fingers turning numb, Valek mostly slid down the side of the building. He hit the ground hard, and pain jolted through his ankles. A few beggars gaped at him, but he didn't care. He spun, getting his bearings. The Citadel's guest quarters were about a block away. Despite the pain, he ran.

Except, he didn't know which one was Gede's. When he neared the row of buildings, he spotted a person. Valek just about tripped over his own feet when he recognized the stout man. Thank fate!

"Things went south at the council meeting," Valek said to Leif. "Where is Yelena?"

Leif just stared at him in shock. But then a nearby window of one of the quarters lit up with a blazing firelight.

"Come on," Valek ordered, running to the entrance.

Locked. He yanked his picks out and opened the door. Inside, a six foot tall fire roared. And standing too close to the flames were Moon Man and Yelena. She yanked on his shoulders, but Moon Man moved deeper into the fire, dragging Yelena with him.

Sitting cross-legged in front of the fire was Gede and two Sandseeds, but they made no move to help Yelena and Moon Man. Instead, they stood and blocked Valek and Leif from the fire.

THE STUDY OF FIRE

Oh no you don't. "Leif, save Yelena!" Valek tackled the closest Sandseed, knocking him into his friend.

"No, Leif!" Gede yelled. "Leave her alone. She's in no danger. Yelena needs to learn."

Leif ignored Gede and darted toward the flames. Valek fought the three men, using all his dirty fighting moves, slamming heads into the floor, and aiming for eyeballs. This wasn't a friendly bout in the training yard. This was back alley brawling. He needed to keep them occupied.

Between punches, he checked on Leif's progress. It seemed to take forever for him to pull Yelena away from the fire. She went limp, and Leif picked her up and headed for the door. Valek continued to fight, giving Leif time to find a safe hiding spot.

Valek tripped one of the Sandseeds, who went flying into a table. Only now did he notice all the furniture had been pushed to the edges of the room. He spotted a pewter candlestick, grabbed it, and promptly used it to bludgeon the remaining two men. They crumbled. Knocked down but not out, Gede pressed a hand to his temple and moaned.

Taking a moment to catch his breath, Valek scanned the room. The fire had returned to a normal size. Moon Man had disappeared. Yelena's cloak and pack sat near the door. He picked them up and left.

It didn't take long to find Leif and Yelena. Leif had only gone a few blocks before hiding in an alley. He sat next to Yelena's prone form.

"Is she all right?" Valek asked, crouching next to her. He smoothed a strand of black hair from her face and checked her pulse. It beat against his fingertips.

"Yes, she's breathing. I had to cut off her air. She wouldn't let go of Moon Man, and he was being sucked deeper into the fire. What the hell is going on?"

"You tell me. Was that the Fire Warper in the fire?"

"I think so. He must have been pulling Moon Man. No way he'd go into the fire on his own."

Valek set down Yelena's pack and cloak. "Leave the Citadel as soon as Yelena wakes. Meet me two miles south of the Citadel."

"But we need our horses and—"

"Do *not* return to the Keep for *any* reason. Understand?"

"Yes."

"Good." Valek had much to do before the night was done.

He returned to the Keep. The stables were located in the northwest, right next to Irys's tower. He had hoped to beat the search for Yelena, but guards filled the campus. Dodging and avoiding the patrols, Valek managed to gather some supplies from Yelena's room before he headed to the dark stables.

Two guards stood in front of the double barn doors. Pulling out his blow pipe and darts, he shot them in their necks. After a count of ten, they wobbled and fell asleep. He dragged them into an empty stall.

Taking a risk, he lit one lantern. The light woke the horses, and they peered over their stall doors.

Valek spotted Kiki right away. Janco called her the magic horse. And for once, he wasn't exaggerating. Intelligence shone from her blue eyes, and he had witnessed her do extraordinary things.

"I need to saddle you and Rusalka," he said to her. "Yelena and Leif needed to leave the Citadel in a hurry. Will you help me?"

Kiki dipped her head and opened her stall door with her teeth. Guess that was a yes. With her help, he saddled them both, filling their bags with feed and supplies for a five-day trip.

"We need to leave the Keep without anyone spotting us. Understand?"

Kiki huffed and nudged him with her nose. He mounted and grabbed Rusalka's reins. Kiki took a circuitous route and frequently paused in large shadows. Eventually, she stopped in the shadow of the Administration building. They were within sight of the Keep's entrance. She cocked an eye and looked at him. His turn.

Despite the late hour, the guards at the gate were still on alert. While the horses waited, Valek searched for Ari in the infirmary. The place was lit up and a few guards milled about. Eventually, he caught sight of him and signaled.

Ari joined him in an empty room. "Is this about Captain Marrok?"

"What have you heard?"

"They just brought him in. He's been beaten, and he's incoherent."

The poor guy. Roze damaged his mind and Cahil injured his body. Valek was surprised he didn't kill the captain. "Are there guards watching him?"

Ari shook his head. "He's not going anywhere. Not anytime soon. What's going on?"

Valek gave him a quick update. "I need you to create a distraction at the Keep's gate," Valek said.

"When?"

"Now."

Ari glanced at the door. "All right. I just helped carry in a couple unconscious men. I could say there's more injured people and I need help."

"Sounds good."

They left the infirmary. Ari ran to the gate and yelled about an emergency, leaving one guard behind. Valek mounted and Kiki trotted up to the man.

He waved his arms, yelling, "Whoa. Stop."

Kiki stopped, reared up, and kicked him in the chest. Hard enough to send him flying into the wall. He banged his head and slumped to the ground. Handy. The horses jumped the barrier with ease.

The streets of the Citadel were also teaming with soldiers hunting for Yelena and Leif. Without being asked, Kiki avoided the searchers. Thank fate her and Rusalka refused to wear horseshoes.

"South gate," he told her.

It took the rest of the night, but they approached the gate without being seen.

"Rather early to be leaving," the main guard at the gate said. "We're on alert."

"I heard," Valek said reasonably. "Do I look like the person you're seeking?"

"No, but you have two horses."

"That I do." Valek leaned forward. "Can you keep a secret?"

The man's hand rested on the hilt of his sword as his expression turned wary. "It depends."

"This extra horse is my soon-to-be fiancé's horse. Well, if she says yes." He winked. "If her father finds out, though…" Valek sliced his finger across his throat. Then he fished out two gold coins and gave them to the guard. "Wish me luck?"

The man pocketed them and laughed. "Good luck." He waved Valek through the gate.

Kiki broke into a gallop as soon as they were out of sight. Two miles later, they found Leif and Yelena's camping spot. He noted they hadn't lit a fire. Smart.

Yelena met his gaze. Her shoulders were slumped, and exhaustion creased her face.

"You know?" he asked.

"Yes."

Valek dismounted. "Good. Saves time. The Citadel and Keep are crawling with soldiers looking for you."

"How did you get the horses out then? A secret spy maneuver?" Leif asked.

"No. A distraction at the Keep's gate, and I bribed the guards at the Citadel's south entrance."

Leif groaned. "Now they'll know where we are."

Exactly. "I want them to think you went south. But you should get as far away from here as possible."

"And go where?" Leif asked.

"Ixia." For now, it was the safest place.

"Why would we do that?" Leif's jaw set into a stubborn line.

To stay alive. "Things are happening too fast right now. We need to regroup and plan. We need reinforcements."

"We should go now," Yelena said.

"I'll meet you at the Commander's castle." Valek handed her Kiki's reins.

Kiki nudged Yelena's arm. "You're not coming with us?"

"No. I still have a few of my corps inside the Citadel. They need to be informed about what's happening. I'll join you at the castle afterward."

Before he could leave, she pulled him aside. They embraced.

"Stay safe," she ordered.

He smiled. "I'm not the one getting pulled into fires, love."

"How did you know I was in trouble?"

"After I heard the council agree to your execution, I had an odd notion the council was the least of your worries."

"Thank you for saving me."

"You keep things interesting, love. It would be boring without you."

"Is that all I am to you? An amusement?"

"If only it was that simple."

Yelena managed a tired smile. "I guess I'm no longer retired."

She had gained some of her confidence back. Good. Valek kissed her goodbye. "Take a roundabout route to Ixia. The borders north of the Citadel will probably be watched."

"Yes, sir."

He watched as they mounted and headed west. Then he began the long, cold trek back to the Citadel. Now that the danger had passed, his ankles pulsed with pain, each step sending a jolt up his leg.

When he reached the gate, the same guard was on duty. "No luck?"

"None." He shook his head sadly. "Her father found out and confiscated our horses. It's a good thing I'm a fast runner."

"Too bad. Are you going to try again?"

"Of course. Love doesn't give up."

~

As he headed to the safe house, Valek passed groups of soldiers still searching for Yelena and Leif. Knowing she was safe outside the Citadel made it worth the long night of dodging patrols. The house was empty. Valek should update his team, but exhaustion had soaked into his bones. And that was when mistakes were made. Best to get a few hours' sleep.

When Valek woke in the afternoon, he changed into nondescript Sitian clothing and went to the market. At first, nothing appeared out of the ordinary, but soon he spotted more Davians. And it didn't take long for Fisk to join him.

"Where's Yelena?" the boy demanded.

"Why?"

"The authorities are looking for her. She needs to leave."

"She's already gone."

Fisk shot him an annoyed glare. "Why didn't you say that first?"

"You're in the business of selling information. I had to make sure of your reasons."

"I would never sell information about Yelena. And I'm insulted that you think I would." Fisk scowled. "Tell her to stay away. And you should leave, too. It's too hot for you both. Consider that *free* advice." Fisk dashed off.

While happy that Yelena had such a loyal ally, Valek hoped

he hadn't just made a new enemy. He headed to the Council Hall. There was significant activity, with people arriving and leaving the building, but Valek didn't want to risk being spotted. Instead, he caught Janco's gaze and signaled. Then he looped around the stables. Brigi hefted a saddle onto a horse's back. She noticed him and gave him a small, relieved smile.

That evening, Janco joined Valek and Brigi for dinner. Valek updated them both on Yelena and Leif's status.

"I'm glad they escaped," Janco said. "Things are getting scary around the Council Hall."

"Scary, how?" Valek asked.

"The place is buzzing with creepy vibes."

Which was Janco speak for magic.

"There's been a lot of emergency missives going out," Brigi said. "The council's messengers have been busy. I don't know what type of messages they're sending. Sometimes I can chat them up and they'll tell me where they're going. And if I flirt, I can get more information. This time, it was all business."

"Can we go home now?" Janco asked.

"Not yet."

Instead of pouting, Janco perked up. "Phew. I thought you were going to try to stop these Daviians with just the four of us."

"We need to find out who is in charge. Roze is either a willing accomplice or she is being manipulated."

"I find it hard to believe anyone could manipulate her," Brigi said.

"If they offer her what she desires, which is to neutralize the threat of Ixia, she might not care how they plan to do it. In any case, we need more details before we can construct a counter strategy."

After having thirds, Janco returned to his post. Valek planned to sneak into the Council Hall during the early morning shift change, so he settled on the couch for a few hours of sleep.

When he pulled up his blanket, the back door opened and then clicked shut. Valek pulled his dagger, but relaxed when he recognized Ari.

"You have news?" Valek asked.

"You're not going to believe this," Ari said.

"Try me."

"A few hours ago, I heard voices in Captain Marrok's room. There's been no guards watching him, and Healer Hayes already checked on him, so I peeked. Two Sandseeds were helping him to stand. They cajoled him into changing and gave him a cloak. I suspected they might be using him for the Kirakawa ritual, so I hid in another room until they passed. I followed them outside and they..." Ari swiped a hand through his short curls. "They disappeared in a shaft of moonlight. All three of them."

If this had been Janco reporting, Valek would have thought a shaft of moonlight was code for something else. "Can you describe the Sandseeds?"

"A big bald man with the blackest skin I've ever seen. And a smaller man with brown hair."

Moon Man and Tauno. While very happy Moon Man survived the fire, why would they rescue Marrok? "Did they say anything about where they might be going?"

"No. I searched the rest of the campus but couldn't find them. On my way back, two horses from the Keep's stable trotted by me. Despite the guards trying to stop them, the horses jumped the gate and headed deeper into the Citadel. Is there something going on that I should know?"

Valek explained about Marrok naming Yelena and Leif as his accomplices. "Moon Man has magical powers, so that probably explains how he disappeared in the moonlight. As for the horses..." Valek shrugged. "He may have called them. Sandseeds have a special bond with their horses."

"This Moon Man must not be in league with the others," Ari said.

"I'm guessing he's being smart and fleeing the Citadel before he is fed to the Fire Warper again." Valek wondered how he had escaped the fire.

"What's our next move?"

"Sit tight for now. See what happens when they discover Marrok is missing. You need to be back in the infirmary before that, or they might suspect you of helping him to escape."

"I'll let you know their response." Ari left.

∼

Valek put the finishing touches on his disguise and headed to the Council Hall. No surprise, the streets were empty. Except, they seemed extra desolate. He also noted the smaller number of beggars sleeping around the building. Janco gave him a woeful look but didn't move from his spot. It had a good view of both the hall and the Keep.

Getting into the rafters was more difficult than any previous time, Valek had to dodge not only guards but a few Daviians. Magic had briefly touched his face when he encountered a warper. The man had given him a hard look. Valek had nodded a good morning and kept walking. Thank fate, the warper hadn't followed.

The great hall was a hive of activity. Messengers arrived and hurried away all day long. The councilors agreed to everything Roze Featherstone proposed. The most frustrating thing was the lack of new information.

The next day, Valek encountered more Daviians when he snuck in. Not a good sign. When he was in the rafters, he realized that while Roze and company were preparing for an invasion, they appeared to be waiting for something or for someone. The Fire Warper? They never said, just talked logistics and strategy.

Ari had reported that Marrok's escape was taken in stride.

No one in authority seemed upset, only Healer Hayes was concerned. He hadn't finished healing Marrok's ribs.

Gabor returned on the twenty-sixth day of the cold season. Ice coated his cloak.

He sagged onto a chair next to the hearth. "It's even colder up north."

"Did you have any trouble getting into Ixia?" Valek asked.

"No. I delivered your message to the Commander and updated Kenda before coming back."

"How did the Commander take the news?" Valek asked.

Gabor scowled. "Not well. Good thing he's not a kill-the-messenger dictator."

"Did he give you any instructions?"

"He said he *trusted* you to take care of the problem."

If only it were that easy.

By day twenty-seven, it was impossible for Valek to reach the rafters. Daviians crawled all over the Council Hall, the Citadel, and, according to Ari, the Magician's Keep.

Magic filled the streets, and at times he had to push through it. On his way back to the safe house that evening, a person stepped from a shadow and confronted Valek.

A broad man pulled his scimitar and pointed it at Valek's chest. "Who are you?"

Unfortunately, it wasn't the man's weapon that made Valek's heart beat out a warning. It was the sticky strands of magic touching his skin. "I'm Ilom Cloudmist, who are you?"

"The person asking questions. Why can I not sense you?"

"Pardon? Sense me how?" Valek opted for ignorance.

"Your thoughts. I am really good at reading a person's thoughts."

"Oh, you're a magician. How...nice?" His voice squeaked as if he were afraid.

"And you are like a ghost."

Shit. "Um, that's...interesting?"

"It is. In fact, you are going to come with me to the Council Hall and talk to my boss about it."

"I am?" He shrank back and palmed a dart.

"You are." The man sheathed his weapon and grabbed Valek's upper arm, pulling him down the street.

Valek jabbed the dart into the Warper's hand.

The man tightened his grip and stopped. Magic slammed into Valek. "You cooperate or you die."

Nice guy. The magical pressure receded. "Okay," Valek said meekly.

"Good." The warper continued to march Valek toward the Council Hall. After a few steps, he staggered and went down on one knee.

"Are you well?" Valek asked.

"I am..." He slumped over.

"Sound asleep." Too bad Valek couldn't erase the man's memory. As soon as he woke, he was going to report the incident to his boss. Valek should kill him, but that would start a manhunt. Instead, he dragged him to a hidden spot and hurried back to the house.

Valek discussed his options with Gabor and Brigi. There was only one—to stay inside for a few days. He didn't like it, but it made the most sense. The warper would prowl the streets with his warper friends, looking for Ilom Cloudmist. Valek just hoped they didn't harm anyone during their search.

Late that night, Gabor returned from his reconnaissance, waking Valek.

"Something happen?" he asked.

"No, but there's too many people on the streets. I don't know if they're vermin, warpers, or the Citadel guards, but they're all very interested in anyone who should be in bed. I hightailed it back here."

And Gabor didn't spook easily. Valek muttered a curse.

The next afternoon Janco arrived with more bad news. "They arrested Bain Bloodgood and Irys Jewelrose for treason!"

That was beyond bad. If they had the power to capture two master magicians, Valek had no chance of stopping them. Time to retreat and regroup.

"Get cleaned up, then talk to Brigi and send a message to Ari. We're bugging out tonight."

Janco hesitated.

"I thought you would be happy to leave."

"I am, but I'm worried about my friends. Some of them have been disappearing."

Valek wasn't surprised Janco had made friends. "As in, leaving because it's dangerous?"

"No. Disappearing. But the others won't leave. They say they have nowhere to go and no money to get there."

"Minel?"

"Still there."

Valek strode to the desk and pulled out their emergency funds. He handed the pouch to Janco. "Make sure they promise to leave the Citadel."

Janco peered into the pouch and then gaped at Valek. "Aww, you old softie."

"Just go."

"Yes, sir."

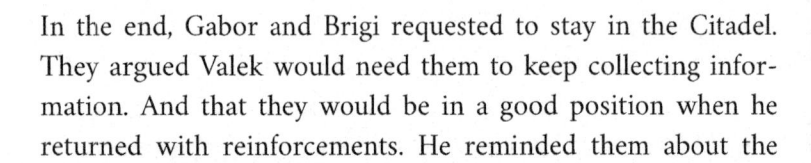

～

In the end, Gabor and Brigi requested to stay in the Citadel. They argued Valek would need them to keep collecting information. And that they would be in a good position when he returned with reinforcements. He reminded them about the agents he'd assigned to watch the Daviians, who had most likely been captured and killed. They countered that they had well-established identities, and Gabor would not stay out too late. "I'm sensing they might enact a curfew," he said.

Valek relented, giving them strict orders to run if they felt unsafe or if their covers were compromised. They agreed.

After dinner, Valek, Ari, and Janco headed to Horses on Mane Street to pick up Onyx and the others. They mounted and walked the horses to the north gate. Valek hadn't wanted to waste time by looping around from another exit. Besides, if the guards at the gate tried to stop them, they would fight their way through. Stealth no longer mattered.

Aside from a barrage of questions about their reasons for leaving, the guards eventually let them pass. They spurred their horses into a gallop. No one said much as they traveled north.

At dawn, Valek turned off the road and found a place to stop and rest the horses. Ari built a campfire while Janco scouted the area, ensuring they wouldn't be discovered.

Breakfast entailed hot tea and travel rations. Valek asked Ari and Janco what they thought of their first undercover mission. He braced for Janco's list of complaints about the weather, and the lack of food and sleep.

They were quiet at first, then Ari said, "It wasn't what I expected. I mean, it was. I knew I'd have to lie and pretend and establish a false identity, but I didn't know I would care."

"Care?" Janco asked.

"I really liked Healer Hayes and some of the medics. I liked helping the patients. I felt bad leaving. I left a note saying my mother was sick, but they'll wonder what happened to me when I don't show up."

"I felt bad, too. I get to go back to my comfy bed, to three meals a day, and to warm fires. And I..." Janco ducked his head.

Valek waited, but when Janco didn't say anything more, he prompted, "You?"

He met Valek's gaze and said in a defiant tone, "I told them to use the money we gave them to come to Ixia. To tell the border guards that Adviser Janco gave them permission to enter, and then for them to come find me at the Commander's castle."

Valek grappled with a response.

"If any of them are captured by the Daviians, they'll tell them about you," Ari said.

Janco huffed. "I doubt it. Half of them laughed, told me I was crazy, but they thanked me for the coins."

"And the other half?" Valek asked.

"Also thanked me and said they would leave the Citadel, but not to go to Ixia. They think the Commander is a tyrant and are terrified. I didn't have enough time to change their minds."

"You won't ever change their minds, Janco," Valek said. "It's a belief based on fear and not on facts."

They finished their meal and set a watch schedule. By midafternoon, they were back on the road. The rest of the trip to Ixia was uneventful and they reached the castle complex late the night before the thirtieth day of the cold season. Officially, the coldest day of the year.

Since they had forgone sleep in order to shorten their trip, Valek sent Ari and Janco to bed when they finished rubbing down the horses. After being welcomed home by the guards, Valek tapped lightly on the Commander's door. No noises sounded on the other side, so Valek turned but paused when the lock clicked open.

The Commander stood in the entry. He wore a set of flannel pajamas and thick wool socks. But his expression was icy.

"Did I wake you?" Valek asked.

"I'd just retired but wasn't asleep. What are you doing here?"

"To report—"

"Valek, you're supposed to be taking care of a very large problem in Sitia."

"It got too hot. I can report in the morning if you're tired."

"As if I could fall asleep now. Come in, I'll get you a drink, you look half frozen."

The whiskey wasn't quite the Ball Thawer, but it warmed him from the inside out. Valek reported what he'd learned in Sitia.

"That tracks with what Yelena reported."

Valek relaxed back into the couch cushions as one worry of a dozen lifted from his shoulders. "When did they arrive?"

"Just this morning. Her and her friends made quite the spectacle. I'm sure the staff are placing bets on how long they stay."

"Friends?" He was confused. Had she introduced Leif as her friend?

The Commander's gaze turned frigid. "You mean you are unaware of her companions?"

Not good. "I sent her and her brother, Leif, here for their own safety."

"They arrived with three others. A magician named Moon Man, a Sandseed named Tauno, and our infamous Captain Marrok."

They managed to catch up with Yelena and Leif. Impressive.

"Yelena and her friends had excellent timing. I just received a letter from the Sitian Council. It warned me about Yelena's renegade status and suggested she and her treasonous companions be killed on sight. Tell me why I shouldn't execute them all?"

CHAPTER 12

Valek's heart paused. Execute Yelena, Leif, and the others? The Commander couldn't be serious. Could he? Best to act as if he was. Jolting his heart back into action, he said, "That's exactly what the Sitian Council wants you to do. Yelena and her companions are a threat to the Daviians. You would be doing them a favor, and not all the councilors are with Roze. Two master magicians have been arrested for treason. We have some allies in the Citadel."

"And according to Yelena, her Councilman, Bavol Zaltana, is also an ally. Yelena wants to return to the Citadel to talk to him."

"By herself?"

"No, she requested your aid and a few of your corps. I told her no, it's too dangerous."

Which just meant she would either go on her own or take her friends with her.

"I offered her a job as my adviser."

"Did she accept?"

"Not yet."

Another clue she didn't plan on staying.

The Commander sipped his brandy. "She asked about her

companions. I told her they could be a part of her staff, but they are not to use their magic against any Ixians without my permission."

That was amazing progress. "Does this mean you're not planning on executing them?"

"For now."

"And you couldn't have led with that?"

The Commander's icy expression melted several degrees. "Where's the fun in that? Although, I might tie Leif up with a big bow and send him back to the Sitians."

"Why?"

"He had the audacity to criticize my way of governing Ixia during dinner."

Ho boy. The Commander did not entertain often. "I'm sure Yelena told him the error of his ways."

"I hope so. We're having a meeting tomorrow afternoon. I want you, Ari, and Janco in attendance. I also want ideas on how to stop these Daviians."

"Yes, sir."

Valek entered his suite. He breathed in the scent of lavender and smiled. The thought of Yelena becoming an adviser and staying in Ixia was a pleasant one. Unrealistic, but a man could dream. He lit a single lantern and trudged up to bed. The crisp sheets were clean and fresh.

Ahhh. He sank into his comfortable mattress—a decadent luxury compared with the couch he'd been sleeping on. Tomorrow night, Yelena would join him. *Ahhh.*

༄

The next morning, Valek stopped in Kenda's office to update her.

"Yeah, Gabor filled me in on the situation. Anything new since then?" she asked.

He brought her up to date. "Any news from our agents sent to the plateau?"

"No." She gestured to the board on her wall. "I've marked them as missing-in-action and presumed dead."

Although he already suspected their fates, Valek slumped in his chair. He would need to inform their next of kins. It was the worst part of his job.

"How about some good news?" she asked. "Trevar and Adrik are becoming Star's go-to recruits. She's still in the preliminary stages of building her network, but they're in the inner circle."

Valek was glad to hear it. "Do they know what she's planning?"

"Her smuggling operation took a big hit. One of her clients fired her. Seems the cargo, so to speak, never arrived in Sitia. The person was supposed to send a letter to the client once safely in Sitia. A letter arrived but without the proper code words."

It must have been Porter. "Do Trevar and Adrik know the name of the client?"

"Not yet."

Valek considered. Porter had been saving young magicians and sending them to Sitia. Why would they go missing? The Sitians should be thrilled. "Kenda, I know who the client is, and I need you—"

"I'm not an idiot, Valek. I've known as well. Don't worry, I won't tell the Commander. I'm glad Porter's helping those poor kids. Do you want me to provide a safe escort for his ducklings? Maybe Trevar and Adrik could impress Star even more by getting her client back and taking his ducks into Sitia."

"That's an excellent idea. But hold off until it's safer."

"And how exactly are you going to make it safe?"

"I'm working on it. In fact, I'm heading to talk to an expert now."

Valek left Kenda's office and searched for Yelena. The

Commander had assigned the group to a guest suite. The main room had a large comfortable couch, a scattering of soft chairs, desks, and tables. Four bedrooms branched off the main area, two on each side. A row of round windows along the back wall let in the early morning sunlight.

Moon Man sat on the couch with Marrok. Tauno prowled from one end of the room to the other like a caged animal. They all glanced at Valek when he entered.

"I'm glad you weren't fried," Valek said to Moon Man.

"I am as well."

"How are you feeling, Marrok?"

Marrok looked at Moon Man in confusion.

"His injuries are healed," Moon Man said. "But his mind has been shredded. I am trying to repair the damage."

"I figured Roze forced him to confess. Can you fix him?"

"I can try."

"Is Yelena here?"

Moon Man chuckled. "I admire your patience. She is not. Leif is in his room if you want to talk to him."

"Do you know where she is?"

"I do not."

He remembered Yelena's comment about them having a falling out. "Why aren't you her Story Weaver anymore?"

Moon Man's humor faded and a deep sadness creased his face. "She has rejected my help. Gede is her Story Weaver now."

"He can't be. Gede tried to feed you both to the Fire Warper."

Grief and a flash of pain sparked in his eyes. "Gede has betrayed my people. He is a warper not a Story Weaver. However, Yelena must reject Gede and reestablish our connection."

Valek considered the night he and Leif saved Yelena. "You escaped the fire. Do you know how to counter the Fire Warper?"

"No. Gede pulled me from the fire. The Fire Warper has no need of the living in the fire world."

"Fire world?"

"There are four facets of our world. The living world, the shadow world, the fire world, and the sky. When we die, our souls can either find peace in the sky or suffer in the fire world. They can also get lost in the shadow world."

"Let's focus on the Fire Warper. Who is he?"

"A soul trapped in the fire world. One who has grown strong enough to heed Gede's call. And once called, he agreed to aid the Daviians for a price."

"More souls?" Valek guessed.

"Yes. Gede and the other warpers have been feeding him souls."

"By using the Kirakawa ritual?"

"Yes. The victims' souls are being fed to the Fire Warper, except for the souls of those who had magical abilities when they were alive. Those souls are being used to empower the warpers."

"Is there a way to stop the Fire Warper?"

"He grows stronger with each soul acquired. Stopping the rituals would keep him from returning to our world, but I fear it is impossible at present."

"What happens if he returns to our world?"

"It will burn."

Okay then. First thing on Valek's to-do list: stop the Fire Warper. Which meant he'd have to stop the rituals. "Do you know where they're currently performing the Kirakawa?"

"No. But I can guess that now that the warpers are in the Citadel, the magicians in the Keep will all become their next victims."

A good guess. However, Valek wondered how the Daviians managed to gain so much power without anyone noticing.

"Before they massacred your people, where did they find their victims?"

"I do not know. I can only speculate that they took those who would not be missed. Those without homes or families. As for magicians, they would have needed to capture those who are young and not under the guidance of another."

Ice coated Valek's skin. Porter's ducklings. But the warpers no longer needed them now that they had an entire smorgasbord of magicians in the Keep. Right?

"How strong does the Fire Warper need to be in order to cross into our world?" Valek asked.

"Much stronger than a master magician. He has gained a great deal of power, but still requires a great deal more."

That was probably what Gede had been waiting for. And now that they controlled the Citadel, they could feed the Fire Warper until he crossed over. Then what? Use him to destroy Ixia, was Valek's guess. "If the world burns when he arrives, then why invite him?"

"Hubris. They believe they can control him."

"Can they?"

"No."

∼

Valek searched for Yelena with no luck. He'd see her at the meeting, which reminded him to inform Ari and Janco that their presence was required. Janco was still sleeping, but Ari said they would be there. Valek then went to his office, took one look at the stacks of reports on his desk, and almost turned around. He built a fire in the brazier and noted Mr. Spider's absence. It was the middle of the cold season, and the freezing temperatures must have killed all the insects.

With a sigh, Valek settled behind his desk. Instead of reading through the files, he stared out the window. The Fire Warper had to be stopped. Despite Moon Man's pessimism, there had to be a way to counter him. If the Fire Warper grew stronger with each soul he acquired, perhaps Yelena could take the souls away from him. She had done something similar to Ferde when he'd performed the Efe ritual. Yelena had pulled the souls of Ferde's victims from him and sent them to the sky. Except for Gelsi's; she'd returned her soul to her body.

Once the Fire Warper was no longer a threat, they only had to deal with all the Daviian Warpers. If they eliminated the Fire Warper before the Daviians killed all the master magicians, then the masters could stop the rest of the warpers. A big if. As the most powerful magicians, the masters were probably going to be sacrificed first.

A knock on the door interrupted Valek's dire thoughts. Brede poked his head inside the room and he gestured him closer.

"I heard a rumor you were back," Brede said. "I'm just checking if you need anything."

"No, thanks. And I won't be here long. I've unfinished business in Sitia."

"Too bad. You've missed out on... Nothing. It's been rather boring around here. Well, except for the arrival of the Sitians. Everyone is abuzz with speculation."

"I'm sure the rumors are outrageous."

"I hope so. Dull rumors are no fun." Brede smiled. "Are you sure you don't have a snake from Sitia for me to study? Preferably one that is still alive. I've been learning a lot about them. Did you know they have these necklace snakes in the Illiais Jungle that strangle their prey?"

"I've heard. Sorry, no critters. Not that I've seen any with this cold weather."

"That reminds me. I'm sorry to say Mr. Spider has passed on to the big cobweb in the sky. But there's good news!"

"Really?"

"Mr. Spider was really Mrs. Spider. And she left a sac of spiderlings. Isn't that exciting?"

"Not if they hatch in my office."

"I'll take the sac outside when it's ready to hatch so they'll be born where they belong. Well, except one. You'll need a Mr. Spider Junior to carry on the family tradition."

Valek laughed. "You really have been bored."

"That obvious?"

"Yes." Valek considered. "Ask Kenda if there is anything she needs to be organized. She loves organization, but she's been extra busy while I've been gone."

"Perfect. Thanks!" Brede dashed out the door.

Valek stood to follow, but the fabric of his pants caught on a nail sticking from his chair and ripped. He cursed. They were his favorite pair, and he'd been meaning to fix that nail for ages. He hurried to his suite to change and took the pants to the seamstress.

Dilana sat at her workstation near the windows. Her curly blond hair shone like gold in the sunlight. Bits of cloth peppered the floor around her. Bolts of mostly black fabric leaned against the wall. Piles of uniform shirts, pants, and skirts littered the floor. When he approached, she cut a thread with her teeth then looked up. With her heart-shaped face and long eyelashes framing honey-colored eyes, she was beautiful.

"You just missed her," Dilana said.

"Her?"

"Oh, come on, Valek. We all know about you and Yelena."

Lovely. "Yelena was here?"

Dilana stood and shook out a pair of black pants before folding them. "She needed an adviser's uniform. I just finished the alterations. Can you give them to her when you see her." She leered.

Lovely times two. "If you can fix my pants." He showed her the rip.

She *tsked*. "These are old. I'll replace them with a new pair."

"No, thank you. The fabric has finally softened to a comfortable level."

"If the Commander complains about your shoddy appearance, you better not blame me, or I'll make your next sneak suit one size too small."

A genuine threat. "I'll take full responsibility."

"Good." She handed him Yelena's uniform. "Now *shoo*, I've work to do."

Valek left. Dilana provided him with all his disguises, and his sneak suits were vital to his work.

He stopped in his office to drop off Yelena's uniform. She hadn't agreed to become the Commander's new adviser, and he doubted she would. The only reason she would need a uniform was because she planned to sneak out of Ixia. Her Sitian clothing would draw unwanted attention.

Valek wondered if she'd leave tonight as he hurried to the meeting. The Commander's war room was located in one of the castle's four towers. Despite the distance, he was the first to arrive. Weak sunlight streamed through the long stained-glass windows that striped the round walls. A large egg-shaped conference table occupied the center. Valek glanced up, checking that no intruders hid in the rafters.

Circling the table, he sat in his place, which was to the right of the Commander's seat at the narrow end of the oval. The Commander arrived next, followed by Ari and Janco.

"Have you determined the best way to counter these Davians?" the Commander asked as he settled in his seat.

"I've a few ideas."

The door to the war room opened. Yelena and her companions entered. No one smiled and tension emanated from their tight shoulders, pressed lips, and stiff spines. They were not acting like a cohesive group. Something wasn't right. When they sat down, they left empty seats between them.

"Valek was just informing me on the state of affairs in Sitia," the Commander said. "Continue."

The state of affairs? Interesting word choice. Had the Commander sensed the friction as well. Valek changed tactics. "I found the situation to be rather ah…unique." He leaned back in his chair and scanned the unhappy faces.

"Unique is putting it mildly," Janco said. He rubbed the scar where the bottom half of his right ear used to be. It was a nervous tick.

"Try alarming," Ari added.

"Alarming would work," Valek agreed. "Taking out the Council wouldn't result in better leaders. In fact, it would have inflamed the citizens to all-out war. And they have some new players who could potentially tip the battle in their favor."

"Players? Try creepy men. Scary magicians. Evil demons." Janco shuddered.

Valek shot Janco a warning look. He was being vague. "I need to obtain more information before I can assess the true nature of the threat and determine the best way to counter it." Which was somewhat true.

"Why have you returned?" the Commander asked even though he knew the answer.

Valek glanced at Yelena. Was all of this for her benefit? "I require more help. Things were getting a little too hot, even for me."

The room fell quiet as Commander Ambrose considered. "What do you need?"

"A few more men, Yelena and her brother."

Leif grunted in surprise but kept quiet.

"She hasn't agreed to be an adviser yet so I can't order her to assist you," the Commander said.

"Then I will have to ask." Valek looked at them.

"Yes," Yelena said at the same time as Leif said no.

"I'm a Sitian, remember? I can't aid Ixia in overthrowing Sitia," Leif said.

Ah, that explained some of the tension.

"I don't want to take control of Sitia," the Commander said. "I just don't want them to invade us, and I will take preventative measures to stop them."

"By helping us, you will also help your country," Valek said.

"We can do it on our own. We don't need you or Yelena." Leif turned to her. "You could never have been a true Liaison, little sister. Ever since we've been in Ixia, you have revealed your true loyalties."

"Is that what you believe?" Her voice shook with her outrage.

"Look at the evidence. At the first sign of trouble, you run for Ixia. We could have returned to the Citadel and explained everything to the council."

With a grief stricken expression, Yelena said, "The council will not believe us. I told you what Irys said."

"But what if you lied? You know I don't have the power of mental communication on my own. You don't trust us, so why should we trust you?"

It was worse than he'd thought. Yelena had not only pushed Moon Man away, but apparently the others as well.

"Believe what you want, then. Valek, can we do without him?" she asked.

"We can."

The Commander stared at Valek. "You *will* tell me your plans before you disappear again."

"Yes, sir."

"Good. You're all dismissed." The Commander stood.

"What about us?" Leif gestured to Moon Man and Tauno. "Can we return to Sitia?"

"Consider yourselves guests of Ixia until this unfortunate incident is resolved," Valek said. If they returned to the Citadel, they would be immediately captured and killed. Staying in Ixia would keep them safe.

"What if we no longer wish to be guests?" Moon Man asked.

"Then you will be our first prisoners of war, and your accommodations will not be so luxurious. It's your choice," the Commander said before leaving.

Leif glared at Yelena. Valek signaled Ari.

Ari nodded and stood. "We will be happy to escort you to your quarters."

Valek shifted his weight as Leif glowered at Ari. Moon Man seemed unperturbed, but Tauno's brow was creased with worry. Eventually, they followed Ari from the war room.

Janco took up the rear guard position. He flashed Yelena a smirk. "Training yard, four o'clock."

"You need more lessons?" She countered with her own smirk.

"You wish."

Her smile faded when the door closed. Not sure what to do, Valek remained seated on the far side of the table.

"Is it that bad?" she asked.

"It's a situation I've never encountered before. I'm worried."

"About Ixia?"

"About you, love."

"Me?"

"I've always been amazed with how you can draw unwanted attention and ire from powerful people. This time, though, you managed to get a whole country upset. If I was the Commander, I would wait out the political strife in Sitia and then offer you to the victors in trade for Ixia being left alone."

"Good thing you're not the Commander."

"Yes. And we should leave Ixia before the Commander figures it out. What are you planning?"

She tried to look innocent. "Me? You're the one with the plan."

"And the adviser uniform you had Dilana size for you? You weren't thinking of sneaking off to Sitia without me, were you?"

She wilted. "Did she tell you?"

"I had ripped a hole in my favorite pants. When I dropped them off, she asked me to deliver your uniform and gifted me with a leer. I would guess the staff is already betting how soon one of them will spot us together." He sighed. "If only intelligence information worked through my corps as efficiently as gossip flowed through the staff, then my problems would be minimal."

Unable to stand being apart for another second, Valek stood. He strode over to Yelena. He leaned on her chair's arms, bringing his face inches from hers. "I'll ask you again. Your plans include me, correct?"

She slumped deeper into her chair.

"Yelena?" His voice held a warning.

"You said you had never encountered this situation before. It's an unknown. I don't want to risk..."

"What?"

"Risk losing you. With your immunity, I can't heal you!"

"I'm willing to take the chance."

"But I'm not willing to let you."

"Sorry, love, that's not your decision. It's mine."

She grumbled. "Okay, I promise not to go to Sitia without you."

"Thank you." Valek brushed his lips against her cheek. His blood hummed with desire.

"What about your plan?" she asked.

"This is my plan." He moved closer and kissed her.

She wrapped her arms around him and started to yank his shirt off.

He pulled away in surprise. "In the war room, love? What if someone comes in?"

She stood and removed his shirt. "Then they'll have a good story to tell."

"Good?" He pretended to be offended.

"Prove me wrong."

Fire raced through his veins. *Challenge accepted, love.*

They ended up underneath the war room's conference table, wrapped in each other's arms. Valek wished they could stay in the bubble of bliss forever. But like all bubbles, it burst. They discussed the events in Sitia.

"I could hardly move within the Citadel," Valek said. "The air was so thick with magic, I felt like I swam in syrup."

"But you weren't detected."

"Not really," he explained about his near miss. "After that, it was only a matter of time. With that many warpers, my presence would have eventually caused a noticeable dead zone."

Yelena was quiet for a long while, then she asked, "Do you know who their victims are?"

"They're probably targeting the homeless. Who would miss a few beggars in a big city? No one."

"What about the need for magicians?"

The magicians from Porter's network wouldn't be enough for all the warpers. "The first year after a magician reaches adolescence is a difficult and vulnerable year. Half the people don't even realize they can access the power source, and the other half don't have a clue how to use it. The warpers could be hunting the streets, looking for someone in that precarious situation."

They also discussed the best way to approach Bavol Zaltana. Yelena believed the councilor believed and supported her, but it would be difficult, but it was important to find out why the councilors agreed with Roze so easily. And hopefully the man also had information about the Daviians' plans.

"I'll leave Ari and Janco here. They won't be happy, but security around the Citadel is too tight, and we're better off just going ourselves. Two of my corps have already been caught." Valek sat up with reluctance. "I have some business to attend to. I'll meet you in my suite later tonight and we can finalize our time schedule. I'll have your belongings delivered there."

"Why did you want Leif to come with us?"

He shook his head. "You wouldn't have agreed anyway."

"To what?"

"To letting Leif get caught and using your mental connection to him to find out what's going on in the Keep. But now you're mad at him—"

"No. He would be killed. I'm not *that* angry with him."

Valek smiled and glanced back at the table when they left the war room. Yet another memory to add to the place. At least this time, no one was set on fire. Well, then again...

Yelena followed him to his office to pick up her uniform. By the time they parted, she had withdrawn from him as if she'd sealed off her emotions. It reminded him of when they'd first met. He wondered what she wasn't saying; what she thought she was protecting him from. The Fire Warper, perhaps?

He tried to catch up on reading the mountain of reports but abandoned the task when his thoughts kept returning to Yelena. A nagging anxiety gnawed on his heart with its sharp little teeth. She had promised to not go to Sitia without him, yet the feeling wouldn't go away. Would she lie in order to keep him safe? He hoped not. Needing to move, Valek gathered supplies for their trip and packed his bag in order to be ready at a moment's notice.

Even when he finished, the uncertainty still nibbled. He decided to go to the stables. Maybe after he cleaned tack and filled his saddle bags with feed, his nerves would settle.

The pleasant smell of earth, hay, and horse greeted him when he arrived. Most of the horses were out in the pasture. Valek grabbed a jar of saddle soap, sat on the stool in the tack room, and worked on the leather. Just like when he was carving, he let his thoughts wander.

Movement out the small window drew his attention. The horses crossed the pasture as if they'd seen something. Valek put down the reins and peeked outside. Yelena stood at the fence, feeding the horses apples. Then she scratched Kiki behind the ears.

An idyllic scene, expect Yelena kept glancing around. She wore a plain gray Ixian wool cloak. Would she hop on Kiki and ride south without him? After patting Kiki on the neck, she turned away. But instead of heading for the castle, she joined in the flow of workers aiming for the south gate.

Valek's thoughts spun. She could be going shopping in Castletown. Or meeting with a friend. She hadn't taken Kiki, so she was not going to Sitia. And Valek would *not* follow her. He trusted her. Except, he also spotted Star leaving the castle complex via the west gate. Both the south and west gates were used by those living in Castletown.

Yelena had been responsible for Star's arrest. If Star hadn't tried to kill her, she wouldn't have been arrested. He suspected Star might try some form of revenge, but he hadn't expected it so soon. Perhaps it was just a coincidence? Star had probably just finished tasting the Commander's dinner. Valek didn't believe in coincidences.

He threw on his short cape and hurried after her. If anything, he might learn what she was planning. Star entered Castletown and strode through the streets as if on a mission, but it didn't appear that she was stalking Yelena.

The streets were busy. Many of the town's residents were hurrying home after work or stopping at the market for groceries.

THE STUDY OF FIRE

When Star reached the Garden District, unease swirled. She was joined by three goons. Too bad none of them were Trevar and Adrik. Why not? If they were Star's go-to recruits, they should be involved. Unless Star knew exactly who they were. Valek suppressed a groan. He'd underestimated the woman again.

Star and her companions slipped into Peach alley. Forty-three Peach Lane was the property Star owned. Was that her new headquarters? Except, they didn't enter the house. The four of them found shadows to hide in instead.

Odd. Very odd. Valek circled around the block and entered the alley from the other side. He kept his distance but was within sight of number forty-three. Settling in, Valek pulled his cloak tighter around his shoulders. The still air smelled heavy, hinting of a potential snowstorm. Lovely.

After an hour, two young teens left the house. When they walked past Star's shadow, she stepped out. Two puffs sounded.

A girl's voice asked, "Did you feel that?"

"Felt like a bee sting, but it's...too...cold," her companion said.

The two girls slumped to the ground. Two goons rushed over to their bodies and picked them up, carrying them from the alley. Star returned to her post.

After a few minutes, Yelena exited the house. Shocked, Valek opened his mouth to warn her as she paused, as if letting her vision adjust to the semi-darkness. Valek snapped his mouth shut. Of course, she knew they were there. He grinned in anticipation. Star and her goon were in for a surprise. Yelena turned to leave, luring Star from her hiding place.

Spinning, Yelena pulled her switchblade from her pocket. Star puffed. The dart hit Yelena's neck. That was unexpected.

Yelena yanked the dart out. "How?"

"Some great magician you are," Star said. "Missing my own tiny talent."

Star had always claimed to have magic, but he'd never felt nor seen it in action. Was the ability to hide from magic her talent? Valek eased closer to the women, debating his next move.

Yelena stumbled and Star caught her. "What?"

Star cradled Yelena in her arms. "Valek's goo-goo juice. Relax, Yelena. Star's going to take *good* care of you."

CHAPTER 13

Star had stolen some of Valek's goo-goo juice and used it to capture Yelena. Valek wondered if Star's tiny magical talent included being able to give his agents the slip. How else could she have gotten the goo-goo juice?

The third goon picked Yelena up and carried her. If they had wanted to kill her, they wouldn't have gone to all this trouble. Curious to see what they had planned, Valek followed the three of them. The streets were empty.

Two horses hitched to a wagon were parked in a dark corner two blocks away. Coffin shaped crates had been stacked inside. The other two goons waited for them. When the threesome neared, they opened the top crate. Yelena was dumped inside.

"Take them to our colleagues in Sitia," Star ordered. "Make sure you prick them with the goo-goo juice every twelve hours until you reach the meeting point."

Two of the goons hopped onto the driver's bench. One grabbed the reins and clicked his tongue. The horses lurched forward.

"What about Porter?" Third Goon asked. "He'll eventually figure out we kidnapped his kids."

Watching the wagon trundle down the street, Star said, "He won't be a problem. Porter can't say or do anything to attract attention because Valek will kill him. Do you know the big oaf actually thought he was in charge of his rescue operation?" She laughed. "He tried to fire me. My people have been smuggling those kids out of Ixia for years."

"He paid you well."

"Yeah, and it was a nice feel good operation until I got a better offer."

They walked in the opposite direction of the wagon, keeping to the shadows.

Valek would bet that better offer was why Porter's ducklings began disappearing. But who was Star selling the young magicians to? He'd bet a year's pay it was the Daviian Warpers, but there was a chance he could be wrong.

Star's goons were taking Yelena to Sitia. They had already planned to go there so Valek decided he'd follow the wagon, find out who the buyer was, and then rescue Yelena and the girls.

In the past, Yelena had understood his tactics. She had even forgiven him for duping her about Butterfly's Dust. She'd understand his decision. Right? He fervently hoped she would.

He raced back to the castle. Grabbing his pack, he shoved in a few more warm layers of clothing, then he ran over to Kenda's office. She was working late as usual.

"Something happen?" she asked.

He updated her.

"I knew we should have killed Star right away. What should I do when she shows up?"

"Arrest her. Only allow her out of her cell to taste the Commander's meals. I'll deal with Star when I return. Find out if Trevar and Adrik's covers have been blown. If not, have them continue their undercover mission. Can you tell the Commander where I'm going?"

"I can, but you owe me a big favor in return. That is, if I survive."

"Add it to the list." He waved and dashed to the stables.

Once again, he appealed to Kiki. She had a magical bond with Yelena. "I need your help. Yelena's been taken and we need to catch up with her captors."

She glanced at her back as if to say, hop on.

"I can't ride bareback this time. This is going to take us a few days. I'll explain everything on the way."

She snorted and pawed the ground. No doubt telling him to hurry up. He saddled her in record time. Then, he put a bridle and reins on Onyx. If, no, *when*, he caught up to and freed Yelena and the girls, he'd need another horse.

Valek had barely settled in his seat when Kiki took off. Without any guidance from him, she flew through the west gate, jumping the barrier. Instead of heading through Castletown, she skirted around the town's edge, aiming southwest. Onyx kept up with ease.

When they reached the Snake Forest, she slowed as she picked her way through the underbrush and fallen trees without making a sound. Magic horse, indeed. Onyx followed her example. They eventually reached a road. Kiki turned left and broke into a trot.

Valek leaned over her neck and whispered. "If this is the road Yelena's on, please don't catch up."

Her ears flattened, but she switched to a walk. He guessed that meant Yelena was nearby. Valek explained to Kiki what he planned to do and why.

"You know I won't hesitate if we see she's in immediate danger."

Kiki's ears relaxed. They located the wagon, and Valek was surprised to see that it joined the queue of caravans going to the border exchange site. Kiki found a spot that they could watch without being seen. While they waited, Valek noted that the goods coming into Ixia were inspected, but the boxes and crates going out were not.

When the wagon reached the front of the line, the border guards glanced at their papers, obviously not reading them. The goons then unloaded the crates and carried them over the border to another wagon. They shook hands with the two large men who had been waiting. Daviians. After the goons were paid, they returned to their wagon and headed north.

The Daviians spurred their wagon team south through the Featherstone Clan's lands. Valek and Kiki followed. The Citadel appeared to be their destination. On the second day, they stopped well off the road to camp for the night. Valek dismounted and snuck closer as the two Daviians set up.

Unfortunately, like the previous night, the two said very little. But they took care of their prisoners, letting them out, taking off the gags and bindings, feeding them, allowing them to relieve themselves in relative privacy. They did this twice a day. Valek hated seeing Yelena and the girls gagged, but he understood why. They were under the influence of goo-goo juice. The drug affected everyone differently, but most felt as if they were very drunk. He mainly used it to interrogate people. The victim couldn't lie very well, and they couldn't stop talking. Sometimes it was gibberish, but Valek had gotten some vital information using the drug.

Valek was about to return to Kiki and Onyx when other voices sounded. A group of people strode through the woods and joined the two Daviians. He counted six with a sinking heart. No way Valek could fight eight.

When the group reached the campfire, the light illuminated their faces. Valek stifled a curse and suppressed the urge to stroll up to Cahil and plunge his knife deep into the man's heart. Standing with the Wannabe King were four of his minions and another Daviian. Magic swept by Valek. There was at least one warper among them.

He tensed for action, but the new arrivals just congratulated themselves on their prizes. They laughed and talked and set up tents. Eventually, they set a watch and went to sleep. Valek debated if he should rescue Yelena and the girls now. They'd been dosed with goo-goo juice. He could prick the guard with sleeping potion, and perhaps the others as well, but it would be hard to get Yelena and the girls far enough away to be safe. Once Cahil woke up and discovered them missing, there'd be a manhunt. As much as he wanted to free Yelena, tonight wouldn't work.

Instead of heading directly south, the group turned southeast and bypassed the Citadel. Valek had been waiting for a better opportunity to rescue the captives, but the next night had all the same difficulties. Perhaps he could exchange the darts filled with goo-goo juice with water while everyone slept. Once Yelena and the girls were free of the drug, it would be much easier to escape.

Except, on the fourth night, they kept Yelena sitting by the campfire and didn't prick her with goo-goo juice. This was new. Valek crept as close as he dared.

"Should not do this," a Daviian was saying. "She should stay under until we reach our destination. Jal is the only one strong enough to counter her power."

Wannabe King said, "I made a promise to her. I want her to know who has her, and what we plan to do to her."

That could be a very big mistake. One Valek had been hoping for.

"Take the gag off," Wannabe King ordered. He stood behind her but stepped into her view.

Yelena took a moment to gather her wits once the gag was removed. She glanced up and saw Cahil's cocky smirk. He kicked her in the ribs. Valek jumped to his feet with his knife in hand, but he was outnumbered. And if the guards started dropping from the sleeping potion, it would warn the others. He settled back.

"That's for hitting me with Curare!" Cahil kicked her again. "And that's just because I can."

Valek promised he would ensure the Wannabe King paid for each kick.

"Cahil," she said between gasps. "You're still…scared. Of me."

Nice, love.

Cahil laughed. "Yelena, you're the one who should be scared." He crouched down and held a dart in front of her face. "*I* allowed you this brief moment of lucidity. Listen closely. Remember what I said to you the last time we were together?"

"When you wanted to exchange me for Marrok?" she asked.

"No. When I promised to find a person who could defeat you and Valek. I've met with success. In fact, you have already had an encounter with my champion."

"Ferde?"

The Fire Warper. And she was well aware of him.

"Act the fool, but I know better. My champion makes you sweat with fear. The Fire Warper has been called to this world with one mission. To capture you. And you're powerless against him." Pure satisfaction shone on Cahil's face. "I will deliver you to Jal and the Fire Warper. Jal will perform the Kirakawa ritual's binding ceremony on you, taking your powers as the Fire Warper claims your soul," Cahil said.

"And what do you get, Cahil?" Yelena asked.

"I get to witness your death and watch your heart mate suffer before he meets the same end."

"But Jal gains power. Do you really believe Jal will let you rule? And what about the Fire Warper? Do you think he'll be content to go back after his task is complete?"

"He has come asking for you. Once he has you, he'll go back. Then Jal rules Sitia, and I rule Ixia."

Hold up. That was the opposite of what Cahil had claimed earlier.

"Before you said you called him. Now you say he has come. Which one is it?"

"It doesn't matter."

"Yes, it does. If you called him, you have control over him."

He shrugged. "Jal will deal with him. As long as I have Ixia. I don't care."

"You should care. The need for power is addicting. Ask your Daviian friends about the history of the Sandseed Clan and the Daviian Mountains. Then you'll realize Jal won't be content with just ruling Sitia. Once your usefulness is gone, you will be too."

There was lots of interesting information in that statement. Valek would have to ask Yelena about it later.

"You're just trying to trick me. I know better than to listen to you."

Cahil tried to stab the dart into her throat. Yelena fell back, but he followed her down and jabbed the metal tip into her skin. She closed her eyes as if defeated.

But then her eyes opened. "Pay close attention, Cahil. You'll see the truth." She went slack, lying there unmoving.

Not goo-goo juice, but Curare. That was worse.

Cahil grunted and stood. "I've seen the truth. That's why I want you dead."

A Daviian joined him next to the fire. "I felt magic. Brief. Did she use her power on you?"

That one was a warper. Valek hoped Yelena had done something.

"No. I got her in time," Cahil said.

They discussed their plans for leaving in the morning. As they set up the tents, the Wannabe King said, "I should kill her now."

Valek rose to a crouch. Alarmed replies told him it would be imprudent. It seemed the Daviians had plans for her.

"Jal needs her, and we do not wish to infuriate the Fire Warper," another said.

"Why should *I* care about infuriating the Fire Warper?" Cahil asked. "*I'm* in charge. He should answer to *me*. He should worry about infuriating *me*, especially after the fiasco in the jungle."

Soothing words were muttered.

"Put her back in the box," Cahil said. "Secure it, just in case we encounter trouble."

Two of the Daviians lifted Yelena and returned her. At least, Valek learned a name. Possibly the leader of the clan? And if this Jal managed to take Yelena's power, they'd become unstoppable.

∼

"Let's get moving. If we push, we can reach the Avibian border by sundown," Cahil said in the morning.

Valek now had a destination.

"Should we check on her?" one of Cahil's minions asked.

"No. She's under Curare now. She can't do anything besides breathe until the potion wears off," Cahil answered. "Finish feeding the girls. We'll let the juice wear off before we prepare them for the ritual."

And he now had a deadline. Tonight.

He followed them as they urged their horses to go faster. Sitting on top of the boxes, Cahil and the Warper added extra weight for the two equines pulling the wagon. The minions ran alongside the wagon like they'd been doing every day.

During the trip, Valek created and dismissed several rescue plans. Eventually, he figured out the best way to save Yelena and the others. Valek told Kiki his strategy. Just in case something happened to him, Kiki would know a safe place to take Yelena and the girls. Now, he only had to wait until full dark before he could make his move.

Cahil and his companions stopped just shy of the Avibian Plains. It was an hour before sunset. Valek wondered why they had come here instead of going to the Citadel. Was this where Jal would join them? Valek dismounted and edged closer.

"We'll camp here," Cahil said. "When you're done setting up, let the girls out. They should be lucid by now and you can get them ready for the Kirakawa tomorrow."

Having them lucid would aid in Valek's efforts.

"What about the Soulfinder?" one of the vermin asked.

"Drakke will give her another dose tonight. Too much Curare could stop her heart," Cahil replied.

Valek waited while they pitched tents and collected firewood. They finished and pulled the girls out. Prepping the girls included stripping their clothing and tying them down by the fire. Valek had to look away as the Warper cut their arms and legs to collect their blood. As much as his heart screamed at him to run in and save the girls, logic overruled. Valek needed to be methodical, and his timing had to be perfect.

When Drakke moved toward the wagon, Valek prepped his blowpipe with a dart loaded with sleeping potion.

The man lifted the lid of Yelena's box, Valek aimed, puffed, and missed. The man grunted as he was pulled off balance. Drakke froze. Probably a victim of the Curare he was supposed to give Yelena. Then, he was hauled inside the box.

Valek silently cheered as Yelena poked her head out. He tucked his blowpipe into a pocket. He'd join her and let her know the plan. Without warning, a flock of bats appeared over the fire. They swooped down on the minions around the campfire, biting their arms as their cries filled the air. Not good.

Cahil and the warper exited one of the tents, and the warper yelled about magic. Yelena must have used her power to create a distraction. Then she popped out of her box and took off in the wrong direction.

His plan was fucked. Valek ran back to where Kiki and Onyx were waiting and mounted Kiki, leaving Onyx behind.

"Go! Go! We'll get between Yelena and the others," he said, pulling his sword.

Kiki broke into a gallop. They raced to the camp. Valek spotted Yelena being pursued by Cahil's minions. Kiki angled to the left to intercept her.

Yelena dove to the ground, rolling into a ball. Kiki cut sharply, avoiding Yelena and turning her side to the minions. They drew their swords and Valek swung his own, pushing them back as Kiki's speed gave him an advantage. Kiki pivoted in another quick turn. Yelena jumped to her feet.

"Yelena!" He yanked her bo staff from the saddle and threw it to her.

She caught it in midair. Kiki spun and Valek slid off her back. He engaged the minions in a sword fight. With four against one, he wouldn't last long. But then Yelena joined with her bo, and Kiki with her hooves. The Wannabe King and the warper hung back, and Valek wondered what they were scheming.

A minion blocked too wide and Valek cut his arm in half. They pressed their advantage as the injured man fell to the ground. Except, Cahil ordered the rest of his minions to disengage. They stepped back. Valek glanced at Yelena.

"The girls are still at the camp," she said.

He nodded and they stalked the retreating men.

The warper threw his arms up and yelled, "Inflame."

Magic pressed on Valek's skin. With a whoosh of hot air, the man on the ground burst into flames. Valek and Yelena jumped back. The poor man screamed and writhed. He stilled as the intense heat consumed him. Acrid puffs of charred flesh reached Valek.

THE STUDY OF FIRE

"Come! Find your soul mate!" The warper's voice cut through the roaring fire.

A man's form coalesced from the pulsing flames.

"What's going on?" Valek asked as nausea churned in his stomach.

"Let's go." Yelena scrambled onto Kiki's back.

Valek hopped on right behind her. Kiki took off.

"What about the girls?" he asked.

"Later."

It was a smart move. They couldn't do anything at the moment, but guilt still welled in his chest. And he couldn't return for Onyx either.

Kiki headed for the farmhouse he had told her about. It was a modest size with flower beds surrounding the structure. The stable, which Valek had praised when he talked out his plan with Kiki, was her first stop. Valek slid off the horse. But Yelena didn't move. She studied the house with a suspicious squint.

Kiki snorted and nudged Valek. He wondered what Kiki was telling Yelena. She had the ability to communicate with Kiki and could magically connect with other creatures, like those bats.

She finally looked at him. "Summer home? Isn't it a little dangerous?"

He smiled. "Safe house for my corps. A base of operations."

"How convenient."

The stable was empty. Valek helped her remove Kiki's saddle and groom her, delaying the inevitable conversation. Valek wasn't looking forward to confessing, but he wouldn't lie to her.

When they finished, she sagged with fatigue. "How did you find me? And your timing was impeccable, as always."

Valek pulled her into his arms. She leaned against him and shook. No doubt the shock of the escape and everything had caught up to her.

"You're welcome, love. I had wanted to sneak in and free you tonight, but you had other plans. I should have been more prepared, but when I saw him poke you last night, I thought for sure you would be out of it." He pulled away. "Let's go inside. I need a drink."

The interior of the farmhouse was decorated like all his safehouses—spartan and utilitarian. Valek lit a few lanterns and poured a couple of drinks. Yelena wouldn't let him build a fire. He understood her fear, but she needed some warmth. Instead, he pulled her close, sharing his body heat as they sipped the brandy.

"General Kitvivan's white brandy?" she asked.

"You remembered!" Valek was pleased. It had been a lifetime ago, when she had learned the taste of all the generals' favorite brandies. Or so it felt.

"There are tastes and smells that call certain memories. White brandy reminds me of the Commander's brandy meeting."

"Ah, yes. And after having to taste all those brandies for the Commander, you drunkenly tried to seduce me."

"And you refused."

And it just about killed him. "I wanted to accept. But I didn't know if your desire was from your heart or from the brandy. You might have regretted it later."

"Enough small talk. Tell me everything," she ordered.

He sighed. "You're not going to like it."

"Compared to what I've just been through these last—what? Three days? I don't even know. It can't be that bad."

"I knew you were swimming in some very dangerous waters," he said, "but I hadn't known they extended so deep."

"Valek, get to the point."

This was going to be bad. Unable to sit still, he stood and prowled the room. "Five days ago, you were taken—"

"Five days!"

Valek put up his hand to forestall her questions. "Let me finish first. You were kidnapped by Star, and the reason she was able to smuggle you so far south, was because...I let her." He paused to let his words sink in.

She stared at him in astonishment. "You set me up?"

Betrayal laced her words, and he felt awful. He hadn't planned for her to be a captive for so long. "Yes and no."

"You need to do better than that." Anger now sharpened her tone.

He hurried to explain. "I knew Star would want to exact some type of revenge on you. She has kept in contact with the underground network, and I allowed her because then I could learn who the new players were. With the Code of Behavior, there will always be a black market for illegal goods and forged papers. I like to keep tabs on the network to make sure things don't go too far, like when Star hired assassins to ruin the Sitian trade treaty. And when—"

"Get to the point."

Right. "Star knew you would be at Porter's safe house—"

"Porter set me up?"

"I don't think so. Are you going to let me tell you or not?" He put his hands on his hips to keep from embracing her and begging for her forgiveness.

She gestured for him to go on.

"I've known about Porter's rescue operation for a couple years and have allowed it to continue. However, recently, his charges have been disappearing and I've been wondering why. But that wasn't the reason I watched the house. I had followed Star and three of her men there and was shocked to see you walk blindly into her trap. Didn't you even see her?"

"She used a subtle kind of magic."

"I haven't felt her, and I've been working with her for a while."

"You didn't pick up on my magic, either. And it flared out of control a couple times within the castle."

"I will keep it in mind," Valek said. "Star's motives for

ambushing you, I understood. The surprise arrived when she and her friends also targeted the girls. I needed to know where they were taking you."

She scrunched her brow. "You could have helped me that night, but instead decided to wait?" she asked in outrage.

"A calculated risk. I wanted to discover the extent of her operation and why she kidnapped the girls. I had no idea you would end up across the border and in the Wannabe King's hands."

Valek knelt in front of her and reached for her hands. She kept them tightly crossed across her chest. Anger flashed in her eyes. He was in trouble. Well deserved, but he had learned so much.

"This wouldn't have happened at all if you told me about your meeting with Porter," he said. They may have been able to come up with a counter plan.

"A *calculated* risk. Like it or not, I'm a magician, and if there's a way to help my colleagues I'm going to try. I wasn't going to tell the Commander's magician killer about it."

Her words were a dagger in his heart. Valek sank back onto his heels. His expression hardened. "Magician killer? Is that what you think of me?"

"That *is* one of your duties for the Commander. I know how you operate. You like to stalk your prey before you pounce. Allowing Porter's network to continue is part of your modus operandi."

Valek kept his expression neutral. He deserved her anger and her censure. She'd been hurt and almost killed. But her words… She didn't know him at all. Did she think he enjoyed killing young magicians? Then why was she even with him?

"How did Star get us into Sitia?" she asked, changing the subject.

Valek said in a flat tone, "Put you into crates, stacked boxes of goods on top, and dressed as traders. They had the proper papers. The border guards did a cursory check and off you went." And they failed to spot the ruse. "The border guards will be taken to task and retrained."

Exhaustion seeped into his bones. He stood. "I was going to suggest we get a few hours' sleep and try to rescue the girls. But since I'm the magician killer, I guess I won't concern myself about their fates." He left the room.

He went out to the stable. Kiki dozed in a stall. Drinking some water and eating a few sticks of jerky, Valek shouldered his pack. No way he'd allow the warpers to kill the girls. Kiki needed to rest, and the Warper camp wasn't that far. Valek slipped from the barn and jogged south.

By the time he arrived at the border, Cahil and the warpers were gone. And so was Onyx. So much for riding to the rescue. The wagon's tracks headed deeper into the plains. Valek followed them. He braced for the Sandseed's protective magic. It swelled and pushed, trying to eject him from the plains. He fought the pressure until it eased, and he continued without trouble.

Until Valek stepped in a puddle of magic. It exploded and he flew through the air, landing hard on his back. He gasped for breath. That was new. And it wasn't Sandseed magic. Had the warpers placed booby traps to keep him from finding them? He wondered what the magic was supposed to do. He sat up and gingerly reached out a hand. The magic had dissipated. But there was no doubt they had set more. Valek considered how to avoid the traps.

He groaned when the answer occurred to him. Untying his shoelaces, Valek pulled off his boots and wool socks. The frosty night air nipped at his toes. He lumbered to his feet. At least the cold sand was soft, but clumps of shrubs, tall grass, and stunted trees grew in the plains. All currently brown and crispy.

Valek laced his boots together and hung them over his shoulder. Thank fate an almost full moon hung in the sky. He walked through the rolling terrain of the plains with care. It slowed his pace. When magic brushed his toes, he pulled his foot back. Sensing the edges with his hand, he skirted the booby traps. At this rate, it'd be dawn before he reached the camp. Good thing, the Wannabe King had said they would perform the Kirakawa ritual tomorrow night.

But he was in luck. He spotted the orange glow of a campfire in the distance. Using the uneven ground to hide him, Valek inched closer. The girls were staked to the ground and two warpers bent over them, cutting into their stomachs. Horror rushed through him. They hadn't waited. He was too late!

Valek yanked his blowpipe out and loaded it. He aimed, puffed, and the dart shot out. It stopped halfway there and fell to the ground. The warpers must have erected a magical barrier. He scanned the camp. A Daviian and a few of the minions watched the ritual, but not Cahil. He must be inside his tent.

The drumming of hooves announced the sudden arrival of Kiki and Yelena. Kiki ran through the camp as if crazed, jumping and rearing, surprising everyone. The minions scattered and dodged her flailing hooves and Yelena's bo staff.

While they were occupied, Valek decided to take care of a problem he should have dealt with long ago. He drew his dagger and snuck into Cahil's tent. It was empty. A horse-shaped shadow loomed, and Valek dove to the ground as Kiki knocked down Cahil's tent. The main pole just missed his head as the fabric draped over him like a blanket. He sighed. Nothing was going right.

To avoid being the next victim, Valek combat crawled toward where the entrance had been. He encountered Yelena's pack on the way and dragged it along with him. Arguments sounded outside. The Daviians cursed and accused the minions for not protecting them. No one noticed Valek as he slipped through the opening. Not yet.

He scanned the area. Yelena and Kiki were gone. Valek

backed away from the camp until he was out of sight. Now if he could reach the safe house without hitting another booby trap, he'd be happy. He slung Yelena's pack over his shoulder.

It was a long, cold slog to the safe house. He kept an eye out for his horse, but no luck. When he arrived, Valek stopped in the stable to check if Kiki was there or if Yelena had decided to leave him behind. Smoke curling from the door was his first warning something was wrong. He ran into the barn. Yelena slept on a stack of hay bales outside Kiki's stall. She writhed as if trapped in a nightmare.

"Yelena!" he yelled, rushing to her side. More smoke poured from the hay. Grabbing her shoulder, he yelped as heat seared his skin.

"Yelena!" No response. He dumped her pack on the ground, picked up a bucket, and poured water on top of her.

Steam hissed. She woke up, choking on the water.

"What?" She sat up. Her clothes and hair were soaking wet. "What was that for?"

"You were having a nightmare," he said.

"And shaking me awake seemed too tame?" She snapped, still angry with him.

Valek didn't answer. Instead, he pulled her to her feet and pointed to the Yelena-shaped scorch mark on the topmost hay bale. The place where she had slept.

"You were too hot to touch," he said in a deadpan.

She shivered.

"I take it your rescue attempt last night has angered some powerful people. I saw you and Kiki create chaos in the camp, ruining my plans yet again. What else did you do?" He kept his expression neutral.

"The Kirakawa ritual traps the victim's soul inside their heart. I was unable to stop the ritual once it started, but I did take the girls' souls before they could be used, stealing the power the warpers hoped to harvest. I carried the girls to the edge of the plains and released them to the sky, where they'll find peace." Sadness and remorse shone in her eyes.

Valek's own guilt churned in his stomach. If he'd been quicker, if he hadn't let them be captured, they would have lived. More proof for Yelena that he was the magician killer.

"I should have let you kill Cahil," Yelena said.

"Why?"

"It would have prevented all this."

"I think not. Cahil's involvement is recent. These Daviians are prepared. They've been planning this move for a while. Cahil wants you dead and wants his throne. I believe the whole Kirakawa ritual sickens him."

"He helped with the kidnapping."

"Because he wanted you. He wasn't at the camp last night. He's probably heading to the Citadel."

"How do you know?"

Valek gave her a tight, joyless smile. "When you stormed the camp, I stole into the tent, intending to put the Wannabe King out of my misery. I had a few seconds to determine he was gone before the tent collapsed on me."

She suppressed a smile.

"But I found that." He gestured to Yelena's backpack.

A happy cry escaped her lips, and she knelt down to check the contents. At least, her pack had given her some comfort. Exhausted, Valek left. The cold empty house matched his cold empty heart. He lit a small fire. Yelena was soaking wet; she'd need the warmth.

There was a bedroom on the second floor loft. Valek changed into clean clothes and wondered if Yelena would join him. After a while, the sound of an opening door reached him. He walked to the railing and peeked over. Yelena stood in the threshold, hesitating. Not wanting to witness her leaving, he walked over to the bed and laid down. He'd find out what she decided eventually.

THE STUDY OF FIRE

∾

The rattle of sleet on the windows woke Valek. Wind keened through the rafters. He rolled over. On the other side of the bed, the unrumpled sheets and undented pillow were a heartbreaking sight. He'd committed an unforgivable mistake. Too focused on solving the puzzle, he'd lost Yelena's love.

Pain sliced right through him, and he allowed it to burn and ache for a few minutes. Then he gathered it and stuffed it deep down inside a box, cutting off all emotions. The Daviians needed to be stopped or more people would die. If Yelena was still here, they would need to work together.

Valek dressed in warm clothes and opened the door. Onyx stood there dripping wet and dragging his reins. The wonderful horse. Valek hugged him then led Onyx into the barn. The noise woke Yelena, who slept on a bed of straw in Kiki's stall. The pain tried to escape its box, but he shoved it back.

He hitched Onyx and rubbed him down before finding an extra saddle in the tack room.

"We need to leave for the Citadel." Valek saddled Onyx. "This weather is good cover."

"How far?" she asked.

"Two days. I have another safe house about a mile north of the Citadel. We can set up operations there."

Yelena prepped Kiki. They worked in complete and utter silence.

∾

Two days later, they arrived at the safe house in the Featherstone Clan lands. Yelena planned to go into the Citadel and contact Councilor Zaltana, finding out why the council followed Roze's orders. And to get a better sense of the danger. Valek gave her a long sleeved plain linen dress and a sand-colored cloak, disguising her as a Featherstone clanswoman.

He styled her hair into an intricate knot favored by the Featherstones and held it in place with her lock picks. It took all his will power not to kiss her neck. When she left, she had said she'd return that night.

She didn't. Unable to sleep, Valek paced. Then he went to the barn and groomed the horses. Twice. What if she'd been captured? He chopped firewood. The sun rose and there was no sign of Yelena. Chopping more wood, he worked until his muscles burned. What if Roze was interrogating her, shredding her mind like Marrok's? Valek walked around the house and barn. How long should he wait before searching for her? Should he take Kiki or go alone? Valek cleaned the tack, mucked out the stalls, scrubbed out the water and feed buckets, and fixed a hole in the siding. What if the warpers had cut out her heart?

By the evening, his body was exhausted, but his mind whirred with a hundred horrific scenarios. He sank onto the couch, deciding he would go to the Citadel at dawn.

When Yelena and Bavol Zaltana entered the house, Valek stared at them. She was alive. He held still just in case it was a hallucination. Bavol spotted him on the couch and balked. Ah, not a vision.

"You set me up," Bavol said, taking a step back.

"Relax, Bavol. If Valek was going to assassinate the council, you would be dead by now. He's helping me."

Valek snorted and was suddenly angry. "I am? Funny how I forgot. Or is it because someone forgot about me?" Sarcasm spiked each word.

"We don't have time for this. The Daviians have kidnapped the councilors' children and spouses. They're threatening them if the councilors don't obey the Daviian's orders. It's not Roze influencing them. I'm going to try to find out where they're keeping the children. I brought Bavol here because I can't use my magic that close to the warpers or they will find me."

Valek's fury dissipated as fast as it had arrived. He had overreacted. At least they knew why the council had agreed with Roze.

Yelena turned to the Councilor. "Bavol, sit down. Close your eyes. Think of your daughter," she ordered.

Valek watched as Yelena's gaze grew distant. She sat still and silent. The minutes stretched and he worried. A familiar scent reached him. It took a moment for him to place it. The smoky aroma of a campfire. Except, only a pile of cold ashes was inside the hearth.

Alarmed, he strode to the window. Smoke billowed from the stable. Valek dashed from the house and threw the barn's doors wide. Kiki was already out of her stall. Flames whooshed up the back wall. Opening Onyx's stall, Valek stepped aside as they bolted outside and toward the pasture. He followed but paused when he spotted a man—a warper—standing near the burning barn. Valek pivoted, reaching for his knife.

"Kiki!" Yelena screamed.

Valek stopped. Yelena ran toward the stables.

"Yelena! She's not there!" he yelled.

But she didn't slow. When she reached the burning building, she dove right into the fire.

CHAPTER 14

*V*alek gaped at the burning building. With no thought to her own life, Yelena had plunged into the flames to save her horse. Breaking from the shock, he raced to the fire, determined to pull her out. But the flames had doubled in size, creating a wall of searing heat. He glanced at where the warper had been standing. The man was gone.

It would cost Valek precious seconds to chase the warper. Instead, Valek ran to the house, yelled at Bavol to help, grabbed a bucket, and then dashed to the water pump. However, a single bucket of water had no effect on quenching the fire. Still, he had to keep trying.

Yelena. Must. Not. Die.

That became his mantra.

Trip after trip after trip, he worked as the flames consumed the wooden structure. Sweat and soot streaked his skin and clothes. Sparks burned holes in the fabric. His world blurred to an orange and black smear. The fire eventually sputtered and died. Not due to his efforts. No. There was nothing left for it to consume. Embers pulsed.

And he had thought losing her love was painful. Yelena's

death took the agony to an extreme level. Too heart-sick to search for her body, Valek stumbled away from the charred barn. Onyx paced nervously in the pasture, but Kiki was nowhere in sight. She must have run off after Yelena... He swallowed. The taste of ashes was thick in his throat.

The house was empty. Bavol was gone. He tried to care, but at this point, nothing mattered. Life ceased to have any meaning. Any joy. Anything.

He washed off the dirt and sweat, changed into clean clothes, and sat on the couch. Valek drew out his cloud kissed dagger. The metal gleamed in the light. So many people had died, either by his hand or because of him. His life was full of death, starting with the murder of his three older brothers. It made perfect sense to end his own life. Go to the fire world and burn for his crimes. He stared at the blade, imagining the perfect angle he'd need to thrust it under his breastbone and into his heart.

Except.

Except, he had saved more lives than he had taken.

Except, if the Fire Warper won, the world would burn.

Except, Valek with his immunity to magic might be able to stop the Daviians.

He couldn't be selfish. He couldn't end his pain. Not yet anyway. He sheathed his dagger and finally succumbed to the exhaustion. Yelena filled his dreams.

∼

A faint crunching sound woke him.

"Kiki," Yelena's voice called.

Valek was at the door without any memory of the trip. Yelena stood at the edge of the ruined barn. A ghost? Her cloak was gone and soot, ash, and burn holes peppered her clothing.

THE STUDY OF FIRE

Her once long black hair had been half burned, leaving an uneven mess of spikes and longer strands behind.

She met his gaze and laughed. Then she collapsed to the ground.

Valek was beside her in an instant. Caressing her face with a finger, he couldn't believe she'd survived. "Are you real?" he asked. "Or just some cruel joke?"

"I'm real. A real simpleton, Valek. I should never have said…I should never have done…" She drew in a deep breath. "Forgive me, please?"

Forgive her? He should be asking for her forgiveness. "Would you promise never to do it again?" he asked, thinking of her diving into the fire.

"Sorry, I can't."

"Then you certainly are real. A real pain in the ass, but that's who I fell in love with." He pulled her close, cherishing the moment. "Why were you so determined to push me away, love?"

"Fear."

"You've faced fear before. What's different?"

"I'm afraid of my magic." The words tumbled from her mouth as if she was finally being honest with him and herself. "If I harvested enough souls, I know I would possess ample power to defeat all the warpers, including the Fire Warper. That's tempting. Tempting enough to want to protect you from *me*."

Valek pulled back and met her gaze. "But all you need to do is ask. We wouldn't hesitate to give you our souls to defeat the Daviians." She already had his heart.

"No. There has to be another way."

"And that would be…?"

"When I figure it out, you'll be the first to know." Before he could comment, she added, "You never answered me. Am I forgiven?"

He sighed dramatically. "You're forgiven. Will you forgive me for not rescuing you sooner?"

"Yes."

"Now come inside, you reek of smoke." He hated the smell.

Valek helped her to stand. She swayed, and he kept his hand on her arm.

"Where's Kiki?" she asked.

"Once you disappeared into the stable, she ran off and hasn't come back."

They entered the house.

"Where's Bavol?"

"The Daviian Warper captured him while I tried to douse the fire. Will they kill him?"

"No. They need him and all the councilors for a while to keep up the pretense that the council and master magicians are in charge."

"How long will it last?"

"Not very."

"Will they come after us here?" he asked.

"No. But we need to retake control."

"We, love? I thought you could handle this by yourself."

"I was wrong."

Valek heated water and filled the cast-iron tub. He removed her burned clothes, and helped her in. While Yelena bathed, he rummaged in her pack, looking for clean clothes. He found a glass statue of a bat. When he picked it up, magic stuck to his skin. Odd.

He returned with the clothes and the bat. "What's this?"

"I visited Opal at her family's glass factory when I was in Booruby. As a fellow artist, what do you think of the construction?"

Valek examined the statue, turning it this way and that. "It's an accurate reproduction. The coloring matches one of the smaller jungle bat species. It's sticky with magic. I feel it but can't see it. Can you?"

"The inside glows as if molten fire has been captured by ice."

"That would be something to see, then."

Yelena touched Valek's shoulder, and his heart tingled. The statue came to life with an inner fire. "Ahh, spectacular. Can everyone see this?"

"Only magicians."

"Good. That lays that debate to rest. I am not a magician."

"Then what are you? You're not a regular person either."

Valek pretended to be mortified.

"Come on," she said. "Your skills as a fighter have an almost magical air. Your ability to move without sound and blend in with shadows and people seems extraordinary. You can communicate with me over vast distances, but I can't contact you."

"An anti-magician?" He rather liked that moniker.

"I suppose, but I'd bet Bain could find it in one of his books." She sighed. "There might be a way inside the Keep. Bavol said that Bain told him an emergency tunnel had been built. It's located on the east side of the Keep and supposedly big enough for a horse."

"What else did you learn from your connection with Bavol?" he asked.

"I was able to connect with his daughter and Councilor Stormdancer's wife, Gale. The Daviians have kidnapped nine children and two adults. They're locked inside a barn. Gale thought they might be in the Bloodgood lands, but she remembered seeing a pond with crimson-colored water. It was shaped like a diamond."

He remembered looking at a map of Sitia, noting the various distinctive features of each clan's territory. "That sounds like Diamond Lake in the Jewelrose lands. It's near the Bloodgood border. The Jewelrose Clan has built a series of

THE STUDY OF FIRE

lakes that resemble shapes of jewels, and the water reflects the colors."

"Why red?"

"Because the Jewelrose Clan is famous for cutting rubies into diamond shapes. The Commander even has a six-carat ruby on a ring, but he stopped wearing it after the takeover. I wonder…" Mentioning the Commander triggered a memory. Valek was wrong, the Commander still wore the ruby but only when he transformed into Signe.

"What?" she prodded.

"Have you shown your bat to the Commander?"

"Yes."

"And?"

She hesitated. Ah, that meant she knew.

"I know about the Commander, love. How could you believe that I spent the last eighteen years with him and not know?"

"I…"

"After all." Valek made a scary face. "I am the anti-magician!"

She laughed. "Why didn't you tell me?"

"For the same reason you didn't." Because it didn't change anything. The Commander was the Commander. And if the Commander wanted people to know, he would tell them. Valek wrapped her glass bat and placed it back into her pack.

"The Commander saw the glow," she said. "I think his body contains two souls, but I have no idea how or why it's magical. And if he does have magic, why didn't he flame out after puberty?"

"Two? Ambrose's mother died during his birth and there was some confusion. The midwife insisted a boy had been born, but later his father held a baby girl. They searched for evidence of a second child but found nothing. They chalked it up to the midwife being upset about losing her patient. Ambrose used to blame this invisible twin whenever he was in trouble, which, from his stories, was quite often."

"Was his mother a magician?"

"She was considered to be a healer, but I don't know if she healed with magic or with mundane remedies."

Valek drained the tub while Yelena tried to fix her ruined hair. Some sections remained long, while others had been burned to stubble.

"Let me, love." Valek removed the brush from her hands. He rummaged around the bath area until he found his razor. "Sorry, nothing else will work."

"How did you get so good with hair?"

"Spent a season working undercover as Queen Jewel's personal groomer. She had beautiful, thick hair." Too bad she was rotten to her core.

"Wait, I thought all the Queen's servants had to be women."

"Good thing no one thought to look up my skirt." Valek grinned as he cut Yelena's hair, transforming what was left of her long locks into a short hair style.

After he finished, Valek said, "This will help with your disguise."

"My disguise?"

"Everyone's looking for you. If I disguise you as a man, you'll be much harder to find. Although…" He studied her face. "I'll use a little makeup. Being a man won't draw unwanted attention, unless they notice you don't have any eyebrows."

She touched the ridge above her eyes with her fingertips. "What should we do first? Try to find the tunnel to the Keep—if it even exists. Or go and rescue the councilors' families?"

"We should—" The sound of distant voices reached him. "Someone's coming."

He signaled Yelena to wait while he went into the living room. Standing next to the door he peeked out, Valek sighed. The door opened. Yelena also hadn't listened to him. Instead of waiting, she brandished her switchblade at the person coming inside.

"What happened to your hair?" Ari demanded. "Are you all right?"

Janco followed him in. "Look what happens when you sneak off without us!"

"I'd hardly call being captured and taken to Sitia inside a box sneaking off," she said, tucking her weapon into her pocket.

Janco cocked his head this way and that. "Aha! You look just like a prickle bush in MD-4. If we buried you up to your neck, we could—"

"Janco," Ari growled.

"If you gentlemen are finished, I'd like to know why you disobeyed my orders," Valek said, stepping from behind the door.

Janco smiled one of his predatory grins as if he had anticipated this question and already composed an answer. "We did not disobey any of your orders. You said to keep an eye on Yelena's brother, the scary-looking big guy, and the others. So, we did."

Valek crossed his arms and waited.

"But you didn't specify what we should do if our charges came to Sitia," Ari said.

"How could they possibly escape the castle and get through the borders?" He didn't have time for their nonsense.

Glee lit Janco's eyes. "That's a very good question. Ari, please tell our industrious leader how the Sitians escaped."

Ari shot his partner a nasty look, which didn't affect Janco's mood in the least. "They had some help," Ari said.

Valek waited.

Ari fidgeted like a little kid about to get scolded. Yelena covered her mouth to keep from laughing.

"We helped them," Ari finally said.

"*We?*" Janco asked.

"I did." Ari sounded miserable. "Happy now?"

"Yes." Janco rubbed his hands together. "This is going to be good. Go on, Ari. Tell him why—although, I think they magicked him." He waggled his fingers.

"They didn't use magic. They used common sense and logic."

Oh? Valek raised an eyebrow.

"There're strange things going on here," Ari said. "If *we* don't put it right, then it'll spread like a disease and kill us all."

"Who told you this?" Yelena asked.

"Moon Man."

"Where are they now?" Valek asked.

"Camped about a mile north of here," Ari said.

The drumming of horses sounded outside. Yelena looked through the window. Valek joined her. It was the four Sitians on horseback.

"How did they find us?" Valek asked in his coldest tone.

Janco seemed surprised. "They didn't know where we were going. I told them to wait for us."

"Isn't it frustrating when no one obeys your orders?" Valek asked.

They went outside. Tauno rode on Kiki and she came straight to Yelena, bumping her chest with her nose. Valek was glad Kiki had returned. According to Tauno, she joined them after Ari and Janco had left.

"We let her lead," Tauno said. "Although, between Marrok and I, we could have easily followed the Ixians' tracks."

The four of them dismounted. By their glares and stiff expressions, they remained angry at Yelena. She avoided their gazes and took the horses over to the burned stable, where she rummaged for brushes. They all tromped inside the house. Valek built a fire and boiled water for tea while Janco regaled him with their adventures. He half listened.

"...six people sharing three horses slowed us down..."

Yelena should be done grooming the horses by now.

"...clueless border guards..."

It was getting dark.

"...and then there was Leif going on and on about how much better..."

It was getting cold.

"...Moon Man telling me I have a complex relationship with my..."

Valek glanced out the window. Yelena worked on the pasture's fence, trying to repair it by pounding on a post with a rock. She was certainly dedicated to avoiding her brother and friends. He left the house. Joining her, he grabbed her arm and removed the rock from her hand.

"Come inside, love. We have plans to discuss."

Reluctance shone in her gaze, but she followed him. The living room conversation died the moment they entered. She sat next to the hearth's fire, warming her frozen and bleeding fingers. She averted her gaze as everyone stared at her, waiting.

Ari and Janco jumped to their feet.

"Did I pass your test?" she asked. "By not diving into the flames."

"That's not it," Janco said. "You have a rather ugly bat clinging to your arm."

Valek had missed the small hand-sized bat hanging from her upper left arm. Yelena offered him an alternative perch and he transferred to the edge of her right hand. She carried the bat outside, but despite shaking her hand multiple times, the creature refused to leave. Instead, it settled on her shoulder. She shrugged and returned inside.

Leif peered at the bat with a thoughtful purse to his lips. Yelena glanced at them. While uncertainty and fear shone in her eyes, determination also emanated.

"Leif," she said.

He jumped as if bitten.

"I want you and Moon Man to get into the Council Hall's library and find everything you can about a tunnel into the Keep." She told them about Bain's information. "Moon Man can disguise himself as a Daviian, and hopefully you won't be caught. Do not use magic at all from now on. It will only draw them to you."

Moon Man and Leif nodded. Valek smiled. His love had returned from her self-imposed exile. The Daviians wouldn't know what hit them.

"Marrok?" she asked.

"Yes, sir."

"Are you able to fight?"

"Ready, willing and *able*, sir."

She swallowed, taken aback by his pledge. But she recovered quickly. "Good. Marrok and Tauno will accompany Valek and me. We'll go south to rescue the hostages."

"What hostages?" Marrok asked.

Yelena explained about the councilors' families.

Ari cleared his throat as if he wanted to interject.

"I haven't forgotten about you two. I need you to go into the Citadel and help organize the resistance."

"Resistance?" Valek asked, thinking about Fisk. "I hadn't heard."

"I put an idea into a merchant's head, and I think if Ari and Janco disguised themselves as traders, they could move about the Citadel. Ari will have to dye his hair. Oh, and find a boy named Fisk. Tell him you're my friends and he'll help you make contacts."

"And when and where, oh mighty Yelena, do we resist?" Janco asked.

"At the Keep's gates. As for when, I don't know, but something will happen, and you'll know."

Janco and Ari exchanged a look.

"Gotta love the confidence," Janco said.

"And when do we start, love?" Valek asked.

"Everyone get a good night's sleep, and we'll begin preparations in the morning. We'll leave early. Do you have enough disguises for four of us, or do we need to get supplies? Money?" she asked Valek.

He smiled. "You mean raid some laundry lines? Steal a couple purses? No. My safe houses are well stocked with all types of items."

Leif was the only one alarmed by his statement. The room erupted with the noise of multiple conversations. Plans were made and actions decided.

Obviously unhappy, Tauno asked Yelena why he was being separated from Moon Man.

"I need a good scout."

"What about Marrok?" he asked.

"We need him just in case they've moved the captives. He can track them to the new location. Don't worry, Tauno, we'll all reunite."

Tauno failed to look reassured, but he nodded and joined Marrok and Moon Man.

Valek turned to Yelena. "We haven't discussed Jal. Sounds like he's the leader of the Daviians. Do you know who he is?"

"I'm assuming Jal is Gede's Daviian name. It makes sense. You can't have your minions calling you by your real name in case there are Sandseed spies. Gede is the most powerful Story Weaver left, and he called the Fire Warper when I was in his quarters. Plus, the fact that he survived the massacre."

"All good points. Also, Moon Man said Gede is no longer a Story Weaver, but a warper since he betrayed their people. I agree with you."

With the small house full of guests, Valek and Yelena didn't have any privacy to do more than snuggle, but considering that he thought she had died, he was blissfully happy just to hold her in his arms all night.

In the morning, Valek transformed his team into members of the Krystal Clan. They wore the light gray tunics and dark woolen leggings that the clan preferred, which matched the short, hooded capes and black knee-high boots.

Before they could leave, Leif handed Yelena a pouch full of herbs. "Since you can't use your magic, you might want to have them. There are directions on how to use each one inside the packet."

"Leif, I'm—"

"I know. Truthfully, I didn't like the distrustful and mean person you became in Ixia. The fire brought my real sister back. So be careful, as I'd like to keep her around for a while."

"You take care, too. Don't get caught. I wouldn't want to tell Mother about it. She wouldn't be pleased."

Leif looked at Ari and Janco. They fought over who would drive the wagon and who would guard it. "Do they always argue?"

Not always.

She laughed. "It's part of their appeal."

Leif sighed. "I'm amazed we made it to Sitia without being discovered." He paused and cocked his head. "I think I'm actually going to miss them."

"I always do."

Valek hoped Janco hadn't overheard her comment or he'd preen. Before they went their separate ways, he said, "Fourteen days, give or take, should be enough time for everyone. Let's meet in Owl's Hill, as this location is no longer safe. There's an inn called the Cloverleaf that is frequented by caravans."

Everyone said goodbye and good luck. Valek mounted Onyx, Yelena rode Kiki, Marrok sat on Topaz, and Tauno rode Garnet. They set a quick pace. Heading west, they hoped to reach the Krystal Clan's border by nightfall. Then the plan was to follow the border south into the Stormdance lands, cross it and the Bloodgood's lands before reaching Jewelrose's border.

THE STUDY OF FIRE

Normally, it was a seven-day journey, but they hoped to make it there in five days.

They created a cover story of delivering samples of quartz, in case anyone stopped them on the road. Valek didn't expect to be challenged, but it was a good idea to be prepared. Which was the reason everyone called Yelena by a new name, so she'd react when they called her Ellion.

Just like the Ixian Military Districts, each Sitian clan had a specialty. The Jewelrose Clan cut and polished gems and stones of all types. They designed and produced almost all the jewelry in Sitia.

Bright sunshine warmed the air and Valek was glad for many reasons. He was tired of the sleet and cold rain. "Let's hope the good weather draws people onto the roads."

"Why?" Tauno asked.

"Then we will be one of many instead of the only ones," Valek explained. He rode next to the Sandseed, and they discussed the best way to find the barn that held the hostages.

In front of them, Yelena and Marrok rode side by side. Kiki occasionally bumped into Topaz when they slowed their pace or stopped for a rest. Valek wondered if the horses were friends or siblings. Yelena's new bat friend hung upside down from her hood. It bumped against the small of her back but didn't appear to be bothered by the motion. It seemed content to sleep. It would be interesting to see what the bat did that evening. Would he leave them?

In the late afternoon, Yelena asked Marrok about his confession.

"Cahil tricked me," Marrok said. "I fell for his lies about remaining with Ferde to discover the extent of the Daviians' operations. Applauded his plan to lure Ferde back to the Citadel. Commiserated over your ill-timed interference. He convinced me to confess, and name you and Leif as accomplices. It would help him persuade the Council to attack Ixia. He promised..." Marrok paused, rubbing a hand along his right cheek. "After I confessed, he turned on me. A mistake I paid for..." He shuddered. "Am still paying for."

Valek thought Roze had used her magic on him to force a confession, but it had been his conscience that caused his reluctance.

"Betrayals are brutal," Yelena agreed.

Marrok looked at her in surprise. "Don't you think leaving us in Ixia was a betrayal?"

"No. That wasn't my intention. I wanted to protect you and was honest with all of you from the start. I just wasn't honest with myself. A mistake."

"You're still paying for?" Marrok smiled. The gesture erased years from his face.

"Yes. It's the problem with mistakes, they tend to linger. But once we're done with the Daviians and Cahil, I will have paid for all my mistakes. In full."

What did that mean? Unease simmered in Valek's chest. Did she plan to sacrifice herself?

"Do you remember your rescue from the Citadel?" she asked Marrok.

He grinned ruefully. "Sorry, no. At the time, I was in no condition to think. Moon Man is a wonder. I owe him my life." Marrok glanced around then lowered his voice.

Valek leaned forward to hear better.

"Being here without him, I feel...fragile. And that's hard for an old soldier to admit."

Conversation dwindled with the daylight. They stopped at midnight. Without any discussion, Yelena fed, watered, and groomed the horses, Marrok prepared a meal, Tauno hunted for rabbits, and Valek collected firewood.

"I'm used to soldiers' rations on the road, so don't expect this to taste like Leif's," Marrok said as he dished out rabbit stew.

THE STUDY OF FIRE

It was a gourmet meal compared to the jerky Valek had been consuming since... Forever. Or so it seemed.

As he ate, he watched Yelena's bat flit over the campfire, feasting on bugs. After dinner, they arranged their sleeping mats and set a watch schedule. Valek set his right next to Yelena's and they shared a blanket. She wrapped him in a tight hug.

"What's the matter, love," he whispered in her ear. "You're rarely this quiet."

"Just worried about the councilors' families."

"I think we have things well in hand. Between my sleeping potion for the guards, your Curare for the warpers, and the element of surprise, we should rescue them in no time."

"But what if one of the captives is sick? Or dying? If I use my magic, I risk letting the warpers know where I am and what I've been doing."

"Then you'll have to decide what is more important—one person's life or the success of the mission for Sitia's future. It's pointless to worry. Instead, use your energy to decide how you would react to each contingency you can imagine. It's more prudent to prepare for all possibilities than fret." Good advice. Valek wished he followed it more often, especially when it came to Yelena. Logic and reason fled when she was in danger. For her, he'd fret all night.

~

Valek looped around their campsite. He stayed far enough away to avoid waking everyone with his footsteps, and to keep his night vision. They hadn't encountered any trouble the past three nights, and tonight remained quiet. He enjoyed the solitude. With no clouds in the sky, the air had cooled considerably. But it was worth it as the stars shone and twinkled like a field of fireflies.

When his shift was over, he crouched next to Yelena and

gently shook her shoulder. "Ellion... Ellion..." He whispered. She didn't move. "Yelena! Wake up."

She pushed his arm away. "Tired," she mumbled.

"Yes, we *all* are. But it's your turn," Valek said.

She blinked at him with heavy eyelids.

He almost relented and let her sleep, but he needed to rest as well. And Tauno was out scouting, so they were down one man. "There's a pot of tea on the fire."

When she didn't move, he pushed her off the mat. Curling in her place, he drew the covers over his shoulder. "Ahh. Still warm."

"You're evil," she said, but he feigned sleep.

However, it didn't take long for it not to be feigned.

Tauno woke them in the morning. He reported that there were no signs of activity along their path to the Jewelrose border. "There is a good site to camp about two miles south of the border," he said. "I will join you there." He left.

Valek watched him go. The last couple days, Valek had been getting a strange vibe from the scout. Perhaps it was due to the stress of being on his own. Or due to a lack of sleep.

They packed up the campsite and followed Tauno's trail. He'd been right, they encountered nothing concerning, and they found the camping site Tauno had mentioned.

While they were setting up, Tauno reappeared with dinner hanging from his belt.

"I discovered the location of the barn," he said, while butchering the rabbits. "It is four miles west of here in a little hollow."

Valek quizzed him for the details. "We'll have to strike in the dark," he said. "We'll go after midnight, leave the horses in the trees, and then attack."

Tauno agreed. He cubed the meat and dropped it into the pot. "I will sleep, then."

While Marrok stirred the stew, Valek prepped the reed

plants, making blowpipes for everyone. Yelena saddled the tired horses. Garnet sighed when she cinched his straps tight.

"It's not far," she said to the horse. "Then you can rest."

When she finished, she joined them by the fire. Valek ate a few mouthfuls of the stew as Yelena filled a bowl for herself. The stew had a strange yet familiar flavor. He stopped eating. What was that taste?

"This is good," Yelena said to Marrok. "I think you're getting the hang of it. What did you add?"

"A new ingredient. Can you tell what it is?"

She took another spoonful, and rolled the liquid around her mouth like Valek had taught her. She swallowed and asked, "Ginger?"

No. The ingredient's name popped into Valek's head. And he knew exactly what symptoms it caused. He dropped his stew. He jumped to his feet and stumbled.

"Butter root!" he cried out in horror.

"Poison?"

"No." He sank to his knees. "Sleeping draft."

CHAPTER 15

Yelena stared at Valek in horror as he dramatically collapsed onto the ground. He winked at her before closing his eyes and pretending to be unconscious. No doubt there was a watcher hiding nearby, waiting for Valek and the others to fall asleep.

Butter Root was similar to the plant he used for his sleeping potion and had the same effect. He wished he'd recognized the taste sooner. Valek fought the waves of drowsiness that threatened to knock him out.

Next to him, Yelena's bowl clattered to the ground as she slumped over. She had eaten less than him, so he hoped she was awake. Had Marrok spiked the stew? Valek peeked. The captain was sprawled on the ground sound asleep. That left— The horses whinnied in alarm.

Ah, the culprit's friends have arrived.

"So easy! All the talk about the Soulfinder and the Ghost Warrior and look at them! Sleeping like babies," a masculine voice said.

"Trust is a powerful ally. Right, Tauno?" a feminine voice asked. She had the same lilt as a Sandseed.

Valek really needed to *trust* his instincts.

"Yes. And trust is blind. No one suspected me, even after the ambush in the plains." He laughed. "Trust is for stupid people. Even the Sandseed Elders had no idea. My ability to find the Daviian camps amazed them."

They chuckled, enjoying themselves.

"We have captured a wanted criminal. That should make the council happy. And we'll bring the Soulfinder to Jal."

He counted the voices around their campsite. There were four of them, good odds for him and Yelena.

"Kill the Ghost Warrior," one of the vermin ordered.

He prepared to move.

"Make sure you cut his throat and collect his blood. It will be just revenge for Alea and her brother."

He wished he could kill those two again. Through slitted eyelids, Valek watched as they lifted Yelena off the ground.

"Now!" Valek yelled, springing to his feet as he drew his sword.

Her switchblade snicked and she plunged it into a Daviian's chest. Valek spun just as Tauno tried to slit his throat with the sharp point of his spear. He blocked and backed up as another Daviian joined the fight. That left one attacker for Yelena.

Facing two opponents with spears was similar to defending against bo staffs. He had fought three people with bo staffs, and this time he had his sword. He silently thanked his seconds-in-command for the practice.

As he engaged with the two, Yelena's attacker ordered her to drop her weapon. As if she'd listen.

Then he said, "You will not be harmed if you surrender."

Yelena countered. "You're not allowed to kill me; Jal wants me alive so he can feed me to his pet Fire Warper!"

Valek approved of her tactic to unnerve her opponent. He concentrated on his own fight. Tauno was a skilled warrior. His friend pushed her magic at Valek, slowing him down. It took

THE STUDY OF FIRE

longer than he expected, but he snaked passed Tauno's defenses and stabbed him.

The woman yelled when Tauno collapsed and attacked Valek with renewed vigor. Her power pressed on his arms. His muscles burned with the effort to move. He ducked and dodged, waiting for the perfect opening.

Across the fire, Yelena and the other warper fought. "Is that all you have?" Yelena's attacker asked. "What about your great soul magic? I think the Fire Warper will be disappointed. Orders are orders." A thud sounded and Yelena collapsed.

Valek went on the offensive and created the perfect opening. The woman was dead in two moves. He turned just in time to see Kiki kick the warper in the head, denting it. Nice. Then he spotted Yelena lying on the ground under Kiki. He raced to her and rolled her over. Cuts oozing blood crisscrossed her arms and legs.

Her pulse was strong and there were no stab wounds. He looked up at Kiki, who kept her protective stance. "What happened?"

Kiki nudged Yelena's forehead. A bright red bruise swelled on her temple. She'd been knocked unconscious. Valek carried her closer to the fire. He checked Marrok to ensure he still slept. Then he grabbed the first aid supplies from Kiki's saddle bags. He found the pouch Leif had given Yelena and sorted through the contents, hoping something would be useful for a headache.

Using a soft cloth and water, Valek cleaned her wounds. He wasn't gentle. She needed to wake up, and he hoped the pain would rouse her. They were running out of time.

He was almost done, when she said, "Ow! Stop that."

"Finally," he said. But he didn't stop. He dabbed at her wounds, finishing the job, then sat back on his heels. "That'll have to do for now. Come on. We need to go."

When she failed to move, he pulled her into a sitting position. Her brow furrowed, and color leaked from her face.

"Here." He thrust red leaves into her hands. "I found them in your saddlebags. The note said to eat them for head pain."

"Go where?" she asked.

Valek yanked her to her feet. "We need to find the barn."

"Barn?"

She was still groggy from being knocked out. As much as he hated to do it, Valek shook the rest of the water over her head. She jolted.

"When the Daviians don't come back with us, the others will know something has happened and will either kill their hostages or move to another location." Valek enunciated each word, hoping she would understand the urgency. "Here." He handed her a set of clean Sitian clothes. "Hurry."

Finally understanding, she changed. Valek stripped the warper, and then dressed in his clothes. Applying makeup, he darkened his skin tone to match.

Once they were both ready, they untied the horses. Tauno must have secured them so they wouldn't interfere in the ambush. Valek mounted Onyx while Yelena hopped on Kiki. They rode the four miles to the barn in silence. Approaching the edge of the woods, they slowed. Valek scanned the barn. Illuminated by the strange red glow emanating from Diamond Lake, two Daviians guarded the entrance.

"Which horse?" Yelena asked.

"Onyx. Kiki is too well-known."

Yelena dismounted.

"Take off your cape," Valek said. "Lie in front of me." He removed his foot from the stirrup.

She climbed up and laid across the saddle. He had cleaned her switchblade. Handing it to her, he said, "It's been primed with Curare."

Valek grabbed the reins with his left hand and held a scimitar in his right.

"Pretend to be unconscious," he ordered as he clicked at

Onyx. He hoped the Daviians would think he was returning from the ambush with the prize.

A whoop of joy cut through the air as they neared.

"Where are the others?" a masculine voice asked.

"They're coming," Valek said in a rough tone.

"Finally! We have her!" another man said, as he tugged at Yelena's prone form.

"Help me."

Valek slid off on the opposite side of the saddle, keeping Onyx between him and the Daviian.

Another person joined in pulling her off. "We'll keep her asleep until she reaches Jal. Get the wagon, you'll leave tonight," the man ordered. He cradled Yelena in his arms.

Valek placed the tip of his scimitar on the man's throat. "Where is Jal?"

The man froze. "At the Magician's Keep. Go ahead and find Jal. Just make sure to take her with you." The man tossed Yelena at Valek and screamed for help.

Shit. She hit him square in the chest and they both went down. But Yelena had been trained well, and she kept rolling until she cleared his body. Just in time for him to twist away from the Daviian's downward slicing blade.

Unable to get to his feet, Valek rolled and scrambled to avoid being cut. The snick of a switchblade sounded, and the man on top of him grunted as Yelena's knife nicked his shoulder. Determined, the man swung his scimitar until his muscles were paralyzed by the Curare.

Yelena grabbed the man's spear while Valek scrambled to his feet. He scooped up his scimitar as four more Daviians with weapons drawn ran toward them.

Valek braced as they collided, and then focused all his energy on fighting off two and sometimes three opponents. Yelena stayed at his side. She killed one man, but before she could help Valek, another person approached.

"Why not use your power to stop me? Afraid the Fire Warper will tell Jal what you're doing?" the newcomer said.

"Give the man a prize. Your intellect is truly amazing," she said.

"Surrender or I'll skewer her," the man called to Valek.

Valek disengaged. A spear hovered in mid-air. The tip was pointed at Yelena's throat. He met her gaze. *Say the word, love.*

"He won't do it," she said to Valek.

"You are right. How about surrender or I will set the barn on fire?" The man was a warper. He pointed to the building. "Do you want to be responsible for the deaths of ten children?"

"No! Don't!" Yelena yelled at the warper. "Let the children go and I'll come with you."

"I know you will," the warper said. The point of his spear touched Yelena's throat. "I am more concerned about the Ghost Warrior." He met Valek's gaze. "Put your weapon down."

Anger sizzled in Valek's veins. He'd like nothing better than to run the man through with his scimitar. However, Yelena and the children locked in the barn depended on him. He bent over and set the sword on the ground, then palmed a couple darts with his left hand. When he straightened, he threw them at the warper. One hit the man's neck, and he jerked in surprise.

"Move," Valek ordered Yelena.

She twisted. The spear's point cut a line across her throat. It didn't look deep, but Valek planned to kill the warper regardless. He stepped closer as the man turned. A loud woosh sounded as bright orange flames spread under the barn's door. The warper finally succumbed to the sleeping potion delivered by the dart. Too late. Smoke filled the air.

"Valek, go!" Yelena waved him toward the building, then whistled for the horses.

He ran to the doors. Fire consumed the dry wood and peeling paint with alarming speed. Once the roof caught, the ten children and two adults trapped inside would be unable to escape. The metal latch burned his hand as he unlocked the doors and wrestled them open. Smoke billowed ominously from inside. Did the warper set another section of the barn on fire?

He rushed in and skidded to a stop. Another structure had been built inside the barn. This one had fresh wood and new locks. Yelena appeared with Kiki and Onyx.

She took one look at it and shouted over the fire's roar. "Tell them to move to the left side!"

Banging on the door, he yelled at those trapped within to move to the left side.

"Now!" he yelled.

Then he ripped off his tunic and yanked his switchblade from its sheath. He sliced the seams of the garment, freeing his hidden lock picks. Tossing the shirt and knife aside, he set to work on the locks, racing the flames that now galloped through the roof's thick beams as if they were mere matchsticks.

A loud bang sounded to the right. Then another, as the horses kicked through the new wood of the interior structure. At least, that's what it sounded like. Valek popped the locks and swung the door wide. Smoke filled the room as flames licked the walls and zipped across the ceiling. It burned his eyes and lungs with its acrid odor, but he waded into the room.

Heat roared in his ears and dulled the cries of the children. Valek found hands and helped them through the hole in the right wall. One of the adults helped, counting kids as they left.

"That's eight," he yelled in Valek's ear. "I've the last two."

"And the Stormdance woman?"

"Got hit by a broken plank," he gestured to the left. "I can't carry her. Too weak." He coughed.

An ominous snap sounded above them, and a beam fell to the floor. No time left.

"Go," Valek ordered.

Staying low to the ground to avoid the thick smoke, Valek

searched with his hands until he found the unconscious woman. He pulled her over his shoulders and stepped toward the hole. A loud crack rent the air. The barn shook and then roared as the roof crashed down on them. A flaming beam hit his temple as they punched through the floor. Darkness consumed Valek before he hit the ground.

Valek woke sometime later. The fire raged about two feet above his throbbing head. Dirt walls surrounded him. He'd been buried alive! Panicked, he drew a breath to scream, *I'm not dead*, but it immediately set off a strong coughing fit which ignited the real pain. Agony shot through his ribs, and it sucked the air from his lungs. His throat burned, and the ache in his head intensified to nonstop hammering. Gasping, panting, he longed to return to unconsciousness.

A light breeze of fresh air caressed his face as a hand touched his shoulder. Yelena?

"Relax," a strange woman rasped near his ear. She lay next to him. "You're safe." Then she gave him a tired half smile. "For now."

Memories rushed back. The barn. The fire. The Stormdance woman. A fist-sized bruise marked her forehead.

"What…how…" Talking over the fire's roar required too much effort.

"I'm a bit fuzzy on the details," she said, touching her temple. "I woke up here with you and the fire—" As if on cue, the flames shifted and burning debris rained down.

Except the breeze strengthened. It extinguished the debris and swept the burned pieces away from them. They landed on a pile. By the size of the mound, Valek guessed she'd been keeping them safe for a while with her magic.

"Can you…" he gestured weakly "…blow all the fire out?"

"I wish. My magic is not that strong. Besides, each time I bring in fresh air for us or use it to blow out the sparks, I'm adding fuel to the fire."

Good point. "So, we wait?"

"And hope my strength lasts. Even then..." She peered at the wall of fire above them. "If bigger beams crash down on us..." Her breath hitched with fear.

"Is there anything I can do to help?" he asked.

"No." She was quiet for a moment, then said, "Did the children...are they safe?"

"Yes, they all escaped along with the man. My colleagues will take care of them."

"Good," she sighed with relief.

Yelena must be frantic with worry. He hoped she hadn't done anything stupid, like rushing into the burning building to save him. Did she even have time before the roof collapsed? Or did she cross into the fire world, thinking he was there? Now he was more than worried. He was terrified. *Don't leave me, love.*

"Where are we?" he asked for a distraction.

"I think it's a root cellar."

They chatted off and on. Her name was Gale Stormdance, the wife of Councilor Stormdance.

"Valek?" she asked horrified. "As in—"

"The Scourge of Sitia?" He kept his tone light.

"Ah..." She grew quiet.

He wondered if he scared her or if she'd fallen asleep. It'd been hours and the fire still burned hot. But a flaming plank fell toward them, and it was whisked away to the pile.

"More like the savior of children," she finally said. "Why are you here in Sitia?"

"It's a long story."

"My appointment with my hair stylist isn't until tomorrow," she joked.

He laughed despite the pain in his head and ribs. "You're not going to like it."

"Try me."

Valek smiled. He was impressed by Gale's strength. "Stop me when you've heard enough."

"Okay."

"I came to Sitia to assassinate all the councilors, including your husband."

She sucked in a breath, and he waited.

"Go on."

He told her about the Daviian Warpers. It helped to keep her awake during the hours. He explained their theories about Jal and that Yelena discovered how the councilors were being threatened.

By the time he finished, it appeared that the active fire was dying down. Even though the embers still glowed red hot, Valek's spirits rose.

After what felt like days, the last of the fire extinguished and they both fell into an exhausted sleep.

～

A crunching noise roused Valek from sleep. He grabbed for his knife, only to find it missing along with his shirt. What?

Daylight leaked through the ashy remains of the barn, reminding him of his precarious situation. A few half-burned beams crossed over the hole above their root cellar. The noise hadn't woken Gale.

Valek pushed up to his elbow. Pain ringed his chest, stealing his breath for a long moment. Cracked ribs. How could he forget? Another muffled scrape reached him. He wondered if it was Yelena or if the warpers had awakened from their drugged sleep. In no condition to fight and with no extra breath to yell, he remained in place. No need to alert the warpers that he still lived. And if it was Yelena...

He sighed. When she had jumped into the stable fire, his world had ended. Valek had spent a long time staring at his knife, working up the nerve to stab it into his heart.

If it was Yelena, it meant she hadn't gone the into the fire world. That she'd be okay for a day or so. He'd catch up, he promised.

∽

Just in case the warpers remained nearby, Valek and Gale waited until dark to move the beams. They crumbled into ash as soon as they touched them, raining down on top of their heads and setting off coughing fits. So much for a stealthy escape. Valek scrambled up from the cellar to defend them, but no one rushed him.

The night remained quiet. Valek shivered in the chilly air. Large burn holes peppered his pants. He smelled burnt hair. Touching his scalp gently, Valek discovered most of his hair had burned off. Lovely.

He called all clear, and Gale climbed up. Her clothing had also been burned and she hugged her chest.

"What now?" she asked.

"We need to find clothes, transportation, and then the location of the children and the Greenblade man. The Daviians think you're all dead, so you'll be safe with them."

"No. I'm going with you to fight them." She held up a hand, stopping his protests. "I know I don't have much power, but I'll do whatever I can to aid your efforts."

He considered her offer. They would need every bit of help they could get. "Thank you."

She waved a hand. "I haven't done anything yet."

"You saved our lives."

"Huh. I guess I did." Then she laughed. "Don't tell my friends at the beauty parlor that I saved the Scourge of Sitia's life. I'll never be invited to another dinner party." Gale tapped a finger on her lips. "Then again, I never really enjoyed them."

Valek clamped down on a chuckle. The movement hurt his ribs too much. Then he began the arduous task of gathering what they'd need to track the others. It wouldn't be easy, but he'd catch up to Yelena as quickly as possible.

∽

As expected, nothing went well. Even after he found Onyx and Topaz, they encountered many obstacles. It ended up taking him and Gale seven days to catch up to Yelena and the others in Owl's Hill, a town east of the Citadel. Except, they were no longer at the Cloverleaf Inn, which added another day. The burns on his skin had healed, but his ribs still ached and protested at every bump in the road.

Finally, he spotted Yelena and his friends near a caravan. They discussed plans. He had hoped that when he died, they'd be able to carry on without him, and it sounded like they already had. Offended at the speed of their recovery, he huffed. Instead of rushing to join them, he stayed in the shadows, listening to them.

"When the riot starts, all the magicians will come to the Keep's gate and help you build and maintain a null shield," Yelena said.

"But it won't last long," Leif said.

"I just need a little time."

"Time for what?"

"To get to the Fire Warper."

A pause. "You can fight him?" Leif asked.

"No."

"Tell me again why this isn't a suicide mission," Leif said.

Yes, love. Tell us.

"I think I can stop him and keep him in the fire world. And in doing so, I think I might be able to pull some of the warpers' powers from them. If Bain and Irys are still alive, and if you round up as many magicians as you can, then you should be able to counter the warpers."

"That's a lot of 'ifs' and 'thinks,'" Janco said.

"And there's no 'when,'" Ari said.

"When?" Leif asked.

"When she returns. There's a *when*, isn't there, Yelena?" Ari asked.

"The only way to keep him in the fire world is if I stay, too."

Anger blazed. No bloody way was she sacrificing her life.

"There has to be another way," Leif said. "You always manage to produce ingenious plots."

"Not this time," Yelena said. She sounded tired and defeated.

Silence ensued.

Gale gave Valek a confused look and whispered, "What are you waiting for?"

"What if we can't counter the warpers?" Leif asked.

"My cue," he said to Gale, then called to the group, "Then you'd better have a person who's unaffected by magic on your side."

Gale rolled her eyes. "Are you always this dramatic?"

"Only when I come back from the dead," he snarked. Then to the others, "Although, this time I would appreciate it if you didn't leave me behind." He stepped into view.

They stared at him as if he was a ghost. Yelena gaped in disbelief and tentatively reached out. He pulled her into his arms, and she pressed against him. Time stilled as they breathed as one. The worry and anxiety of the past week melted away.

The others disappeared and when he kissed her, Valek poured his heart and soul into that kiss. Yelena hugged him harder as if she'd received the message. Pain ringed his chest.

He pulled away, breathless. "Easy, love." The words turned into a coughing fit.

"How did you survive the fire?" she asked. "The roof collapsed, and you didn't..."

"Two things happened at once." He explained how the beam crashed down and they fell into the root cellar. Valek rubbed his ribs and grimaced.

"You're hurt and I can't heal you!"

"Just bruised." He ran a hand gently over his head. A healing gash marked the right side of his head. When he'd found a mirror, he'd cut his hair. The Commander would be pleased to see it was now military regulation short.

"Why didn't I see you the next morning? Why didn't you call out?"

His hand went to his ribs again. "I didn't have enough air to yell, and Gale needed all her strength to keep us alive."

"Why couldn't she blow the fire out? Or save the children?"

"Her powers are limited. It's all part of her weather dancing thing." He gestured past the wagon, where Gale held Onyx's and Topaz's reins. "You can ask her. I've brought her along." When he saw Yelena's questioning look, he added, "We're going to need all the help we can get."

"Did you learn anything else?" she asked him.

"Yes. Finding clothes when you're half naked is harder than you think. And scared horses can travel pretty far in the wrong direction before you find them." He studied the group of horses. "Onyx and Topaz are fast, but there's nothing like a Sandseed horse when you're in a hurry. And despite your detour to Booruby, love, I had a hard time catching up."

"You could have found a way to tell me you were all right. I've spent the last week in utter misery."

"Now you know how I felt when you jumped into the stable fire. And you know how I'll feel if you don't come back from fighting the Fire Warper."

She opened her mouth then closed it. "You were eavesdropping."

"I had hoped to hear everyone discussing how much they missed my altruistic qualities, my legendary skills as a fighter and as a lover." He leered. "Instead, you're making plans for tomorrow. Interesting how life goes on in spite of itself."

Valek sobered and stared at her intently. "With all that planning, love, I'm sure you can figure a way to return."

"I'm not smart enough," she said in frustration. "I don't know enough about magic! I don't think anyone does. We're all just bumbling along, using it and abusing it."

"Do you truly believe that?"

"Yes. Although, I'll admit to being a hypocrite. First sign of trouble and I fall back on using magic. When I think about magic, all I see is the harm it has done to this world."

She sounded just like the Commander.

"Then you're not looking in the right places." Valek studied her dubious expression. "Think about what you said to the Commander about magic."

"I tend to agree with the Commander about how magic corrupts."

"Then why did you mention to the Commander how magic could harness the power of a blizzard and save his people instead of discussing the possibility of using power as a weapon? If magic corrupts, then why hasn't it corrupted you? Or Irys? Moon Man? Leif?"

"We haven't let it corrupt us."

"Right! You have the choice."

"But it's a very tempting choice. Power is addictive. It's only a matter of time."

"Oh yes. Sitia has been battling warpers for ages. Though you wouldn't know it from all the peace and prosperity hanging around." Valek's tone dripped with sarcasm. "Let's see, how long ago did the magicians use blood magic? I think Moon Man told me two thousand years. Then you're right! It's only a matter of time. A matter of two thousand years. I'll take those odds any day."

"I never realized how annoying you can be."

"You know I'm right."

"I could prove you wrong. I can be corrupt." She leered at him.

Desire shot through him. Valek glanced at Janco and the others. They milled around a small fire, trying to appear nonchalant as they listened to every word.

"Not in front of the children, love. But I'll hold you to that."

Yelena and Valek joined them. Tauno wasn't the only one missing. "Where's Moon Man?"

"He was captured by the Daviians yesterday afternoon," Leif said. "After finding no information about a tunnel into the Keep, we met with an old magician in hiding. He only had vague details, but he taught me how to create a null shield." He shook his head in disgust. "And since I'm a genius, I practiced. The magic called the warpers, and we were attacked as soon as we left his house."

"How did you get away?" Valek asked.

"An unruly mob arrived. In the mass confusion, a guy pulled me free from the riot. I hid, but Moon Man wasn't so lucky."

Valek glanced at Yelena.

Sadness lined her eyes. "I hope he's still alive."

"That's why we're camping with this caravan," Ari said. "If they interrogate Moon Man, they might learn about the inn."

"What's the plan for tomorrow?" he asked.

"We're going to storm the Keep," Yelena said.

"Funny."

"Oh, she's *dead* serious," Leif said. "We're going to hide in those coffins—"

"Crates," Ari corrected.

"Says the man who gets to drive the wagon. Janco and

THE STUDY OF FIRE

Marrok will be on horseback—part of the caravan. Once inside the Citadel, Ari will drive the wagon to the Keep, which, by the way, is surrounded by a protective magical barrier. Oh, and you're gonna *love* this," Leif said, parroting Janco. "At the Keep, he will inform the Daviians that he has captured the powerful Soulfinder and would like the bounty of five gold coins. Thank you very much."

"And that's when the citizens will riot, creating a distraction," Janco said.

"And I'm supposed to create a null shield to protect us once we're inside the Keep," Leif said.

"A null shield you just learned how to create?" Valek asked.

"That's the one, but Yelena will call the other magicians to help me maintain it."

"And that's when I heard the rest of your plans." He turned to Yelena. "Keep thinking about your exit strategy once you defeat the Fire Warper. Please."

She nodded, but the sadness in her eyes remained.

∽

The next morning, they prepared to join the caravan. Valek was standing next to Yelena when Janco snarked, "You ever notice how couples start to look alike?"

In a deadpan, Valek replied, "Yes. In fact, I was just thinking how much you and Topaz resemble each other. It's uncanny."

Ari chuckled at Janco's chagrined expression before saying, "The caravan is leaving soon. What part of the line do we want to be in?"

"Near the back, but not the last wagon," Valek instructed. "When we're out of sight of the gatehouse, head to the Keep."

"Yes, sir." Ari snapped to attention.

"We don't know what we'll encounter inside the Keep. Listen

for instructions, and follow orders even if they don't make sense," Valek said.

"Yes, sir," everyone said in unison, including Gale.

Before they assumed their positions, Yelena handed three glass statues to Leif and another three to Gale.

"What are these for?" Leif asked.

Yelena explained that she'd stopped in Booruby to visit Opal. "I discovered I can use her glass animals to communicate with other magicians far away, without using my own magic. When Opal blows into the glass, instead of air, she blows magic, trapping it inside."

Valek remembered the brief glimpse of the trapped magic he'd gotten with Yelena's help. Beautiful.

"Keep one each, but give the rest to Moon Man, Irys, Bain, and Dax if they're still alive," Yelena said. "I think I can use the animals to communicate with you when I'm in the fire world."

That would be helpful, but Valek hoped she would find a way to come home.

"Come on, you first." Yelena gestured Leif to the cart.

With a grumble, Leif, and then Gale, laid down in the row of boxes in the wagon. Valek met Yelena's gaze and held it a moment. *Come back to me, love.* Then he laid down. The top closed and the darkness was instant. After a few moments, his eyes adjusted. Light shone through the cracks in the crate.

Thumping sounded above him as goods and Yelena's crate were loaded, followed by a pile of rugs to conceal everything. The wagon lurched. Valek reviewed the plan as they trundled closer to the Citadel. The caravan planned to enter through the south gate, as it was the closest to their destination.

A couple hours later, the wagon jerked to a stop. Then voices sounded. This was it. If they were discovered, all bets were off.

Something banged on wood. "What's in this one?" a man asked.

"The finest silk sheets woven by the Moon Clan, sir," the

owner of the caravan replied. "Perhaps you care to purchase a set? Just feel the fabric and you'll know your wife will be most anxious to try them out."

The man laughed. "I'll not be spending a month's pay for a night with my wife. That's why I married her."

More laughter, then the Citadel's guard asked the owner a bunch of standard questions. He answered without hesitating. After an age and a half, the wagon finally moved. They had made it passed the gate. Soon, the sounds of bartering, children shrieking, and the general buzz of people gathered in one area reached him. They were in the market, where Ari was signaling his resistance force to riot when the wagon entered the Keep.

They turned a corner and came to an abrupt halt. Ari cursed as the jangle of many horses echoed on the cobblestones.

"Oh no. This will not do," the Wannabe King called out.

CHAPTER 16

Valek rolled over in his crate and rested on his elbows and knees. He slid the panel below him open, then he eased onto the cobblestones.

"I assume you have Yelena hidden somewhere in your wagon," Cahil said.

"Have who, sir?" Ari asked, playing innocent. "All I have are goods for the market."

From his position, Valek counted horses. Five. They stood in a semi-circle, blocking the front of the wagon.

"For the market? The market you just rode through without stopping to unload? I don't think so. Despite your disguises and weak attempts to explain your presence, I know who you are and why you're here. In fact, I was sent by Jal to come and escort you to the Keep."

Valek combat crawled to the back of the wagon, where Janco and Marrok remained on their horses. Keeping the pile of goods between him and Cahil, he climbed the stack, stopping short of the top. Ari shifted his weight while Janco met Valek's gaze. Janco signaled, *Not yet.*

"Relax," Cahil said. "I'm not here to capture you. I'm here to join you. And I hope for the sake of all our lives you have a decent plan."

Join us? No way Valek would believe a word that man said.

"A plan, sir?" Ari asked.

Cahil snorted with exasperation. "Yelena! Leif!" he called. "Come out and tell your big northern friend I'm telling the truth. Look for yourselves."

Janco signaled. *Go.*

Valek climbed on top of the wagon.

Cahil said, "My people have not drawn their—"

He launched into a diving tackle, knocking Cahil off his horse. The Wannabe King yelped as they hit the ground with a thud. Valek yanked his dagger, pulled Cahil to his feet and pressed the sharp blade to the man's throat. His minions froze.

Ari pulled off the rugs and helped Yelena from her box. Leif, Gale, and Janco joined Ari with weapons in hand. However, Marrok stayed on Garnet.

"Tell me why I shouldn't cut your throat?" Valek asked Cahil, even though he was pretty sure this was going to end with the Wannabe King's death regardless.

"You won't get into the Keep without me," Cahil said. He kept still and held his hands up and away from his body.

"Why this sudden change of heart?" Yelena asked.

"You were right," he said as if in pain. "They're using me and..."

"And what?" she prompted.

"The rituals and killings have gotten out of hand. I can't be a part of it anymore." He looked at Marrok. "I wasn't raised to be a killer. I was raised to be a leader. I'll earn my throne the old-fashioned way."

Although the expression on Marrok's face never changed, his body relaxed.

"How do we know you're telling the truth?" Ari asked.

"Yelena knows through her magic."

She shook her head. "I can't use it. It will alert Jal and risk the mission."

"She already knows you're here. You have thwarted her a number of times. Although it will be more difficult now, as she has gained an incredible amount of power through the Kirakawa ritual."

"She?" Valek and Yelena asked in unison.

"We thought Jal was Gede," Yelena said.

Cahil blinked at her for a moment in shock. "You didn't know? What else don't you know? You were planning an attack at the Keep, right? I thought you had it all figured out."

"You thought wrong," she said, annoyed. "We had to guess about the state of affairs inside the Keep."

"Then here's a way for me to prove my loyalty. I'll tell you what's been going on and will help you get inside. Agreed?"

Valek and Yelena exchanged a glance. *Could they trust him or not?*

"Do I still get to kill him?" Valek asked, hopeful.

"At the first sign of betrayal, yes," Yelena said.

"What about after this is all over?"

"Then it's your call."

He grinned. Valek never took pleasure in killing, but Cahil's death might be the first.

Cahil stared at them. "Hold on. I'm risking my life to help you. I'd like some guarantees."

"We've come to a point where there are no guarantees. For any of us," she said.

"That's not very encouraging," Cahil said.

"It's not supposed to be. You should know what happens when you play with fire, Cahil. Eventually, you'll get burned. Now, tell us what you know," she ordered.

Valek removed his knife from Cahil's throat and stepped back. Cahil scanned the area. They had attracted quite the crowd, but there were no Daviians among them.

"Where are all the warpers?" Yelena had made the same observation.

He gave her a sardonic smile. "They're all at the Keep. Roze plans a massive Kirakawa ritual using all the magicians she has captured to empower all her favorite warpers in one sweep. And you're to be the coup de grâce."

Ah, so Roze was the Daviians' leader. Valek had suspected she was working with the Daviians, but now that he knew her real role as their leader, it made sense. Kudos to her for keeping it a secret for so long.

Yelena paled. "Roze?"

A superior expression settled on Cahil's face. "Yes, Roze Featherstone, First Magician. Also known as Jalila Daviian, First Warper and founder of the Daviian Clan."

All color drained from Leif's face. "But how? Why?"

Valek remembered Yelena's brother worked with Roze on criminal cases. Poor guy had just received a massive blow. Betrayal seemed to be the theme for this mission. First Star, then Tauno, and now Roze. Valek wondered how long she'd been planning this coup.

"I had no idea until Ferde was caught," Cahil said. "She asked me to rescue him in exchange for the council's support to invade Ixia. I thought it was an undercover mission to learn who else was behind his bid for power. Though, when I discovered the truth about Roze and the other warpers, I must admit it didn't bother me at the time. She promised to attack Ixia and make me king."

"How many warpers are inside and who are the victims for the ritual?" Yelena asked.

"Six very powerful warpers, including Roze and Gede. They have been very careful about who they allow to increase their powers, keeping crucial information about the Kirakawa ritual to a select few. There are fifty Daviian soldiers and ten medium powered warpers. Two of those warpers are scheduled to be given master-level powers during the massive ritual. The victims for this ritual will be the three other masters—who are incarcerated in the Keep's cells—Moon Man and the councilors."

Sixty-six against seven. Perhaps they should recruit a few dozen people. Too bad, they had no time.

"What about the students?" Yelena asked.

"The older apprentices have been put in the cells. The younger ones obey out of fear."

"How does Roze plan to control the master magicians?"

"She has the power, but I think she does plan to prick them with Curare to save her energy. Once they are tied down, a dose of Theobroma will weaken their defenses."

"They seem to have an unlimited supply of Curare," Yelena said wryly.

"Gede Daviian has provided the drug for them. He also helped recruit dissatisfied Sandseeds to the Daviian Clan. And having a pet Fire Warper has made him the Daviians' most valued member."

Gede and Roze had to be Valek's first targets. That was, if he could get close to them.

Yelena appeared to consider Cahil's words. "How do you plan to get us inside?"

"As my prisoner. She knows I went to find you. I'll bring you to her. Since my feelings for you haven't changed, I won't have to act like I hate you. Sensing nothing wrong, Roze will probably order me to take the rest"—Cahil pointed to Ari and Janco —"to the cells."

"Why would I cooperate with you?"

"Because I'll have Leif, and I'll make a bargain to keep him safe in exchange for your cooperation."

Valek hated to admit it, but Cahil's strategy had a small chance of success.

"Cahil, when you take the others to the cells, can you free everyone inside?"

"As long as Roze is occupied."

Valek smiled. "What's the plan, love?"

~

Back inside his crate, Valek wondered if they would survive the day. Yelena sat with Cahil on his horse. Ari and Marrok had their hands tied behind their backs, acting like prisoners. Leif rode on Kiki with a minion who held a knife to his throat. Janco and Gale hid in the other crates.

The wagon moved slowly. Valek straddled the open panel, watching the cobblestones. They went through the Keep's gate without pausing. The resistance force had been updated to wait ten minutes after they entered the Keep before rioting. Cahil had said the Daviians had built a large bonfire in the grassy glen between the apprentice barracks at the very center of the Keep.

Valek poked his head out. When he spotted the side of the dining hall, he dropped to the ground. The wagon continued toward the Apprentices' wings. He hustled over to the building's shadow. There was no one in the area. *Good.* He kept to the shadows and moved closer to the glen. There were enough trees and shrubs to hide him from sight.

However, it didn't matter if he was hidden or not. Everyone's attention was on Cahil and Yelena. The glen had been covered in sand. He wondered if that was Avibian sand. Blood stained it, and stakes had been driven into it. A bonfire roared in the center. The killing ground for the Kirakawa ritual.

Valek's heart sank when he recognized the next victim staked in the sand. Moon Man. Bloody cuts crisscrossed his abdomen, legs, and arms. Although in pain, Moon Man still managed to smile at Yelena. "Now we can start the party," he said.

Here we go.

Roze frowned at Moon Man, and he writhed in agony. Gede stood beside her. Other warpers ringed the fire pit, watching with predatory gazes.

"I see you finally managed to get something right, Cahil," Roze said. "Bring her here."

Cahil dismounted and dragged Yelena from the horse, dropping her onto the ground. When he leaned over to yank her to her feet, Valek saw him whisper something to her. Then Cahil clamped his hand around her arm and pulled her to Roze. They stopped a few feet from the fire.

Roze gestured to a couple of nearby warpers. "There are two hiding in the boxes. Take them."

The warpers and a few soldiers advanced on the wagon. After some banging and lots of cursing, Janco and Gale were hauled out.

"There are three compartments, but one is empty," a warper called.

Roze looked at Yelena.

"For me. So I could get inside the Citadel," Yelena said.

"At this distance, Yelena, do you realize your mental defenses are nothing but a thin shell? I will see your lies before you can form them in your mind. Remember that."

She nodded.

Roze laughed and ordered the soldiers to take the prisoners to the cells. "I'll deal with them later."

Although they had wanted Cahil to escort the prisoners, the change didn't ruin their plans. Once the wagon was out of sight, Roze peered at Yelena and the Wannabe King.

"Your capture was too easy," she said. "You must think I'm a simpleton. No matter, I've only to expand a sliver of power to find out what you're planning." Roze stared intensely at Yelena.

"Why?" Yelena asked.

"Nice try. You are in my power now. Sitia is saved."

"Saved from me?" Yelena sounded incredulous.

"Saved from you. The Commander. Valek. Our way of life is secured."

I wouldn't count us out just yet. Where was that bloody riot?

"By killing Sitians? Using blood magic?"

"Small price to pay for our continued prosperity. I could not let the Commander invade us. The council failed to see the problem. I created the Daviians as a backup years ago—a hidden weapon for when we needed them. It worked. The council eventually agreed with me." Roze's words dripped with smug satisfaction.

But she didn't mention the hostages. Was that not part of her plans?

"The Daviians forced the council to agree with you. They had their children," Yelena said, picking up on the same thing as Valek.

Roze shot Gede a venomous glare. He kept quiet, but he stiffened.

"Are you sure you have control of the Daviians?" Yelena asked.

Nice, love. Keep her talking.

"Of course. And once we choose a new council, we will attack Ixia and free them. They will welcome our way of life." She smiled, a true believer of her own twisted ideals.

"So you saved Sitia? Tell me, how is sacrificing the council different than Valek assassinating them?"

Another point to Yelena. But she had gone too far. Goaded, Roze frowned, and Yelena jerked in pain, collapsing onto the sand. Valek curled his fists. If he was fast enough, he could kill Roze before anyone could stop him. Too bad, it wasn't part of their strategy.

"Isn't *choosing* new councilors the same as *appointing* generals?" Yelena asked, once she recovered. Then she arched her back and screamed in pain. Valek stepped from his hiding spot, but Yelena relaxed.

"Would you care to ask anything else?" Roze's cold tone promised more pain.

But Yelena wasn't intimidated. "Yes. How are your actions different than the Commander's?"

Roze narrowed her gaze.

Yelena rushed on. "You want to protect Sitia from the Commander, but in the process, you've turned into him. You're worried the Commander will invade Sitia and turn your clans into Military Districts. But you're planning to attack Ixia and turn his Military Districts into clans. How is that different? Tell me!" Yelena demanded.

Valek silently cheered as Roze gaped and floundered. "I'm... he's..." Then she laughed. "Why should I listen to you? You're a Soulfinder. You want to control Sitia. Of course you would try to sway me with your lies."

Next to her, Gede relaxed and chuckled. "She will twist your words. You should kill her now."

Roze drew a breath.

"Wait for the ritual! I have something you want," Yelena said.

"What could you have that I cannot take from you?"

"According to the ritual, a willing victim releases more power than a resisting one."

"And you will submit to me? In exchange for what?" Roze asked.

"For all my friends' lives."

"No. Only one. You choose."

"Moon Man, then." Yelena stood.

Roze pointed. "Lie in the sand."

"Can I ask another question first?"

"One."

"What happens to the Fire Warper after this ritual?"

"Once you're dead, our deal is complete. We have promised

him your power and we have fed him in exchange for knowledge about the blood magic. He will then have enough power to rule the underworld."

A shout echoed. Magic swelled, pressing against Valek's face.

Finally. He peered over a bush. The sounds of a clash south of the glen drew everyone's attention. Valek spotted Janco, Ari, and others fighting the Keep's guards in the open area north of the dining hall.

Roze turned to the commotion and gestured to her warpers. "Take care of them." Unconcerned, she faced Yelena, "You know they will not get close to us. My warpers and I have enough power to stop them."

"Yes, I know."

"But I don't think you believe it. Watch what I can do. This used to drain me of energy. Now it takes only a thought." Her gaze went to Moon Man.

His face paled, and his body jerked once then stilled. The shine in his eyes dulled as he died. Valek stifled a cry of dismay. He'd liked and respected Moon Man.

Yelena dove over the Story Weaver's body. Valek hoped she had collected the man's soul.

Gede gasped. "He was for the ritual."

Roze laughed. "Don't worry. She'll now give me two sources of power when I cut her heart out."

"We made a deal, Roze. My cooperation for Moon Man." Yelena's voice shook with fury as she brushed the sand from her clothes.

"And you won't cooperate when I press a knife to Leif's throat?" Roze asked. "You're too soft, Soulfinder. You could have raised a soulless army. They would have been undefeatable. Magic doesn't work on them. Only fire."

Another cry sounded. This one was fainter. The rioters.

A Daviian raced toward Roze.

"Now what?" Roze asked him.

"The Keep's gates are under attack," he said, panting.

Roze glanced at the warpers fighting with the Keep's magicians. "There is nobody left to rescue you," Roze said to Yelena. She then redirected a few warpers from the battle to deal with the revolt at the gates.

"Roze, you haven't figured everything out."

She looked dubious. "What have I missed? Valek? Oh, I know he's here. Magic might not affect him, but Curare will do the trick."

"No. The Fire Warper."

"What about him?"

"You haven't taken into account that he might have different plans than you."

"Don't be ridiculous. Gede and I feed him. We give him his power. Who else would help him?"

"I would."

Yelena bolted toward the fire. For the second time, Valek watched as she disappeared into the flames. A scorching heat encircled his heart. The burning pain fueled his anger.

He edged around the glen and loaded his blowpipe. When he neared the melee of warpers and magicians, he targeted the warpers until he ran out of darts. Then he pulled his sword and waded into the fray despite being vastly outnumbered. They just needed to give Yelena some time to deal with the Fire Warper. He didn't know how she planned to do it, but he trusted her.

As Valek fought, he caught glimpses of the others. Gale swept warpers off their feet with sand-filled whirlwinds. Ari went down and lay frozen. Janco's sword blurred with the speed of his attacks. Magic pressed on Valek from all directions, impeding his movements as if he'd fallen into a giant vat of honey.

Cahil and Marrok also fought the Daviians. Bain toppled after a dart pricked his neck. Once Roze joined the fighting, Irys was ensnared in some kind of magical hold. Leif cried out and collapsed. One by one, Valek's teammates were immobilized and dragged to the glen, where they were staked to the sand. He fought four opponents while darts whizzed past his ears. Keeping the warpers between him and the guy with the blowpipe, Valek ducked and dodged.

His energy drained at an alarming rate. It was only a matter of time before he joined the others in the sand.

Come on, love. A little help. But he'd no idea what she could do from the fire world. If anything.

The magic surrounding him increased tenfold. Breathing became extremely difficult. He met Roze's powerful gaze.

One last move. Valek jerked as if struck by a dart. He slapped a hand to his neck, cursed, and then dropped to the ground as if paralyzed.

Roze yelped and everyone turned their attention to her. She pushed up the sleeves of her dress. Black liquid oozed from her arms, dripping onto the sand. Then Gede shrieked as black stains spread on the sleeves of his tunic. The smell of rancid blood filled the air.

Valek guessed that Yelena had somehow managed to take the stolen souls from the warpers, removing their power.

The magic around him disappeared. He hopped to his feet with a sudden burst of energy and attacked the distracted warpers. After he killed number four, he spun to find the man with the blowpipe, but he'd run off.

Irys had gotten free and freed Cahil, Marrok, and Gale. They attacked Roze together. As the First Magician, even without her enhanced magic, she was still a formidable opponent. Valek moved to join them. It didn't take long to knock her unconscious.

Valek moved to slit Roze's throat, but Irys stopped him.

"She must be tried for treason," she said.

He gestured to the carnage. "This isn't enough evidence?"

A sad smile briefly touched her face. "Our country has been betrayed. We need time to process and mourn, and to do things the Sitian way. We have special cells in the Keep that neutralizes a magician's magic. Together, Bain and I have enough power to hold her when she's not in the cell. The traitors will be hanged."

"You have a year. If they're not dead by then, I will kill them," Valek promised.

"Understood."

Valek glanced around. Marrok and Cahil untied those who had been hit with Curare. "Do you have any Theobroma to give them?" The drug was an antidote of sorts for the Curare. They could melt it and drip it into the mouths of those who had been paralyzed.

"Yes." Irys strode away.

Those who'd survived began the long, arduous task of checking bodies and cleaning up. Four warpers, Gede, and Roze had survived the battle. They were carted to the special cells. As for their team, they had only lost Moon Man. Only. As if that word somehow made it sound better. It didn't. The Story Weaver would be mourned and missed.

Later in the day, a long line of groundskeepers carrying buckets approached the bonfire. When one threw water on the fire, Valek raced over.

"Stop!" he yelled. "No!"

They peered at him in confusion.

Irys joined him. "What's wrong?"

"Yelena hasn't returned yet."

Her expression softened. "She might not—"

"She *will*. This fire stays lit until she's home. Promise me."

"We'll keep it burning for now. Eventually, we will need to extinguish it and go on with our lives." Irys stared at the flames. "If only we had some way to communicate with her."

That reminded him. Hope surged through his heart. "Where's Leif and Gale?"

"Leif's in the infirmary; he has a number of lacerations. Gale left to reunite with her husband. Why?"

Valek was in too much of a hurry to answer. Instead, he turned and ran to the infirmary. All the rooms were filled with the injured. There was also an open area of examination tables for minor wounds. Leif sat on one of them.

Leif perked up when he spotted Valek. "Yelena?"

"No sign yet."

Leif deflated.

"What did you do with those glass animals she gave you?" Valek asked.

"Oh, that's right! Ah… They're in my pack. Which is…" Leif cast about. "So much has happened." He rubbed a hand through his short brown hair. "It's in the wagon!"

"Where's the wagon?"

"Last I saw it was parked next to the Administration building."

"Thanks." Valek ran into Ari on his way out. It was like hitting a brick wall.

"Whoa," the big man said, steadying Valek.

"Are you injured?" So focused on Yelena, he hadn't checked on his seconds.

"No. I'm just helping out. With so many wounded, the healers could use it. I even drafted Janco."

"I'm sure he was thrilled." Then Valek realized why there were so many in need of care. "The resistance?"

Ari frowned and his brow creased with grief. "Yeah. Without magicians on their side, they were hit pretty hard. About a dozen casualties."

"And you feel responsible?"

"Of course. I motivated them. And it didn't matter in the end. We didn't need them."

"We did. They pulled warpers from our fight, which gave us more time to keep them busy while Yelena did her thing."

"Besides saving us all, what *exactly* did she do?"

"I'm not sure. We'll have to ask her when she comes back."

"Will she?"

"She will." Valek refused to believe otherwise.

He found Leif's pack in the wagon and returned to the infirmary. Handing one of the glass statues to Leif, he said, "See if you can talk to Yelena."

Leif stared at the turtle for a long moment. His shoulders slumped. "No answer."

"She might be busy, keep trying."

"For how long?"

"For as long as it takes." Valek almost snarled. Almost. She was Leif's sister, and he was hurting as well. "Does it take a lot of energy?"

"No."

"Then how about once an hour?"

"All right, I'll try again."

Valek had two more statues. He found Irys in her office. With her elbows on the desk, she rested her head in her hands.

She looked up when he approached. Her face was lined with exhaustion. "There is so much to do. I don't know where to start."

"Start with a council session. Explain what happened, assure them that their children and spouse are safe, and then delegate. Make a list of what needs to be done, then let each councilor handle a task. You can't do everything."

She gave him a tired smile. "Did you need something?"

He handed her a glass hawk. "Opal made these. Apparently, they contain magic that you can use to communicate with other magicians. Yelena thought you might be able to reach her in the fire world with these."

Irys stared at the statue with a rapt expression. "It's beautiful. Is that why you took off so fast?"

"Yes. I remembered she had given three to Leif and three to Gale."

Irys jerked in surprise.

"Yelena?" he asked.

"No. Leif. We'll have to take turns trying to reach Yelena. Who else has one of these?"

He set the last one on her desk. "Give this one to Bain. I'll get the others from Gale. Zitora should have one as well."

"Third Magician is in the infirmary. She was seriously wounded in the fight."

"I'm sorry to hear that. Yelena also mentioned someone named Dax. I can see if Gale can use the magic inside. If not, are there others who can use them?"

"We've a number of magicians who are strong in mental communication." She wilted. "We had. I don't know who is left."

"You will. Remember when we defeated Brazell?"

"Yes."

"It took me, the Commander, his advisers, and Ari and Janco three months to get everything sorted. Just take it one day at a time."

"Thanks, Valek. Speaking of the Commander, can you please let him know that the Sitian Council would like to reestablish a relationship with Ixia?"

"I will send a messenger." Plus, he needed to check on Gabor and Brigi.

"Oh? You're not returning to Ixia?"

"Not until Yelena is back."

"Won't the Commander—"

"I don't care."

She studied him. "You helped save Sitia. You're welcome here. In fact, you can stay in Yelena's rooms."

Better than the couch in the safe house, but the simmering in his heart flared to a blaze. Would sleeping in her bed without her be too painful? "Thank you. I'll also help where I can."

"What about your companions?"

"I will give them the choice to stay in Sitia or go home."

"They're excellent fighters. We're going to be sending units of soldiers to root out all the Daviians and could use their help. Cahil has volunteered to lead this effort."

"You trust him?" Valek asked in a neutral tone.

"Yes. He allowed me to read his thoughts with my magic. He made a big mistake, but he recognized it and made amends by fighting on our side."

"Uh huh." Valek still wanted to kill him.

"I need him," Irys said, correctly reading his expression and flat tone. "His people are highly trained."

"If he sets one toe in Ixia, he's a dead man."

"I'll let him know."

∼

Valek returned to the infirmary. Ari and Janco were helping with the wounded. He told them his plans to stay until Yelena returned. "You can return to Ixia or remain here."

"What would we do here?" Janco asked.

"Irys said she could use your fighting skills to help round up the Daviians."

"That sounds fun."

"What about the wounded?" Ari asked.

"I doubt you will leave right away. I'm sure you can work here in the meantime. Up to you."

"We'll talk it over and let you know," Ari said.

"All right." Valek checked the patient rooms. He hadn't known about Zitora; who else had he missed? Each one contained at least two beds. Some had three.

He found Gabor in one of them. His left arm was bandaged and secured to his chest in a sling, but he was awake and sitting up. Unlike his two roommates who were unconscious.

"How are you?"

"Other than a broken arm and clavicle, I'm fine. The healers normally wouldn't waste their energy healing my injuries with magic, but since I'm a Sitian hero, they will. But I have to wait until after the serious cases are taken care of first."

"And Brigi?" Valek asked.

"She wasn't injured."

"Good to hear. What have you been doing since I left?"

"Mostly, we laid low. Pretended to be going about our business. We heard a rumor Yelena was spotted at the market and after that there were murmurings of a group of people planning a revolt. Brigi and I made some inquiries, but when we saw Ari and Janco dressed as merchants and leading the revolution, we joined up."

"How did the riot go?"

"At first, we had the element of surprise and the momentum. The guards at the gate were no match for us. But then the warpers showed up and it turned into a bloodbath." He shuddered, then winced. "After that, it was a blur. One of the warpers used his magic to pelt us with anything he could find—rocks, sticks, and one small stone statue that hit me right here." He touched his left shoulder. "I fell back and blacked out. Woke up here."

"Where's Brigi?"

"Probably at the council's stables, soothing the horses. With all that noise and the smell of blood, we could hear how upset they were. Brigi loves horses more than people."

"More than you?" Valek guessed.

"Well, let's not get too crazy." He grinned.

"When you're healed, come find me. I'll need you to take another message to the Commander for me."

Gabor groaned. "No rest for the wicked."

"You and Brigi can take some time off once the Sitian Council is back on their proverbial feet."

"Thanks, boss."

Valek left to search for Gale. The government residences behind the Council Hall all had flags that represented the clans. The one for the Stormdance Clan was easy to figure out. It had two lightning bolts and storm clouds in the center.

Councilor Stormdance opened the door and peered at him with suspicion. "Can I help you?"

"I'm here to talk to your wife."

"Why?"

"Leuel, let him in," Gale said. "That's Valek."

The Councilor reached out and grabbed his hand, shaking it. "Thank you so much for rescuing my wife."

"It was a mutual rescue. She fought bravely today."

"That's my lady. Come in, come in. What can we do for you?"

If he'd knocked on his door a day ago, Leuel would have called the warpers to arrest Valek. *My how times have changed.*

"Gale, do you still have those glass animals Yelena gave you?"

"Oh, I forgot all about them. I'll get them for you." She hurried from the living area.

"We sent a message to Kell Greenblade that it is safe to bring the children home," Leuel said. "It will be a big relief for all the councilors. We've all learned a valuable lesson to not leave our families unprotected."

Gale returned with the three statues.

"Can you access the magic inside?" Valek asked.

"I can, but I can only use it to enhance my magic, which doesn't include mental communication." She handed them to him.

He thanked her and returned to the Keep. Irys and Bain stood near the glen, overseeing the gruesome task of collecting the bodies. Valek gave Irys the statues, and she promised to distribute them.

"We're going to set up a schedule," Irys said. "With six of us, we can each try to contact Yelena once an hour. That's every ten minutes during the day. Since I'm a night owl, I'll try while the others are sleeping."

"Thank you. Also, thanks for the offer to stay in your tower. Could I bunk in Yelena's old room in the Apprentices' wing instead? It's right next to the bonfire."

"Of course. No one has been assigned that unit this term." She glanced at the wings which bookended the glen like a set of parentheses. "There are only a few apprentices left. Since they were more of a threat than the new students, the warpers targeted them first." Irys rubbed her eyes.

"We're having a council session tomorrow morning," Bain said. "You are invited to attend."

"Ambush?" Valek asked with a smile.

"Not this time. Unless you plan to carry out the Commander's orders to assassinate us?"

Ah, yes. Just because Bain had been paralyzed with Curare, didn't mean he couldn't hear. "I do not. And the Commander has no interest in taking over Sitia. It's just that when it became apparent you'd lost control, he worried the warpers would attack Ixia. With good reason, because that's exactly what they planned. Did you know about the snake?"

Irys and Bain glanced at each other.

"What snake?" Irys asked.

Valek explained about the present the Commander had received.

Irys's shoulders drooped. "He'll never trust us again. So much for reestablishing a relationship with Ixia."

"I don't know. The Commander is rather sensible. Plus, the person responsible for the breakdown of communications has been caught and will be executed. That will definitely help."

"Roze fooled us all," Bain said. "We knew she hated Ixia and feared you and the Commander, but we had no idea she'd go to such lengths to gain enough power to launch an offensive on Ixia. I just started investigating, but it appears she'd been scheming for decades. She might have been working with Kangom when he'd kidnapped those Sitian children and smuggled them into Ixia all those years ago."

Kangom was also known as Mogkan, and one of those children he'd snatched had been Yelena. Valek's stomach clenched. If Mogkan hadn't taken her, Valek would have never met her.

"Did you find out how Roze convinced the Sandseeds to become Daviians?" Irys asked.

"Roze's mother was born a Sandseed. She left the clan for unknown reasons. Eventually, she married Roze's father, Julian, and they settled in the Featherstone lands where Roze was born. Due to that blood connection to the Sandseeds, the protective magic has no effect on Roze. With her mother's family still living in the Avibian Plains, Roze managed to recruit a number of dissatisfied clan members to join her." Bain sighed. "It's going to take us months to untangle all her lies and schemes."

"As the Commander is fond of saying, power corrupts. You'll need to be more vigilant in the future, First Magician," Valek said.

Bain jerked in surprise. "I never *wanted*, nor did I ever *expect* to become First Magician."

"That sentiment will make you a most excellent one."

"Any suggestions on how to be more vigilant?"

"Organize a committee to check in with your magicians that are out in the world from time to time. If they know you're interested in what they're doing, they might not get into trouble. Also, if they're lonely or afraid, you can help them. It's what I do with my agents in the field."

"We'll take it under advisement."

～

When Valek arrived at the great hall, most of the councilors gasped in dismay. Irys and Bain hadn't yet arrived, but Councilor Stormdance jumped to his defense.

"He saved your children, Councilor Greenblade's husband, and my wife," Leuel said. "He saved Sitia from the Daviian Warpers."

"I helped," Valek said into the silence. "Yelena used her Soulfinder magic—that same magic that you're all terrified of—to save us *all*. Sitian and Ixian. If she hadn't, we'd *all* be dead."

Irys and Bain arrived soon after, and the council session began. They explained to the rest of the council about Roze's ill deeds, her plans, the Fire Warper, and Yelena's heroic sacrifice. Valek filled in a few of the gaps. They would need to search Roze's office and figure out just how she'd been able to fund her new clan. Bain presented the list of tasks the master magicians had compiled and started to delegate.

Councilor Krystal shot Valek a nasty glare. "Is this how it's going to be? You order us around like we're your advisers?"

"No, child," Bain said. "We are assigning tasks. If you do not like the task you've been given, please swap with another. We all have to do our part to recover from this tragedy."

Bain tended to call everyone child, but in this case, it was the perfect word for a belligerent councilor.

During the very long meeting, Valek made suggestions about their security procedures that, if they enacted, would make it harder for him to sneak in. However, he didn't tell them about the rafters. Magic hid the ropes, so it was pretty secure overall. Chatty guards, though, needed to be a thing of the past.

~

The next few days fell into a routine, with council sessions dominating most of Valek's time. He sent a healed Gabor to Ixia with a message for the Commander. Ari and Janco had decided to stay in Sitia until Yelena returned. They would join the hunt for Daviians, once Cahil was ready to go. The Wannabe King had found a great deal of useful information in Roze's tower about the Daviians and was using it to map out a plan of attack.

Amid all the planning, organizing, and activity, Valek's heart burned. No one had been able to contact Yelena in the fire world. The pain was constant. He imagined his heart resembled a blackened hunk of wood with an orange ember pulsing deep inside. At times, the ember was a faint simmer. But it would unexpectedly blaze red hot and furious. During those episodes, Valek had to find a quiet corner and lean on the wall as sweat formed on his brow and his legs threatened to collapse.

Gabor returned to Sitia with an official response from the Commander. He offered to send Ambassador Signe to aid the Sitian Council. Valek was surprised by the Commander's gesture of goodwill. Especially since Signe was the Commander's alter ego. Of course, the council debated the offer for a week. While frustrating, it was good to see the council had bounced back from the horrors of the Daviians. In the end, they decided to accept the Commander's offer and sent an official invitation to Ambassador Signe.

For Valek, time no longer flowed smoothly. It jerked and paused and zipped. Whenever the council or the master magicians would suggest it was time to extinguish the bonfire, or stop trying to reach Yelena, Valek would remind them all of her heroics. Each time, though, it took longer to convince them.

Two weeks after the massacre at the Keep, Councilor Harun Sandseed approached Valek. "You are invited to the burial ceremony for Moon Man."

CHAPTER 17

"I'll be there," Valek said, as the fire in his heart pulsed with heat. "When and where?"

"We plan to leave in two days for the plains. Moon Man's body has been preserved by magic; we did not wish to bury him until our home had been cleansed. My people have messaged me that all is prepared for the ceremony."

Valek mounted Onyx two days later. He steered his horse to join the growing line of mourners. The entire Sitian Council and their spouses sat on their horses. Ari, Janco, Leif, Marrok, and Cahil were in attendance. Yelena would have wanted to be with them. Perhaps that was why the burn in his chest had spread throughout his body and settled deep in his bones.

Moon Man's body was wrapped in a linen sheet and secured to Kiki's saddle. No one else rode her. She led the procession to the south gate of the Citadel, and then headed southeast.

The morning sun swept the cold air away and returned the colors to the landscape. A bright blue sky arced overhead with not a cloud in sight. Valek wondered if the perfect weather was compliments of the Stormdance Clan.

When they crossed into the Avibian Plains in the afternoon,

Valek thought the Sandseed horses would use their gust-of-wind gait and leave the rest to catch up. However, they stayed together. And the protective magic did not attack.

That night, they made camp. It was a quiet group. Even Janco was subdued. Only a few people in attendance really knew Moon Man, but they were all there to honor his sacrifice for Sitia.

The somber mood lasted until Harun settled by the fire and said, "Let me tell you about a man named Moon."

He regaled the rapt audience with Moon Man's exploits. From a precocious child to a rebellious teenager, and to the strong warrior and skilled Story Weaver he'd become. Laughter filled the air.

~

They reached a small settlement late the next day. Eight tents with animal designs painted on the fabric ringed a fire pit. The air smelled like sage, and a few horses grazed nearby. They were greeted by the clan's new elders. Fourteen Sandseeds had survived the Daviian massacre. The clan planned to repopulate by inviting other Sitians to join them. Bloodlines did not matter to them as much as living on the plains. When enough grains of sand were in a person's teeth, they'd become a Sandseed.

Janco muttered to Valek, "I think I qualify as a Sandseed. I've swallowed about a pound of the stuff."

Once again, stories about Moon Man were told around the campfire. They focused on his deeds and his accomplishments, on his contributions to the clan. Valek stared at the dancing flames and willed Yelena to come back.

You have so much to offer this world, love.

In the morning, everyone was led to a large area of just sand, which was unusual. They stood in a semi-circle facing Harun, who cradled Moon Man's dead body. The sheet had been removed and there were no visible wounds. Moon Man appeared to be sleeping.

Magic swelled, and the sand in the center of the semi-circle undulated. Soon, the hiss of moving grains sounded and a hole appeared. It was about seven feet long by three feet wide and two feet deep.

Harun lowered Moon Man into the hole, then arranged his limbs so he looked comfortable. He stood and the sand hissed again, just covering Moon Man's body. One of the Sandseeds approached each mourner with a bucket, encouraging them to dip their hand inside and withdraw a fistful of something that turned out to be seeds.

"Moon Man was born from these sands, and now he has returned to these sands," Harun said. "He contributed to our way of life while alive, and he will continue to nourish our sand for our future generations. Thank you, Moon Man, you will be missed, but never forgotten. Stories of you will be told to all those who come after you." He opened his hand and spread the seeds over the buried body.

He invited the mourners to approach the grave and sprinkle their seeds into the hole. Tears blurred Valek's vision when it was his turn.

He knelt on one knee. "You were a true warrior, protecting us, helping us, and giving your life for us. I'm truly glad that I was able to call you my friend."

When everyone finished, more sand flowed back into the hole, completely filling it. Within seconds, Valek could not tell that there had ever been a hole in that spot.

Next, Kiki and two other horses approached. They held buckets in their teeth. When they neared Moon Man's grave, they set the buckets down and knocked them over with a hoof. Water ran out, soaking into the sand.

The significance of the action hit Valek hard. He glanced at the nearby plains, seeing the grasses, shrubs, and small trees with a new understanding.

Irys pulled a folded piece of silk from her robes. She opened it, revealing Moon Man's grief flag. Embroidered in silver on the indigo-colored silk were things that had a significant meaning to Moon Man. Indigo was his favorite color, and in the center of the flag was a full moon with streaks of moonlight emanating from it. Around the moon was a scimitar, a horse, a flower, and the silhouettes of three people standing together. The border of the flag was a braid, representing his Story Weaver abilities.

There wasn't a flagpole to raise the flag. Instead, Irys held it above her head and a sudden breeze pulled it from her hands. Gale smiled as it fluttered higher and higher, symbolizing the release of Moon Man's soul to the sky.

A meal and more stories followed the ceremony. Laughter, tears, and a few cheers sounded. Valek hadn't really considered an afterlife before Moon Man had explained the different worlds to him. And with Yelena being a Soulfinder, he was comforted by the knowledge that Moon Man was at peace in the sky.

~

They returned to the Citadel and picked up where they left off. Ari, Janco, Cahil, and Marrok headed out with ten teams to round up the Daviians who had escaped or were in hiding. Each team had seven people and one magician. Ari and Janco had been unhappy to be assigned to Cahil's unit. But once Valek explained that they could ensure the Wannabe King behaved, they perked up. Especially when Valek gave them permission to kill the man if he showed any signs of colluding with the enemy. Valek wished them good hunting.

Ambassador Signe arrived the next day. Valek dreaded

having to update her. So much had happened, was still happening, that he didn't have the strength to go over it all again.

He joined Signe in the office the council provided for her. Sitting on the chair in front of the desk, Valek met Signe's gaze. Her features were an amazing transformation from the Commander. There was a family resemblance and the same gold-colored eyes, but that was all. Signe's long hair, softer features, and curves just didn't match. Not that Signe's appearance mattered to Valek, but he remembered Yelena had said the Commander could see the magic inside Opal's glass animals. And maybe, just maybe the Commander used a one-trick power for this transformation. Which Valek did find interesting.

"Are you well?" Signe asked.

Surprised, Valek blinked. He'd expected to be ordered to report. "No. It's been a grueling few weeks."

"You haven't been sleeping." It wasn't a question.

"Not well."

Signe stood and poured Valek a drink. "Here, something from home."

He sipped the Ixian fire whiskey and sighed.

"Gabor's report was very thorough. But he only had vague details on how Yelena stopped the Daviian Warpers."

"Right now, all we have are guesses."

"She hasn't returned?"

"Not yet." He took a bigger swallow. The heat sizzling down his throat was no match for the bonfire in his heart.

"She's stubborn, intelligent, and determined, she'll find a way. In the meantime, the only thing I need to know from you is if the Sitian Council can be trusted."

Valek appreciated the pep talk. "At this point in time, they can be trusted."

"And in the future?"

"That's harder to determine. The councilors are elected; new people might be voted in. The master magicians are down to three. Zitora Cowan is now Second Magician, but she's very young and impressionable. She looked up to Roze, swallowed all her lies. Zitora could become bitter and disillusioned, or she could learn from the experience and become stronger. Time will tell. And another magician, who we know nothing about, might pass the master-level test and join their ranks."

Signe dismissed him soon after. Valek crossed to the Keep. He spotted the dining hall and wondered when he had last eaten. When he couldn't remember, he altered his path.

Halfway there, Leif ran up to him. "Yelena! I contacted Yelena!"

Joy energized him in an instant. "What did she say? What's going on? Is she coming back?"

Leif held up his hands. "I only want to say this once, so let's go find Irys and Bain."

Within half an hour, they'd assembled in Bain's office. Valek sat on the edge of his chair.

"It was my turn to try to contact my sister. And like the billion and one times before, no response. I was about to disconnect when she said hello." Leif pressed his hand to his chest. "I nearly fell out of my seat. I asked her to come back, but she said she can't. I asked her why, but she wanted an update on what's going on here first." He huffed. "Typical. I told her everything and then she finally said she couldn't return because someone has to keep the Fire Warper from regaining power."

Bain interrupted. "Did you tell her about the texts? That we burned all the books on blood magic to prevent anyone else from learning those rituals. It about killed me, but it had to be done."

"I did. But she said there are others like Roze and Gede who know how to perform the ritual, and, after we execute them, their souls will be sent to the fire world and will be able to communicate to anyone in our world who is determined to seek them out. Like Gede did with the Fire Warper. She's afraid it will happen again. So, I responded by saying she was the Soulfinder, and asked her why she couldn't send those souls somewhere out of reach."

"And what was her answer?" Valek asked.

"That those souls don't deserve to be in the sky." Leif threw up his hands in frustration. "Then she ended the communication."

They remained quiet for a while.

Bain broke the silence. "Bright side, we can talk to her. Perhaps we can help her figure out a way to return."

Valek had mixed feelings. He wanted to be selfish and tell her to not worry about someone else contacting the Fire Warper, that they'd deal with that person like they had with Roze and Gede. On the other hand, Roze and Gede had killed so many before they could be stopped.

Over the next few weeks, Yelena talked to Irys, Bain, and Leif through the glass animals. Irys figured out that the magic encased inside the statues would eventually run out. It was a sobering discovery.

The trials of the Daviian Warpers began. For once, the Sitian Council was in complete agreement. All six were sentenced to death, including Roze. They would be hanged on the same sands where they had killed Moon Man and so many magicians. The sound of hammers striking nails as the gallows were built competed with the roar of the bonfire.

After the bodies of the traitors were burned into ash, the fire would finally be extinguished. Valek tried to argue, but even Yelena had agreed that it was time. It helped that she thought she could use any fire to cross over, but she still intended to ensure Roze, Gede, and the other warpers didn't try to reach out from the fire world.

They committed the crimes, Yelena saved the world, and she was being punished for her heroic deeds. Valek hated the world sometimes.

He lay on the bed that still smelled of Yelena and stared at the ceiling. Valek didn't know if he could survive in a world without her. Would extinguishing the bonfire douse the burning in his heart? Would he return to the cold, emotionless assassin he was before she entered his life. Or would that pain be with him forever, consuming his soul until there was nothing left but a hollow husk of a man?

Someone banged on his door. Valek jumped to his feet and opened it. Leif stood on the other side, bouncing on his toes.

"She found a way! She thinks it might work, but it might not. No sense getting our hopes up." He grinned. Obviously not taking his own advice.

"Slow down. What might or might not work?"

"Sorry. Yelena's return from the fire world. Let's go wake Irys and Bain."

Valek trotted after Leif, trying and failing to keep his expectations in check. They woke Bain and he mentally called Irys, who joined them in Bain's office in record time.

"Wow, did you fly here?" Leif asked the Third Magician.

"On wings of magic," Irys said. "Now, talk."

"Yelena figured out a way to return to our world, but she isn't sure it will work," Leif said.

"We'll try it regardless," Bain said.

"Yelena believes that when Roze and the others die, she'll be able to capture their souls and imprison them in Opal's glass statues."

"How?" Bain asked.

"This is where she's not so sure it'll work. Since Opal can trap magic in her glass animals, Yelena theorizes she will be able to also trap the souls. And if they're trapped in there, they won't be able to communicate with anyone."

"But Opal isn't a Soulfinder. Can Yelena transfer the soul to Opal?" Irys asked.

"That's the this-might-not-work part."

"What do we need to do?" Valek asked.

"We need to bring in a kiln, and all the equipment needed for glass blowing. And we need Opal."

"I'll contact the local glassblower's guild," Irys said. "I'll ask them to provide the equipment."

Valek stood. "And I'll fetch Opal."

"Uh, that might not be a good idea," Leif said. "You'll probably scare her."

"I'm not letting any harm come to the one person who might be able to save Yelena."

"I understand that, but what if her parents refuse to let her come with you? Are you going to kidnap her?"

Of course, he would. Valek huffed. "Then join me. Rusalka is a Sandseed horse. I plan to ask Kiki if I can ride her so I can cut through the plains."

"That's a good idea. When do you want to leave?"

"Now."

Leif grumbled but left to pack his bag. Valek stopped by Ambassador Signe's guest quarters. Two guards stood outside the door. One raised an eyebrow when Valek approached.

"This better be important," he said.

He handed the man an envelope. "Please give this letter to the Ambassador when she wakes."

He looked relieved. "Yes, sir."

Valek went to the stables next. Kiki looked over her stall door when he entered. Her ears drooped and she gave him a morose nudge, like she had done every day he'd visited for the last couple weeks. Feeding her a peppermint, he explained about Yelena's plan and how they had to get to Opal as fast as possible.

"You're the fastest, Kiki. Will you come with us?"

She practically knocked him over in her hurry to leave her stall. He laughed for the first time since Yelena had gone to the fire world. He was almost done saddling Kiki when Leif entered. When he finished, Valek helped him get Rusalka ready.

Finally, they mounted, and Kiki took off with Rusalka right behind her. Normally, she'd walk through the Keep and the Citadel's streets. This time, she jumped both barriers and broke into a gallop as soon as they cleared the east gate. Valek just held on.

A half-moon shone in the night sky. It was almost the end of the warming season, so he had left his heavy cloak back at the Keep. He tried not to think of all the time that had passed without Yelena, but the answer popped into his head: sixty-four days.

When Kiki reached the Avibian Plains, she switched to her gust-of-wind gait with a slight hitch in her step. The sands beneath her hooves blurred into a river of wind. They flew. Valek had only experienced it a couple times. Each time was as thrilling as the first.

Eventually, Kiki slowed, and the world snapped into focus. The sun was low in the sky and both horses' sides heaved. Valek had no idea how far they'd traveled, or even if it was the same day or the next.

Valek walked with them as they cooled down. "Don't kill yourselves," he said to Kiki. "Yelena would be very upset if you died on this mission."

Then he wondered if horses had souls. He guessed that since souls seemed to have magical power, that the Sandseed horses with their magical gust-of-wind gaits would indeed have souls. He'd have to ask Yelena. And for the first time in a very long time, he had hope that he would have another conversation with her. Once the horses were taken care of, they made camp.

Kiki woke them when it was time to go. Another thrilling ride was followed by another stop. When they halted for the third time, Valek saw buildings and farms in the near distance. From the position of the sun, he guessed it was mid-morning.

Leif pointed to a collection of buildings. "That's Opal's family's glass factory." Then he glanced at Valek. "Let me do the talking."

"Have you met them before?"

"When we were in Booruby hunting Cahil and Ferde, Opal invited us to have dinner with her and her family. She has quite a bit of guilt for pricking Yelena with Curare."

"It wasn't her fault. She was a victim."

"That's what Yelena told her. But emotions and logic don't always align."

True. They left the horses to graze in the plains.

Leif led him to the house. "We'll talk to Opal's mom first. The others are probably in the factory, and they won't be able to hear us."

"Why not?"

"Those kilns are loud. To melt sand, limestone, and soda ash into glass, they need to be heated to twenty-five-hundred degrees. I know that temperature is unfathomable. Let's just say, it's bloody hot."

"Bloody? You've been hanging out with me too much."

Leif grunted.

"How do they get it that hot?" Valek asked.

"They burn white coal. It burns hotter than black coal and is much cleaner." Leif knocked on the front door.

After a minute, an older woman answered the door. "Leif! What a surprise. Come in, come in." She ushered them inside and offered them a cool drink. "Mara's working, but I can fetch her."

Valek wondered if Mara was Opal's sister.

"We're not here for Mara. Your daughter, Opal, is needed at the Magician's Keep."

"Opal? Why?" She glanced at Valek.

"I'd rather explain it to the entire family, if that's possible," Leif said.

After an hour—it seems that working with glass wasn't something that could be put down at a moment's notice—the family arrived. An older man sat next to Opal's mother, and three siblings filed in after him. The beautiful teen girl gave Leif a big smile. Her younger sister, who must be Opal, had long brown hair and sad eyes. A young man, around ten years old and with a mop of brown hair, gave Leif a high-five. They all sat down in the comfortable living room, staring at Leif and Valek with concerned expressions.

"Ah, Jaymes and Vyncenza," Leif said to Opal's parents, "Please meet Valek."

Here we go.

Jaymes was on his feet in an instant. "Why did you bring him into our house?" he demanded.

Leif held up his hands. "He's helping me. Yelena needs Opal's help, and we're here to escort her to the Keep."

"Me?" Opal asked. "Why? I'm..."

"The only person in all of Sitia that can help," Leif said.

"Are you sure?"

"Yes." Leif explained about Yelena's determination that Opal's glass animals contained magic. Then he told them of her plight. "She believes that she can transfer a soul to you, and you'll be able to trap it in a glass prison."

Watching their expressions, Valek knew Leif had just overloaded Opal's family with too much information.

"Opal doesn't have magic," Vyncenza said. "She's been tested."

"She doesn't have any of the traditional skills." Leif agreed. "However, she could have a one-trick power. Regardless, her abilities are needed at the Keep right away."

Leif answered a bunch more questions. Opal shrank back into the cushions of the couch as her family discussed the situation, circling around and around with the same concerns.

Valek finally lost his patience. He stood and the room went

silent. "Opal, Yelena needs your help to return to this world. She's my love and I promise that I will protect you with my life if need be. Will you help her?"

"Yes," she said softly.

Her parents immediately expressed more concerns. They demanded to come along, which would considerably slow down their return trip.

"Yes, I'll help," Opal said louder.

"You can't go alone," Jaymes said.

Valek should have just kidnapped Opal.

"Mara can come with me. She's eighteen." Opal turned to Leif. "You have two horses, right?"

Leif glanced at Valek.

"This isn't going to be a holiday trip," he said. "We're covering a great deal of ground each day. If she can sit on a horse for that long, then Mara can come along."

Both girls looked at their father.

Jaymes sighed. "Leif, I'm holding you *personally* responsible for the safety of my daughters. Understand?"

In that instance, he sounded just like the Commander. Valek hid his grin.

"Yes, sir," Leif said. His expression turning queasy.

"And you." Jaymes turned to Valek. "I expect *you* to keep *your* promise."

"Yes, sir."

Vyncenza insisted they eat a hearty lunch before setting out. It was a good idea, and the horses needed to rest, yet every part of Valek yearned to get going. After the delicious meal, the girls each packed a small bag of essentials, and Leif updated Opal's parents on the Daviian situation. Valek strode out to the plains to check on the horses. He groomed both and fed them some grain.

Finally, everyone was ready. They mounted. Opal behind Valek on Kiki; Mara holding onto a blushing Leif on Rusalka. A couple of things clicked, and Valek realized Leif was sweet on Mara. Ah, young love.

The horses broke into their gust-of-wind gaits. Despite the extra weight, it took them almost the same amount of time to return to the Keep. They arrived in the early evening. Kiki headed straight for the glen. Irys, who had been overseeing the installation of the glass making equipment, hurried over.

"That's amazing," she said.

Leif said, "Well, it took a bit to convince Opal's parents—"

"Not that. You were only gone six days."

It took five days for a normal horse traveling on the road to get to Booruby from the Citadel. To go there and back.... Valek patted Kiki's neck. "Extra peppermints, apples, extra everything for the magic horses."

Opal and Mara slid from the saddles. They inspected the equipment. All Opal's hesitation, worry, and uncertainty during the last two days disappeared when she picked up a blowpipe. It was fun to watch the fifteen year old give orders to the older glassmakers.

"Yelena said she wanted to test her theory," Irys told Valek and Leif.

"How?" Valek asked.

"Before we execute the others, she wants to send the Fire Warper into the first glass prison. If it works, then she knows she can do the others."

No one said, "And if it doesn't," but Valek could tell that they all thought it.

"When?"

"When Opal and Yelena are ready."

It didn't take long for Opal to prepare, but she approached them before she started. "Just so you know, it will take twelve hours before we'll know if this worked."

"Why that long?" Valek asked in a reasonable tone even though his heart thumped its impatience.

"The glass needs to cool slowly, or it'll crack. If it cracks, then the soul trapped inside will get free."

A good reason, and it brought up another concern. "What happens if years from now, it's dropped or crushed? Does glass get old and brittle?"

"Glass is an amazing material," Opal said. "As long as it's thick enough, it can withstand being dropped. And it doesn't get brittle with time. I'll make animals that don't have long legs, that are more blob-like so there's less risk of one of the limbs being snapped off."

"We'll ensure they're protected and in a secured location," Irys said. "No one will be able to touch them."

Noble aspirations, but in Valek's experience, nothing was impossible to steal.

Opal returned to the kiln. She picked up a metal blowpipe, then opened the small door. Inside, a searing bright orange glow pulsed. Opal dipped the end of the pipe into the cauldron of molten glass and rolled it with her fingertips.

"She's gathering a slug of glass," Leif said to Valek.

Withdrawing the pipe, she sat on a bench and worked on the molten glass, shaping it with a long pair of metal tweezers.

"Jacks," Leif explained.

"How do you know?"

He blushed. "I've been doing some research. So, I...have something to talk to Mara about."

Adorable.

After Opal created an ugly stout pig, she stood and glanced at Irys. The Third Magician stared at the glass hawk she held in her hand. When Irys nodded, Opal bent and blew into the opposite end of the blowpipe. She jerked as if injured but continued. She used the jacks to squeeze the glass at the end of the pipe until it was narrow. Then, she took it over to a metal tray that had some sort of lumpy substance on the bottom. She tapped the pipe with the bottom of the jacks and the pig fell into the tray. Carrying the tray to another smaller kiln, Opal opened a drawer and inserted the tray before pushing it inside.

"That's the annealing oven. It'll slowly bring the temperature of the pig down to ambient, which takes about twelve hours."

Twelve hours of hell.

"We might as well take care of the horses in the meantime. Maybe get some sleep," Leif said.

"I'm not letting that annealing oven out of my sight."

Leif gestured. "There are plenty of guards."

"I'm not trusting anyone. This is too important."

"All right, I'll take care of Kiki and get Opal and Mara settled in one of the Keep's guest suites." Leif brought Valek his pack before he led the horses to the stable.

Valek set up a makeshift camp in the sand and settled in to wait. A few hours had passed when Leif returned with a hot meal and an extra blanket.

"Thanks," Valek said.

"Do you want me to take a shift so you can get some sleep?" Leif asked.

"No."

"Ari and Janco are back, how about I ask them?"

"Leif, do you really think I'll be able to get any sleep tonight?"

"No, I suppose not."

Time ceased. Valek swore the moon hadn't moved at all. His thoughts whirled as his heart continued to burn. If this didn't work, Yelena would remain trapped. And he would... No, not going there. This had to work. Had to. Otherwise, it was unthinkable.

∽

Valek's vigil ended a few hours after dawn. Before the time was up, people joined him on the sands. Opal, Mara, Leif, Irys, Bain, and the entire Sitian Council attended. Ari, Janco, and even Fisk and his guild members waited. Cahil showed up with his minions. An older couple held hands. The woman bore a striking resemblance to Yelena—they must be her parents. Ambassador Signe and her adviser hung toward the back of the crowd.

Everyone who cared about Yelena had come. And it was quite a crowd. Valek marveled. Less than two years ago, Yelena had nobody. She'd been all alone and on death row. And now... A lump formed in his throat, but it wasn't caused by grief. No, it was caused by gratitude. Yelena had found her family.

Opal squared her shoulders and approached the annealing oven. Pulling on a pair of cotton gloves, she opened the drawer and picked up the pig. Every single person in attendance held their breath.

CHAPTER 18

Opal raised the pig into the air. Cheers erupted from the magicians. He couldn't see anything different about the statue, but Valek guessed the experiment had been a success. He locked his knees as his emotions pushed to escape their box.

Keep it together. She isn't here yet.

Opal returned to work, gathering a slug of glass as the traitor Roze Featherstone aka Jalila Daviian, was brought to the gallows. Under the magical control of two master magicians, she was forced to mount the gallows' steps. The noose was tightened around her neck and the executioner stepped back.

Roze's expression contorted with rage. "You all will *burn!*"

When Opal finished the statue and prepared to blow into the pipe, the floor opened underneath Roze's feet. She fell until her body jerked to a sudden stop.

Once again, Opal jolted as if stung, but she focused on her task, finishing the piece.

Gede was next, followed by the four warpers. After placing the last glass animal into the tray, Opal sagged onto the sand.

Everyone turned their attention to the bonfire. Seconds turned into minutes.

Come on, love.

"Yelena!" Leif shouted, pointing to the black shape stepping from the flames.

Yelena's cloak caught fire, and she dove to the sand, rolling to snuff it out. She stood up with a chagrined smile, wiping the sand from her clothes.

Valek's heart lurched as if it, too, rolled to extinguish the flames that had been consuming him from the moment she disappeared into the bonfire. He released his tight hold, and his emotions surged through him in one powerful wave, overwhelming him. Weak with relief, he sank to the sand.

Yelena's parents pounced on her, followed by Leif and Irys. Valek knew he wouldn't be able to get close to her for a while. Plus, he wasn't going to let those six glass prisons out of his sight. He could wait a little bit longer. When they reunited, he wanted her all to himself.

He kept guard and watched as she was surrounded by her family. Watched as the bodies of the traitors were burned in Yelena's bonfire. Once they had turned into ash, the bonfire was finally extinguished. Thick, oily smoke boiled from it and clung to the ground until Gale Stormdance created a fresh breeze to whisk it away.

Valek watched as the councilors left for the Council Hall, and Fisk and his guild headed out. Watched as Ari and Janco joked with Yelena before she rushed to the stable, no doubt checking on Kiki. Yelena then disappeared with her parents toward the Keep's guest rooms.

As the day wore on, Valek remained in his camp. No one paid him any attention. He'd become part of the scenery.

Twelve hours after Yelena returned, Opal, Mara, Irys, and Bain pulled out the six glass animals. By the satisfied smiles of the magicians, Valek knew they all contained the traitor's souls.

Opal carefully set them into a box that had been lined with a spongy material. The box was closed and locked.

THE STUDY OF FIRE

Valek joined the group. "What do you plan to do with them?"

Irys and Bain exchanged a glance.

"They will be locked inside the safe in my office," Irys said. "The council will decide on their final resting place."

And having all those people know their location was basically announcing it to the world. Valek couldn't leave them in the Sitian's hands. Too dangerous. But he nodded as if it sounded like a great plan. Irys and Bain headed to the Administration building, where they both had offices. Except, Valek had years of practice at spotting a lie. And Irys wasn't a very good liar. The glass prisons weren't going to the safe in her office.

Opal and Mara turned toward the guest quarters.

"Opal," Valek said.

She looked back.

"Thank you."

"You're welcome."

∼

Valek sat on the fourth set of stairs in Irys's tower, waiting for Yelena. She had a busy day visiting with everyone and night had fallen. The soft sound of her boots on the stairs below him sent a fire through him. The good kind of burn.

She entered her rooms, and he padded down to the third floor. Standing at the windows with her back to him, she opened the shutters to let the air in. He approached.

Without turning, she demanded, "What took you so long?"

Valek pressed against her back, wrapping his arms around her stomach. "I could ask you the same thing." He spun her around. "I didn't want to share you, love. We have a lot of catching up to do." He leaned in and kissed her, wishing the moment could go on forever.

Eventually, she pulled away and laid her head on his chest. His heart, full of joy, flipped in his chest. "That's the second time

I lost you," he said. "You would think it would be easier, but I couldn't douse the burning pain. I felt like my heart had been pierced by a spit and was cooking over a fire." He tightened his grip. *Please don't leave me again.* "I would beg you to promise never to disappear again, but I know you won't."

"I can't. Just like you can't promise to stop being loyal to the Commander. We both have other duties."

He huffed with amusement. "We could retire."

"From being a Liaison, but not a Soulfinder. There are many lost souls to guide."

Valek drew back enough to study her. "How many? It's been a hundred-and-twenty-five years since Sitia crisped the last Soulfinder. Hundreds?"

"I don't know. The Soulfinders documented in the history books were really Soulstealers. Guyan Sandseed could have been the only true Soulfinder in the last two thousand years. Bain would delight in helping me with that assignment. But I will need to travel around Sitia and Ixia to help them all. Do you want to come? It could be fun."

"You, me and a couple thousand ghosts? Sounds crowded," he teased, even though he longed to say yes a thousand times. "At least you already found one soul, love."

"Moon Man's?"

"Mine. And I trust you not to lose it."

"The only magic to affect the infamous Valek."

She studied his expression. "How old were you when the King's men killed your brothers?"

He peered at her. It was a strange question.

"How old?" she asked again.

"Thirteen." The second worst day of his life.

"That explains it!"

"Explains what?"

"Why you're resistant to magic. Thirteen is around the age when people can access the power source. The trauma of seeing your brothers killed probably caused you to pull so much power you formed a null shield. A shield so impenetrable you can no longer access magic."

She sounded so confident, but that was quite the leap in logic. Or was it?

"After a season in the underworld, you're now an expert in all things magical?" he asked.

"I'm an expert in all things Valek."

"Analyze this, love." He drew her close and kissed her. Deepening the kiss, he pulled her tunic up.

She stopped him. "Valek, as much as I want you to stay, I need you to do a favor for me."

"Anything, love."

She smiled. "I want you to steal those glass prisons. Hide them in a safe place where no one will find them. Don't tell me or anyone else where you put them."

Yelena had also figured out the danger. "You don't want to know. Are you sure?"

"Yes. I can still be corrupted by magic. And if I ever ask you for their location, you are not to tell me. No matter what. Promise."

"Yes, sir."

"Good."

"It may take me a few days or weeks. Where will you be?"

"I'm going to continue being the Liaison between Ixia and Sitia. I plan to commandeer a certain cottage in the Featherstone lands and declare that parcel of land neutral territory."

"Commandeer?" He smiled.

"Yes. Having safe houses for Ixian spies in Sitia is not very friendly. Spying on each other is not conducive to the type of open dialogue I want between the two nations."

"You'll need to rebuild the stable. Hire a lad," Valek teased.

"Don't worry. I already have a houseboy in mind. A loyal and handsome fellow, who will be at my beck and call."

Valek raised an eyebrow as desire sizzled on his skin. "Indeed. I'm sure the boy is most anxious to attend to his duties."

He slid a hand under her shirt, caressing her skin. She took a step back, but he snaked his arm behind her, stopping her.

"You need to finish one job before you begin another," she said.

"The night has just begun." He pulled her shirt off. "Plenty of time to take care of my lady before I run her errand."

His lips found hers, then he nuzzled her neck. "I must." He paused to place a line of kisses down her chest. "Help my lady." He picked her up and laid her down. "To bed."

Yelena melted and pulled him down with her, helping as he removed her clothing. This time, when they joined together, something shifted inside him. She fit right into the gap in his heart. Without her, he was incomplete. Without her, life was empty. Without her, there'd be no joy and no reason to live.

In that moment, he realized Yelena was truly his heart mate. There'd be no other. Ever. And he'd do anything and everything in his power to ensure she stayed with him. In this world and into the next.

EPILOGUE

Valek found the seven glass prisons in the Keep's special cells underneath the Administration building. It was the only logical place, as Irys's safe could easily be cracked. As much as he hated to leave Yelena after being apart for so long, Valek had promised her he would find a better hiding place for the glass statues.

He packed his things and saddled Onyx. After stopping to give the Ambassador another letter, he headed north. The letter said that the Commander had summoned him home, and to please let the others know where he'd gone.

Heading north through MD-7, Valek mulled over where to hide the prisons, dismissing various locations as soon as he thought of them. When he reached the border to MD-8, he turned Onyx east, thinking the thousands of caverns in the Soul Mountains would be a great hiding place. Except, an earthquake might trigger a collapse and crush them. Stopping at a travel shelter in the middle of MD-6, he considered his options. And then it dawned on him.

It didn't matter where he hid them. If someone threatened

Yelena's life if he didn't tell them the location, he would tell them. She was more important.

Valek returned to the castle. Ambassador Signe had arrived a few days earlier. Of course, the Commander sent a messenger to the stable with a summons for Valek to report in right away. Valek shouldered his pack and went straight to the Commander's office.

"Where have you been?" he demanded.

Valek placed the box of glass prisons on his desk.

"Is that—" The Commander glanced at him. "The Sitian Council suspected you stole them. It made it very difficult for Ambassador Signe to work with them. What are they doing here?"

"They need to disappear, somewhere no one can find them," Valek said. "I can't hide them, because I can be compromised. Yelena is beyond precious to me. No one has that type of leverage over you. And I know you'll tell no one."

"Consider it done."

A MOMENT OF PEACE
Created by Hillary Bardin
Commissioned by Tasha McIlwaine

THANK YOU

Thank you for reading *The Study Fire*, the final book in Valek's Adventures. If you like to stay updated on my books and any news, please sign up for my free email newsletter here:

http://www.mariavsnyder.com/news.php

(go all the way down to the bottom of the page)

I send my newsletter out to subscribers three to four times a year. It contains info about the books, my schedule and always something fun (like deleted scenes or a new short story or exclusive excerpts). No spam—ever!

Please feel free to spread the word about this book! Posting honest reviews are always welcome and word of mouth is the best way you can help an author keep writing the books you enjoy! And please don't be a stranger, stop on by and say hello. You can find me on the following social media sites:

- Facebook (https://www.facebook.com/mvsfans)
- Facebook Reading Group - Snyder's Soulfinders (https://www.facebook.com/groups/SnydersSoulfinders)
- Goodreads (https://www.goodreads.com/maria_v_snyder)
- Instagram (https://www.instagram.com/mariavsnyderwrites)

ACKNOWLEDGMENTS

Once again, I have plenty of people to thank for helping me make this the best book possible. Most of them have been mentioned in many of my acknowledgments since they continue to support me and my writing career. A career that I'm still a bit surprised has worked out so well. Considering I failed spelling and grammar in elementary school, I had no clue that I'd eventually be writing for a living.

Eternal thanks to:

My creative team: Dema Harb, Joy Kenney, Martyna Kuklis, Hillary Bardin, Cindy Tynga, and Raphael Corkhill.
My editorial team: Nat Bejin, Elle Callow, Reema Crooks, Reilly Gahagan, Brittany Clevenger, Krystal Nesbit, Rodney Snyder, and Jenna Snyder.
My publicity team: The staff of Cupboard Maker Books.
My supportive friends: Christine Czachur, Judi Fleming, Kathy Flowers, Michelle Haring, Amy and Bruce Kaplan, Mindy Klasky, Brian Koscienski, Jenn Mason, Jeri Smith-Ready, Kristina Watson, and Nancy Yeager.
My loving family: Rodney, Luke, Jenna, Mom, Pop, Karen, Chris, Amy, and Kitty.

ABOUT MARIA V. SNYDER

When Maria V. Snyder was younger, she aspired to be a storm chaser in the American Midwest so she attended Pennsylvania State University and earned a Bachelor of Science degree in Meteorology. Much to her chagrin, forecasting the weather wasn't in her skill set so she spent a number of years as an environmental meteorologist, which is not exciting...at all. Bored at work, and needing a creative outlet, she started writing fantasy and science fiction stories. Twenty-four novels and two short story collections later, Maria's learned a thing or three about writing. She's been on the *New York Times* bestseller list, won a dozen awards, and has earned her Masters of Arts degree in Writing from Seton Hill University, where she is now a faculty member for their MFA program.

When she's not writing, she's either playing pickleball, skiing, traveling, taking pictures, or zonked out on the couch due to all of the above. Being a writer, though is a ton of fun. Where else can you take fencing lessons, learn how to ride a horse, study marital arts, learn how to pick a lock, take glass blowing classes and attend Astronomy Camp and call it research? Maria will be the first one to tell you it's not working as a meteorologist.

Printed in Dunstable, United Kingdom